CITY OF DEMONS

Kevin Harkness

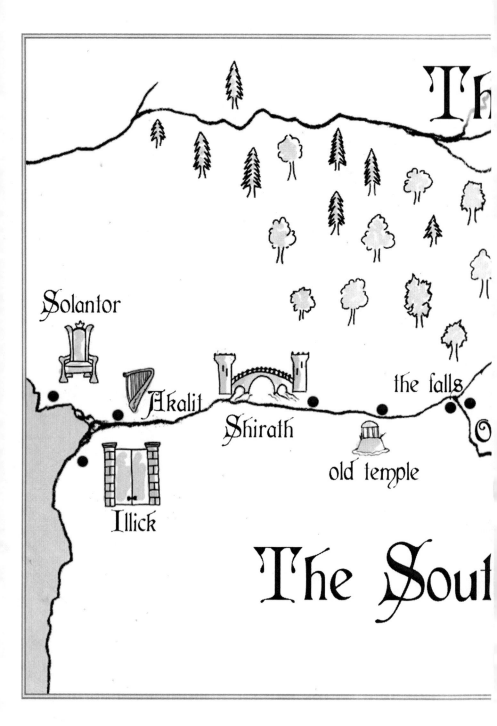

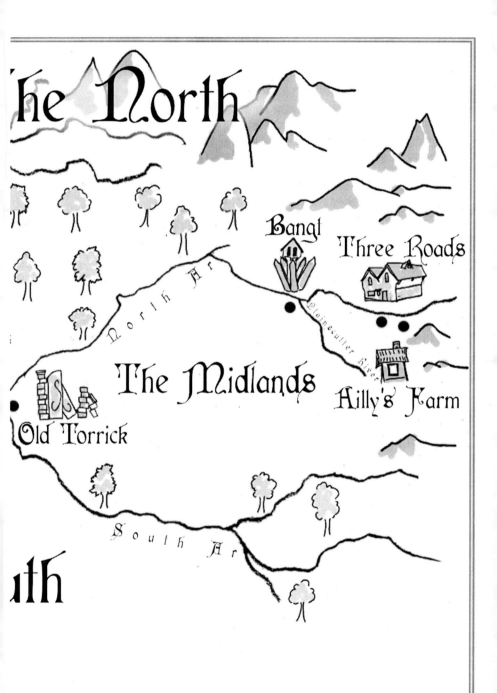

Praise for *City of Demons*:

"*City of Demons* is a fast-paced page turner of a fantasy novel, with rich characters, vivid, evocative settings and a deep vein of universal truth. Bullied by a brutal father, Garet yearns for a life that matters. When their farm is attacked, he must face his new destiny. His quest to defeat the demons, both within and without, that stand in his way sweeps the reader along on a wild ride. The writing is infused with emotional intensity and a deep understanding of human nature. *City of Demons* marks the debut of a fresh, new voice in fantasy writing."

Wendy Phillips, Governor General's Literary Award winning author of *Fishtailing*

"*The door latch started to rise, pushed up by a long, curved blade slid between the door and the jamb. The latch cleared its hook, and the door opened a crack. The thin blade was joined by three others, and Garet saw that they were not knives; they were a set of claws, attached to a bony, mottled arm.*

And for Garet, a change comes. Forced to leave the isolated farm where he has grown up with a cruel father, he must travel beyond the mountains that have been—in his lifetime—borders of safety. But the world beyond is filled with the terrifying and the new: demons, whose power is Fear.

Garet reveals an ability with demons, and is chosen to become a Bane, a demon-fighter. But being chosen does not make the training or the task any easier. His tutor, a young woman named Salick, and the small company of Banes become family, and they make their way to a new city, and a new life.

City of Demons is a terrific debut novel. Lock the doors before you set out on this journey. Pick it up and turn the pages, and be pulled in by that bony, mottled arm. You will not put it down again."

Alison Acheson, author of *Molly's Cue*

CITY OF DEMONS

Kevin Harkness

TYCHE BOOKS LTD.

City of Demons: A Novel

Published by Tyche Books Ltd.
www.TycheBooks.com

Print ISBN: 978-0-9878248-4-4
Ebook ISBN: 978-0-9878248-5-1

Printed in the United States, United Kingdom and Australia
First Printing: 2012

Cover Art by Malcolm McClinton
Cover Layout and Map by Lucia Starkey
Interior Artwork by Galen Dara
Interior Layout by Tina Moreau
Editorial by M. L. D. Curelas

Contents

Acknowledgments I

1: The Unexpected Hero 1

2: Strangers at the Gate 14

3: Out of the Hills 23

4: The Demon Jewel 35

5: Lessons 40

6: An Unfriendly Wager 49

7: Old Torrick 62

8: A Change of Masters 75

9: The Falls 82

10: Symbols and Stars 87

11: Demons and the Dead 100

12: Shirath 115

13: The Palace Plaza 126

14: A New Life 139

15: City Lessons 147

16: A Change in Circumstances 159

17: New Freedoms, New Problems 175

18: The Mechanicials 189

19: Plots and Swords 200

20: Meetings and Mysteries 230

21: Claws in the Night 250

22: The Banehall Besieged 259

23: A New Hallmaster 283

24: The King's Chambers 295

25: Swords In the Banehall 314

26: The Caller's Claws 329

27: The Temple 347

Author Biography 353

Acknowledgements

This book is dedicated to my wife, Cecilia, and my son, Thomas, for their support and love; to the three muses: Wendy, Karen, and Jenny for their inspiration; to Alison Acheson for her advice; to Margaret Curelas and Tina Moreau of Tyche Books for trusting their luck; and to all the writers and all the readers.

~ Kevin Harkness

The Unexpected Hero

"Get up, you lazy pigs!"

The words, which came out as "Geryupyalazpigs," crashed through Garet's sleeping brain. He stiffened and cracked open one eye. His father's own eyes glared back at him over the top rung of the ladder. Garet kept still and squeezed his eyelid down to the limits of secret sight. With a sour grunt, his father climbed down from the sleeping loft to transfer his loud ill-wishes to his wife.

He would have to be extra careful around his father today.

Garet was always careful around Hilly. The big man so obviously disliked his youngest son that Garet had once asked his mother if Hilly was really his father. He had been too young then to realize the insulting nature of the question, but his mother had merely sighed and pointed out that although Garet had a thick head of hair as black as her own and had a smaller build compared to his older brothers, who had all seemed determined to catch up to their father in girth and height as soon as possible, he still possessed his father's grey eyes and high cheek-bones, as well as, she said dryly, a certain stubbornness—especially when facing a difficult problem.

Garet shook his head at recalling this conversation. Everyday was a problem, made bearable only by the presence of his mother and sister in this rough farmhouse. With his father safely out of reach, he pushed back the itchy blanket and sat up. After a stretch and a tug at his hair, cut short and roughly, for the shears were the same ones they would use to trim the sheep in the spring, he put his bare feet into his shoes, feeling the cold floor through a hole in one tattered sole. Something moved near the toe. He hastily pulled the shoe off and shook out a long, green sting-bug that had crawled inside during the night. A shudder ran through him at his close call.

A snicker sounded from across the loft. His older brother Gitel, sliding to the floor from the top bunk, exchanged a knowing look with his twin, Galit, in the bunk below. The two of them laughed their way down the ladder.

Not chance, Garet thought. *Deliberate.* A sting from the fierce little insect, now hissing on the floor, would not have gotten him off work today. No, his father would not put up with such "laziness" and "wool gathering" for a mere sting. But the pain from his swollen foot would have made each step a torment until well after the sun dropped behind the western hills.

His little sister, Allia, reached out for the bug. Although still small enough to be tied by a long cord to her bed for safety's sake, she had never feared anything in her life. She wobbled full tilt at anything fate put in her path. She almost had the enraged insect in her hands when Garet hauled her back by the cord. Howling in indignation, she flailed her arms and the sting-bug waved its antennae in equal anger until Garet brought his other foot, shod in an unbroken shoe, down on the creature. Allia was silent for a moment, then bent down to look at the slimy mess now covering the bottom of Garet's shoe and the rough planks of the loft's floor. Sting-bugs always had more juice in them than you expected.

"Rain at harvest time now," said a quiet voice behind him.

He looked around and saw his mother's head and shoulders, her small, strong hands holding the top rung of the ladder. He lowered his eyes. He didn't know if she believed in the old wives' tale that killing a sting-bug would bring autumn rains to rot the grain in the field, but he knew that his mother hated to kill any living thing. Her husband often railed against this weakness: "What, woman? Do you think the chickens and sheep will cut off their own heads just to suit your tender heart?" And if he was feeling particularly cruel after killing one of the old hens he would seize her long-fingered hands in his gnarled, bloody ones and lecture her about the duties of a farmer's wife. She never talked back—he could be fast and cruel with those bloody hands—but only lowered her eyes and nodded silently. Garet's heart would burn for his mother's shame, and at night, in his narrow bed, he would call on the spirits of the great Northern heroes in the ballads. He would beg for the strength to change his life, to help his mother, and if his mood was black, he would ask for his father's death.

Garet met her eyes and defended his actions. "Allia was reaching for it. I didn't have any choice!"

His mother nodded. She knew that, like herself, Garet had no real cruelty in him, and that for both of them, choices were rare.

"It can't be helped then. Come down to breakfast."

Garet untied Allia's cord from the bedpost and wrapped the end around his wrist just in time as his sister flew at the ladder, missed as usual, and was only saved by a quick tug on her leash.

"Garet! Let go!" Allia fell to the loft floor and tried to wriggle out of the loop tied around her waist.

"Come on, little dragon." Garet picked her up and Allia immediately stopped squirming and clamped two pudgy arms around his neck.

"Let's go eat," he said, smiling at her fierce little face.

"People?" Allia's startling blue eyes fixed on his.

He smiled. "No, you're still too small a dragon for human meat. It's porridge until you get your full growth." It was an old game they played, but one that pleased them both.

Allia allowed herself to be carried down the ladder into the single room of the log farmhouse. The front half was all brightness and morning noise. The table never seemed big enough for his father and hulking brothers, now tearing at the bread on its clay platter. The back of the cabin was windowless and dark. It contained their parent's large, lumpy bed, his mother's spinning wheel, and a trapdoor to the root cellar. Garet's older brothers hinted at a chest of copper coins buried under the potatoes and onions, but they didn't dare the threat of their father's fists to try and find it. Garet often thought wistfully of that treasure. *What could I do, if I had enough money to escape from this farm,* he wondered. Buy passage on a coastal trading ship and go north like his oldest brother, Axil, to fight the dragons? Go west to the demon cities of the coast and find work? Someday, he promised himself, he would leave this place but, as always, the thought of leaving his mother, whom he loved, and his sister, who loved him, made him turn away from such thoughts, and he climbed down towards the heat and light of the small, busy house.

The low sun of morning streamed in through the open door. It shone on the copper pots on their hooks, the painted clay jugs and plates, and on his mother's worn, white apron. The breakfast had been laid out on the sturdy trestle table. Bowls of porridge, topped with green onions and a few dried flakes of salt fish—for his Northerner parents would not live without some fish, even in this land-bound house—a loaf of dark bread now torn into chunks waiting to receive butter, and mugs of milk, were all laid on the scarred planks. His mother moved silently among the three men already savagely devouring their shares. She would eat later when the house was quiet.

"Get to table and eat," roared Garet's father as the boy settled Allia in her seat and tied the cord around the chair's back. "You're to help your brothers gather wood for charcoal."

Gitel and Galit looked knowingly at each other. Garet winced. His brothers, using pinches and slaps as measures of persuasion, would make him do all the gathering of wind-fallen wood. And if his father complained at the end of the day that there was not enough, they would innocently blame it on his laziness and swear that what had been collected was due to their labours alone. Such lies often meant another slap for Garet, this time from his father. When the twins did allow Garet to stop working, they would force him to wrestle or box, practicing for their chief amusement of fighting with other farm lads. No drinking party at the trading post or rare social gathering in those lonely foothills was complete without a brawl. Garet never hit back, because experience had taught him that too much resistance meant a real beating. Instead, he kept his wits about him and twisted and dodged as best he could. His brothers thought this was great fun and bet each other as to who would catch him first. If Garet was lucky, they were too tired by the time they did catch him to do much damage. Garet might be thin, but he had wiry muscles from doing his own and his brothers' work; he also had black and blue patches from their sport with him.

The torments had gotten worse since Axil left for the north. Before his eldest brother fled the same mixture of brutality and boredom that choked Garet, the twins were afraid to harm him, openly at least. Axil, unable to protect his mother or himself from his father's anger, had done what he could to keep Garet safe. Bruised and disheartened, he left one night, a year ago, with only the clothes on his back and a bundle of food that his mother claimed he had stolen, so as to deflect her husband's rage. Before he went, he told Garet, "Get out! Get out as soon as you're old enough to earn your way. There's no life for you here!"

Garet had been only fifteen then. Now, at sixteen, he was old enough to follow his advice, if he dared. With Axil gone, the twins had welcomed their new freedom. They eyed him now, grinning.

Before he could think of an excuse for his father's deaf ears, his mother spoke softly, "I think Garet had better take the sheep to the hill pasture to fatten them up." Her voice was quiet and toneless.

Garet held his breath. His mother rarely contradicted his father. Hilly glared at her, but she stood deferentially, head bent down and slumping her shoulders as she usually did around her husband.

"The good summer grass is about gone," she said, not quite looking at the glowering figure seated at the head of the table. "We'd best graze off the rest of it, before autumn."

Faced with an undeniable truth, her husband chose, as he always did, to meet it with scorn and anger.

"What difference is it?" Hilly finally growled. "He's no use working at the hard jobs anyway. Geyahh! You're treating him like he was Southern dandy, or a girl!"

In his father's view, Garet was small, timid, and skittish. Hilly's attempts to "train-up the boy" had, in his own definite opinion, come to nothing.

Garet blushed hotly while Allia swelled up for a tantrum on behalf of her beloved brother, playmate, and protector, but was distracted when Gitel dug an elbow into Galit's side, provoking a spew of porridge back into his bowl. Allia switched her glare to the twins.

"If he were a girl," Gitel said, "we could marry him off, see, and maybe make some money on the deal."

His father roared with laughter but Gitel's own guffaws were cut short by a wooden spoon slapped down on the back of his knuckles.

"You little nit!" Gitel raised the wounded hand while Allia waved her weapon, looking for another opportunity to strike.

Hilly laughed even louder, if possible, and grabbed the twins, one choking and the other cursing, by their fist-lumped ears. He pulled them outside, dragging them in the direction of the tool shed. His mother closed the door and leaned against it for a moment, pushing at it as if she would keep those loud, cruel men, her own husband and sons, from returning. Then she turned and, after giving Garet a soft pat on the head, and kissing the triumphantly crowing Allia, started clearing the dishes. Breakfast once again survived; it was time to get on with the day's work.

And so it was that Garet was with the eighteen sheep the family owned, watching them graze on the hillside the day that his life changed. The pastures above the farm ran steeply to the crests of the surrounding hills. A smart shepherd sat above the sheep on one of the innumerable boulders these hills spawned, so that any chasing would be downhill and not up.

Below his perch, the farm lay scattered like bits of wood left over from a creek's spring flood. There was not much to look at. Beyond the cabin with its swayback roof, a sheep corral, a few sheds, and a cow barn were placed with a fine lack of care. Wooden fences ran haphazardly, jumping and diving over the uneven terrain. The numerous holes in these barriers were patched with old tree stumps or woven plugs of brambles. The whole farm wore its neglect and indifference like an old, shabby coat, and surrounding it for as far as he could see were only trees and stony hills. Garet knew his father liked this isolation, and, although his wife might have craved other farmwives to talk to, it mattered nothing to Hilly that the nearest company was three hours walk away, at Three Roads tavern.

But no neighbours meant no help either. It seemed a wonder to the boy sitting on the boulder, arms wrapped around his knees, that they grew enough to keep them alive through each winter, though it was often a near thing. A late spring might see his mother taking him far up the wooded slopes to pick wood sorrel. If they were lucky, they would run across rabbit tracks. Then his mother would put aside her reluctance to take a life and show him how to track the small animal to its rough tunnel and pull it out with a noose of flexible spruce roots. Those rabbits and his father's luck with a bow had often meant the difference between mere hunger and slaughtering their sheep to survive. If the sheep ever were lost, his father would have to go back north and admit defeat or maybe even move west, to the river cities to work for a rich man, two things his father would rather die than do.

Garet stirred on his perch. The thought of the wider world thrilled him, perhaps because he knew so little about it.

He did know that it was a world of two great threats. In the North, a place of deep, narrow valleys, where cold rivers tumbled to an even colder sea, dragons harried the fishing boats and fired the ripe grain in the field. In the South, a land of fertile soil and broad rivers, demons hunted people through their strong-walled cities. No, it was not a safe world out there, but those people, even though harried by one or the other of these terrors, still managed to live their lives. And at least they had lives.

Although he had never been farther than Three Roads, he had also heard enough to know the general geography of the Midlands. The Ar, the same river that fed the fertility of the South, split into North and South branches, collecting the waters of these foothills and the farther mountains. This twinned river enfolded a wide plain of gentle climate and rich soils. For a hundred years, people had left their hazardous lives, mostly from the cities of the South but also from the North and the rest of the known lands, and plowed and built until farms dotted the wide prairie. No dragon flew past the endless forests that separated their bleak mountain nests from the Midlands to burn the rich grain fields. No demon clawed at a house door closer than the fortress of Old Torrick, where the two rivers met and gave themselves, through a roaring waterfall, back to the Ar. Generations of men and women had lived peacefully and profitably here. Demons and dragons had become the tales of a winter's evening, bringing wide eyes and a child's playful shrieks, but no real fear.

Garet slid off the boulder and rebuilt his small pile of stones. Whenever a ewe strayed too far, he threw a stone over its head to strike the ground beyond. The animal, as stupid as Gitel and Galit put together, would run from the noise and crowd back into the small flock. There, attracted by the sweet grass of late summer, the sheep would munch contentedly until some new whim sent one of them wandering. Garet sighed. His mother had sent him up to the field early, with a packet of bread and a jug of water. The message was clear: stay up there all day, out of your father's way.

With the sheep temporarily content to feed in a group, he leaned back against the boulder and drifted into a pleasant daydream. It was a familiar one about stealing his father's coins and buying a horse from a Midland farmer to ride, oh to ride all the way along the North Ar to Old Torrick. From there, to gallop past the tumbling waters of the Falls to the first big city of the Southerners, Shirath, the "City on the Two Banks." He had heard tales of that city from plainsmen come trading two years ago at the Three Roads tavern for hill country wool. They spoke of Shirath's beauty, of her lively markets, and of the three great, arched bridges that spanned the Ar to make it one city instead of two. With no experience of the wide world, Garet could not even guess if the merchants' houses, as the traders claimed, were covered with gold and staffed by bejewelled servants, or if the number of storytellers in the market was always greater than the number of listeners. In his fantasy, Garet stood in the middle of three such storytellers, all vying for his attention with tales of heroes, dragons, and demons.

A distant sheep 'bahhed' and Garet came back to his unheroic reality and the pile of stones. It took three well-placed missiles to guide the latest woolly adventurer back to the flock. With the truant returned, Garet settled down again to his dream of wealthy cities—until the next ewe strayed and 'bahhed' him back to his life. The rest of the long day teetered between daydream and dull reality.

The breeze on the hill finally turned, signalling the approach of evening. Garet kept one eye on the cabin, looking for his mother to wave him down for the day. Sitting hunched beside the boulder, he slowly released his dreams and concentrated on reality. As the fantastic images faded, he knew in his heart that he was not destined for an exciting life. He was no hero from his mother's Northern songs. His hands were callused from wielding a shovel, not a dragon-killing spear. His clothes were hand-me-downs and hung loosely, giving him a scarecrow look. No, he did not seem designed for adventure, and, if he were honest with himself, he would have to say that his life would likely be spent in these lonely hills, farming and working until he died, perhaps of boredom.

Now, as the sun slid past the brow of the hill, turning bright day into sudden twilight, Garet climbed the boulder again to look for his mother or brothers to wave him down for supper. No one appeared and Garet finally decided to get the flock headed downhill before it became too dark to see. The sheep were uncharacteristically nervous as they neared their pen. Every other day they trotted happily into the corral, knowing that Garet would mix their ration of grain with some expensive, tasty salt to keep them healthy. Now they milled and crowded from one side of the enclosure to the other, calling to him in plaintive voices.

Inside the cowshed, their milk cow, Saliat, lowed just as nervously. She pranced and pushed against him so urgently that Garet bent to check her udder, but his mother had already milked her dry. The frightened beast then laid her big, soft head in the crook of his arm and rolled her eyes. "Shhhh, shhhh girl, shhhh," Garet said to calm her, but she kept butting into him until he had to leave the poor thing uncomforted, still moaning and staring in her stall. A shiver ran up his back as he walked to the cabin; every animal on the farm was at the point of panic. The chickens buzzed like feathered bees from roost to roost in their coop. The two sows and their piglets backed into a corner of the sty and bared their teeth at Garet as he walked by. The dog, a skinny mongrel with only three legs that his father kept, "just for the bark," whimpered and hid under the steps that led to the farmhouse door.

Garet slipped inside and felt the heat on the left side of his face from a roaring fire in the hearth. His father, who ordinarily wouldn't waste a twig more than was necessary for cooking or heating, especially on a warm summer night, was just pushing in another log. He levered it with the poker between hearth's stone teeth and glared at Garet.

"You're late—as usual. Help your mother." He poked the log furiously and Garet saw sweat beading on his forehead and upper lip.

Garet looked to his mother, but she didn't acknowledge him. She seemed unaware that he had even entered the house. Twisting a washcloth between two white-knuckled fists, she stared out into the twilight beyond the open door.

The dog yelped. Gitel and Galit clattered into the house as if they were being chased by all the people they had ever offended. Galit slammed the door behind him and threw the latch. The cabin fell into shadow; the one small window, covered with a thinly scraped sheep hide, let in barely enough light to show his mother's twisting, wringing hands. The fire only confused his sight with its dancing patterns of light and shadow. Without a word, his father took down the winter lamp from the mantle and lit it.

Garet was dumbstruck. No one, especially someone as stingy as his father, wasted lamp oil. Every winter they were treated to lectures about how the expensive oil must be traded all the way from the dry lands south of the Midland Plains, its price increasing with each mile travelled. And yet with twilight still brightening the sky, the winter lamp blazed on the mantle! He shivered, despite the heat of the fire. This was so strange; what was happening to them? Only Allie seemed immune to whatever fit had gripped his family and was now jumping under his own skin. Tied to her chair and fixing the door with her usual savage glare, she held a wooden spoon ready in her hand.

His mother finally stirred herself to put the food on the table, and they all sat in silence. The dinner was a fine one, for late summer was a rare time of plenty. It consisted of a stewed hen, who had ceased to lay eggs thus sealing its fate, new potatoes, and greens that his mother grew in the farm's kitchen garden. But the dinner had no taste for Garet. He could barely force any food past his chattering teeth. The muscles of his shoulder knotted under a nameless dread. His brothers jumped at every clink of a fork against a plate. In desperation, he tried to break the mood by daring to talk directly to his father.

"Father, the sheep are gaining weight." There was no response, and he tried again. "Will we take the yarn to Three Roads to sell this year?" This was more than he usually said to his father in a week, and to ask such a foolish question— after all where else would they take the yarn—usually meant a clout to the ear. But any response, even a slap, would be better than this stretching silence.

His father slowly turned to face him, but his eyes were as wide and staring as the cow's. Garet felt his stomach knot. Then the dog yipped and shrieked right outside the door. Garet jumped back, turning his chair over. The only other person who moved was Allia, who twisted her head to look at him, as he backed up to the cabin wall, crowding the pots hanging on their hooks.

The door latch started to rise, pushed up by a long, curved blade slid between the door and the jamb. The latch cleared its hook, and the door opened a crack. The thin blade was joined by three others, and Garet saw that they were not knives; they were a set of claws, attached to a bony, mottled arm. That arm now slid through the crack and felt along the wall. The door opened wider and a head out of a nightmare followed. It was narrow and ridged. Bony crests ran from a sloped forehead to the flattened crown. Instead of a nose, it thrust forward a leathery beak. Two black eyes, showing neither whites nor pupils, peered into the room. The mouth opened to reveal a narrow tongue flicking in a bed of needle teeth.

The creature pulled itself inside, and now Garet saw blood on its beak and tufts of fur and feathers stuck to its spidery hands. It was skeleton-thin and moved quickly, sometimes like a child on two gangly legs, sometimes on all fours, like some freakish hunting cat. The small part of Garet's mind that could still think knew what it must be: a demon! A demon where it had no right to be. This was the Midlands. Here all were safe from both the demons of the South and the dragons of the North. But the demon ignored the impossibility of its presence and climbed onto the crowded table, skittering over the dishes.

A low moaning filled the room, and Garet's horror increased. The man Garet had thought he feared more than anyone or anything else in the world could only whimper as the creature walked his table. His two brothers sat as rigidly as their father. As the demon passed the twins, the sharp smell of urine bit the air. The demon sniffed at it, seemed to grin, and continued towards Garet's grey-faced parents. Its thin arm slowly lifted and reached, almost delicately, towards his father's clenched face.

"Nnn—Nnnn, Nnnno...," his mother seemed to push out the syllable by sheer force of will. Her head jerked from side to side.

The creature paused, as if surprised at this discourtesy, and the curved claws changed their course from the man's face to the woman's. A hot anger erupted in Garet's belly, warming him and loosening his muscles. He began to burn with an incredible rage: anger at the creature for threatening his mother, anger at his father and brothers for doing nothing, and anger at himself for his fear of the thing. That last anger was the strongest. It fought with the horror that came off the demon like a foul wind. He hated this fear, and all the others of his life. He saw his terror of the demon as being no different from his fear of his father, his brothers, and his bleak future. A battle raged inside him, as if every fear he had ever felt filled his chest, and the anger boiled up to meet it.

The curved knives were an inch from his mother's eyes when Allia yelled. The demon paused. Though small, his sister could shake the roof when she wished. She brought her spoon squarely down on the creature's other hand. She was no amateur at this, and the spoon hit a knuckle. The thing gave a piercing shriek. The raised claws now twisted to slash at the child.

Garet moved without knowing it, without knowing that he could. His forgotten hand had been on a copper pot, heavy as a paving stone, and he grabbed the handle and flung it at the creature. It was more effective than he could have hoped. The heavy bottom of the pot brushed past the spindly arm and smashed into the side of the vicious beak. Garet heard a crack—he didn't know whether the pot's handle or the thing's head was broken—and the demon was flung between his two brothers into the hearth's crackling fire. His body now free, Garet scrambled over the table after the beast. He had no weapon or skill, so he did what he could. As the creature tried to crawl out of the flames that were consuming it, he used the long poker to shove it back in and hold it tight against the blazing logs until its hideous, whistling shrieks stopped.

Strangers at the Gate

Nothing was the same.

The moon had passed from new to almost full, and the beast had been buried, twice now. The first time had been the night the demon invaded their home. Garet had dragged the charred body out the door, past the torn remains of the dog, and had buried it between the outhouse and the manure pile. Looking down on it in its grave, he was again struck by its appearance. He could not call it an animal, for what mere animal could have paralyzed a man like his father. Hilly claimed to have fought against the dragons in the North. His sons might have thought it a lie, but their mother had quietly confirmed it. She had met Hilly when he was a member of the brigades, men who climbed the sharp cliffs above the northern sea and hunted dragons among the rocks. Two years before, he had set three arrows in a charging hill bear that had been after the pigs and laughed as it collapsed and died a few feet from him. And yet this huge, violent man, who was three times the size of this gangly creature, had sat frozen while its claws reached for his eyes.

Not an animal then, Garet thought, *and not really human either*. There were vague similarities. It had two arms and two legs. The spindly hands had four fingers and a thumb, although each was tipped with a sickle claw. Its general shape, although exaggerated, was similar to his own. Indeed, when stretched out in the cold moonlight, its torso and limbs were a deformed mockery of a young child. But all such resemblance ended with the head. The long, flattened

14

skull was curved at the back, hanging over the spine like a round stone. Starting at the brows, the face narrowed into that cruel beak. Steeling himself, Garet had pried open its mouth with the shovel and seen that the thing's tongue, swollen in death, was neatly split at the tip to give it a forked, snake-like look. Its many teeth fit together as closely as the blades of a pair of shears. He was glad enough to cover the corpse with a layer of concealing dirt; for even in death, he still felt a wrenching fear of it.

The need for a second burial quickly became apparent. Only Garet could bear to come near the thing's grave, though even passing near the spot made his stomach flip. This made its resting place beside the privy an urgent problem. Hilly and the twins had bolted from the cabin as soon as Garet had dragged the corpse outside. They did not return until the next evening, stinking of the rotgut liquor that Pranix, the owner of the Three Roads tavern, sold to the unsophisticated hill farmers and any ignorant traveller. Hilly was a friend of the tavern keeper; though hardly close enough to beg a free drink. Garet wondered where he had got the money. Upon their return, they had made a beeline for the outhouse, jostling and cursing each other. But a good five yards away, they had all shuddered to a stop and stood weaving and belching a moment before stumbling down to the bushes behind the chicken coop. On hearing that the demon was buried near the privy, Hilly clouted Garet's ear, much harder than usual, and demanded he move the body before breakfast. There was a new look in his father's eyes. The contempt was gone and had been replaced by something else—hatred?

He had wrapped the stiffened corpse in an old, ragged sheepskin and dragged it to the far edge of the sheep pasture. The fear of being near it came on him again and he sweated from more than the effort it took to get the corpse up the hill. The new grave was shallower, due to the rocky soil, and Garet rolled several large stones on top of it to keep the animals away. He needn't have bothered. When he brought the sheep up after breakfast to continue grazing off the last of the summer grass, none of the ewes would go within fifty feet of the pile of boulders. *If I could bury a dozen of those things around this field,* Garet thought ruefully, *I'd never have to throw another stone.*

For the next two weeks, life seemed both better and worse for Garet. It was now easier to avoid his father and brothers. Indeed, it seemed that they were intent on avoiding him. Not a word was yelled at him during meals. No sting-bugs or other practical jokes tested his finely-developed sense of caution. His brothers even gave up using him as a training dummy. But this new freedom was tainted by the way they looked at him when they thought he wasn't looking back. He caught it from the corners of his eyes or in the reflection of the copper pot hanging again on its hook behind the table. Their eyes held fear and hatred. Fear? Of him? His mother's and Allia's treatment of him was unchanged, unless you could count a warm gratitude and pride that coloured every word or look his mother sent his way. His little sister seemed unaffected by these earthshaking events. She yowled and twisted, hugged and demanded as much or as little as before. *After all,* thought Garet, with one of the few smiles he had in those weeks, *what was a mere demon to a child who risked sudden death a dozen times a day?*

As the moon passed into its dark phase, word came from Three Roads that Demonbanes had ridden from the cities of Old Torrick and Shirath. They came to track the demons that had attacked not only Hilly's farm but also farms and villages throughout the Midlands. Garet heard this from his mother, who had it from the tavern keeper's wife.

Returning from delivering eggs to the trading post, she told the family, "Trallet says there have been attacks all through the Midlands. Many have died. Pranix has gone to the Rivermeet." She looked at Hilly. "Will you be going?" It was a direct question for someone who usually hedged her speech in 'ifs' and 'perhaps' to avoid challenging her violent mate. Since the demon's attack, Garet had seen his mother become more confident, as if she too were tired of her fears.

If it was a direct question, it was also a fair one. Hilly was the unofficial leader of the hill farmers near Three Roads, if only because his temper meant no one cared to disagree with him. The village of Bangt, where the North Ar was fed by the Plainscutter River, hosted the Rivermeet every year. The hill farmers would need representation, and none would trust Pranix, the tavern keeper who overcharged them for trade goods and underpaid them for their wool, to look after their best interests.

Hilly, however, sneered at the suggestion. "What can a hundred fat Southerners do about," and here he stumbled, for he never spoke of that fearful night, "...about anything!" He stomped out the door, and the twins slouched after him.

His wife sighed and said, more to herself than to Garet, "They'll be off to the tavern now, trying to get free drinks." Her expression showed that this was unlikely, and Garet had to agree; Pranix and Trallet's stinginess was legendary.

Garet also sighed. With Allia taking up so much of her mother's time, most of the work of the farm now fell on his own shoulders. His father and brothers disappeared for whole days at a time. He knew they did this to avoid him. He also knew that when it came time to dig up the root crops and store them, or plow the land in the spring, the farm would need their strength. Maybe he should leave, finally fulfil one of his daydreams and escape from this life. With so many said to be killed on the plains, there must be a place for a farm lad used to hard work. If their farm failed because he stayed, he would end up hurting his mother and Allia. He could not bear the thought of them with the pinched faces and bloated bellies of starvation. He remembered all too well the children of less fortunate farmers who came begging at the farm gate in the early spring when the poor suffered most. If Hilly was around he would chase them off with curses, but if his mother was alone, she would give them some of her gathered wild greens or a scrawny chicken to take back to their homesteads.

Garet's time in the sheep pasture was now spent considering possible, rather than imaginary, futures. These weeks were like living through the low part of winter, between the great events of harvest and spring. But in all the fantasies he had created on this boulder, he had never foreseen how frightening real change could be. Now that he had finally played the hero of his daydreams, he feared that his reward would be to lose all that he loved along with all that he hated.

A week after the news from Three Roads, strangers came riding between the low hills to the gate of Hilly's farm. From his perch on the sheep pasture boulder, Garet could see his father gesture angrily at the four figures, who had not bothered to dismount. The party consisted of an older man mounted on a tall black, a young woman or older girl on a smaller grey, and two boys, younger than Garet and riding together on a big, brown farm horse. The twins had swaggered over to join their father, and all three now seemed to be shouting at the older man. His father repeatedly pointed at himself and waved his arms. Whatever response he got must have displeased Hilly for he shook his fists at the unmoving figure on the black horse.

The girl urged her mount up beside his, crowding the twins back. The older man merely kicked the sides of the big black. Hilly jumped out of the way as the party rode through the gate and towards the farmhouse. For a long moment, Garet saw his father stare after the riders. Then, Hilly lifted his face to the sheep pasture. Across that great distance, father and son looked at each other. Garet ducked his head as his father spat in the dirt of the trail and turned away. With the twins following, Hilly walked quickly back the way the strangers had come, in the direction of Three Roads and the tavern.

His mother appeared at the door of the cabin, waving her hand to signal him down from the pasture. Garet eyed the sun, still too high above the hill's brow to bring in the sheep, and knew that he was being called to a meeting. *Perhaps the new life starts here*, he thought. A stray breeze played with the back of his neck. Nervously, he picked up a handful of stones and began the laborious process of aiming the sheep downhill.

When he had corralled the sheep and reached the cabin door, he saw his mother seated at the table with Allia twisting in her lap, facing the older man. Garet slipped quietly inside and made his way around the table to his mother's side. His back touched the heavy pot he had thrown at the demon, and for a wild moment, his hand itched to pick it up again and drive these strangers from the house.

The old man gave no indication that he felt endangered. Stiff as a plank, he sat across from Garet's mother and sipped his tea. There was no sign of the two younger boys, but the girl, tall, blond and no more than a year older than Garet, stood just as stiffly behind the grey-haired man. Garet couldn't help staring. Their clothing was well made but dusty. They each wore a coloured sash over a long, purple vest, a black, high-collared shirt, and grey trousers tucked into high, black boots. The girl's sash was green, the old man's blood red. The girl noticed his open examination and gave back an icy glare.

The old man put down his tea. "Mistress Allaina, at the tavern it is said that there was a demon slain here."

Garet's mother straightened as if to match the posture of the man opposite and replied, "Yes sir."

Garet prayed that she wouldn't expose his actions on that terrible night until they knew what these strangers wanted, but his worries were interrupted by an indignant outburst from the girl.

"A Bane of the Master Mandarack's rank is to be addressed as 'Master', not 'sir'—farmwife!" The last word was delivered dripping with contempt. She took a step forward and Garet, less intimidated by someone so near his own age and size, stepped up to shield his mother from her anger.

The old man raised his right hand, and Garet saw that the other hand lay twisted and curled in his lap, the whole arm seeming dead to use. The girl immediately stopped her forward motion and retreated to her station behind her "master". She appeared to be grinding her teeth. Her blue eyes were blazing, and her blond hair, so typical among Southerners, shook in its braids.

"Salick," said the seated man, his good hand still raised, "Mistress Allaina is from the North, and has—or so it is said at the tavern—lived isolated upon this farm since she came south." He looked a question at Garet's mother. She gave a brief nod, and Garet was surprised to see that she was also angry. The old man continued, "It is neither surprising nor disrespectful that she is unaware of our traditions...or of how to speak in such a situation."

The older woman blushed slightly, barely noticeable against her dark complexion, but Salick's fair skin turned dark red and Garet thought Master Mandarack's comments were more for her benefit than for his mother's. Having no other place to put her anger, the girl glared once more at Garet, but he had already returned to his mother's side, his attention back on Mandarack.

"I spoke to your husband." Was that slight twist of his lips a judgement? "And he claimed to have killed the demon himself. Indeed, that is what we first heard in the tavern." His hand rose again, this time to forestall Allaina's protest, which was accompanied by the rapid banging of Allia's spoon on the table. Mandarack patiently waited for the noise to end. "After a moment's speech with him, it was obvious that he was claiming another's due." The man's eyes, grey as a threatening cloud, shifted to Garet. "But I think the one who did the deed is in this room."

Garet felt his mother's hand grasp his own and, with that encouragement, he stepped forward.

"My lord," he spoke as loudly as he could, "I killed the beast," and here his voice faltered, "but I don't know how..."

Salick looked at him with open surprise, but Mandarack only nodded his head as if he had expected the demonslayer to be a skinny, ragged boy not yet seventeen.

"Demons destroy people by fear as much as by claw or beak, lad. Only those who can bear that fear become Demonbanes. Were you not afraid?" The pale eyes held him and demanded an answer.

Garet swallowed. "Yes, my lord, I was as afraid as the rest of my family." He would not mention Allia's courage or her role in defeating the demon. He needed to find out their interest in him before he would risk his sister.

The old man raised the cup and took an appreciative sniff of the contents. "Mint, and strawberry leaves; a refreshing drink, Mistress." He fixed Garet with his pale eyes again. "Lad, if you were as 'afraid as the rest of your family', you would be dead, and I would now be hunting the beast through these dark hills. Were you afraid in," he paused to find the right words, "a true proportion to the danger the demon represented?"

Garet thought for a moment before answering. "I feared it more than I thought I should, at least, when I had time to think about it." He swallowed and continued, "But I thought it was only because I was a coward." For some reason it became extremely important not to look at the young woman standing across from him.

Mandarack shook his head. "You are no coward," he said firmly. "A demon's power is that it makes men and women fear it more than is...necessary. Much more." He took another sip of tea. "Any of you, well almost any of you," his lips twitched into a slight smile at Allia who lifted her spoon threateningly in response, "could have killed such a small demon as was described at the tavern." He glanced over Garet's shoulder. "Your mother herself could have dispatched it with one good blow from that pot."

Garet barely kept a smile from his own lips as Mandarack unknowingly named the very weapon he had used to dispatch the demon.

The old man continued, "No, it is not strength, or rough courage, or even the weapon that matters. Fear is the key. Demons are covered with it like a stench. It strikes all those who are near." He raised his cup slightly off the table, as if in a subtle toast to the boy in front of him. "Only those who have known fear as a constant companion and refuse to give in to it can stand up to the special terror a demon brings."

Mandarack stood, and the girl at his elbow opened the door in preparation for their leaving. It was obvious from her twitching nose that she wished to be gone from this poor house as soon as her master allowed it.

"Mistress Allaina," Mandarack spoke to his mother as an equal and she rose and stood straighter than usual in acknowledgement, "the demons that have long plagued the cities of the South have appeared in the Midlands for the first time in history. We need all who can be trained to fight against them. It is the custom in the South to take those who can withstand a demon's fear and train them in the Banehall of their city." He glanced around the cabin. "There has never been a need for a Banehall in the Midlands, so we are taking any likely candidates to Shirath for training. As you are a

Northerner and a stranger to our customs, I feel that it is right that we should ask your leave to do so."

Garet's mother swayed a bit and grasped the back of her chair with both hands. "You mean to take Garet to Shirath? How will he live? Who will care for him?"

Mandarack appeared not to hear Salick's snort. "Banes are well supported by the city they live in, Mistress," he replied. "Your son, if he becomes a Bane, will never lack for food or the means to live. If he cannot pass our tests, I will guarantee his safe return to your farm." He held his good hand out towards her. "It must be your decision, Mistress."

It seemed an eternity of time to Garet as his mother stood looking at her son, searching his face, and perhaps looking inside her own heart for the strength to say what she must.

"My Lord Mandarack," she said facing the grey-haired man again and putting her own hand in his, "as you have said, I do not know all your ways, but if you promise to give my son a better life than he would have here, you may take him."

Mandarack merely nodded, but Salick's nose twitched again, and her expression seemed to say, "A better life than this? Any life would be better!"

Out of the Hills

The Plains were a revelation to Garet. He had spent his life trapped within the dark green hills that surrounded his father's farm. Even Three Roads, the nearest thing to a village within walking distance, was hemmed in by those forested ridges, which ran for ten days' travel from the edge of the prairies to the far mountains.

Now his eyes ran along lines that did not end in a humped, green wall. Sometimes flat, sometimes gently rolling, the land was a continuous surprise. Even the colours were different. The grass, long enough to tickle the belly of the horse he rode, glowed golden in the setting sun. The wind sent great waves of the nodding, seeded stems bowing and straightening all around him. Looking up, the blue arc of the sky seemed deeper, wider, and more vibrant. And just when he thought that blue and gold were the only colours left in the world, they would ride through a patch of wildflowers, red poppies and tall, purple lupine, that stretched half-way to the horizon.

The only visible barrier as the small party rode west was a thin line of clouds hovering above the distant horizon. At times the limitless views led Garet to think they made no progress at all, and the horses only walked in place while the sun swept overhead. Then he felt exposed and naked, a worm crawling across a giant's table. At other times, when the swaying of the horse lulled him into drowsiness, he felt his spirit flow out over the plains, bending and swaying on the endless grass, and then something like peace came into his heart. Most of his time, however, was not spent in contemplation of the landscape, but on more immediate, personal concerns.

It was two days since he had left his home, and all the day dreams he had spun of riding away to adventure and independence had not prepared him for the two things most on his mind: his loneliness and the pain in his backside.

Although all the boys had tried riding neighbours' horses at Three Roads, Garet had never ridden for more than a few minutes. Now, after two days of riding, the chafing of the saddle on his bottom and thighs had made life miserable and walking almost impossible. The night before, Salick had been forced to steady him as he hobbled from his mount to the camp they had made. It had taken over an hour for him to recover and walk downwind far enough to attend to his body's needs. Salick had haughtily informed him that the discomfort would disappear as soon he became used to riding. Garet, after another full day in the saddle, felt that becoming used to riding might take the rest of his life.

Mandarack signalled to Salick and pointed over to their right. In the distance, a line of trees seemed to magically appear out of the dry grass of the prairie. The elderly man, relaxed and seemingly immune to saddle sores, turned the head of his lean, black mare and trotted towards the distant trees. Salick signalled the younger boys, Dorict and Marick. Both rode the same horse, a brown plough horse that Marick claimed was the stupidest animal he had ever seen. Dorict pulled its blocky head to follow Salick's lead. The mare placidly obeyed. Stupid or not, the animal was the only one of the four that could bear to drag, although on a very long rope, the corpse of the demon. The two Banes, perhaps two or three years younger than Garet, had somehow found the corpse and prepared it while he talked with Mandarack and Salick. The other horses, the two ridden by Mandarack and Salick and the pert brown pony from Three Roads that Garet suffered on, stayed far ahead of the mare as Marick yipped in his high voice and jammed his heels into its barrel ribs to urge it to a reluctant trot. The bundled corpse bounced and swung behind them, knocking down great swaths of the tall grass.

Garet turned the head of his pony to jolt after Salick's mount. An hour passed before the trees grew near. The sun would soon be resting on the clouds lining the horizon. Now he could see that the trees grew out of a river valley that cut a curved line through the plains. The banks of the river slumped down from the flatlands at a steep angle and they had to ride a good mile before they found a path gentle enough for the horses to manage. The other side of the river boasted a small farmstead, but no smoke rose from its clay and stick chimney, and no animals sheltered in the large corral. Like all the farms they had passed, this one was deserted. *Where have all the people gone*, he wondered. Had the demons killed them all? He desperately wanted to know this and a thousand other things. What would happen to him in Shirath? Why did Mandarack, Salick, and the two boys all wear different coloured sashes? And just who was Mandarack? How could he ride up to Pranix, himself just returned from the Rivermeet, point to a horse and take it without paying? The tavern keeper, who could blister skin with his curses, had merely grumbled under his breath and saddled the mount for Garet's use. Everything that was happening around him grew out of some mystery that no one would bother to explain!

His loneliness rose up and, for a moment, he forgot the pain of riding. He bent over the horse's neck and felt a knife-sharp longing for the simple, reassuring threads of his lost life: his mother putting dinner on the table, her quick hands moving in the light of the winter lamp; his sister banging the table with the rough wooden dragon he had carved for her; even his father and brothers coming roaring in from the fields. Tears fell on the pony's neck, and it tossed its head at the unexpected wetness.

"Are you sick?" Salick asked sharply. She had dropped back beside him, their mounts brushing each other on the narrow trail along the river's edge.

Garet remained silent, bent over the pony's neck. He would not give this arrogant, unpleasant girl the pleasure of seeing him cry.

"No," he grunted.

Salick said nothing else, more evidence, Garet thought, of her dislike. She nudged her horse past the pony, taking up her accustomed place behind Mandarack. When the party came to a flat spot nestled in the curve of the river, Mandarack dismounted. Garet envied his obvious lack of discomfort. He gingerly swung his own leg over the pony's rump and slid down to the ground, remembering this time to keep a grip on the reins so that no one would have to chase down his mount. To his surprise, he could manage the pain well enough to stand on his own. Delicately, with tiny steps, he led the horse to the river's edge and let it drink. Marick came up beside him, leading the stout mare. The demon's corpse had been left on the prairie, some distance from the head of the trail.

"Still bowlegged?" The younger boy's joking tone could have been either a friendly jibe or callous insult.

Garet only nodded, still unsure of how to respond. Marick puzzled him. Like the twins, the small Bane took every opportunity to poke fun at Garet. He had laughed openly when, at the end of the first day's riding, Garet's legs gave out, and he lowered himself from the saddle straight into a surprised squat on the ground. And when Garet's horse had run away the night before, forcing Dorict to chase it for a half a mile, the small boy had collapsed in whoops and howls of mirth until even Salick, too busy supporting Garet to help catch the pony, had cracked a slight smile.

And yet for all that, Marick's enjoyment of Garet's mistakes had none of the cutting cruelty of his brothers' laughter. As far as the younger boy was concerned, Garet had joined them for the sole purpose of increasing Marick's own enjoyment of life. And that enjoyment was obvious in everything he did. He chattered at the silent and irritated Dorict on their shared horse and cheerfully dismounted to help whenever the demon's corpse became tangled in a patch of brush. Unintimidated by Salick's dour presence, he often teased her by snapping to attention or bowing at every word she said.

He even found his own mistakes hilarious. At their noon break that day, he had stepped off his horse into a warm pile of droppings left by Mandarack's tall black. A shocked yelp had turned suddenly into a rush of gasping, wheezing laughter at his own predicament. The fit went on so long that the Master himself walked back to look down on his helpless apprentice. Marick had looked up from his undignified position, flat on his back with one reeking boot in the air and gasped out at the Bane, "Master, I've found something you dropped." Dorict's and Garet's jaws both dropped; Salick turned a deep shade of purple as she choked on a withering reprimand. Mandarack, however, merely regarded the boy, who was still wheezing as if he had run all the way from the foothills, and turned back to attend to his mount. This set off a whole new round of gasps and howls from Marick, and it was some time before they could get any work out of him.

Marick now squatted easily by the river, grinning at the creaks and groans produced by Garet as he lowered himself down on his haunches. They drank from their cupped hands before the horses had a chance to muddy the water. The cool water was a blessing after the late summer heat of the prairies. The two finally straightened and led their horses back to the wilting trees bordering the campsite. Garet's resemblance to an old man as he stood up set Marick chuckling again, and for a moment Garet thought that if he held his hands out to the boy, as to a roaring fire, the heat of Marick's good cheer would banish the pain of his isolation.

His next encounter, however, brought him back to reality. Dorict called to him, "Get some firewood. Salick says we'll camp here tonight."

This was the longest speech he had received from Dorict so far, and Garet decided to risk a question. "What is this place?"

If Dorict heard the question, he did not bother to reply. Instead, the boy went back to his mount and pulled off the saddlebags stuffed with the food so reluctantly supplied by Pranix. Garet looked over to the others and saw Salick staring at him, waiting for him to obey the order. With a sigh, he picked up the hatchet and limped off to start picking up deadfalls and knock dry branches off the heat-struck trees.

The fallen leaves and brown ferns brushed against his canvas pants, the only ones he owned that were long enough and whole enough to qualify as decent clothing. The pants, along with a wool tunic that itched in this heat, his tattered shoes, and a few copper coins pressed on him by his mother at their parting were all the reminders he had of his old life. After delivering a second armload of firewood to his indifferent companions, Garet found himself wandering farther away from the camp, westward along the riverbank. He stopped picking up branches and stood looking out over the water.

The river broadened at this point, coming out of the narrow curve that had created their campsite. Farther along, above the trees, a thin column of smoke rose from an unseen fire, but Garet was too heartsick to wonder who else might be left in this demon-cursed country. It felt better just looking at the river and trying not to think at all. The twilight had turned the water to a fine, grey satin. The surface rippled and flowed in and out of itself, gliding over logs and sandbars. Dragonflies flitted a touch above the water, chasing clouds of busy gnats. Leaning his shoulder against a slanting birch tree, Garet ran his hand over the scarred bark and felt the tears rise up in him again.

Standing there, really sobbing at last in the privacy of the sheltering trees, Garet did not hear the light, precise footsteps behind him.

Mandarack's dry voice reached him through the sound of his own weeping. "Do you desire to go home, boy?"

Garet turned quickly, wiping his tear-stained face with the back of his sleeve. The Bane stood in the shadow of the trees, his calm, pitiless gaze demanding an answer.

"Why wouldn't I?" he spat. The bitterness of his own answer surprised him but did not faze the old man.

"Can you go home?" Mandarack's voice kept the same dry tone.

Garet's mouth flew open to shout, "Yes!" but he closed it before he spoke the word. Could he? His mother and Allia would accept him, of course. His mother might be disappointed that he had not been able to escape the farm, but she would not—could not—turn him away. But what of his father and brothers? With a sinking heart, Garet realized that he could never return to the farm. It had only been a

28

comforting fantasy, like one of his sheep pasture daydreams. Looking miserably at Mandarack, Garet wondered, *why do I always want to be somewhere else? Stuck on the farm, I wanted to be a hero on his travels. Now I am a hero, and I just want to be back on the farm!* As he thought this, a small fire of determination, similar to the one that had helped him fight the demon, blazed in his belly. He stood straighter to face the old man.

"No, Master," he tried to speak as evenly as the Bane, "I know I can't go back to the farm. My father wouldn't have it." There, that was it. He had no place to go but forward, though maybe not in this unpleasant company.

Mandarack raised an eyebrow and, as if able to guess his thoughts, observed, "And yet you are unhappy here. Most children, you know, dream of becoming Demonbanes." He paused. "But I forget how you were raised."

Garet bristled slightly at this easy dismissal of his life. Mandarack noticed the resentment and raised his eyebrow again. "That's good. Anger is better than sadness, at least in our profession. It has its uses." He reached across with his good hand and drew up his crippled arm to cross both at his chest. "My mind has been much on what is happening in these Midlands. And it has been many years since I have worked with initiates..." he saw Garet's look of confusion, "...those who are beginners in the Banehall."

Turning to look at the river, his voice became less dry and more gentle. "There is not much ease or choice these days for any of us, but if one thing could be changed, and I can make no promises," he waited to catch Garet's nod of understanding, "what would it be?"

Garet now knew better than to ask to return home. And he guessed that no one could demand friendship. However, there was one thing he could ask for—the one thing that could help him to live in this new life.

"Master," Garet replied quickly, "I want to know all the things you do." He stumbled at Mandarack's surprised look, "No—not that exactly." He searched for the right words. "I need to know whatever someone my age should know about demons, the South, Banes, Shirath..." his voice rose in frustration, "about their life!"

Mandarack considered the request while Garet leaned back against the tree, shaking with the effort of freeing his emotions. Above his head, a flock of crows cawed and spun their way from the river towards the open plains.

The grey-haired Bane had already turned back towards the campsite. "I will instruct Salick to answer any questions you might have," he said over his shoulder. "Ride beside her tomorrow. Learn quickly. You have only a few days to make up for a lifetime of ignorance." He had gone a dozen paces when he realized Garet had not followed him. He turned towards the boy and saw him looking up at the mass of black birds. "What is it now, lad?"

Garet lowered his eyes. "Master, crows should fly to their roosts at this time of day." Dusk had settled around them, muting the colours of the small valley. "No crow would sleep on the open ground. Why would they fly away from their nests?" The flock poured across the sky above them, obscuring the face of the pale, full moon.

Mandarack did not answer. He stood, with his eyes closed, turning his head slowly from one side to the other, as if listening to a distant sound or seeking out a barely discernible scent. The movements became smaller and smaller until he faced the thin column of smoke that rose, almost invisible against the darkening sky, a quarter mile away. Garet, looking in the same direction, felt a tingling in his belly, a nervous fluttering.

Mandarack opened his eyes, looked for a moment at the smoke and turned quickly towards their camp.

Garet hurried behind the tall man, trotting to keep up with his long strides. The Master, usually invisible in his calmness, seemed to grow and crackle with impatient energy. Salick looked up as they came into camp. She ran over to their pile of gear, laying her hand on the long, leather case still tied to the saddle.

Mandarack shook his head, "Not yet. The demon is not so close. Bring the weapons and come with me." He quickly made his way up the embankment. Salick followed with the case and Dorict fished a long pole out of the pile, one end covered in a leather bag. Marick hurried over and grabbed the hatchet from Garet's hand. For once the cheerful apprentice looked serious. Dorict plucked a wide-bladed knife from a saddlebag. All three Banes scrambled after Mandarack, leaving Garet to follow empty-handed. At the top of the cut, he pried a fist-sized rock out of the dirt and ran after the Banes before the deepening night could hide them from his sight.

They ran, making surprising speed for such a disparate group. Garet's sore muscles warmed and loosened as he followed. Clouds danced across the moon's face. In moonlight and shadow they sped along the top of the river cliff until they arrived at the source of smoke. It was a homestead much like the farm he had seen across the river: a sod cabin with a thatched roof, a mud and stick chimney, a beehive shaped bread oven near the door, and a corral beside the house. But this chimney still produced its thread of smoke, and the corral was not empty, though it contained nothing alive. As Garet took in the clawed and chewed remains of four cows and their calves lying in pools of their own blood, the fear that had been growing as they neared the farm threatened to come pouring out of his stomach and onto the ground at his feet. Salick noted his distress, and although she was green-faced herself, sternly signalled him to cover his mouth to keep from vomiting.

Mandarack held out his right arm, the left hanging limply at his side. Salick opened the case she carried and brought out a length of metal, bright in the moonlight. Oval at one end and sharply pointed at the other, it looked like a narrow shield. Mandarack slipped his arm through a loop at the blunt end and gripped a smaller loop nearer the point. His forearm was now covered in gleaming steel from his elbow to a foot below his knuckles.

Salick put out her hands to Dorict. The boy thrust the knife into his belt and nervously untied the bag at the end of the pole he carried. He handed her a queer, three-pronged spear. With a thrill of recognition, Garet thought, *I've heard of this in the songs of the Sea Lords. A trident!* The shaft with its barbed tines was taller than Salick as she held it nervously before her. Garet glanced at Dorict and Marick. Each bore a weapon now, Dorict a knife and Marick the hatchet. Garet hefted the stone he had dug from the dirt; it had a comforting weight. He looked up to see Mandarack staring at the rock in his hand. After a slight hesitation, the old man nodded, but then waved the three boys back with his shielded arm. The moon peeped through a rift in the bank of clouds. There was no sound; even the crickets had left off their chirping. The world seemed to be holding its breath as the Master and his apprentice approached the closed door. At a nod from Mandarack, Salick poked it open with the prongs of the trident.

The night exploded.

Salick and Mandarack jumped back as the door slammed closed. The frame did not stop it, and the planks continued to bow outwards from some hideous pressure within. Now the frame itself broke and brought the sod wall with it. Beams cracked, and the turf roof fell in. Something immense pushed its way through the debris and out of the ruined farmhouse.

The demon was huge. It towered above the five humans ranged against it. Garet could easily have walked under it without brushing the distended belly with his head. Its breath reeked of fresh blood, and drops of it slid off the hooked claws at the end of each spindly leg. The demon's head was small in proportion to the mass of its chest and stomach but it was still eerily familiar to Garet. The black eyes were smaller and set under larger ridges, these rising up into wickedly sharp horns; the beak was shorter and stronger, and yet it was kin to what Garet had slain. Shaking itself free of the roof beams, it battered through the remains of the wall and attacked.

Mandarack waved them all farther back and engaged the demon. Moving with a grace and economy of motion that would have been impressive in a man half his years, the Demonbane easily avoided the slashes of the creature's front legs. With the quick, precise movements of a sparrow flitting from branch to branch, he sidestepped each vicious attack. Garet soon saw the strategy behind his jumps and twists. Mandarack was leading the creature into the corral, where it soon stumbled over the broken rails and dead cattle in its pursuit of the old man. He had still not used the shield to either protect himself or attack the thing.

When the creature inadvertently hooked a back leg into the gutted body of a calf, Mandarack shouted, "Now!"

Salick ran forward and thrust the trident through the fence rails. She pinned the demon's other back leg between the weapon's tines and, with a strength not apparent in her slim form, twisted the shaft to lock the leg and drag it towards her.

The creature, already overbalanced, tried to jerk the leg back in its fury to catch the old Bane darting just out of reach.

Salick, gasping with the effort of restraining the beast, called out, "Dorict, Marick!"

The two boys dropped their weapons and ran to her, wrapping their arms around her waist and shoulders. After a moment's hesitation, Garet dropped his rock and joined them, grabbing the remnant of the shaft that stuck out behind Salick's hands and twisting hard in the same direction. With a crack, the thing's leg twisted and it crumpled screeching to the ground. Mandarack fell on it like a bolt of summer lightning. A strong thrust of his shield arm drove the triangular point into the demon's neck. Garet couldn't tell if the thing's throat was cut, but the blow ended the fight. Its free legs clawed the ground as it wheezed and struggled for breath. The younger Banes kept a tight hold on the trident. Mandarack stood, as poised and relaxed as the leader of a harvest dance, shield raised for another blow. But it was not needed. The clawing slowed, then quickened again into spasmodic jerks. Finally, the demon slumped in death, one leg still hooked in the calf's body.

The younger Banes relaxed, and Salick untangled her trident. Marick smiled at Garet. "Lot of good that rock would have done!"

Looking at the size of the creature slumped on the ground, Garet could only nod his head in agreement.

Dorict punched Marick on the shoulder. "Fool! He had nothing else!"

Marick kept on smiling, used to Dorict's disapproval.

The larger boy turned towards Garet and said approvingly, "Well killed."

Garet, still breathing hard from the effort of holding the beast, mumbled his thanks.

Salick agreed, perhaps a bit reluctantly, "When you helped us, well, you did the right thing."

Marick added wickedly, "For once."

"Salick."

Mandarack's dry voice interrupted them. The old man was breathing a bit harder than usual, but seemed otherwise unruffled by the battle. Salick handed her trident to Dorict and helped her master remove the shield from his arm. The Bane then put his hand on Salick's right shoulder and repeated the words Dorict had used, "Well killed, Salick." His apprentice swallowed and looked fierce as she fought back tears. He did the same with Dorict and then Marick, both of whom swelled visibly at the praise. Garet tried to step into the background, but Mandarack's firm touch on his shoulder stopped him.

"Well killed, Bane."

The Demon Jewel

The small party of Banes walked slowly back to the campsite, each wrapped in his or her own thoughts. Mandarack's silence had become a wall, and even Salick did not walk near him. He had not allowed her or the others to examine what lay beneath the skewed and fallen roof of the poor farm. After crawling back out from under the broken rafters, he had walked away without a word or sign. Salick had rounded up the others and followed.

Garet felt the queasiness in his stomach fade as they left the body of the demon behind them. Why did demons still terrify him when they were dead, he wondered as he walked behind Marick. True, the queasiness and jitters had been stronger when the thing was alive, but even now the creature's corpse was horrifying. How could he know where the demon power started, and his own natural fear of a thirteen-foot tall nightmare left off?

At the camp, Dorict and Salick washed the weapons in the stream. From his voluminous saddlebags, Dorict produced a soft cloth and dried them. The weapons were then replaced in their leather sheaths. The younger Banes soon got out their bedrolls; no one wanted dinner after what they had seen. The silence of their master was a blanket over all of them, and even Marick bedded down without his usual banter. Mandarack sat with his back to the distant, slain demon and stared into the fire. When Garet woke in the grey light of dawn, the old man was still sitting there, staring into the dead embers. It was impossible to say if he had slept at all.

After a cold breakfast, Mandarack drew Salick aside and spoke softly to her. Garet watched her nod, uncertainly at first but then with more enthusiasm and agreement. She waved and Garet came over, yawning after his fitful sleep. He had dreamt of returning home, but the small cabin was empty. The hearth was cold, and spider webs covered his mother's pots and pans. As he put his hand on the loft ladder to search for his family, a shiver of fear came over him, and with the slow sureness of dreams, he realized that a demon waited for him in the loft. Sleep had not been easy after that. Waking and seeing Mandarack's silhouette in the light of the dying fire had reassured him, and he had eventually drifted off into other desperate, though unremembered dreams. Salick's stern expression did not help his nerves and he wrapped his arms anxiously around himself as he stood before her.

"Come with me," she commanded, "and bring the hatchet." She began the climb to the top of the hill.

Mystified, Garet asked Dorict for it. The younger boy retrieved the small axe from his saddlebags and handed it over.

"Right. We should have thought of that last night," Dorict yawned, "but, you know, it was too...too..." He flushed and turned away to busy himself with saddling the horses.

Still confused, Garet followed Salick, hatchet in hand, back to the ruined farmhouse. She skirted the building, face turned aside, and walked resolutely up to the sprawled form of the demon.

Garet decided to begin his education. "Salick, why do I still feel afraid of this..." Words failed him in describing the thing before them. Faced with what it was and what it had done, even the word 'demon' seemed inadequate.

Salick held her hand out for the hatchet. She seemed to weigh her words as carefully as he had last night. "Garet," she said, with none of her usual disdain, "Master Mandarack has asked me to tell you 'what any Southerner would know.' But this goes beyond common knowledge. It is a thing known only to Banes." Her eyes narrowed and she was the old Salick again. "And you will never speak of this to anyone outside the Banehall!"

Garet nodded, and when she kept glaring at him, belatedly added, "I promise."

Salick returned his nod and knelt beside the demon's head. She pushed it over and raised the hatchet to strike it above and between the eyes. She explained her purpose between strokes.

"The ability to project fear is common to all demons." *Thwack.* "Although some are stronger than others." *Thwack.* Her words had the quality of a recital, as if she were repeating something she had heard many times. "Each kind of demon possesses an organ, called the demon's jewel, in its forehead." *Thwack.* The hatchet had split the skull of the creature, and Salick pried the blade back and forth to widen the opening. Garet strove to keep his breakfast in its place. "The size of the jewel is what really determines the level of fear felt by any human or animal and the distance at which that fear will be felt." Her tone changed to one of disgust as she pushed her fingers into the opening and probed inside. "The demon you killed was a 'Shrieker;' they have large jewels." Her look indicated that Garet was not to let this go to his head. "Of course, the one you killed was not particularly large. This," she tapped the strongly ridged head with the blade of the hatchet, "is a 'Basher' Demon." An unwelcome memory of the creature plowing through the wall of the farmhouse rose in Garet's mind. Salick continued, "They have a relatively small jewel." With a wet, sucking sound, she pulled a small blue sphere from the gaping wound in the demon's head.

The 'jewel' was neither shiny nor particularly gem-like. To Garet, it looked like a stream-smoothed pebble. Salick handed it to him. The bottom of his stomach dropped as the jewel's surface touched his flesh. Curious, he experimented with holding it close to himself and then far away. There was a slight but noticeable difference in his queasiness. He next placed it a hundred paces from the creature and slowly backed away. The fear did decrease with distance from the stone, and no longer increased with closeness to the demon's corpse. Salick watched these activities curiously. Finally satisfied, he handed the stone back to her.

She wrapped it in the cloth Dorict had used to dry the Banes' weapons. "The strongest sensations come from touching the jewel with your bare hands."

He had to agree. Touching the jewel made him feel as if he were falling from a great height. His stomach made desperate attempts to get past his clenched throat.

The demon's carcass still lay splayed out over the gutted cows. The clouds of the previous night had retreated again to the horizon, and it promised to be another hot, sunny day. By noon the demon would no longer need its jewel; the stench would drive away anything with a nose. But plundered of its jewel, the corpse no longer had any particular terror for Garet. One of his questions had been answered. He took the hatchet from Salick and wiped the blood from it on the grass with a grim smile. Handling demon bodies was becoming second nature.

Not as repulsed by the corpse, Garet realized that this was the first time he had seen these creatures in daylight. Leaving Salick waiting impatiently outside the corral, he examined it.

The first thing that struck him was the colour. He had never seen the Shrieker, save in the uncertain light of the winter lamp or later when it had been charred black by the fire. The ridges that swept up from the hatchet wound on the Basher's head were a startling shade of blue, but the rest of the head, along with its back and the outside of its legs were a deep, dry-blood red, fading to a light pink on the rest of the body.

Prodding the skin while Salick wrinkled her nose in distaste, he discovered it to be as tough as boiled leather. No wonder Mandarack had waited to strike a vulnerable spot. Even a sword slash would be of little use against this natural armour, for he could see that the shield had crushed the throat, not cut it. The legs, at first sight so insect-like, were actually jointed in the same fashion as his own. Although freakishly long and thin, the bunched muscles of its back and shoulders explained the incredible strength the demon had shown last night. As if to offset the length of its limbs, the demon's fingers and toes were shorter than a Shrieker's but much more heavily clawed. Garet swallowed hard as he saw the dried blood and long strands of blond hair stuck to those terrible weapons.

He straightened from his examination, expecting to find Salick fuming in her impatience. Instead, she was staring upriver, past the collapsed house. The crows that had alerted them to the demon's attack were back. They circled nervously in the air above a stand of birch some distance from the house. A crowd of them would land in the branches but then others would suddenly take flight, creating an unending chaos of broiling, noisy birds. Garet realized that they were poised between a fear of the demon's jewel and a hunger for the small mountain of carrion meat in the corral.

She turned from the crows to glance at the demon's body. "Come on, Garet. They'll eat it now." She looked somberly at the collapsed house. "They'll eat everything."

Lessons

Salick seemed to have completely accepted Mandarack's order to tutor Garet. Although she often rolled her eyes or shook her head at the depth of his ignorance, she answered all his questions as fully as possible. In the next two days of riding, he learned more about the South than he had in all the previous years of his life. Not that it all made sense. Each piece of information, although freely given, stubbornly refused to connect with any other piece to make a sensible whole. Why did Shirath have sixteen 'Lords' and only one 'King,' a young man named Trax? Why were Banemasters equal to lords even though they had no section of the city, a 'ward,' Salick had called it, to rule? Why did Salick seem to think that the Shirath Banehall was as powerful as the King if the Ward Lords were less powerful than King Trax? The more he heard riding at Salick's side, the more questions poured out of him.

Marick had soon recovered his good humour. He found Garet's endless curiosity and Salick's determined patience hilarious. From his position, perched behind Dorict on the stout mare, he would ask his much less patient companion outrageous questions. He had run out of questions about Dorict's parents, siblings, cousins of various degrees, and had just finished exploring his feelings about personal hygiene. Dorict endured the assault with mounting irritation.

"Tell me, friend Dorict, what is that thing at the end of your arm? You know, with the five fingers?" Marick spoke loudly enough for the two older apprentices riding ahead of

40

him to hear his innocent tones. He continued his imitation, "Tell me, good sir, what is its use?"

Even Salick had to laugh when Dorict showed him one such use by reaching back and twisting his tormentor's ear. After yelping and breaking free, Marick asked, with even more innocence if possible dripping from his words, "Pray sir, and what purpose does that action serve?"

Dorict growled, driven to a rare state of exasperation, "With you, it serves no purpose at all. Fool!" He squeezed the reins in his hand and looked appealingly at Salick and Garet.

"Marick!" Salick had erased the smile from her face and spoke sternly to the irrepressible boy. "Recite the names of Banehall Lords from the Founding onward."

Marick put on a face of pure suffering and started the list. "Shirath Banehall was founded in the First year by Banfreat the Baker. He was followed by Moret, the son of a lord, and then by..." The boy's voice droned on in the background and Dorict looked his thanks at Salick.

"How many Banehall Lords are there?" Garet asked.

Salick replied, "Seventy-four. So you can continue with your questions. I'm sure you have more," she added dryly.

Garet reddened but pressed on. He would not waste this opportunity to prepare himself for whatever awaited him in Shirath. Behind him, Marick droned on, "...and he was replaced by Torinix, who often drank to excess, and later by Sharict, who weighed five hundred pounds..." Dorict's pained expression showed his opinion of Marick's changes to the list, but he obviously preferred the droning character assassination to another torrent of foolish questions. The mare clopped along happily, ignoring both its passengers and revelling in the absence of the weight of the demon's corpse. When they had returned from the farmstead, Salick had removed the Shrieker's jewel, larger and smoother than the one she had cut out earlier, and rolled the now harmless corpse over the lip of the embankment into the trees, covering it with loose dirt and leaves. The bag with the two jewels now jounced and skipped effortlessly at the end of the mare's rope.

"Salick," Garet began, "you've told me about the city, and I thank you, but I think I must see it at work for it to make sense to me." Salick considered this and nodded at the logic of it. He continued, "But there are other things I need to know. If I am to be a Demonbane," a glance at the tall girl showed no objection, "I need to know about the Banehall."

Although Salick rolled her eyes, she appeared to enjoy playing the expert to Garet's ignorance. She glanced up at the position of the sun and decided that there was time for a long explanation before their noon break. A glance ahead at Mandarack to make sure she was not needed was followed by a quick order directed to Marick to begin his list again, "Properly, this time!"

Satisfied, she continued, "When the demons came to the South, six hundred years ago," her voice dropping again into the rhythm of an oft-told tale, "those men and women who could bear to face them joined together to protect their families and neighbours. We did not live in large cities in those days. Each lord lived in a high-walled keep and fought for land to give to his supporters and to house his serfs and slaves. There was no peace in those days, and any lord strong enough or arrogant enough could call himself a king. Such men use fear on others, but have little need to conquer it within themselves, so they were among the first to die or be driven from their homes."

She paused, closing her eyes to search for the thread of the tale, and Garet imagined her sitting on the floor as a child, long arms wrapped around her knees, listening to her parents' stories as he had listened to his mother's songs. Salick opened her eyes again. "A third of the people died. A third fled to the North, preferring to fight the great dragons and suffer through the deep snows of winter." Here she looked at Garet, studying his black hair, rare in the South, and darker skin. Garet suspected she was looking for the Northerner in him, and he refrained from telling her that most Northerners were as blond as she was.

"The last group, only a third of the people who had lived in this land before the demons came, banded around those few who could fight back. These men and women became the Demonbanes, and were honoured in the land. They hunted down the demons, following the wake of their fear."

Garet thought of the great sweep of crows fleeing the Basher Demon the night before.

"No family was safe without a Bane nearby, so all the South—farmers with their cows, weavers with their cats, lords with their hunting falcons—gathered into five great cities: Solantor the Great, where the High King lives; high-walled Illick; Akalit, the city of music; Shirath of the two banks; and Old Torrick." Her voice lost its cadence and she continued conversationally, "I love Shirath, but one day I hope to visit the Banehall in Solantor. They say the market is bigger than all of Shirath, and the palace walls are draped in cloth-of-gold." She paused, perhaps embarrassed to forget her role as teacher. "Each city took only as much land as could be patrolled by its Banes. The nobles who survived were each given a section of the city to rule. The king's family was chosen from them."

Garet considered this. "Do the lords still fight each other?" The closest thing in his experience to such a 'Lord' was Pranix, the Three Roads tavern keeper. Such a man would never allow another to rule over him. And if all lords were like this, then only blood could set a crown on a king's head.

"No," Salick replied, "the king prevents it."

"There are sixteen lords and only one king," argued Garet. "What prevents the lords from killing the king if they wish it?"

"We support the king."

Ah, Garet thought, *of course.* The Ward Lords might squabble and brawl like his brothers at a harvest festival, but the Demonbanes were the foundation of the city, more powerful and more necessary than either the lords or the king himself. Without considering the diplomacy of his question, he blurted out, "Why don't the Banehalls rule the cities then?"

Salick seemed shocked by the suggestion. "We are Banes, not kings!" Seeing Garet's confusion, she relented and tried to explain, "Garet, you cannot be a Bane and any other thing. There is no time. There are no Bane-tailors or Bane-merchants. We train; we patrol; we fight. That is our life. If we stop to live any other life, people die." She looked at her master, his horse reined in for a moment while he drank from a leather flask. "Not that there aren't some Masters who would make better kings than many whose bottoms have warmed the Shirath throne!"

Mandarack signalled a general halt, and the horses were led down to the river to drink. They had already passed several more houses this day, each abandoned but with no sign of a demon's attack.

Dorict pulled out the last of the Three Roads food and said, "I hope we get to the crossing today, or we'll have a hungry night." Broad shouldered and stout, Dorict did not sound as if he enjoyed the prospect of a missed meal. When the horses had finished drinking, he took the reins from Garet and led both mounts back up to the prairie to graze.

"If only Dorict could eat grass, he could always be happy here." Marick had divided the food and now stood there holding out Garet's portion.

Although still wary of Marick's knife-like jibes, Garet decided to risk asking why they couldn't cross the river now. They had passed two or three places already that the horses could have managed.

Marick surprised him with a straightforward answer. "This isn't the right river!" He waved a hand at the nearest bend. "This little thing is called the Plainscutter. It joins the North Ar at a town called Bangt. That's the only place to ferry across the North Ar for fifty miles. We don't really want to cross the river, but a barge should be waiting there to take us to Torrick." Then the sly smile returned to his face. "Unless, of course, you have become too attached to riding."

To his own surprise, Garet laughed and was rewarded with a friendly punch from the younger boy. Something had changed between him and his new companions. What had been, at best, a reluctant tolerance of his presence had become acceptance. Ever since he had seized the shaft of that trident, to join three other pairs of arms twisting in and around each other, his status had risen from that of a backcountry farm boy who claimed to have killed a demon, and a small one at that, to what Master Mandarack had called him as they stood beside the hulking body of the farm-destroyer, a Demonbane.

Marick continued, "I doubt that you'll have to give up your horse tonight though." He looked at the low angle of the sun. "I'm sure Salick will convince the Master to halt for the night if we find shelter."

"Why?" asked Garet. "Wouldn't it be better to be in a safe place, rather than camp out here and meet another demon?"

Marick stretched his short body into an uncanny imitation of the lean Salick. Speaking through his nose, he lectured Garet, "My dear boy, you are not thinking like a Demonbane. It is our job to kill demons, not hide from them!" With a grin, the boy continued in his normal tone. "And better any demon runs into us than some poor farmer chasing his cows. Besides, Mandarack may fight like a demon himself, but he's older than time, and had best take it easy."

Anything further that Marick might have said was cut off by two slim hands coming up from behind him and grabbing his ears. He started to twist, but the fingers only squeezed tighter.

"Ow! Salick! What are you trying to do? I can't be a Bane if I've got no ears, can I?" he protested as the tall girl dragged him to his feet.

"Well, my little Bane, if you've got time to gossip, I suppose I'll just have to find a job for you." Her eyes were narrowed and her cheeks red. Garet guessed that she had overheard Marick's remarks about Mandarack. "Something to get your mind off your betters, I think." She handed him the hatchet. "Start finding wood for tonight's fire. You can carry it beside the horses until we reach some shelter."

Marick, instead of protesting at the unfairness of his punishment, merely winked at Garet and whispered to him, "That'll teach me to keep my mouth shut or my eyes open." The boy trotted off to where the trees straggled over the lip of the river valley.

Unpredictable, thought Garet. He could never guess what Marick's reaction would be in any situation, but he found himself liking the young Bane more and more. What would it have been like to have him for a brother instead of Galit and Gitel? More practical jokes maybe. But they might have been

45

ones you could laugh at too, and maybe you could play one yourself and get a laugh back instead of a beating.

Salick interrupted his thoughts. "Don't listen to Marick's foolishness. He rattles on like the Ar in spring flood!"

Garet had to ask, "Is Master Mandarack really all right?" The old Bane was responsible for this new life of companionship and adventure. What would happen to him if Mandarack died?

Salick puffed up, ready to attack and then seemed to deflate. She answered in a lowered voice. "Marick was right about one thing, the Master is no longer young." She glanced around to make sure they were alone. "It's true that I worry about him; he takes too much on himself. If we don't look after him, well...we should find a place to rest for the night."

Garet was surprised at the trust she was showing in him, to reveal so much of her fears. "He's like your father, isn't he?" he ventured.

Salick gave a half-hearted bristle and grumbled, "Better than my own father, anyway." She stomped off towards the horses and called to Dorict to help her re-load the bags.

And mine too, Garet thought.

They rode on for the rest of the afternoon but found no likely place to rest. Now many of the homesteads were a mess of tumbled turf walls and charred roof-beams. Others had a stink of death about them that hurried the small party on. As the sun dipped towards the west, they came upon a farmhouse that appeared to have escaped the demons' attacks. Larger than most, the simple corral typical of Midland farms was here replaced by a substantial barn and several sheds. The house itself was timber framed with thick walls made of pressed mud and clay. The outside was whitewashed and glowed in the low rays of the sun. Instead of thatch, curved red tiles covered the roof. Everything spoke of prosperity and comfort, down to the broad vegetable garden flanking the painted wooden door.

"No dead cattle, no corpses. A cheerful place to rest. Shall we, Master?" Marick asked as he trotted alongside the horses, branches bundled under each arm.

Mandarack nodded and dismounted slowly from his horse. Garet guessed that the effort of killing the demon and travelling across these plains had indeed taken a toll on the old man's body.

"It will do. Salick, scout the area. Take Garet with you." The Banemaster walked towards the well, but Marick dropped the wood with a crash and ran ahead of him to lower the bucket and draw up water for his master to drink.

The truth is in the deed, thought Garet. No matter what the impudent boy said, he loved his master as much as Salick did. He dismounted and followed his tutor in a wide circle around the farm. Salick stopped often to examine tracks on the ground, but to Garet they looked like the tracks of cows and dogs. Reassured, they moved on to examine the barn then returned to the house.

A resident cat acted as their host that evening, giving its haughty approval to their presence by rubbing against their legs and hopping into their laps at the least convenient moments. Marick put his wood in the hearth and lit the fire while Dorict searched for some food. Luckily, the speed of the owner's departure meant that some provisions had been left behind. The stout boy, much cheered by what he found, began peeling potatoes and carrots.

Garet was used to kitchen work and lent a hand. The vegetables were soon cubed and boiled in a blackened pot over the fire while Dorict rolled out flour and water into thin disks. "If we had some herbs," the young Bane told Garet, "and some honey, I could show you the bread we eat in Shirath."

"There's green onions in the garden," Garet offered. He pulled some from the wreckage of the hastily dug plot, another sign of the speed with which the farmer had left. The chopped green stems were added to the flat bread, along with a touch of sugar that Salick had found in the bottom of a crock. Dorict set them in a frying pan that he had heated in the centre of the coals, and a wonderful aroma soon filled the abandoned house. They sat down to a better supper than Garet had tasted since their journey began.

Filled to the brim with Dorict's cooking, the Banes sought an early bed. Mandarack took his blanket to a back room that must have once housed the farmer and his wife. Salick, Dorict, and Marick arranged cushions and rugs around the banked fire and soon drifted off to sleep. Garet had a problem. The cat was firmly planted in his lap and showed no signs of moving. After waiting until all his companions were breathing deeply, he gently lifted the cat down to the still form of Marick. The creature gave him one unfathomable look from its green eyes and then snuggled against the boy's chest.

Garet crept about looking for another rug to cushion the polished plank floor. He had not had a chance to examine the house before this, what with helping Dorict prepare supper, and he was struck with how familiar the place looked. It had the same basic arrangement as his own home: a long bottom floor, although the lower sleeping quarters were here enclosed by a plastered wall; a loft that had once held beds small enough to be put on the owner's cart when he fled this place; a kitchen hearth no deeper or wider than his mother's; and here and there, an abandoned pot or wooden spoon that touched his heart with their homely familiarity. He reached down and picked up a straw doll, wrapped in a bit of cloth for a dress. Garet held the lost thing and thought of his sister calling his name to come play. He put the doll back where he had found it and, picking up a straw mat rolled up in the corner, turned to join the others in sleep. He saw a gleam in the fire's uncertain light but couldn't tell if the two eyes looking at him were the cat's or Marick's. Whoever they belonged to, they shut again and Garet drifted off to sleep.

An Unfriendly Wager

The next morning saw the party of Banes finally arrive at the village of Bangt. Mandarack had roused them at dawn, and they had chewed on Dorict's slightly stale disks of bread while riding. The trail widened as it joined other tracks heavy with the prints of cattle and the ruts of laden carts. Here the river they had followed for two days, the Plainscutter, met the North Ar, making it wider and calmer for a part of its journey to the western sea. The foamed staircase of rapids and the sandbars upriver to the east, which confounded even the smallest boats upstream, disappeared. Here, the river matured into a stately, sober current that minded its manners until it quickened again at the great falls near Old Torrick.

At Bangt, plainsmen and traders could cross on barges hauled to the other side by thick ropes. It was a small place, by the standards of the South, but Garet had never seen so many people in his life. Once a village little bigger than Three Roads, Bangt had swelled to become a crowded refugee camp. The appearance of the demons had finally driven the scattered humanity of the plains together. Farming families, who had once dotted the prairie on isolated homesteads, now huddled around the few wooden buildings that made up the original village. Every available patch of ground grew a makeshift tent crafted from canvas, rough-cut boards, or even sheaves of bound wheat. Small children sat in front of these poor shelters, thumbs in mouths, as if still stunned by the loss of their homes. A gang of men and women were pulling logs from rafts nosed into the riverbank. These logs, probably cut in the foothills Garet had so recently left, were being used to raise a wooden palisade around both Bangt and its mass of uprooted humanity.

"Wooden walls!" mocked Marick as the group made its way to the hustle of activity along the river. "A Basher would smash through that in a minute."

"Look before you talk," Dorict replied dryly. He pointed to the patch of ground before a completed section of the wall. A group of boys, too young to lift the heavy timbers making up the wall, were busy sharpening six-foot long stakes. The stakes were planted, sharpened ends angling out and up, in a broad belt protecting the palisade. In front of that, another group of teens laboured in a half-dug ditch. "Even a Basher would have a hard time building up enough speed for a charge. We might learn something from these Midlanders."

"But they've pointed them the wrong way," Salick noted. "They'll never trap a demon with the spikes facing out, could they, Master?"

Mandarack had paused to examine the defenses. "They build against their fear," he replied. "When a Banehall is established here, we will teach them how to guard against demons." He slapped the neck of his horse with the reins, but the party's forward progress was interrupted by the flustered arrival of a young woman, dressed as a Bane and in age a match for Salick.

"Master Mandarack!" She stopped to catch her breath but flashed a smile, first at Salick, then at the younger Banes. "You're here! The barge is ready to take you on to Torrick. Supplies are hard to get." She waved towards the mass of refugees while gulping for more air. "But there's enough to get you to the Banehall." Her message delivered, she straightened and stood respectfully, waiting for a reply. She was a typical Southerner, blond hair, tall and slim, with bright, blue eyes. She noticed Garet's examination and smiled again, revealing dimples in her cheeks. Garet blushed and looked away.

One of the great trials of Garet's existence, at least from his point of view, had been the lack of young women in his life. Aside from his mother and sister, he might go weeks without seeing another woman of any age. The other farmers kept their daughters away from Three Roads and from other farmers' sons, so the only example of the other sex he had a chance to see had been the women who worked in the tavern at Three Roads. But they were wolf-like, eyeing the passing traders as if they were dinner, and therefore more frightening than attractive. Trallet, the tavern keeper's wife, was the worst of these. She covered her face in rouge and powders to hide her age, but she achieved only a harsh mockery of youth. Salick, the only other young woman he knew, was Trallet's opposite. She disdained makeup and hid what might have been a pretty face behind such deadly seriousness that he did not dare to think of her romantically. Besides, his relationship with her was now one of student to teacher, a relationship she was unlikely to let him forget.

The young woman standing in front of them now, long braids whipping around her cheeks in the prairie wind, wore neither rouge nor a grim expression. She smiled, not to entice him, but from a pure love of this moment in her life: the blue sky, the excitement of the camp around them, and meeting old friends, for she and Salick now hugged each other and fell to talking. For perhaps the first time in his life, Garet understood just what beauty meant. He blushed even more and busied himself with a perfectly good knot on his horse's rein.

"Vinir! I didn't know you were sent here." Salick looked happier than Garet had ever seen her. She grabbed Vinir by her shoulders, giving the other Bane a shake.

"Easy there!" Vinir replied, freeing herself and brushing the hair out of her eyes. "I need to complete my duties. Master, is there anything else you'll need?"

Mandarack shook his head. "No, Vinir. Tell me, are you to be posted here permanently?"

"No, Master!" the reply was emphatic. "I have no wish to live in a wooden city." She reached over and ruffled Marick's hair, acknowledging his nod of agreement. "Besides, I'm really only here to help the Golds and Reds." She scanned the horizon beyond the camp. "They're still out, hunting down the last few demons or guarding the feeding cattle." With a slight bow to the Master, she motioned to a narrow lane between the tents, and the party followed her.

The press of people parted like a bubble around them and Garet wondered nervously if the refugees blamed the Banes for the arrival of the demons. Mothers cowered as they approached and held their children to themselves as if the Banes were demons themselves. He caught at the reins of his mount, and the mare flicked its head about, rolling its eyes nervously. An old man spat on the ground but turned and vanished into a tattered tent. Garet swallowed. He felt his shoulders shaking and then caught himself. Why was he so on edge? The people avoiding the party looked as afraid as he felt. With the beginnings of understanding, he turned and saw that Dorict had moved from his distant position in the rear to right behind Garet.

Was Dorict afraid of losing them in the crowd? The usually calm boy's face was strained and sweating. In his arms, he held a coil of rope and the ragged sheepskin bundle containing the demons' jewels. Garet swallowed. He slowed his breath and tried to see this anxiety as a thing outside himself, emanating from those two small spheres the younger Bane carried. Ignoring the reactions of the people around him, he concentrated until he could will the jangling of his nerves to stop.

They ate a quick meal on the riverbank near the docks. Mandarack had directed Dorict to tie the sheepskin package by its long rope to the bow post of the barge they were soon to board.

"Isn't there a place prepared for..." Salick pointed with her chin at the young Bane tying off the rope.

"Not yet," Vinir replied. "There's been no time for anything but saving as many people as possible. We may have to send them down to Old Torrick for a while," she added between mouthfuls of warm bread stuffed with spiced beef. She handed another piece to Marick, who had not stirred from her side since they started eating.

All too soon, Vinir saw them off at the ferry dock, hugging Salick and weeping in a way Garet found confusing. His mother had not wept at his departure. Girls were perhaps more complex than he had thought.

The flat-bottomed boat they had been lent was a cargo barge, one of many that Salick assured him travelled back and forth to Old Torrick without accident or loss of life. Garet distrusted the craft right away. He had never been on a boat, the streams near his home were small enough to be jumped over, and it felt very strange to have the boards beneath his feet tip back and forth. Capable of carrying many tons of wheat or other goods, this barge was empty except for the Banes, their meagre luggage, and the four young men assigned by the village elders to work the long, sweeping oars. With a chorus of good-natured curses and insults, the oarsmen bade goodbye to their fellows on other boats and, with their muscles bulging under their tunics, forced the barge out into the slow current.

Garet sat in the bow and watched that current bear branches, leaves, and himself down the river. After initial misgivings, he had to admit that this form of transportation was much more comfortable than riding a horse. He had not been heartbroken when they left their mounts with Vinir. This floating was especially easier on his backside. He could sit with his legs stretched on the bench seat, a saddlebag or blanket for a pillow, and look at the trees leaning out over the water on either side. A breeze ruffled his hair and, rocked by the river, Garet fell into a state of neither waking nor sleeping, a state of near perfect rest, while the oarsmen lazily swung their oars to keep the barge off the muddy banks.

With the river so willing to do most of the work, the young men leaned on their oars as much as they pushed them, putting their shoulders into it only when the boat was in danger of grounding. Between these bursts of energy, they gossiped and laughed at each other's rude jokes.

Marick cocked an ear critically at the Midlanders' attempts at humour but soon rolled his eyes at their crudeness and lack of imagination. Dorict, like Garet, seemed lulled into a trance-like state by their gentle passage. Salick and Mandarack were quietly discussing the battle with the demon two nights before. Vinir's eyes had widened at the report of their encounter with the Basher. "You, just a Green and these two Blues, and him just a..." she stopped, stalled by Garet's lack of formal status. "You actually killed a Basher?" Her reaction led Garet to suppose that the lower ranks did not usually fight demons. But, he reasoned sleepily, with the Midlands overrun for the first time in hundreds of years, the Banes of the Southern cities might be spread too thinly to follow old rules. He closed his eyes but kept his ears open to listen to Mandarack instruct Salick.

"No," the dry voice was a welcome alternative to the rough laughter of the oarsmen, "if you had attacked the demon's body from behind, I doubt that the combined strength of all four of you would have punctured its skin. And the attempt alone would not have even distracted the demon."

"I think that I would be distracted by a trident in the, ah, back," Salick replied.

Garet's ears pricked up. Not only was the subject fascinating, but also this was the first time he had heard Salick contradict her master, even if indirectly. He waited for Mandarack's response.

"Bashers are stronger than most other demons, but they have simpler minds. They can only concentrate on one thing at a time. If there is a threat, or a potential meal, in front of them, nothing on earth can distract them. That is why your entanglement worked. It had no concern at all for its legs. Although," he added, "you were even more successful than I expected. Compared to what you were able to accomplish, stabbing it would have been as helpful as a mosquito bite." He held up two fingers. "Whenever two Banes must take on a large demon, one Bane traps, and the other kills." Garet opened one eye a crack. Mandarack had leaned back against the gunwale and closed his eyes, signifying that the lesson was over.

The harsh laughter of the boatmen erupted again, and Garet heard the word 'Demonbane' punctuating their mockery. The muscular young men had made no secret of their surprise at the less than heroic appearance of these demon hunters. The leader of the group, a broad-shouldered brawler with a bent nose, spoke again, loudly enough to be easily heard by the Banes at the opposite end of the barge.

"Demons must be as dangerous as worms if a skinny little crow like that can eat them up!" Garet reddened, knowing that his black hair, so unusual in the South, made him the 'crow.'

"Heaven's shield!" the young man continued. "A broomstick girl, three puppies, and an ancient! Not a one of them would be a match for my own granny. And she's eighty-three!" More jeering laughter.

Marick started up, a biting retort on his lips, only to be restrained by Salick's warning hand on his shoulder. They both looked to Mandarack for advice or censure, but the old man's eyes were still closed, and his grey head rested on the palm of his good hand.

"Easy, Marick." Dorict had left his contemplation of the water to warn his mercurial friend. "This lot has obviously never met a demon. I expect most of the survivors haven't. They've only heard of them, or they wouldn't be alive to mock us."

Salick took up the argument. "I agree. Marick, they've never experienced the demon's fear. And, if they're from up-river, we're probably the first Demonbanes they have ever had a good look at. If you returned here in a year, they'd show you as much respect as you'd receive on the streets of Solantor itself!"

"All right!" The small Bane shrugged off Salick's hand. "It's just hard to get along with such fools!"

Garet was a little surprised to see the lack of sympathy in Dorict's and Salick's faces, until he remembered the idiotic pranks Marick had subjected them to on their journey across the prairie.

Dorict, a hint of satisfaction in his voice, observed, "Well, as a fool yourself, you'd probably get along with them better than anyone else."

Marick's answering glare suddenly dissolved into a thoughtful expression. Then he grinned, and when he saw Dorict's worried reaction, transfigured his face into a picture of pure innocence. Now even Salick looked nervous. As Marick casually climbed over the bulkheads towards the curious oarsmen, Garet realized that he was starting to worry too. Only Mandarack seemed unconscious of the approaching disaster.

Marick's actions, however, seemed as innocent as his expression. He made himself at home in the stern and, as the sun slipped over the top of its arc and the shadows of trees lengthened on the river, mixed easily with the young men. He laughed at their poor jokes and readily agreed with their outrageous conceptions of what life was like in the great cities of the South. When they mocked him about his small size, he nodded sadly and praised their great height and bulging muscles.

The three young Banes seated in the bow, filled with nervous anticipation, watched Marick ingratiate himself with the plainsmen. By the time the sun in its descent turned the river from silver to gold, the oarsmen had steered the conversation again to the matter of killing demons.

"Well, my little warrior," teased the Midlander with the bent nose, "frighten us with a tale of all the terrible demons you have slain." Loud snorts and digging elbows were exchanged by his friends.

Marick leaned in towards the group and lowered his voice as if he were dispensing a great secret. "Most people don't know this, but demons are not all that hard to kill."

Dorict and Salick looked at each other.

The young men leaned into their new friend's circle of confidence and nodded for him to go on. *Trapped*, thought Garet.

"We Banes really do have an easy life," Marick continued in his conspiratorial stage-whisper, "free food and lodging, people bowing down to us, women..." At that point, the four young men turned their heads to look at Salick. Garet felt a hot flush of anger and was surprised at the strength of his reaction. He needn't have bothered though. Salick's eyes would have frozen fire, and the four young men quickly turned back to Marick.

"In fact, all we need to get our pay, and that is no small amount," a pause to wink at his listeners, "is bring back a small trophy from the poor creatures."

Dorict and Salick looked questions and incomprehension at each other.

Marick pointed to the rope tied to the bow post. The bundle containing the demon jewels was so light that it drifted well ahead of the heavy barge.

"The trophies we collected on this trip are in a package at the end of that rope. We sometimes use them to play a wagering game in the Banehalls." Marick grinned up at the large Midlander. "Of course, you have to be brave to try it."

The other three oarsmen immediately dared their leader to display his courage. He waved them off and put his beefy hand on Marick's slight shoulder. "How much money do you have to wager, little demon killer?" The oarsmen were busy emptying out their waist pouches and adding their copper coins to make a small pile in the big man's other hand.

Marick looked contrite. "I'm afraid this trip has exhausted all my own money, friend. But!" He hopped his way back to the bow and, grabbing the startled Garet, pulled him over the benches to confront the Midlanders.

"My friend Garet still has some coins left," Marick reached for Garet's pouch, "don't you?"

Garet could only stand there as Marick casually emptied his pouch of the few coins his mother had pressed into his hand when he left the farm. They were Northern coins that Garet realized his mother must have hidden from her husband for all the years she had lived in the South. Their dragon symbols and heroes' profiles caught the ruddy light as they lay in Marick's palm.

Marick made a great show of examining them. "I make this out to be four silvers, don't you?"

The oarsmen, unwilling to reveal their ignorance about foreign exchange rates, nodded sagely. Their leader counted out the equivalent in coppers bearing the gate of Old Torrick on one side and a crown on the other. Marick piled them together with Garet's coins on the bench that ran across the barge at midships. He motioned Dorict to pull in the rope. Dorict looked to Salick, who looked to Mandarack and found him still asleep. She bit her lip and, after a long hesitation, nodded at Dorict. The stout boy shrugged and pulled on the rope. The package rose dripping from the water and with slow, deliberate fingers, Dorict untied the sheepskin and gave it to Marick's hands.

The young Bane's smile seemed a little forced as he returned to the waiting Midlanders, but his voice had lost none of its persuasiveness. "Now both of you hold out your hands. That's it, hold them steady now."

The slow dread that accompanied the closeness of the jewels was at least familiar to Garet. He willed his breath to slow and his pulse to stop beating at his temples. The Midlander looked green but kept a shaking hand outstretched. Marick, his grin changing from friendly to contemptuous, dropped the jewels, one in each of the player's hands.

The touch of the jewel on his flesh constricted Garet's chest and seized his heart in a rough grip. Knowing he had conquered the dread before, he willed himself to relax to the point where he could breathe again. When, after a time he could not calculate, he had some control of himself, he looked over at his opponent.

Marick was taunting the man who had dared to insult a Demonbane: "Why, what's wrong, friend. A big barge-hauler such as yourself can't be afraid, can you?" His voice dripped with sarcasm. "Could it be that a little crow is braver than a huge pig like yourself?"

Garet tried to focus on the Midlander. The change in the man was sickening. His tanned face had turned pale. His eyes, so confident before, were starting out of his head. His teeth were clenched so tightly that a thin trickle of blood dripped from the corner of his mouth. With a thrill of horror, no doubt exaggerated by the jewel in his own hand, Garet saw that his opponent wasn't breathing. His lips were blue, and he was beginning to sway on his feet.

Marick started to speak again but stopped as Garet moved stiffly forward. The younger Bane stared unbelievingly as Garet reached out with his free hand and took the jewel from the Midlander. Released from the touch of the powerful stone, the poor man collapsed in a heap, drawing in huge gasps of breath at Garet's feet. His friends, still under the spell of the jewels, could barely move to help him. A wave of relief passed through Garet as Dorict came up, swept the jewels into their wrappings and quickly lowered them back into the water.

For the rest of the dying day, the Midlanders huddled in the stern and the Banes stayed in the bow. When they nosed into the riverbank to camp for the night, the Midlanders tied up the boat and moved a good quarter mile away, under a stand of willows, to make their camp. After a quiet dinner, Mandarack, who had roused himself as they landed, told them to make ready for bed while he walked a while on the plains above the river. Salick started up but he motioned her to stay and was up the bank before she could protest.

As soon as he was out of sight, the four Banes, by some unspoken agreement, all came to the small cooking fire. Dorict spoke directly to Marick, and the usually calm boy was shaking in his anger.

"Marick, I've known you a long time, but this is the cruelest joke you've ever played!"

The younger Bane ducked his head and gave a muffled reply, "I know." There was a sniffle and Garet saw that he was crying. "I didn't want to hurt the oaf, just teach him a lesson!"

Salick, her usual air of stern competence replaced by uncertainty, put her hand on his arm. "I know, Marick, we all did." She looked at Garet and Dorict and they nodded. "But that's no excuse—for you or for me." She put her hands on his temples and lifted his head so that she could look into his reddened eyes. "I should have stopped you," she confessed and then smiled at the stricken boy, "after all, everyone knows you have no sense."

Marick smiled a bit through his tears but shook his head. "I do have some, at least usually enough to know when I've gone overboard. It's my fault, Salick, not yours." He glanced up the trail Mandarack had taken for his stroll, "But what puzzles me is why did the Master let me go so far." The little Bane buried his face in his arms again.

"Marick, he was asleep!" Garet said.

"No, Marick's right, Garet." Dorict was also looking thoughtfully in the direction Mandarack had taken. "He must have known what was going on. Bringing those jewels past him would have woken a first year Black Sash from the dead."

"Why would he want me to do that to the Midlanders?" Curiosity had roused Marick from his unaccustomed humility.

A spark of an idea came to Garet, and he asked Salick, "What's the biggest danger right now for the Midlanders? Aside from meeting a demon."

"Ignorance," she answered promptly. "They have no idea of how much danger they're in. Vinir said it took a half-month just to convince them to give up their farms and build walled towns. If they truly knew the risk of living without Demonbanes, they would never have been so stubborn."

"Exactly," Garet agreed, "and our little 'game' will be told and re-told to both ends of the river within a week. People will see that if a big brawler like him couldn't bear the touch of even a tiny part of a dead demon, a 'trophy,' then the power of demons is too great to deny."

"And the necessity of the Banes," Dorict added thoughtfully.

"And so the advice of the Banehall will be heard, rather than ignored." Salick looked at Garet with grudging respect. "That must be it. The Master planned it all. He used Marick to prepare the Midlands for the Banehalls we will build here."

Dorict looked at his young friend. "It must be reassuring to know that even a fool like you has his uses."

Marick, still feeling the temporary burden of his sins, refused to answer the jibe. Salick, however, seemed her old, confident self again. Reassured of Mandarack's infallibility, she bounced up and started shooing them all to their bedrolls. "Everyone to sleep! We'll want to be rested when we arrive at Old Torrick tomorrow." She even slapped a yawning Garet on the back. "It's not the Shirath Banehall, but any hall is a home to us."

Garet fell asleep wondering about this home he had never seen.

The largest of its foul kind, the Basher Demon can o'er turn a laden cart and kill many at a single charge.

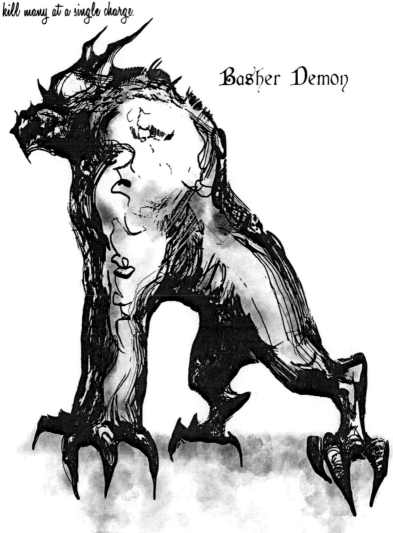

Basher Demon

Heaven favours us by making it a stupid brute that cannot see beyond its intended prey. Attack in groups, some from behind, and be quick.

Old Torrick

The name, "Old Torrick," was easy to understand as the city appeared around a last bend in the river. So ancient that it seemed to grow out of the riverbank, the city's stone walls slumped between slanted towers before almost meeting at a broken gate. Salick had already told Garet that Torrick was the oldest of the five cities of the South. It was also the smallest; barely twenty thousand people lived within its walls, although a few thousand more lived in the rough villages of miners scattered below it, at the foot of the Falls.

The decrepit appearance of the fortress was sharply contrasted by the bustle of activity around its stone wharves. The barge was soon tied up beside a small flotilla of other such boats, most of them in the process of being unloaded. Most carried tightly bundled sheaves of hay; a few others bore thatch-covered piles of winnowed grain. Men and women, dressed in the rough clothes of labourers, called to each other as they lifted out bags and bales to set them in piles on the wharf.

Their own crew had disappeared as soon as they scooped up the coins Mandarack had left on the stern bench. They were the same coins Marick had won from them the day before. Garet had no idea how Mandarack had got hold of them, but suspected Salick had arranged it. During the exchange, Marick had hidden as the bent-nosed leader swept up the coins and walked, stiff-backed, down the stone quay with his fellows. The small Bane snaked his head around Salick's elbow and stuck out his tongue at the departing

Midlanders. Salick slapped him on the top of his head in reproof.

"Ow!" Marick yelped. "There's no need for that, Salick. You'd have done it yourself if you weren't so stiff!" Salick raised her hand again, genuinely angry, but Marick was saved by his master.

"Marick," Mandarack called from where he was conversing with the dock master, a portly man with a sheaf of linen pages in his hand. "Take the package and run ahead to the Banehall. Wait for us there."

Caught between Salick's hand and his master's commands, Marick scurried off with the dripping sheepskin. Garet saw him run in wide curves around the workers on his way down the dock.

The dock master respectfully accepted Mandarack's signature on one of his sheets and, handing back the ink pot and quill to a child apprentice younger than Marick, strode back to oversee the noisy chaos of the workers. Garet watched him, trailed by the child, thread through the shouting lines of longshoremen, carrying their bags of grain and towers of hay on broad shoulders. As each pile of the plain's wealth grew on the dock, cargo nets were hauled, bumping and catching, up the inclined blocks of the wall, and the party of Banes followed them, climbing a stone stair wide enough for three to walk abreast.

Each block in the wall was the height of the already vanished Marick, and Garet wondered at the effort needed to build it. Dorict saw his awed regard. "Torrick needs this wall to keep the river from eating the earth out from under the city." He motioned down to the river current pushing the barges against each other. "It's the same with every city in the South. They're all on the Ar."

At the top of the wall, a cobblestone lane peaked and slumped its way to the city gate. Mandarack paused, perhaps to catch his breath, although his face showed no strain at the steep climb, and Salick hovered protectively near him. Garet himself was glad of the chance to lean against the bags of grain stacked at the top of wall and wait for his legs to stop burning. *Horseback riding and climbing stairs*, he wryly observed, *must use the same muscles.* After a minute, the old Bane led them slowly to the city's entrance.

There was as much activity here as there had been at the wharves. A crazy weaving of scaffolding left only a small path for passing under the gate's archway. Men and women, many of them wearing round, bronze helmets, hauled up a new panel of stout timbers to replace a rotted patch on the ancient gates. The right wing of the gates was in pieces on the ground. More workers were perched on the scaffold, using picks and crowbars to pry out hinges that leaned at odd angles from the stone.

"Old Torrick had little use for gates these last few hundred years or so." Salick pointed at the helmeted workers. "Those are miners. It's good to see that the King of Torrick and his lords are serious enough about rebuilding their defences to disrupt their main source of income!" The workers noticed the Banes and stopped their activity to sketch hasty bows. Mandarack nodded back, and they quickly returned to their tasks.

"Money's no good if you're dead," Dorict said, and added for Garet's sake, "The nobility of Torrick is famous for paying more attention to their own purses than the state of their city." A metallic groan cut off Dorict's words as the workers freed one of the massive hinges.

"Were there no demons in this city, as in the Midlands for these past six hundred years?" Garet asked the younger boy. They moved under the shadow of the gate and entered an arched, stone tunnel.

"Not as many as in Shirath," Salick replied before Dorict could speak. "They were lucky to fight three a year. That's as many as show up in a bad week in a city like Shirath or Solantor. That's why the Banehall has less influence here than in the other cities."

Garet swallowed. Three demons a week! His distress must have been obvious for Dorict smiled and said, "Don't worry, there are over two-hundred and forty Banes in Shirath. You won't have to kill them all yourself!"

Relieved, Garet turned his attention back to their surroundings. The tunnel seemed to burrow through the thick walls of the fortress before ending in another, this time intact, gate. *The walls must be forty paces thick*, he marvelled.

"Salick," he asked, "does every city have walls this thick to keep out demons?"

But it was Mandarack who answered, his voice floating back in the gloom of the tunnel. "The Torrickmen from ancient times have not farmed, nor made, but have dug their wealth from the ground. Almost all the copper and iron, and most of the gold of the South come from this city. Such wealth bred enemies before humanity found itself faced with a greater threat. For six-hundred years now there has been no war. Piracy on the seas, occasionally. Bandits from the deserts and mountains, certainly. But no war. These walls, Garet, were built to keep out an older fear." His voice paused as they passed under a spiked gate, rusted but still ready to drop down on some long-vanished attacker. As they moved deeper into the tunnel, it echoed hollowly off the curved ceiling. "They were built to keep out other men."

The inner gate opened out on a large market, larger than the muddy field occupied by Three Roads Village. One-storey shops were built leaning against the inside wall in a ring around the square. Clusters of pole and canvas stalls, advertising everything from sweets to iron goods, filled the centre Aside from a few old men and women lounging in the doors of the outer shops, nothing moved or made enough noise to mask the sighing of the wind. Dust devils played among the colourful canvases draping the stalls.

Salick stared at one group of stalls, near the south wall, that had been smashed flat. Broken poles stuck out of the torn canvas. A cracked sign lay on top, advertising perfumes.

"I suppose there's nothing like a Basher to take the profit out of a market day," she mused. The wind shifted and a powerful mix of blood and perfume assaulted them. "Gyaah!" Salick retreated from the stench with Garet and Dorict close behind, holding their noses. "The poor Banes who killed that demon must have suffered!" Garet nodded agreement, hands over his mouth and nose, his eyes watering.

As they followed Mandarack across the deserted market, leaving behind the sickening reek of perfume soured with demon blood, the obvious wealth of the city impressed itself upon the new Bane. A market day here could bring all the Midlanders within a week's journey, all with money for Torrick's lords. *What would happen now*, thought Garet.

"Salick, if the demons have returned to the Midlands and Old Torrick, won't the people here have to give up trade for farming?"

Salick looked at him curiously. "Why would that be? Trading has always gotten them what they wanted. Besides, everyone knows that Torrickmen are too lazy to farm."

"Well," Garet reasoned, "trade will end, or at least be hurt by the loss of farms in the Midlands. What they're unloading at the docks must be the last of the spring wheat planted last fall; the fall harvest of summer-planted wheat may rot in the fields if people dare not travel too far from towns like Bangt."

Dorict agreed. "That's the truth, Garet. And they'll get little help elsewhere. What surplus Shirath and the other cities grow is stored for their own use or traded North for fish and tin."

"But who here knows how to farm?" Salick mocked. "You can't take a miner and tell her to grow wheat!"

For once, Garet refused to retreat into his customary silence; if Salick could argue with Mandarack, he could do the same with her. "If they want to eat next year, they'll have to," he retorted and then went on more thoughtfully, "or they might take some of those homeless farmers we saw at Bangt. Or at Three Roads." He felt a sharp pain in his chest as he thought of his mother and sister crowded into those rough tents. But in fact, he had no way of knowing if his father had even decided to leave the farm and take his family to live behind those wooden walls. They might still be isolated on their farm, easy prey for demons. Thankfully, Salick interrupted his thoughts.

"It's a good idea, Garet. I'll mention it to the Master when we're settled in the hall." She looked at him with a certain surprise. "You've got a good head on your shoulders..."

"For a poor Northerner farm boy?" Garet was surprised at the resentment in his voice, but he was tired of being an outsider and was still distracted by his thoughts about his family.

"That's not what I meant." Salick's voice became as dry as her master's, and Garet realized he had offended her by rejecting her rare show of approval. "I was going to say that you had a good head on your shoulders for someone who has never had a reason to use it." She turned on her heel, and Garet knew that their relationship had just taken a giant step backwards. "Keep up now. We don't want you lost on your first time in a city," she called over her shoulder as she strode off after Mandarack.

Garet stood for a moment, cursing himself for lashing out at the very people he now depended on. He felt a hand on his shoulder.

"Don't worry," Dorict whispered. "She'll forgive you when she's had a chance to think it over. Salick hates to admit mistakes, but she's fair-minded for all her pride." The young Bane trotted off after Salick, the saddle bags bouncing on his shoulders.

With a sigh, Garet ran after him, catching up at the far wall of the market. The party now entered a narrow lane running between rows of narrow, two-storey houses. Ropes strung across the street from the upper stories fluttered with drying sheets, tunics, and stockings. Small children dashed madly under their feet, crossing from one house to another as if they owned them all. Older siblings chased after their little brothers and sisters half-heartedly, if at all. As the Banes passed by, these minders grabbed their charges to force them into wobbly bows and curtsies. Mandarack nodded back with the same dignity and regard he had shown the dock master. The younger Banes copied him as well as they could. Giggles erupted behind them, and the endless chase resumed.

After many twists and turns, the lane opened onto another square, much smaller than the market plaza. A fountain with a broad, round curb squatted in the middle of the courtyard. Women of all ages crowded around it, washing clothes, yelling at their friends, and shouting for their children to-come-get-the-basket-and-smartly-now! They rivalled the longshoremen on the wharves for their noise and energy. Mandarack, Salick beside him now, led the others past the cheerful din to the biggest building in the square.

Built of the same rough stone as the walls, the Torrick Banehall took up the whole west side of the courtyard. Red paint peeled from the door frame; half its second storey windows were boarded up; at their feet lay a cracked roof-tile. Mandarack looked grimly at the rundown building.

"This is disgraceful!" Salick exclaimed. "Every Banehall and every Bane is insulted by this." She stopped as Mandarack raised his hand.

"This is not our Hall, Salick," his voice was harsh, "but, under Heaven, things will soon change here. They must!"

"Hadn't you already stopped here on the way into the Midlands?" Garet asked Dorict, too mindful of Salick's present annoyance with him to risk asking her.

"No," the boy replied, staring distastefully at the rundown building. "We were in too much haste and passed by Torrick at night on horseback. You save no time taking a barge against the current!"

The door burst open, shedding a few more chips of paint, and Marick bounded down the steps. The sheepskin package was gone. "Master! I spoke to Hallmaster Furlenix and a cart is ready to take us back tomorrow. There's beds for all of us and better food than we've had lately, and you're to make your report to the Hallmaster before you go to your bed!"

Salick bristled at the impertinence of either Marick, the Hallmaster, or both. Even Dorict narrowed his eyes in anger at the order given to their master. Marick waited, obviously enjoying the effect he had created. Mandarack only gave a slight snort and answered, "Very well, Master Marick." The usually dry voice held a hint of banter. "Perhaps you could conduct us to our duties."

With an elaborate bow, Marick led them into the Banehall. The interior was as shabby as the outside. Mandarack stopped in a spacious room just inside the door. They faced a staircase leading up to the second storey. To the right, a hallway with rows of doors on either side stretched to the end of the building. To the left, an opening led to a dining hall, where Garet could see very young black-sashed Banes laying out plates and bowls.

"That's servant's work," Salick hissed. She looked at Garet, her anger at him forgotten in her general disgust with the Torrick Banehall. "Garet, you are to do no such work while you are here. No first level Bane should have the time or energy for the setting of tables!"

"Am I a Black Sash, Salick?" he asked carefully, hoping for an answer and not another eruption.

"Yes, Garet, you are a Black Sash," Mandarack answered in her stead. "And, as Salick has instructed you, you will not do servant's work, even if you are told to by the Master of this Hall!"

"But you should get some proper clothes," Salick said, and looked to Mandarack, who nodded before he walked off down the hallway. Salick looked around for someone to help them. The hall was deserted. The Black Sashes had finished their work and run up the stairs. Her face reddening, Salick opened her mouth to shout when a voice called out.

"Don't yell! I'm sorry I've left you standing here, but everything has been in an uproar for the last month." A short young man wearing a sash of muted gold trotted out of the hallway. "Please forgive us, Green, but this place is currently held together with string and spit, as they say." He grinned at them and introduced himself. "I am Boronict, and I'm at your service." His head bobbed up and down in a quick acknowledgement of his guests.

Salick introduced herself and the younger Banes and, somewhat impatiently, requested rooms, water to wash with, and a set of clothes for Garet.

"Of course," the young man said. "Please follow me!" He led them up the stairs into a warren of halls and rooms, most of them, it seemed, unused. He directed Salick to a dormitory for female Banes, but Marick spoke up quickly when the Gold turned to the three boys.

"Don't worry, Boronict. I've already found a place for us." He shepherded the other two past the surprised young man and down another hallway. Stopping at a narrow door, he pushed it open on squeaking hinges and pulled Garet and Dorict inside. "I found this while waiting for you snails. Now, this is comfort!" He flopped down on a sagging bed, sending up a fountain of dust from the mattress.

Dorict dropped the packs on the floor, creating another cloud. "Marick, why did you bring us to this rat hole?" A row of beds took up one wall. A small hearth and a curtained window faced the door, and a jumble of mismatched dressers, desks, and wobbly chairs took up the rest of the space. The stocky Bane wrinkled his nose at the musty smell of the long-abandoned room.

"Use your head for something other than eating, Dorict! Boronict would probably put us in with a bunch of lowly Black Sashes." He grinned at Garet. "No offence," he said, making a great show of adjusting his own blue sash. "And if he did, we'd probably have to go to early practice tomorrow. And we'd probably have to fight our way to the best beds." He swept back the curtains and the late afternoon light flooded the room through cracked window panes. "In here, we can at least be near each other."

"A comfort, I'm sure," his friend replied and pulled a mattress off a bed to beat the dust from it. "Garet, open those windows before we choke to death."

Garet did so, then helped the younger boy kick and punch the mattresses, taking the opportunity to ask more questions. "Dorict, I know that a Black Sash is lower than a Blue, and that a Red Sash is the highest."

Marick interrupted. "Not really. A Banehall master has a red sash with black borders."

Dorict ignored him. "That's right. Black sashes are for beginners just entering the Banehall."

"That's so they can wipe their hands on them after dinner and not look messy. Blacks are usually just kids," Marick explained.

Dorict continued ignoring him. "Blacks study the basics of demons, some have to be taught to read and write. That takes a while. They also have to get in physical shape for the next stage."

"Much harder for some than for others, I'm sure," Marick observed.

His overweight friend was hitting the mattress harder than necessary, but didn't lose his train of thought. "Blue Sashes train in basic weapons and tactics. When they're proficient, they become Greens." A silence followed. Dorict and Garet turned towards the youngest Bane, expecting another comment, but Marick merely grinned and stuck his tongue out at them.

Scowling, Dorict resumed his explanation. "Greens help Golds with patrols and learn how to track demons outside the walls. Golds, like Boronict, patrol the fields and wards. When they're good enough, they might lead teams to make kills, but mostly they assist the Masters." He glared at Marick, waiting for either sarcasm or silence. The young Bane replied with a rude gesture.

"Garet," Dorict growled, "please take this fool out to find your uniform before I see how much dust I can beat out of him!"

Marick bowed; he liked nothing better than getting his usually placid friend's goat, and led Garet out the door. They went down several halls, turning and twisting until Garet was totally lost.

"Marick," he complained, "do you really know where you're going?"

"Of course. I used to live here, you know."

Garet stopped in surprise and put a hand on the Blue's shoulder. "Then why are you now at Shirath Banehall?"

"Had to leave," the cheerful Bane answered as he resumed his trot along the hallway. "Misunderstanding with the Masters here."

As they reached the end of the hall and stopped at a massive iron-studded door, Garet mused that it would be very easy to arrive at a misunderstanding with his chaotic little companion. Pushing open the heavy door, Marick and Garet entered a large, low room lit weakly by the angled light from its high windows. Every surface—tables, side boards, and chairs—was covered with the Banehall's stores. Pots and pans tumbled onto the floor to fight for space with stacks of linen writing-sheets, piles of paired boots, and twisted wreaths made of different coloured sashes.

Marick approached an older master sitting behind one of the burdened tables. As they neared him, Garet was shocked to see that the right side of his face was furrowed by deep scars. The old wound sealed his eye socket and his right sleeve was pinned and empty.

"Marick, is that you?" the old man inquired waspishly. He glared at the boy from his good eye. "How did you get back here?"

"I'm just passing through to Shirath, Master Senerix," the young Bane assured him. "This is a new Bane, Garet. Master Mandarack wants a uniform for him."

The glare remained on Marick. "If Mandarack is his master, than Shirath can cloth him." He took up his quill and continued writing on the sheet in front of him.

"Of course, Master," Marick said agreeably. "But if the Hallmaster comments on Garet's lack of proper clothing at dinner tonight, should I direct him to you for an explanation?"

Senerix stopped writing but refused to look up. After a moment, and very unwillingly it seemed, he rasped out, "Very well, but from the used piles." The quill pointed to a far corner. "If Mandarack wants new clothes, he can provide them himself."

Garet stiffened at the rudeness of the man and steeled himself to make some reply. What grated most was Senerix's total dismissal of him. He didn't enjoy being the topic of a conversation when he should have been a participant. However, Marick obviously knew the old man too well to challenge his petty victory and, after a hasty bow, dragged Garet over to a pile of hand-me-downs in various stages of disrepair. He kept Garet over on Senerix's blind side and began a loud, rambling lecture about the generosity of the Torrick Banehall while they rummaged through the pile. Another Bane, a Green, came in with a new pile of sheets to drop on Senerix's desk. The sheets slid over onto the floor, and Senerix spluttered angrily at the young woman.

"Now!" whispered Marick and dived for the piles of new clothes, stuffing a tunic, pants, and black sash down the front of Garet's wool shirt. He hastily measured a pair of shiny new boots against Garet's foot and, tucking them under his arm, bolted for the door with Garet in panicked pursuit. A querulous voice rose behind them, but Marick's twisting and turning soon had them out of danger.

The two thieves didn't stop until they had burst though the door of their room, startling Dorict who was in the midst of laying a fire in the hearth.

The stout boy gasped, hand on his chest. "Marick! You'll be my death one day!" Dorict said, and fell back onto one of the considerably cleaner beds.

"Did you think I was a demon coming to get you?" Marick laughed at his friend. "Besides, what are you doing lighting a fire when it's summer?"

"Trying to drive the mustiness out of this room. We won't sleep in this smell."

Marick nodded. "Oh yes! I found this in the storeroom." He pulled a short candle out of his pocket and passed it under Garet's nose. It had the aroma of sweet herbs. "Senerix's rat-hole could use a little freshening up too, but I'm sure he won't miss just one candle." He handled it over to Dorict, who quickly lit it from the small blaze he had built. Immediately, the air seemed more fragrant, and the mustiness was driven away.

"That's nice," observed Marick, "much better than that perfume in the market! Now Garet, let's get you looking like a proper Bane." He pulled out the stolen articles from inside Garet's shirt and smoothed them out on the bed.

Garet changed quickly, while Dorict, with Marick's unhelpful suggestions, laid out their bedding. The loose grey pants felt no different than the ones he had brought from the farm, except that they bore no patches or tears. The high-necked tunic, on the other hand, was a revelation in luxury. Made out of a soft, thin cloth for which he had no name, it settled its black length over him like a cool wave. He buttoned up the collar and wished for a mirror to catch the expression on his own face as much as for the look of all this finery. The vest, purple and trimmed with gold thread at the collar, followed. Finally, Dorict helped him arrange the black sash around his shoulder. He then assisted him with the boots, which for all their shine, were stiff and uncomfortable. Marick then turned Garet towards the window, which the fading light outside the Hall had turned into a cracked and wavy mirror.

"Now, here's a Bane!" exclaimed Marick. Dorict nodded, just as pleased with the effect.

Who is that person, Garet thought, looking at the strange image facing him. *Where is the farm boy?* He smiled at the thought of the sheep's reaction to his new clothing, and the dignified young man in the window smiled back at him. *Am I a Bane now?* He tentatively reached out a hand towards the reflection, and Marick slapped it playfully.

"Don't worry! It's not an illusion. You're one of us now." He punched Garet on the shoulder.

"Of course," Marick added, in a voice remarkably like Mandarack's, "as a mere Black Sash, you will have to obey our every whim." Dorict sniffed at this frippery.

Garet smiled with them and adjusted his sash, feeling his future in the weight of his new clothes.

A Change of Masters

The evening began as an exercise in staying out of sight. Garet refused to leave the room until driven out by his growling stomach. He slunk down the stairs behind Dorict and Marick. As they entered the wide dining hall, he pulled them to the last table, far away from Senerix. The scarred Bane sat behind a long, polished table on a dais at the front of the dining hall. He was hunched in his chair, scanning the room with his good eye. Garet ducked and took a chair that allowed him to sit with his back to the man they had cheated. Marick sat beside him, also hiding his face from the high table. Dorict, the only one with a clear conscience, sat across from them.

The table was loaded with steamed greens and salt beef. Bread was piled in central dishes and the quick hands of the Black and Blue Sashes surrounding the Shirath Banes scattered them with showers of crumbs as they tore it into individual portions. Dorict used his size to shoulder up to the platter and retrieve a whole loaf, round and with a rough letter cut into the brown top.

"That's the sign for a Banehall," Marick informed Garet as the apprentices divided the loaf into three roughly equal pieces.

"I thought it meant treasure hall," he replied, holding his piece up to Marick's to examine the complicated, and now somewhat mangled glyph. "See here. The box on the right means hall, doesn't it? But the left hand part means gold or treasure."

Dorict looked at Garet as if he had grown wings. "You can read!" he exclaimed, shocked out of his usual calmness. "How under Heaven did you ever learn to read on that pest-hole of a farm?"

Garet blushed. It was not a skill he boasted about, mainly because his father had no taste for "scribblings 'n time wasting." His mother had taught him to draw the symbols common to both the South and the North. She had spent many mornings with him, before he had been old enough for much farm work, dipping her long finger in water and tracing each word on the table top. He had practiced this skill on the hillside, scratching lines in the dirt to escape the mind-numbing boredom of watching sheep chew their mouthfuls of grass. Trying to remember enough symbols to write out one of his mother's complex Northern songs of dragon fighters or forest magic had pleased his mind in a way that herding sheep never could. His mother's pride in his ability and her joy at being able to pass on the learning of her own childhood had strengthened the bond between them. Was she thinking of him now, he wondered.

"I learned from my mother," Garet said, and the sad shading of his tone prevented even Marick from ribbing him about his surprising skill.

Dorict only said, "Blame the baker's hand. That's 'claw', not 'gold' on the side."

As they ate their dinner with a speed possible only to young boys, Garet twisted his head around to catch glimpses of the high table. It was occupied solely by Red Sashes. A portly man sat at its centre, his belly straining at a red sash bordered in black. He shovelled his food as if he were trying to match Garet and his friends, despite his grey hair and wobbling jowls. Mandarack sat to one side of him but only picked at his plate. A slight woman with grey hair cut shorter than he had ever seen on a woman was leaning over and talking to him. Mandarack engaged her in quiet conversation throughout the meal. Garet was curious but didn't dare observe them more closely for fear Senerix would spot his turned face. Dorict ignored their plea to spy for them while he ate but was more accommodating when he had finished his second plate.

"They're still talking," Dorict reported in a low voice. "Isn't she the weapons trainer for Torrick?"

Marick risked another look and nodded. "That's right. Corix. She's a terror to her students and very unfair to the younger Banes!"

"In other words, she didn't let you get away with anything, eh?" Dorict smiled and continued his report. "Two other Reds are leaning in for a listen. Now she's waved Boronict over."

"Why him?" Marick demanded. "He's only a Gold."

"I'm sure your old teacher won't mind if you ask her," Dorict offered and smiled at Marick's answering glare. "Now shut up and let me look. Hmmm. Boronict's gone out of the hall. Some Golds are following him. Now she's talking to Furlenix, the Hallmaster. They're arguing...well, you can hear it yourself."

Dorict was right. The Hallmaster's voice was loud enough to be clear even at the back of the hall.

"This is Torrick Banehall! Not Shirath!" His jowls shook as his words rang out over the hushed dining hall. "Master Mandarack's advice is not welcome!"

Their caution forgotten, Marick and Garet joined the whole hall in staring as Mandarack rose, nodded calmly at the sputtering Hallmaster, and left with Corix at his side. There was a flurry of indecision at the high table. In the end, the outraged Hallmaster was left with only Senerix and a few other ancient Reds sitting forlornly at the high table.

"Come on," whispered Marick as he grabbed his friends' arms and dragged them into the crowd of different coloured sashes funnelling through the dining hall doors. They had barely squeezed through the opening when Garet felt a hand fall on his shoulder. He froze, expecting the rasping, querulous voice of Senerix demanding back his new uniform, but it was Salick's voice that cut above the hubbub and arguments swelling around them.

"Come on! Let's find some place where we can talk," she shouted.

Marick led them through the press of bodies and up the stairs. The halls were no less crowded here. Golds ran back and forth with scrolls of paper. Knots of older Reds argued among themselves, the lesser ranks looking nervously on. With a few twists and turns, the Shirath apprentices were safely inside the room the three younger Banes had appropriated.

"I would guess that Marick has something to do with this," Salick said, looking around appreciatively: a small fire crackled cheerfully in the hearth, the beds were free of dust and covered with their own blankets while the mismatched chairs were drawn cozily around a table near the hearth. "Quite homey. And to think I'm sharing a room half this size with three other Greens!"

"You can bunk with us, Salick," Marick quickly offered. "No one will know in this mess. But tell us what you think is happening!"

Salick took a chair and looked out on the candle lit windows in the houses across the fountain square. "I think Mandarack proposed something—I wasn't near enough at my table to hear what—but I'm sure that's what started this riot." She looked sharply at Marick. "Go find Boronict. He's friendly to us, and he might know what's going on."

She had hardly finished speaking before Marick was out the door. Dorict closed it hurriedly before the arguments and what sounded like fist fights entered the room. Had they just heard the thud of someone hitting the wall?

"Salick," Garet asked, "why is there any argument at all? I mean, isn't Furlenix in charge of this Banehall?"

Salick paused before answering. "Garet, a Hallmaster is not a king. He or she is chosen from the other Masters. They can choose someone else, if there is dissension."

Garet thought about this. "But, Salick, wouldn't such a fight keep the Banehall from fighting the demons, and Torrick unprotected?" The image of the ruined stall in the marketplace rose in front of his eyes, and he shuddered.

"Not necessarily," Salick replied. "Each Master is responsible for his or her own patrols and trains their own students—above a certain level, of course." She adjusted the green sash around her shoulders. "But someone has to control the rest: who takes a watch in case of sickness, whether or not the division of duties is fair, and who should take on special jobs like training Blacks and Blues or keeping records and such."

Dorict turned from where he was listening at the door and added, "The Hallmaster is also the Banehall's voice when we talk to the King and his lords."

Garet nodded, understanding a bit more of this new world.

"Then a Hallmaster's power is really limited," he said.

Salick shrugged. "It depends on how many Reds support you."

The noise swelled in the hallway again, and Salick twisted her hands nervously. "Maybe it was a bad idea to send Marick into this kind of chaos. Do you think we should...?"

Before they could decide whether not to set out and rescue their companion, the door flew open and Marick dragged in a harried looking Boronict.

"What is it, Salick?" the anxious young Gold demanded. "I'm...we're all in the middle of something here!"

"What is that 'something,' Boronict?" Salick asked, grabbing his arm to keep him from leaving again. Marick slammed the door and put his back to it, a determined look on his face.

"I suppose you'd better know, since it's partly your fault," Boronict said, a wry smile on his face.

Salick stiffened. "How can you accuse us of..."

"Hold on, Green. It's not you. It's your Master! He's set the wolf among the sheep tonight." The young man wiped his forehead and gratefully accepted the cup of water Dorict handed him. "Master Mandarack has convinced Training Master Corix and several other Reds to vote on a new leader for Torrick Banehall!"

"Well, it's about time," said Marick, still guarding the door. "All Furlenix does is eat and eat and then eat again. This Hall's gone downhill since I left!"

Dorict rolled his eyes at this arrogance, but Boronict bowed, a touch of irony in his voice. "No doubt we have lacked your noble example. Though I believe most people think that the disappearance of petty crime has almost made up for it."

Marick blushed and, surprisingly, bowed in return.

Boronict continued. "Many of the Masters have been dissatisfied with the leadership of this Hall." His eyes flashed and his voice rose. "The King and nobles have taken away many of our privileges in favour of their profit. As long as few demons attacked, we could manage without proper walls between neighbourhoods, without enough horses for patrols of the mining villages, even without enough labour to keep up our own hall." He looked at the door, anxious to be gone. "Salick, the Reds know that Furlenix is not the Master to face this great change in the Midlands. By the end of this night, there may be some bent noses, and maybe one or two broken ones, but there will be a new Master in this Hall!" He strode to the door and picked up Marick, gently depositing him to one side. "I hope it's Corix. She's not the most pleasant person to work with, but then, these are unpleasant times." With that, he darted out the door and back into the arguments and shoving in the hall.

The shouting continued long into the night. The four young Banes listened intently whenever the wash of sound increased or when they heard furniture breaking. Finally, as the city watch called out the third hour past half-night, a silence descended on the Banehall. Marick stuck his head outside the door, despite Dorict's hissed warning.

"Not a soul in sight," Marick reported. "I'll be back!" With that, the boy sped down the hall before Salick could catch his shoulder.

"Demon take that boy!" Salick hissed and darted after him.

Garet and Dorict looked at each other. Both were more cautious than the others, but tonight they were just as curious. With a slight movement of his chin, Garet suggested, and with an answering grimace, Dorict agreed. They moved out into the corridor as quietly as they could, though their footsteps seemed loud in the new silence.

They caught up with Salick at the top of the main staircase. She held a wriggling Marick, staring over the balustrade. Dorict wrapped a thick arm around Marick's neck and muttered threats in his ear. But his friend tore free and pushed his face between the slats. A crowd of Reds with a dusting of Golds on the fringes huddled around the woman who had been talking to Mandarack earlier. With her short, iron-grey hair framing a severe face and her fists planted firmly on her hips, she made an imposing figure. The others quieted as she began to speak, raising her voice to reach those in the back and, unintentionally, the four students on the upper landing.

"Furlenix has agreed to step down as Hallmaster and take the position of Archivist. Taraox will leave that position to supervise the Blacks and Blues, and Praxilit will replace me as Training Master." Her eyes swept the crowd in front of her, stopping here and there to momentarily pin a single, reluctant man or woman. Garet could see a few backs stiffen at the uncompromising tone of their new Master, but Corix held them with her narrowed eyes, her short hair seeming to bristle at any sign of resistance. Daunted, the Reds murmured agreement and began to disperse, the Golds trailing in their wake like fall leaves.

Salick pulled them away and quietly led her small group back to their room. She pushed them inside and closed the door, warning them to get some sleep. Her attitude was one of extreme concentration.

"Salick," Marick called as the door swung closed, "do you think this is happening at the other Banehalls?" His tone lacked its usual confidence; he sounded like the child he was, in need of reassurance.

Only Salick's hand was visible, curled around the edge of the door. It was a small hand, but it was tracked by scars that Garet realized must come from constant training with weapons. Salick's voice came softly through the narrow crack. "Not yet. Things are most dangerous here, on the edge of the Midlands. The others won't feel the change, not yet." With that half-comfort, she closed the door and left the three boys to think their way to sleep.

The Falls

The excitement of the night before and the few hours of
sleep before dawn left the Banes tired and subdued as they
waited for Master Mandarack in the front entrance of
Torrick Banehall. Garet and his two young friends had eaten
quickly in the kitchen under Salick's impatient eyes. She had
been up even earlier than they had, or perhaps had never
gone to bed, for her eyes were red and puffy, and she yawned
between orders to the other three to hurry up, "lest the
Master be kept waiting."

Breakfast was cold tea and dry bread, left over from the
night before. Dorict stayed behind to beg a packed lunch
from the yawning cooks while Salick and Garet carried
saddlebags down the stairs to the front hall. Marick had
disappeared. He joined the rest in the front hall some time
later, looking pleased and secretive. Salick gave him a
calculating look but was prevented from investigating by
Mandarack's arrival. He was accompanied by Corix and a
scattering of tired, grim Reds. Garet saw that Corix's red sash
was now trimmed with a black border.

"The Gold you met yesterday, Boronict, will be taking you
to below the Falls shortly," Corix informed the younger
Banes, "just as soon as I've had a talk with him." Her grey
eyes, no less sharp for the bags under them, swept the young
Banes, lingering for a long moment on Marick. "He will
accompany you to the villages below the Falls but no
farther." With a slight, stiff bow to Mandarack, who returned
it just as precisely, she turned and, dividing the Reds like a

wind cutting through the prairie grass, disappeared back into the depths of the hall.

Marick stepped out from behind Salick and grinned at the new Banemaster's back. Salick took this opportunity to cuff him lightly on the back of his head.

"Oww! Salick, I didn't do anything! I..." he started to hide behind Dorict, but one glance at his friend's face sent him to Garet's side instead. "Besides, we'd better set off if we want to make the Temple by dark, and if I know this Hall, the horses won't be hitched yet and the cart will have a broken wheel, and..."

Garet yawned and grabbed him by the elbow, dragging the still-protesting boy out the door as the party, following Mandarack, left the Banehall. A clammy fog had settled on the town, and for a moment Garet missed his old wool shirt. His new vest left his arms bare save for the thin, shiny cloth of his tunic.

Despite Marick's misgivings, the canvas-roofed cart was in one piece and hitched to a pair of large grey horses. Boronict joined them in a few minutes, silent and wrapped in a great black cloak.

Once out the gates, he turned the horses away from the road they had come up on the day before and took a rutted path towards the west. As they got farther and farther from the city walls, two things changed: a heavy mist rose and the great roar of water made normal speech impossible.

"That's the Falls, of course," Marick yelled in Garet's ear. "We have to go down the Miner's Trail to the bottom. Unless you'd like to swim over!"

The Trail was a dizzying succession of narrow switchbacks, all wrapped in mist until, for one glorious moment, the wind shifted and cleared the air for a view of the Falls.

Garet was glad of the sight, though it was terrifying in its grandeur. Far above them now, the North and South Ar joined and launched themselves together from a channel cut into the cliff top. All white foam and noise, it beat into the pools below, falling five times the height of the walls of Old Torrick. The wind died and the mist returned, but Garet knew he would never forget that one glimpse.

At the bottom of the trail, they heard the ring of hammers on anvils and the shouts of men and women, but saw nothing more than the ten feet of road ahead of the cart. Boronict kept driving until they came out of the mist on the road to Shirath, the sound of the Falls now soft enough to talk over. The Torrick Bane climbed down from the wagon and stood without speaking.

"Thank you for the help," Salick said as she jumped down to join him. The other Banes followed.

She smiled and waved her hand back at the wall of mist. "If we tried to get through that on our own, we'd have been very lost or very wet! You're a good guide. Maybe Corix would let you take us all the way to Shirath."

No smile answered her jest and the younger Banes crowded around Boronict pelting him with questions. "Heaven's shield! What's wrong, Boronict?" piped Marick above the rest, and the young man looked sadly down at him.

"I'm afraid you will have to go on without me. You see, my life here has ended. I can no longer stay at Torrick Banehall."

Salick's arm dropped and she gasped out, "But why? What could you possibly have done to get tossed out? Is Furlenix back in charge?"

Boronict shook his head, raining drops of water upon his interrogators. "No. It's Corix who's sent me off. You see, the reason you had to wait for me at the Banehall was that she wanted to see me about a,"—the young man's face turned a deep red—"well, about a love letter!"

Marick's mouth dropped open and the colour drained from his face.

Boronict put a limp hand on the young boy's shoulder. Marick flinched. "You see," he continued sadly, "someone left a letter on her desk professing a passionate love for her."

Garet couldn't help blurting out, "But you couldn't have written such a letter, Boronict. You and Corix..." He couldn't finish, but shocked murmurs showed that the idea of the steel-spined Banemaster inspiring a romantic passion in anyone—and most especially in a young, good-natured man like Boronict—was impossible. Mandarack stood beside the cart, listening in his calm way.

"Well, Garet, that's the problem. You see, someone signed my name to that letter. Corix was furious. I've never seen her so mad. And now I must leave Torrick Banehall forever." A tear welled in his eye, and he stood with his head hung down, hand still on Marick's shoulder.

Marick grabbed Boronict's other hand and erupted in a torrent of words. "Oh no! Boronict. I wrote that note! I didn't think Corix would really think it was from you. Oh, it was just a joke! Please, let me write another note, or I could even go back with you and explain it to Corix. Oh, Boronict you can't stop being a Bane because of me! Ow!"

The hand on Marick's shoulder was suddenly clamped on the back of his neck. "Which is as much as Master Corix and I thought, my little friend." Boronict was grinning from ear to ear.

Marick wriggled but couldn't break the young man's grasp. "That's unfair, Boronict! You never would have found out if you hadn't lied to us about getting kicked out of the Banehall. That was a cheap trick!"

Boronict's smile did not fade. "High praise—from a master of cheap tricks! But I wasn't lying about leaving the Banehall." He released Marick and opened the heavy cloak. Instead of a gold sash hanging from his shoulder, a blood red sash was revealed.

Marick's mouth dropped open and even Salick was struck dumb. A dry voice spoke behind. "Congratulations, Boronict. When Master Corix told me she intended to promote you and send you to Bangt as part of the new Banehall, I thought it was a very reasonable decision."

Boronict bowed at the compliment and smiled down at Marick. He extended his hand. "No hard feelings, Marick?"

The young Bane closed his mouth with an audible snap and ruefully held out his hand. "I can see that I taught you Torrickers too well when I was there. Good luck in Bangt."

The other Banes joined in the congratulations. Garet offered his own warm regards, for he liked the friendly manner and sharp wit of the young man. When the group had quieted, Boronict snapped his fingers.

"That's right. Garet, Master Corix sent this for you to study on your way to Shirath. The rumour is that you can read." He pulled out a small book from an inside pocket of his cloak. Its cover was moist from their passage near the waterfall, but Garet could make out the words on the cover: *The Demonary of Moret*.

Marick groaned when he saw it. "That old thing! I swear, Garet, I almost went back to the streets rather than try and puzzle out what old Moret was talking about."

Salick interrupted. "Garet," she instructed him, in her serious 'teacher' voice, "that is the first book that Blacks study at the Banehall. You will be tested on its contents before you can wear the Blue."

He looked at the slim volume in his hand. Many times on his father's farm, he had dreamed of reading a book. His mother had spoken lovingly of the books her own merchant father had collected. Some passages concerning the great battles between famous heroes and equally infamous dragons she could still recite from memory. Now he had such a book, in his own hands. Garet felt at once close to his mother and yet achingly distant. Tears welled up in his eyes as he thanked Boronict. Salick, perhaps sensing his emotional state, told him to put the Demonary safely in his pack. Gratefully, he left the others and brushed past Mandarack to huddle over the luggage until he could control himself.

By the time he returned, the Banes were ready to take their leave of Boronict. The luggage was loaded into the cart and the canvas rolled back to admit the warm sunshine. The iron-rimmed wheels ground against the stones of the road as they set off towards the next city on the river, Shirath.

Symbols and Stars

The slow, steady progress of the cart was a relief to Garet. After so many new experiences, painful, frightening, or merely confusing, finally he had a chance to digest it all. The cart soon left the cobbled lanes of the mining villages and now travelled on the great paved road that Dorict told him stretched from the Falls, past Shirath, to the great sea itself.

The road was a marvel to Garet. Used to hill paths and mud tracks, he had never imagined as great a construction as this. Three carts wide, it sloped from a slightly raised centre to gravel-filled drainage gutters at the edges. Every foot was paved with squared and smoothed stones, though it was rutted in some spots from centuries of use. The first Overking of Solantor had commanded each city to contribute to its construction. Every city of the South was either on it or only a ferry boat ride away from it. For six hundred years, the goods of the cities and the mines had passed from the falls to the ocean on this highway.

"Why not use another boat?" Garet asked Salick.

"There are some stretches of shallows and rapids that would stop us or turn us over," she replied. "And there are rare cases of water demons this far up the river. Believe me, Garet, you do not want to try and fight a demon from a rocking boat!"

Dorict curled up and dozed against the luggage. Marick sat in the driver's box and honed his wits by pestering Salick. Mandarack sat stiffly across from Garet. The old man's eyes were closed, but Garet felt sure that he was not asleep. As the

87

wheels turned, the harvest sun beat down on the cart's canvas, the grain-drying sun to the people of the Plains. But here there were no homesteads or farming villages. Save for swatches burned bare by lightning strike, the land nearest the road most resembled the prairie in its tall grass and late summer flowers. Farther back, groves of ancient apple trees endured the birch and aspen growing in their midst. Those ghostly orchards and the hedges that marched single-mindedly straight across the fields were the only clues that this land had once been farmed. Now the road cut through a wilderness that only half-remembered its civilized past. Wild rose and poplar trees grew in the ancient furrows. Behind it all, green mountains flanked the broad river valley.

Twisting to get the sun off his face, Garet opened his pack and, after gently moving Dorict's elbow, took out the Demonary. The cover was of blackened leather, tooled and pressed to form the symbols of the title. Although the edges were frayed and the spine shiny with bending, each page was complete and unstained as he fanned the pages. He held it reverently and promised himself to keep it just as well as its previous owner. He opened the book.

Laying the Demonary carefully open in his lap, Garet began to read. The symbols were not as graceful as his mother's or even his own, and the lines sometimes wandered from straight to slanted. With a twinge of disappointment, Garet realized that the book was probably the copy work of a young Bane, not the work of a true book maker. The illustrations were another matter, though. Each one had been drawn in a confident hand and with much detail. They were not on the paper of the book itself but had been pasted on the back of various pages throughout the Demonary. Each drawing showed a demon. The variety was bewildering. At least twelve different types were shown, maybe more, as some illustrations were collections of different parts of demon bodies and must have represented more than one demon.

As the sun cut across the heavens, Garet read through the book as a traveller in the desert takes a long drink from an oasis pool. A thirst for something greater than his own poor life had been building in him for years. In the kindness of his mother's eyes, in the brief protection given him by his eldest brother, and even in his sister, Allia's, careless courage, he had seen a nobility in the world that spoke against everything his father cultivated on that drab prison of a farm. And he wanted that nobility—to serve it, or if he was worthy, to live it. In teaching him to read, his mother had fed that hunger, and now he devoured each symbol and illustration. He heard no sound or voice and even Marick gave up trying to bother him. At last, as the shadows lengthened across the road, he closed the worn cover and looked up. Mandarack's eyes were upon him, grey and calm.

"I hope it was what you were seeking, Garet," the Banemaster said.

Garet saw that everyone else's eyes were on him. Dorict's were as calm as his Master's. Marick's blue eyes were full of lively anticipation. And Salick's? To Garet's surprise, they seemed to show concern, as if she feared he might be disappointed. He took a deep breath and gathered his thoughts.

"It is, Master," he replied, looking up to meet that calm regard. "I just don't know how to take it all in." He felt as if he had eaten past full or taken in too much air at a single breath and now struggled to hold it.

"We have all felt some of that," Mandarack said, leaning forward to emphasize his words. "In the Hall we call it our second birth—into a very strange life, I suppose. Most find it as difficult as their first birth." He leaned back again. "But we all grow into it." A short yelp told Garet that Salick had forestalled Marick's attempt to enter the conversation.

"You have come farther than most to this new life. We have never had a Bane from the North."

"I was born on the Plains, Master," Garet replied in a soft voice.

The grey eyes closed again. "Yes, Garet, but only for your first life."

His voice had the hush of evening in it, and Salick soon found a beaten down patch of earth beside the road to stop at for the night. The ground was a maze of ruts and well-used fire pits. Wood had been stacked near the central pit, and the young Banes quickly set up camp. As true night fell, they ate well of the supplies Boronict had placed in the cart and then laid their blankets down beside the dying fire. Dorict had dragged Marick off to help with the washing of pots. Mandarack, as was his habit, had walked beyond the circle of light and was looking up at the stars, his good arm clasping the withered one behind his back.

Garet took this opportunity to ask Salick some questions he would have been embarrassed to ask Mandarack.

"Salick?"

She looked up from the fire to regard him, the light chasing shadows across her face.

He swallowed and pressed on. "Salick, there seems to be something wrong with the Demonary." He paused, waiting for an explosion of passionate defense, but the Bane only raised her left eyebrow.

"Some of the symbols were strange, though my mother swore she had taught them all to me." Salick nodded at him, and he continued. "And the drawings do not match the text." His frustration boiled up and into words. "There is no order to it! Moret starts talking about a "Glider Demon" and drops it in mid-sentence to describe a Basher, while the drawing is of something called a "Squeezer," which is never described in the book!" He thumped the ground with his fist, raising a little cloud of angry dust. "It's like sitting in the tavern at Three Roads and listening to six conversations at once. You can't make sense of it." He looked warily at Salick, but to his surprise, she was smiling.

"I believe you, Garet. That book was probably the copy work of a Blue or Green and was made from a copy by another Blue or Green. And so on, back a hundred years! Each student's mistakes were lovingly preserved, or added to!" She stretched out on her blanket and said sleepily, "Honestly, I think a Bane learns nothing until they become a Green and apprentice to a Master. Master Mandarack has taught me more in one year than I learned in six years from those musty books!"

"But they should be useful!" Garet protested. "What is written in a book should be true!" He had no other way of expressing his deep sense of betrayal, something that he had not dared express to Mandarack. "Don't you see, Salick?

Writing is rare. It takes so long to learn it, and so few people ever do. Whatever is written must be...beautiful!" He blushed at his own passion, and Salick shook her head.

"Garet, there is no use getting upset. I sympathize! I cursed the Demonary myself when I was a Black, but you will have to puzzle it out for yourself the way we all did." She rolled over, her back a definite sign that the conversation was over.

Garet could not resist one more comment. "Well, at least this copy should be fixed. It's a disgrace!"

"A good idea." Mandarack had come back unnoticed to the fire while Garet had been complaining to Salick. "You should practice your writing as well as your reading. Salick has some writing materials. You may start tomorrow." The dry voice had no hint of irony.

A clanging of pots signalled the return of Dorict and Marick. The smaller Bane laughed. "Never complain yourself into more work, Garet!" He set the pots by the fire and climbed into his blanket, but stopped his movements, open-mouthed at Garet's reply to Mandarack: "Thank you, Master. I look forward to beginning." Marick sadly shook his head and, looking over at his fellow Blue, said, "He'll never make it in the Hall, Dorict. The first rule is to never volunteer for extra work!" Dorict shook his head as well, although it was perhaps as much at Marick as at Garet.

The next morning Garet sat cross-legged on the floor of the cart, using his seat as a writing table. The Demonary was open on the bench and an ink pot held down a sheaf of papers. With a short brush, of a size to fit in a traveller's writing case, Garet carefully soaked it in the ink according to Salick's instructions. His first attempts at writing symbols were marred by the way the brush fanned out and smudged the word if he used too much pressure. This had not been a problem for him before. No matter how hard you pressed with a wet finger, it still made a finger-shaped mark, not a black blot the size of his knuckle.

When his practice characters finally became readable, he inked in the title of the book on the top of the first page. Then he paused. For all his complaints, he was unsure about how to fix the book. A thought scratched at him like a claw:

maybe he was unworthy to fix it. Maybe the problem was in him and not in the Demonary. Why should he think that he knew better than the Banehalls? But he pushed that thought down deep and remembered that Salick had agreed with him, and Mandarack had approved of his plan. It was shoddy work, and that had never been tolerated on the farm, even by his mother. Garet remembered her gentle scoldings, "Now Garet, if you write in such a sloppy hand, no one will think you educated, and they will blame your teacher, and that's me!" Nothing, not even his father's beatings, could have made him work harder to perfect his writing skills. At least in that, he could improve this book. The title page he had written was already an improvement over the blocky, childlike writing of the unknown copyist.

But what about the mangled information? If he just copied it again, albeit in a better hand, his main complaint would go unanswered. Mandarack's order had made it clear; it was his own business and no one else's. If he wanted it fixed, he had to figure out a way of fixing it himself. He sighed and wished the Demonary were like one of the ballads he had learned as a child. They told a story that made sense. The hero, his companions, the dragon they were to kill, each was introduced in verse after verse of poetic description. By the end of the song, you could see it all so clearly in your head. There was a definite beginning, middle, and end. To hear one of those songs was to live it like a second life!

He paused, the brush still in his hand, poised above the ink bottle. Well, why not like a song? Each demon could be like a dragon in a ballad, given its description and strengths and evil deeds all in one place, not scattered throughout the book. He could make a page for each one, and try to copy the illustrations on the back, each picture with its rightful description.

He dipped the brush and wiped the excess ink off the tip as Salick had shown him. At the top of a blank page, he wrote "Basher." Picking up the Demonary, he leafed through the pages for the six different references to this particular demon he had seen. At each page, he wrote down the information on his copy, being careful not to repeat the original's mistakes in writing and grammar. He did not try to give his own descriptions the chanting rhythm of a heroic ballad, but instead tried to write as if he were explaining the creature to someone else. He asked Dorict and sometimes Salick about words he could not read, and once had to nervously ask Mandarack about a confused reference to poison in a passage about a "Crawler Demon." Before he knew it, the morning had passed, and they were stopping to take their lunch.

The road had wandered closer to the river here. Dorict and Garet beat a path through the tall grass and filled buckets for the horses and bottles for themselves. The water ran fast, and they could hear the hiss and clatter of a set of rapids downstream.

Returning to the cart, they sat with their backs against the stones of a long-tumbled wall and ate leisurely. Garet's mind was still dizzy with the countless facts about demons he had been hunting out of the book, so to distract himself, he asked Salick about a minor matter that had been puzzling him since they left the falls.

"Salick, why are there no cities in this valley? It looks like many people lived here once, and the soil is good." He picked up a handful of the dark earth and compressed it into a loose ball. The shape held until he dropped it back onto the ground: a sure sign that it would grow a good crop.

Salick paused before answering. "We don't learn anything about this part of the valley in the Halls, Garet." She looked over at Mandarack. "Master, did many people live here before the demons came?"

The old man nodded. "Six hundred years ago, the upper valley was as rich and populous as the Midlands. The farms in this area looked to the Lords of a large town we will stop near tonight." He answered Salick's look of surprise. "There is, of course, no town there now. Only the Temple remains, and the town's name, Terrich. The rest of the town, all the buildings and walls, went to make part of the road we travel on." Garet looked at the grey, square blocks surfacing the road and tried to imagine them upright, in a high wall.

The Banemaster continued, "After the demons appeared in the South, those who survived gathered in large groups, protected by the first Banes and ruled by the surviving Lords.

Some Lords would not submit to the common good and tried to live without change in their fortresses. When they could not convince the Terrich Lords to help the new cities under the shield of the Overking, the Banes abandoned them to their fate. Without the Banes, demons hunted the Terrich Lords through their own streets like rabbits." His dry voice, so at odds with the terror he described, held them motionless. "The few peasants and townspeople who survived fled that madness and came for help to Shirath. In those chaotic times, it was a month before a force of Banes, drawn from each city, could ride out to search the town. What they found is written of in the records of the Shirath Banehall. There was no one left to save. The demons had done their work. The town was burned and the walls toppled to keep other fools from using it as a false sanctuary."

The young Banes blanched at the thought of a city's population killed in such a horrible fashion. Garet blurted out, "How many demons did the Banes have to kill?"

Mandarack replied, "There is no mention of that in the records. Perhaps when the Banes arrived in force the last demon had left to hunt for new prey."

"But Master," Garet objected, "to kill a town full of people, there must have been many demons. Did they all attack the other cities?" he asked, unaware of Salick's glare and the younger Banes' look of incomprehension. Even Mandarack seemed to wonder at the question.

"I am not sure of your meaning, Garet."

"Well, it's said in the North a dragon in its rage will not stop attacking a village until all are dead, and then it moves on to a new village. That is why they must be killed. Don't demons continue to attack until they are killed?"

The old Bane seemed troubled by the question, and Salick hissed at Garet, a look of fury on her face.

"Forgive me, Master." Garet hastily added, "It's a foolish question. I am ignorant of these things and will study more." He crouched against the wall and wrapped his legs with his arms, wishing he could disappear.

Mandarack held up his hand to stop Salick's intimidation. "No Garet, it is a very interesting question indeed. But I'm afraid that I have no answer for you." A trace of a smile lifted a corner of his mouth. "I too am ignorant of these things and must study more."

Salick stared at her Master, open-mouthed, and then quickly busied herself packing up their cooking things. Marick winked at Garet conspiratorially while Dorict shook his head and went to help Salick. Mandarack walked thoughtfully to the river and regarded the water. Garet followed Marick to see to the horses.

"Garet!" Salick's strong hand grabbed his shoulder and pulled him around. Her eyes were bright with fury and she fairly spat out her words. "Why do you ask questions that no one can answer, not even..." Her lips compressed, and Garet knew that her anger was born of her concern for her master's honour and reputation. She could not bear to see her master bested by any situation. "What is the use of such questions?" she demanded.

Now used to Salick's moods, Garet gathered his courage to answer her back. "I ask such questions because I have to know, Salick. You Southerners are all practically born with this knowledge. You learn it from your parents the way I learned about dragons and farming and tracking rabbits. If I ask questions which cannot be answered," his voice rose in frustration, "it's only because I'm ignorant of what I must know!" He shook off her hand and stomped to the cart to take his place on the floorboards. He avoided Salick's eyes as she helped Mandarack mount and then silently took her place on the driver's bench with Marick. The young Bane wisely restrained from commenting on the air of obvious ill-feelings.

The long afternoon of writing and reading, swaying back and forth in the back of the cart, worked the irritation out of his mood. By the time they stopped, he had wheedled out full descriptions of seven demons from the confusing pages of the text. The concentration he had spent on the text had also lessened his frustration with Salick. Mandarack had looked over his shoulder once or twice but had made no comment. Dorict, bored with the long ride, had asked Garet for the finished pages. He read them through in his slow, careful way and nodded at him.

"I wish I had had this when I was a Black Sash. The tests would have been much easier." He handed back the pages. "You know, when you get through this, I could give you a few Blue texts to rewrite."

Marick rolled his eyes. "Dorict, why don't you do it yourself? I swear you'd starve if your hunger wasn't just slightly greater than your laziness!" The small Bane grinned at Garet. "Maybe we should call this the Garet Demonary from now on."

Garet's protest came a split second before Salick's outraged gasp. He quickly denied the compliment. "Marick, I didn't write any of this, I just organized it so that it was easier to read. I got the idea from the songs my mother used to sing to me."

Salick had rounded on Marick and Dorict. "Don't you two fill his head with praise! Garet is still just a Black Sash; he has the same duties, responsibilities," her tone turned acid, "and limitations of any beginner in the Hall."

The way she had stressed the words limitations and beginner, told Garet that Salick had not forgotten their argument. He crouched down over the papers, and tried to block out her anger by concentrating on some cryptic comments about a demon called a Scraper.

Despite his concentration, he could not avoid hearing Marick's return jibe: "If we all stuck to our limitations, Salick, Dorict and I would be back in Shirath practicing beginning weapons, and you would be holding the reins for some Gold while older Banes got all the fun. You hate limitations as much as I do!"

Because she made no response, Garet did not know whether Salick agreed or disagreed.

He was glad when, in the early evening, the cart shuddered to a halt. The road had moved away from the water for most of the afternoon. It had cut straight across a bulge of land that squeezed the river into a bow-curve of white, foaming rapids. Now the road and river met again: the road giving up straight lines for gentle curves and the river leaving this first set of rapids for a calmer, more stately flow.

The sun was still high in the sky, so Garet was surprised when Salick unhitched the horses and the two younger Banes started unloading their blanket rolls and cooking gear.

"Marick, aren't we going on 'til dark?" he asked.

"What's this?" cried Marick in mock indignation. "A mere Black Sash asking questions? Learn your place, underling!" Further comment was forestalled by Dorict's hand giving the little Bane a sharp push between the shoulders.

"There's no better place to stop along this stretch," Dorict told him. "We'll stay at the old temple tonight." He shouldered a load of pots and food. "Too bad we can't take the cart any closer." He puffed as he clambered over a curb of stones on the north side of the road and pushed his way through a bramble of low bushes.

Garet picked up the remaining stores and followed him through the waist-high brush. A screen of encroaching brambles had long ago reduced a lane of paved stones to a tumbled miniature of the rapids they had just passed. He heard Dorict ahead of him cursing softly as he maneuvered around flipped cobbles and out-thrust roots. Now the brambles were replaced by a grove of hoary old oak trees that made a green tunnel over the path. Any flat area was thick with rotted acorns and dry leaves.

Suddenly, the grove ended. In front of them a moat was crossed by a graceful arch of stone that sprang out from beneath the shadow of the oaks. The water circled the green mound of an island. Mandarack and Salick, leading the horses, were already on the island, and the three others hurried to join them.

The island was as round as a cart wheel and rose gently to form a low hill. The grass was still green and lower than in the lands they had passed through, but the honking of the geese swimming in the moat told Garet what had been cropping it short. On the crest of the hill stood an astonishing structure, a square building fashioned of many white pillars instead of walls. Its domed roof was a startling shade of blue, a shade that seemed to have captured the colour of the twilight sky a minute before it turns to black. The beauty of that solitary, elegant building caught in Garet's throat for a moment, and he could only stare at it, his shoulders draped with bags and bundles.

Responding to Marick's impatient call, he shifted his load and walked up the hill to a small, paved plaza in front of the building. As he neared the top, the ruins of a crumbled wall appeared to the north over the ring of trees. The remains of many campfires showed that this was a favourite stop for travellers. Garet saw that none of the fire-rings were made of the white and blue stones of the structure. Instead, someone had carried stones from the road to line the blackened circles. He understood their labour. No one who saw this temple, for it could be nothing else, would want to tear it apart. He saw that Mandarack and Salick were already inside, and the other two Banes were sitting on the top of the low steps, wrestling with their boots. He sat beside them, feeling foolish, and took off his own. Barefoot, he stood up. Dorict smiled at his confusion and led him between the pillars and beneath the dome.

The white stones of the floor were smooth and cold on his feet. The marble had been polished to reflect the sunlight up onto the curved ceiling. Garet gasped as he looked above his head. The ceiling was covered with patterns of bright crystals. At first it was too overwhelming to make sense of, but soon he caught one familiar shape, and then another. These were the stars! Sure now, he looked for the Southern Swan and the Winter River, but could not find them. This was a high-summer sky. The Ploughman chased his running Ox, and the Dragon circled the North Star. If he wanted confirmation, he could look outside in a few hours and see them in the real sky.

"Have you been in a Temple before, Garet?" Mandarack asked him.

Caught slack-jawed and staring, Garet had to tear his eyes from the beautiful ceiling to answer him. "No, Master, I have never been in a place like this. At Three Roads they had a tent with a blue roof for the festivals, but this..." his voice trailed off as he turned slowly, looking back up at the dark, deep blue of the re-created sky.

Mandarack looked up as well. "Heaven is always above us, Garet. It guides us, comforts us, and gives us its beauty."

With his shadow of a smile, he looked down at Garet's bare feet and said, "That is why we stand this way, our feet touching the earth as we look up to the beauty above us. They seem so separate, but it is we who join the two by being of the Earth but yearning for the Sky."

Garet turned and turned to view every constellation. Mandarack's words, the soft sound of his feet, his very breath echoed down from the dome. He felt dizzy and overwhelmed by a sense of awe that he had never felt before.

"Does Heaven judge us?" he asked in a low voice. Garet had known men at Three Roads, drinking companions of his father, who would curse their luck at dice and then, glancing up at the smoke-stained tavern roof, softly call on Heaven to forgive their sins.

"Yes," Salick answered from the shadows. She was standing between the pillars, hand resting lightly on one fluted surface.

"Many believe so," Mandarack said, "but, Garet, we are all judged by what we bring to our lives: courage or cowardice, intelligence or stupidity, kindness or cruelty. In the end, we are known, and judged by what we do." He raised his good hand to the dome and then slowly knelt to touch the floor. "And Heaven always sends us opportunities to show others our true selves." He glanced over at Salick and stiffened, then quickly rose to his feet. She was staring in horror at her hand, for the shadowed pillar had been painted with blood.

Demons and the Dead

Dorict and Marick came at Garet's call. Mandarack was examining the blood on the pillar.

"It's very fresh," he said. The Banemaster scanned the surrounding trees. "Get your weapons. We'll scout the area."

The party quickly put on their boots and armed themselves. Salick pressed the hatchet into Garet's hands. "Unless you'd prefer a stone," she said sarcastically, but Garet could see how shaken she was. Although he knew little of the faith of the South, he could imagine how wrong it must feel to find proof of violence on holy ground.

Mandarack split them into two groups. He would take the two Blues and the horses back to the cart and scout along the road. Salick and Garet were to circle the ring of oaks and meet the others at the cart. The old Bane settled the shield on his good arm and led them back through the trees. Dorict and Marick pulled at the horses' reins, keeping as close as possible to the others.

After they separated, Salick was as silent as the trees, moving slowly along the outside of the grove, her head constantly swivelling and her trident held ready. The brambles caught at their tunics, and they froze at each twig's snap when they pulled their clothes free. The hatchet felt awkward and useless in his hand. He trembled a bit with anticipation, yet there was none of the dread that Garet had experienced in previous encounters with demons, and he was not surprised when they circled the woods without encountering anything. Remembering the odd behaviour of the birds at the ruined farmstead, he paused for a moment and listened. Salick tugged at his sleeve, but he stayed motionless. There were birds moving on the forest floor and in the trees. Now and then a tentative trill sang out over their heads. Salick, at last understanding why he had stopped, listened as well. She shrugged her shoulders and motioned to him to finish their patrol and return to the road. The others were waiting by the cart.

Mandarack was grim. "Come with us." Dorict and Marick also followed, both clearly shaken.

Salick and Garet knew better than to ask and fell in with the shivering Blues behind the Banemaster. A trail, smashed through the berry bushes a hundred paces from where they had stopped, led from the road towards a copse of greyish-green poplars.

Garet knelt down and touched a dark stain on the dirt. His finger came away red. The old man looked grimly at the stain and led them through the smashed bushes, his shield held clear of the thorns. Before he followed and despite Salick's jibe, Garet picked up a good-sized stone to put in his tunic pocket. He had little faith in his ability to use the hatchet against any of the demons listed in the Moret's book, but at least he was sure of his skill with a rock. Fifty more paces brought them to the dusty island of trees. A body lay hidden in the brambles just in front of the poplars. It was a young man, a few years older than Salick, dressed in a blue tunic. His throat was cut in three precise parallel curves from just under one ear to the other. *Too precise and knife-like for a bear*, Garet thought, *and too big to be any other natural beast.* There was no doubt in his mind as to what had done this. The man's eyes were wide and staring, as if he still felt a horror of the demon that killed him.

Garet's stomach twisted, and he savagely fought to control himself. Salick's lips were pressed and her cheeks pale. Mandarack waved them into the poplars and stood in the centre of the small grove, his shield braced against a tree and his eyes looking down at a second corpse, this one clad in the clawed remnants of a black tunic and a shredded gold sash.

"Cassant!" Salick cried. She sobbed and stabbed her trident into the ground. "Oh, Cassant! Master, how could this be? Cassant was a Gold. How could he be killed?"

Mandarack's voice was harsh. "Any Bane can die beneath a demon's claws, Salick, even a Gold, even a Master, but something else disturbs me even more than the death of someone from our Hall." He slid the shield off his arm and kneeling, gently turned the corpse over. "See here, the back is where the killing blows landed. There are little but scratches on the front of his body." He slipped the shield on again and said quietly, perhaps to himself, "Why did he not face the beast?"

Could the demon have crept up on him? But before Garet could ask Mandarack, he remembered the gut-wrenching effect of a demon's approach. The Gold would have felt the demon long before he saw it. How could it have attacked him secretly from behind?

"Garet," Mandarack's sudden call brought his attention back to the Banemaster. "I think you have some skill in tracking animals. Check the trail and tell me what you see."

Garet followed the smashed passage through the bushes carefully, but most of the tracks belonged to him and his companions. Only one or two stretches showed the running strides of other feet. While casting along the sides of the trail he spotted a glint of metal beneath the bushes. It was a long spear. A hook of bright metal swept back from where the point joined the shaft, the Bane's weapon perhaps. He carried it back to the others.

"Master," he said when he rejoined Mandarack by the entrance to the poplars, "two people ran quickly down the trail."

"Ran?" asked the Bane, his eyes holding Garet's and demanding confirmation.

Salick stared at him, mouth open.

Garet nodded. "Yes, sir, and quickly too. The prints are far apart and the dirt is thrown back for a good distance at each step." He paused to slow his breath. "I saw a scuffed track behind them; something clawed the ground, but what it was isn't clear." He held out the spear to the old man. "And there was this."

Salick leaned close to Mandarack's ear and whispered urgently.

"No," he replied clearly. "I do not know why a Bane would run, Salick, or drop his weapon. But we must find out." He turned to Garet. "Keep the spear for now, lad. You might need it before we can leave this place." Garet handed his hatchet to Marick and gripped the unfamiliar weapon tightly in both hands.

The five Banes half carried, half dragged the corpses of the two men to the road and laid them in the back of the cart. The horses shied away from the smell of the blood, making the cart jitter and sway.

Mandarack closed the eyes of the young man and slipped his hand into the shield again. "Dorict, Marick, stay here with the cart," he instructed. "Do not try to fight anything that might appear. If you are attacked, cut the horses loose. They might draw off the demon and allow you to escape. Make your way back to Old Torrick if we are separated. Do you understand?"

"Of course, Master," cried Marick, his face white, "but what will you and Salick and Garet be doing?"

"We hunt," the old Bane replied shortly. Before he led Salick and Garet back down the trail, he turned and told Dorict, "If we do not return by evening, light the lanterns and start back to Torrick. Ask Hallmaster Corix to send as much help as she can."

Dorict nodded nervously and clutched at the reins to quiet the shifting horses.

The three Banes, Mandarack in the lead and Salick bringing up the rear, quickly retraced their steps to the poplar trees. The brambles caught at the shaft of the spear in Garet's hand, until Salick's whispered, "Hold it up, you fool!" He blushed and raised the weapon above his head.

At Mandarack's direction, Garet and Salick circled the grove looking for clues as to where the demon had gone. Salick found some blood on a patch of dry moss, and Garet was able to make out enough scrapes and scuffs to lead them to the north end of the grove.

The tracks went lightly through the brambles, though here and there, the soft earth showed a full print.

"Master," Garet called softly, "come and look at this." He was crouched between the bushes above a set of prints. A nearby spring had seeped into the soil and softened it to the consistency of porridge. Two sets of tracks were clearly pressed into the earth. Both were of long, narrow feet whose claws cut thin lines in the dirt at each step.

Mandarack lowered himself carefully and examined the tracks. Salick hovered nervously.

"Master," she asked, "did the demon pass here twice?"

Mandarack scanned the trail. "No," he said. The point of his shield hovered over the marks. "See there where the larger tracks cover the smaller set, while here it's the smaller set on top." He pushed himself up, using the shield as a support. "There were two demons, Shriekers I believe, on this trail, travelling together." He tapped the shield lightly against his boot to knock the dirt from its tip.

Salick stared at him, open-mouthed. After a moment she swallowed and tightened her grip on the trident.

Garet scanned ahead. "Master," he said, "why can't we feel them? Are they too far away?"

"I don't know," Mandarack replied softly, turning his head this way and that as he had on the night he had detected the Basher. "It's almost as if..." His voice trailed off.

No noise broke the silence for a long minute, then Mandarack spoke again, "Salick, what do you feel from the direction of the setting sun?"

The shadows of leaves made crisscross patterns on her face as she swivelled towards the low sun and closed her eyes.

"Nothing, Master." A pause, then: "But it feels...dead!"

"That is what I sense. Not a feeling, but the absence of all feeling."

Garet had been trying to sense anything in the same direction and came to the same conclusion. It was like closing your eyes and turning from sunlight to shade. Something was missing, although he had no clear idea of what it was.

He opened his eyes. The trail led west to the ruins he had seen beyond the temple. Mandarack followed his glance.

"That is the old temple market. It was never dismantled, but is mostly in ruins now. Stay close to me." He moved carefully towards the jumble of walls and collapsed buildings. Salick and Garet exchanged quick glances and followed.

The market had once been a large walled compound which, like the market of Old Torrick, was ringed with stalls and buildings. The wall itself had been breached by weather and time in several places, and few of the shops had more than two walls left upright. The three Banes crouched just inside the market wall, behind a half-collapsed tea house and listened. Now no bird sang, no animal called. But still there was no sense of fear. The only sound was the brush of branches from the overgrown, ornamental trees against the walls. At the Master's signal they slipped between the shops and looked out into the compound.

The remains of buildings and galleries crusted the inner walls, leaving only narrow alleys between them. What walls were left were covered with faded paintings and deep carvings of the constellations. *That's why these buildings weren't torn down to help build the road*, Garet thought; they were too holy to be disturbed by anything but time. A substantial building, boasting a complete front wall, but no roof, dominated the north end of the compound. Between it and the ruined gate to the south lay nothing but cracked flagstones and a dry fountain.

"That would be the Market Master's building," breathed Mandarack, pointing with his chin to the north. "The blank feeling lies in that direction." Now, Garet could easily feel the wrongness of that dead area.

Salick must have felt it as well, for she wrinkled her nose at the large building as if it held something foul.

Mandarack turned to face them. "If the demons are both here," he said slowly, "they might seek such a shelter for a lair."

"You're not sure, Master?" This burst out of Garet without thought. But a panic filled him at Mandarack's uncertainty. If the Banemaster was not sure, what chance did they have?

Salick's hand clawed at his shoulder, and her voice whispered harshly in his ear, "Keep quiet, idiot! No Bane has ever faced two demons before. Not even the greatest. Demons never appear together!"

They moved inside, hugging the shop wall and keeping low to take advantage of the piles of stones and the long shadows cast by the wall. The overhanging trees shaded the inside of the Market Master's ruined mansion. Each remaining window was a blind eye staring out into the still-bright square. As they crept along, Garet could feel the dread growing in him. The dead feeling was gone. Even with his new techniques of self-control, he could barely force himself forward. Was this the effect of the demons or of his loss of faith in Mandarack's limitless knowledge? He looked across at Salick. Her skin was pale and beads of sweat dotted her upper lip and forehead.

At least I'm no worse off than she is, thought Garet, and the thought calmed him enough so that he could push the fear down and hold it in his belly. The ease with which he accomplished this told him that it was mainly his own doubts he fought. They were at the last tumbled shop before their goal now. At least twelve running paces separated them from the nearest window. Something clicked on the stones to their left. The old Bane waved them up to crouch beside him. He whispered his instructions, his voice so low that Garet had to read some words from the movement of his lips to get the entire message.

"Garet and I will go through the front entrance. I think we will be attacked by at least one of the demons right away. They are close. Salick, you go through the far window on the right and make your way to the entrance from the inside. If both demons are attacking us, you can come out and pin one down with your trident. If you are attacked inside the building, defend yourself until I can assist you." He saw their understanding and stood up. "Now, Garet."

Three paces behind and with the spear held ready, Garet followed the old Bane at a slow trot across the intervening space. As they approached the entrance, an arch of stone long empty of any hinge or door, Garet caught a glimpse of Salick's dash to the far window.

The Bane stopped a few paces from the door and held up the shield. There was a scuttling. Mandarack set his feet and called to Garet, "To the side now, boy. Careful with the spear!"

A red blur came out, not from the door, but from the crushed walls to the left of the building. It was a Shrieker, claws lifted and whistling its horrible cry. It charged straight at Mandarack, only to be batted away by the upraised shield. The old Bane swung to face the demon, and again Garet was reminded of the movements of a bird. The Master froze into the terrible stillness of a river heron, metal beak raised to stab the thing that scampered back towards him. The shield cut downwards, but only chipped the flagstones as the beast changed direction at the last minute, charging Garet.

Shaking himself out of his stupor, Garet yelled and launched himself, spear first, at the demon. It swerved around the point on all fours, tearing out more chips of stone as it dug in its claws for traction. Garet swung the point wildly after it, but succeeded only in unbalancing himself, and he dropped to one knee. The creature turned and was running at him again. Mandarack shouted something that Garet could not understand. As the creature approached, claws held out, the only thing he could think to do was to fling the spear cross-wise at it, so that the middle of the shaft caught the demon on its knees. With a squawk, the thing tripped and rolled completely over Garet, its claws whisking past his ears.

Mandarack was as taken aback as the demon and belatedly swung at the beast as it rolled, ball-like, past his legs. The demon untangled itself just before it hit the stone stairs of the building and scuttled around Mandarack, just out of reach of the shield, to attack Garet again.

Without thinking, Garet rolled to the left, and came to his feet in a crouch as the demon streaked by, missing him by inches. It turned, barely staying upright in its speed, and leaped at him. Without hesitation, Garet rolled under the flying body of the beast to come to a crouch behind it. Finding itself clawing air instead of its intended victim, the demon twisted around and shrieked its frustration.

But it had forgotten Mandarack in its anger, and that was the creature's undoing. The poised shield lanced down to pin it against the ground. The old Bane leaned into the shield with all his weight until, with a horrid screech from the demon, the point tore through the leathery skin of its back and dark blood flowed out over the stones of the square.

Garet's chest heaved as he tried to catch his breath. Even without using fear, the demon had nearly won the battle.

"Garet," the Bane gasped, "go find Salick. Help her. The other demon must still be inside."

Leaving Mandarack to his grim task of holding the demon down until it was dead, Garet ran inside the shadowed building, bruising his shins against fallen beams just within the entrance. Wincing, he climbed over them into an open space and stopped for a moment to let his eyes adjust to the dim light. The roof had been replaced by a thick net of vegetation, filling the building with cool, green shadows. Mounds of old leaf litter covered the floor and rearranged themselves into new piles at every little breeze.

Garet could see the main hallway leading away from the lobby and, at the end of it, the window Salick must have entered. He moved quickly. No need for silence as the other demon must know they were there. It was probably fighting Salick now, but he couldn't hear her calls or the creature's hissing screams—and there was still no telltale aura of fear to tell him where to run.

Checking each flanking room quickly, he arrived at the end of the building without finding Salick. The window she had entered faced a fallen wall in the back of the building. A trail had been beaten in the brush under the trees.

She's chased it. He jumped over the rubble and started running down the trail only to stop dead. Salick's trident was lying in the beaten earth. *No!* His mind whirled to that other weapon, the spear he had left in the courtyard, and what had happened to its owner. Empty-handed, he tore down the trail, branches whipping at his face and arms. The ground dipped suddenly and deeply into a trickle of a stream. Garet jumped it and scrambled up the other side, breaking out of the forest as soon as he gained level ground.

Salick stood in the middle of a glade. Wild grain brushed the sides of her vest leaving their golden seeds stuck to the purple cloth. Hands slack at her sides, she faced the far end of the field where the trail continued under the dark brows of the forest.

Garet opened his mouth to shout, but the cry died in his throat. The dead feeling of the air, the blankness they had felt ever since coming near the ruins was gone. Peace flooded through him, and he knew he was being called home. His mother was there, and Allia. His father and brothers were away hunting. Dinner was on the table, and the three of them would laugh and joke in the warmth and peace of the cabin. Would his father return? No, his heart said. There would be no pain, no fear, only peace.

But the thought of his father made him pause. For a brief moment the feeling of peace disappeared and he saw in amazement that he was halfway to where Salick stood in the middle of the field. He must help her against the demon. The demon? The thought of the demon, like the thought of his father, seemed to lessen the feeling of happiness that filled the clearing. No, said the voice in his mind. There is peace, only peace. He shook his head and concentrated on the image of the Shrieker he had just faced. He imagined its cruel beak, its curving teeth. In his mind, he heard its shrill call. Holding the image between himself and the forest like a shield, he moved to Salick's side. Her face was empty of personality, its normal intensity erased by whatever spoke in her own head.

Garet scanned the woods opposite, searching for the physical reality of the demon he held so firmly in his mind. Sometimes the image wavered and he saw the cabin and his mother, but he gritted his teeth and thought, *no! I've given up that life. I can't go back!* He focused on the demon's yellow eyes, pupilled like a cat's, and then suddenly saw two such eyes staring back at him from the shadow of the trees.

Salick gave a little moan and took a half-step forward. Distracted, Garet lost his concentration and was also pulled forward, until he built up the walls of his mind again. He had to stop that lying voice. In moving, his hand had brushed against a hard object in his tunic pocket. The stone! He had forgotten picking it up when they first took the trail of the murdered Bane. He fumbled it out and weighed it in his hand. Rounded and heavy, it brought back the memory of all those lonely vigils on the steep pastures of the farm. Even more than the image of the Shrieker, the strong memory of those dull days protected him from the eyes watching his struggle.

As he had ten thousand times before, his hand whipped around in a great arc, and he stepped into the throw, putting his shoulder and hip behind it. He had not lost his skill. A whistling screech sliced the air. An echo of some fierce pain brought Garet to his knees, both hands pressed to his temples. When he looked up, the thing that had been waiting for them was crashing through the trees. It paused for one brief instant to look back, and Garet saw that one of the yellow lights had gone dark, leaving only one shining eye to glare at him before it turned and escaped into the darkness of the forest.

He heard Salick gasping and turned towards her. She was lying in the grass, as if the breaking of that false voice had flung her back like wind-tossed straw. Her face was white with shock, and she stared into the darkening sky with genuine terror in her eyes.

"Garet! Salick!" Mandarack's voice called from the trail behind them. In a moment, the old man came running through the trees, breathing hard and leaving a trail of blood dripping from the tip of his shield.

"Here, Master!" Garet pushed himself to his feet and held out a hand to Salick. She grasped it quickly, as if she were drowning rather than lying on her back in a green field. He pulled her up and held her steady. Her anger with him seemed forgotten, and she did not brush him off, but seemed content to lean on his shoulder as he led her back to where Mandarack stood, his grey head twisting back and forth in search of their enemy. The old Bane examined them both carefully. He nodded distractedly at Garet's rushed report of the encounter while he looked them over for any injuries.

"Should we track it now, Master?" Garet asked. "I'm sure it's wounded."

"No." The order was quick and certain. "This demon is different. Coming after you, I felt no terror, but a pull, a desire to give in and stop fighting." He looked into Salick's eyes, and she gave a nervous nod of her head. "We go back," he said, and turned to walk quickly down the trail. His voice drifted back, "Whatever all this means, pursuing this creature now would be folly. We must return to the Banehall as quickly as possible."

They jogged around the ruins to cut the forest trail and return to the two young Banes waiting on the road. While the others loaded the cart, wrapping the two bodies in blankets, Mandarack directed Salick and Garet to check along the road for any clue to what had happened to the rest of the victims' party. The paving stones gave no sign, but the softer gravel of the edge showed where a cart had been hurriedly turned and driven back towards Shirath. Where they had completely left the road and ploughed into the soft earth, the ruts still had their ragged, fragile edges, not yet blunted by wind or rain. He told Salick that a cart had cut these marks not more than half a day before. Salick whispered in response that the blood on the corpses was still sticky to the touch. For a moment, she squatted beside him in silent, grateful companionship. When they returned to the cart, Mandarack listened to their report and then waved them aboard. With no more delays, Salick slapped the reins on the broad backs of the horses, rousing them to a more than willing trot.

A red sunset fell around them and lay bright upon their companion river. It was a lovely summer evening, but the Banes were only concerned with their pursuit of the missing cart. With the bloody and confusing events of the evening, there was no thought in Garet's head of using the remaining light to continue his studies. Alongside Dorict and Marick, he huddled near the driver's bench, avoiding the bloody bundles that jostled each other on the floor of the cart. Mandarack lay on the opposite bench, exhausted from the battle, but with his shield in easy reach of his good hand. Salick halted the horses only once, to light the cart's lanterns. The yellow glow cast only a feeble illumination ahead of them, and she reluctantly slowed the horses so as to keep the cart on the winding road.

It was well that she did. As they slowed on a hairpin curve, Dorict shouted and pointed towards the river on their left. The brush and grass of the road's shoulder were roughly parted, and two wheel ruts were cut in the dark earth. Salick tied off the reins and, taking one of the lanterns from its hook, leaped down from the bench. In a moment Garet and Marick were beside her. Peering down the embankment, they could just make out an overturned cart many feet below them. Marick ran back to the cart and returned with a length of rope that had lain coiled beneath the driver's seat.

"Dorict, tie one end to the wheel," Marick said. "Quick, give me the lantern and I'll go down!" His voice was high and excited. Salick gripped him by the shoulder and shook him.

"Marick! This is no game. Be careful or I'll..."

Marick grinned at her as he tied the rope around his waist. "Or what? You'll kill me? Not if I kill me first!" With that, he placed the lantern's wire handle between his teeth and held the rope with both hands as they lowered him down the embankment.

"Farther down," he called, and they lowered him until the rope was taut from the wheel to the dark below. "That's it!" Marick cried, and the rope went slack. The circle of yellow light bobbed and wavered towards the riverbank. It paused there for a long time and then slowly returned to the foot of the hill. At a tug on the line, they pulled Marick back up.

"No use," he called awkwardly, the lamp again held in his teeth, as they pulled him up the last few feet. He teetered on the edge, and then there were three arms steadying him and Mandarack, who had come up silently behind the younger Banes, asked, "How many?"

"Only one, Master. Not a Bane," Marick replied. Tears streaked his dusty face. "Slashed by claws. I think she bled to death while she was driving back for help." He paused for breath. "Both horses died in the fall. Should we bring up the body?"

Mandarack did not reply for many seconds, but stood listening to the sound of the water brushing the bank. "No," he said. "We will report this to the Banehall and the King's guards as soon as we can. I still feel that we should return immediately."

They drove on throughout the night, changing drivers, and dozing fitfully beside their stiff, silent companions.

Though it be small in comparison to all other demons—save for Rat and Crawler Demons—this creature is faster, more cunning, and more deadly than any other a Bane may face.

Shrieker Demon

The most common of the plague that has sickened Shirath from my green years to my grey. Indeed, the first demon killed by my Master, Banfreat, was a Shrieker, so called for its foul voice.

The beast is sly and will attempt to escape, climbing walls and trees to avoid death if the fear does not freeze its prey.

Shirath

"The jewel!" Marick cried. "Master, we left it in the Shrieker you and Garet killed!"

They had travelled through the night, Dorict spelling off Salick at the reins. Garet looked up out of a fog of half-sleep at the younger Bane's shout.

"Not forgotten, Marick," replied Mandarack softly and fell silent again. The old man wore his weariness like a heavy cloak. The long night's ride, coming so quickly after the battle with the Shrieker, had taken its toll on him. Even Marick did not dare to question him further.

Not forgotten, Garet thought. He yawned and tried to fold himself into a less uncomfortable position. Had the Banemaster intentionally left the Shrieker and its powerful jewel in the ruins of the market square? Before the battle, the beast's ability to provoke fear had seemed stopped by that strange "dead" area. But thinking back, Garet now recalled that when they skirted the walls of the market on their return, he had felt the power of the jewel, as if that deadness had been dispersed when he had driven off the other beast.

He accepted the water flask handed to him by Dorict and yawned again. If the jewel were still powerful, it would be a danger to anyone who wandered nearby. He took a sip and handed the flask to Marick before returning to his thoughts. Yes, the dead demon was a danger, as long as it kept its jewel hidden within its skull. On the other hand, what sane person, man, woman, or child, would, or even could, approach a demon's jewel? He looked across at the old Bane. Did

Mandarack want the area to remain undisturbed until it could be reported to the Banehall of Shirath? Wrapped in a blanket, their Master nodded with the sway of the cart. *What we found and fought,* Garet realized, *must have been so unusual that even the Master is unsure of how to deal with it.* That was another unsettling thought.

Now unable to sleep, he climbed onto the driver's box beside Salick, carefully avoiding the two blanket-wrapped bodies rocking back and forth on the floor of the cart. Salick moved over to let him up on the plank seat.

"Do you know how to drive a cart?" she asked.

Garet could see her eyes were red and puffy from her long efforts during the night. "No," he replied. "We were too poor to have a cart." He was too tired to be angered by her half-hearted snort of contempt.

"How did you run a farm without horses and a cart?" she asked.

"We mostly ran sheep," he replied. "We plowed a few small fields with the milk cow and carried the sheep's wool and the yarn my mother spun to Three Roads on our backs."

Salick shook her head. "I didn't know people could live like that." She slapped the reins to keep the horses moving.

"Like what?"

"In such poverty!" she replied.

Garet thought for a minute. He had seen only bits and pieces of the lives of the people they had passed on this journey, so he had little to compare with his previous life except for his mother's songs of the North and the traders stories of the South. The hymns to the Dragon Heroes never mentioned something as ordinary as farming, and after seeing Old Torrick, he was beginning to think that the tales of gold covered buildings and legions of storytellers were just stories to impress ignorant hill farmers. Nothing he had seen so far had led him to believe that a Southerner's existence was as luxurious as he once thought. Although, he had to admit, even the ragged children who ran the back alleys of Old Torrick looked better fed than the poorer farmers of the foothills.

He looked out over the road ahead and was gathering his thoughts to answer Salick when she broke out into a tumble of words.

"Garet, I'm sorry. I know it was not your choice to live that way. It's just that I've never seen anyone in such want before. Your mother looked so thin, and the cabin you lived in was one good storm away from falling down." She half turned towards him, her shadowed eyes open and apologetic. "The other Plains farmers looked so prosperous. I mean even the refugees were fat and healthy! And in Shirath, no one goes hungry. If there are those too old or ill to please their Ward Lord, the Banehall will give them our extra food. Everyone else is looked after by their Wards or the King."

Not everything she said made sense to him, but he realized she was trying to understand him at last, not condemn him.

"Salick, why would the Banehall have extra food? Do they charge for killing demons?"

"No!" Salick drew back, her eyes wide. "No Banehall would dare! Though," her voice dropped, "six-hundred years ago some of the first Banehalls tried to do just that." She shrugged. "It didn't work. People were all working together to survive the coming of the demons, and those few Halls were finally forced to give up any claims to a special reward. They had to trust that if they did their job and looked after the people of their city, the people of the city would look after them." She smiled. "Anyway, we're better off now. People really want to keep us healthy so we can catch the demons quickly. You can't patrol through a ward without old grannies and bakers putting food into your hands. We just drop off what we don't need on our night rounds."

Garet felt better about the Banehall, hearing of this generosity. "No one is poor in Shirath then?"

"Not like you were," she replied honestly. "But think of this, Garet, the demons are so great a threat that we only survive by working for each other, not for ourselves. The Banehall knows that; the King and his lords know that; every citizen of Shirath knows that." She looked thoughtfully at the road ahead. "I hope the farmers of the Midlands know that too."

Garet had his doubts. Isolated on their own farms, each man his own little king, it would take much to get them to cooperate in the way Salick described. But if the threat of claws in the night was enough to change Shirath, maybe it could do the same for the proud farmers of the Plains. He smiled to think of Pranix, the tavern keeper, giving away free food and drink from gratitude. He would probably rather face a demon bare-handed.

"What's so funny?" Salick asked suspiciously.

Garet told her and she grinned. "I remember him. Only the promise that Three Roads was going to become a protected outpost kept him from bursting when he found out he had to supply us."

"What if he had refused?" Garet asked.

"Well, in Shirath, that could lead to some pretty severe punishments. Not cooperating for the city's good can get you hauled in front of your Ward Lord. Your family might have to live in a smaller set of rooms. You can lose a good work assignment or, if you have a trade, be kicked out of your guild. If you still resist, then you can be whipped or imprisoned, and if after all that you still refuse to work for the city's good, you can be banished."

Garet shuddered at the thought of being alone and unprotected, outside the city walls, night after night.

Salick continued, "Pranix's wife saw the light before he did and screamed at him until he agreed." She shook her head at the memory. "I'd rather fight another Basher than live near that woman."

Garet nodded in agreement. "Until the demons came, Trallet was probably the most dangerous creature on the Plains!"

They both laughed, bringing Marick up to lean over their shoulders.

"What's this," the boy asked, "laughing and pleasantries between such mortal enemies?"

Garet shoved him back onto the side bench. Salick looked daggers at the boy and then turned resolutely to the front, cheeks flaming under her blond braids.

Garet groaned inwardly. It seemed every time Salick began to ease towards him, something brought their friendship to a grinding halt. And he wanted Salick to like him. She was his best guide to this new world: not much older so they could talk easily, and diligent about preparing him for his duties. He had to admit that he already liked her. In many ways, she reminded him of his sister, Allia. Salick had that same fierceness of manner that he admired in his little "dragon." And, like his sister, she was quick to attack whatever or whoever irritated her.

Dorict took the reins again to allow Salick another fitful nap. Garet stayed on the driver's bench and asked the younger boy to show him how to guide the horses. By the morning's end, he had the trick of steering the cart, a matter of convincing the horses to keep moving and not interfering too much with their own good sense. He found that he had so little to do that the hot sun and the swaying of the cart kept him on the verge of sleep himself.

He was jolted back to wakefulness when Dorict put a hand on his arm and said, "There, Garet, we're nearing the city!" He pointed to a forest that rose before them and grew to the very edges of the road.

Garet furrowed his brows and tried to see the city beyond the trees, but this new forest blocked everything beyond it. Then he noticed something odd about the trees; they were growing in regular rows, like a crop of grain planted in plowed furrows. He had grown up surrounded by trees but had never seen anything like this. There was no underbrush, giving the forest an almost naked look. *As if it was weeded*, Garet thought, *and someone was farming these trees like any other crop.* He looked questioningly at Dorict.

The younger Bane smiled back. "Not like the woods near your farm, eh? These are the tree plantations of Shirath. Each tree is planted like a rose, and cared for just as lovingly."

"Ignore him, Garet," Marick called from behind them. "His family are all loggers. He heard nothing but talk of trees and lumber until we rescued him for the Hall."

"Does your family live near here?" Garet asked, and then he blushed at his obvious mistake.

"Well, no," Dorict replied, ignoring Marick's chuckles. "They live in Shirath with everyone else. Sometimes, though, in the winter and spring, many loggers and their families live in the woods for weeks at a time, protected by Banes, of course."

The woods surrounded them now, rank upon rank of grey trunks under a deep green canopy. Mandarack roused himself and called a halt for lunch. Leaving their grim cargo in the cart, they sat under the trees.

"There is no use in arriving at the Banehall too tired to talk," Mandarack told them. "We will rest here for an hour or so to regain our strength." He lay down beside them and only roused the party when the sun had moved three hands widths across the sky. He moved more easily and Garet was sure that for once, the old Bane had slept as long at they had.

"Come along, the city waits for us," Mandarack said. They pushed themselves up from the dry ground, brushing leaves and ants from their tunics. With Salick at the reins, they urged the cart horses out from under the cool shade of the forest and back into the mid-afternoon sun.

The forests ended abruptly, not petering out as they did at the borders of the Plains, a lone tree here and there like stragglers following a crowd. The cart passed that border and broke out into broad fields of grains. Beyond those waving heads of wheat and oats lay more trees, this time trimmed orchards of apples, pears, and cherries. Driving on, they came to the first of these groves. The smell of apples was as strong as wine to the younger Banes, and they drank it in with great gulps. Stacked baskets of the fruit lay under the nearer trees, waiting to be picked up, but as yet, they had seen no other sign of the citizens of Shirath.

Now, beside the road, they passed the first sign of human habitation. It was an outpost, a kind of fort, surrounded by a timber and stone palisade. A call rang out, and they saw a figure with a black tunic and a green sash waving over the tops of the logs. Salick waved back, but at Mandarack's nod, kept driving towards the city.

The smell of green apples was replaced by the scent of pears, and then by no scent at all, only the long cool leaves of cherry trees. Now apples again, but a redder, bigger variety. They were ready to harvest as well, for ladders were placed between the rows, and here and there a fallen fruit lay under its tree.

Garet swayed on the cart's seat, overwhelmed by the sights and smells around him. *It's a farm,* he thought with wonder, a farm bigger than any he had ever imagined, a farm for a whole city. And it was also prettier than any thing he had ever seen. Even the Plains, with their golden grain and bright flowers, even the Falls, with all their power and song, were nothing to this ordered, beautiful garden. Salick cursed under her breath and pulled at the horses to keep them from snatching apples from the baskets set by the side of the road.

The fruit trees ended, and what they had only been given glimpses of became clear. The walls of Shirath rose in front of Garet, barely a mile away.

"Sit down! You'll fall off the cart!" Salick yelled and pulled Garet back down by his sleeve.

He landed off-centre and had to grab onto the side-rail to catch himself. Absently rubbing his elbow, he stared at the city.

Shirath rose beyond a complex pattern of vegetable and grazing plots. People moved among these plots, herding cattle, carrying loads, and working in the fields. Garet observed them eagerly. These were the men and women of Shirath, the people he would now help protect from the demons, his people. At a distance, they looked no different from the men and women of the Plains, save that their clothing was brighter than the simple blue and grey tunics of the people he had seen at Old Torrick. Bright oranges and reds vied with sky blues and vivid yellows on the backs of the workers, though many of the younger men had removed their tunics in this heat and worked bare-chested. They came alongside a tall, middle-aged woman stepping along the road with a basket of tomatoes on her head. The collar of her light blue tunic was embroidered in a pretty pattern of running deer and twining flowers. She dipped a curtsy without missing a step or endangering her load, and smiling, continued on her way towards the city.

With his black tunic and black hair, Garet felt like a shadow on a sunny day among these colourful, blond men and women. *Like a crow,* he thought, remembering the insults of the barge men. Marick noticed him slouch down in the seat and pull his arms across his chest. The small boy gave him a thump on his shoulder and a grin of encouragement. Garet forced himself to straighten up.

They passed more people, each one giving the group a short bow or curtsy, more in greeting than in deference, it seemed, and if Garet was stared at, it was no more or less than his friends and guardian. He took comfort in that as the cart rumbled along.

When they neared the city, Garet saw why it was called "the city on two banks" and "the city of the bridges." The Ar River, which their road now rejoined, cut Shirath cleanly in two. The high, white walls curved in a great half-circle on each side of the river. They did not end at the river, however, for the walls followed the banks to seal off each half as if it were a separate city. These walls, each facing its twin across the Ar, were broken by Shirath's three arched bridges, the last barely visible in the distance. But even from so far away, Garet could see much movement and activity on the spans.

"There, Garet!" Marick yelled, pointing at a herd of sheep being driven back into the city from pasture. "If you ever get homesick, you can guard the shepherds."

This speech was cut short when Dorict dragged the laughing Bane back into the cart's box, but Garet, looking at where Marick had pointed, did indeed see two horses pacing the sheep, and on each a Bane, one a Gold and the other a Green. Now that he had noticed them, he looked at the fields and saw more scattered among the workers, some on horseback and others on foot.

They passed a line of fishponds set between the road and the river, and Marick called out to a Green lounging against the frame of a water wheel. The young woman waved her hand in reply. She yelled something, but the clacking of the wheel and the noise of the water pouring from its buckets into the ponds drowned out her words.

A pair of young men pulled in a net from the nearest pond. They carefully separated out the small silver fish from the larger carp and released the little ones back into the water. The bigger fish were hauled in baskets up to the road and dropped into large clay pots, half-full of water. There, they swam frantically about, slopping water over the side and occasionally jumping out, only to be quickly grabbed and put back in.

"Carp are best this time of year." Dorict sighed. "Do you think that the Hall will have fish tonight?" The young Bane was more animated than Garet had ever seen. *And why not,* he thought. *Dorict is coming home.*

"Easily enough!" Marick yelled and prepared to jump off the cart, but Salick grabbed him by the collar of his tunic.

"Oh no you don't!" she said as she hauled him over Garet's lap to sit between them. "No more rule breaking. We're back in Shirath now and anything you do reflects on our own Banehall." Her look was meant to terrify, but Marick only smirked.

The walls were very close, and Garet had to stretch his neck to see the tops of them. No guards patrolled the heights. There were no watch towers or arrow slits, or any of the other things he had seen in the walls of Old Torrick.

He turned to Salick. "How can these walls keep the demons out?" He pointed to the nearest section. "Look! It's so rough here that a Shrieker could easily use its claws to climb up to the top and get in."

Salick was giving him the look she wore to inform him of his ignorance, but before she could lecture him, Mandarack spoke. "You're right, Garet. These walls are not designed to keep demons out, but to keep them in." He smiled slightly at Garet's shocked expression. "It sounds foolish, doesn't it? But Shirath is built so as to allow Banes to easily trap and destroy the demons as soon as they are discovered."

"But Master," Garet replied carefully, "in Bangt, they were making ditches and rows of sharpened logs. And Old Torrick's walls were built to throw back an enemy, both the rebuilt sections and the older parts."

Salick was listening now.

Mandarack shifted on the bench, careful not to nudge the wrapped bodies lying on the floorboards. "In Bangt, they were building for their fear, not their real danger—though if reversed they could prove to be useful. And the walls of Old Torrick were rebuilt partly from tradition. Torrick is the only one of the Five Cities that is older than the demon's arrival six hundred years ago. The Lords and people of that town value that history. That is why they rebuild their walls in the same manner as before." He paused to nod at a Red riding in the opposite direction. "And the Torrickers do have other concerns besides demons."

Salick bit her lip for a moment and then asked, "What concerns could they possibly have? I mean, Master; what is there to fear that's worse than a demon?"

Mandarack turned slightly to face his apprentice. "The Torrick lords, in truth, have much to fear from the miners they cheat and the Plains people who now demand adequate protection. For many years the rulers of that city have used their position at the boundary of the South and the Midlands to enrich themselves."

Garet remembered Dorict's comments on the greed of those lords. "Even now," Mandarack continued, "the lords may still believe in that threat more than the increased danger of demon attack." He shrugged. "Every thief wants a well-locked door for himself, as they say."

The Midlanders were not the only people who would have to learn how to work together, Garet realized.

Behind the Red they had passed, a line of men chained together, ankle to ankle, shuffled off the road to let the cart go by. There were about twenty of them, and many had the veined noses and slack eyes of heavy drinkers. Two young men with truncheons guarded them, one at the head of the column and one at the tail.

Mandarack's words had brought them level with the walls. There was a gap between the city and the river and it was through this space, three carts wide, that the road continued. With the high wall on his right and the wide river on his left, Garet felt as small as a crawling ant. The people on the road, in their bright tunics, stood out against the grey flagstones like spring flowers growing from rocks.

They soon came to the first bridge, arching above the road to a twin path on the other side. Salick made to turn onto it, but Marick grabbed her wrist and looked pleadingly at Mandarack.

"Master, can't we take the Main Bridge?" He waved at the road ahead with his free hand. "This is Garet's first time in the city, and we'll still have lots of time to get to the Hall before supper!"

Mandarack thought about it for a moment and said, "Very well, but go on foot, you, Garet, and Salick." He then looked at the quiet boy sitting across from him. "Dorict and I will take the cart to the Hall. That may not be delayed."

Salick looked down at the wrapped corpses and nodded. The rest, even Marick, blushed to realize that they had forgotten the tragedy that had marked their journey home. Salick pulled back on the reins and handed them to Dorict as she stepped down. Garet and Marick joined her beside the cart.

"We'll be there for dinner!" Salick called after the cart as it rumbled onto the bridge, but Marick was already pulling her and Garet down the road to the middle bridge, a much wider arch that joined the two halves of the city at its centre point. They swerved around single men pulling handcarts of vegetables and groups of old women leading goats and sheep on tethers. Marick seemed to instinctively know which twists and turns would get them to their destination in the least time. Garet felt as if he was flying through the thickening crowds on the road, and turning his head, he saw that even Salick's cheeks were flushed and her eyes bright with excitement.

The Palace Plaza

When they reached the centre bridge, Marick pulled at Garet to hurry, but he resisted for a moment, wishing to look around before the small Bane had him running again. Two ramps, one on each side of the bridge, took travellers up from the level of the road to the higher gate and bridge. The gate itself was of iron-reinforced wood, and of a size to dwarf even the gates of Old Torrick. Garet judged that twenty men could have joined hands and walked through it without brushing the posts.

Guards stood at the head of each ramp, tall men in bronze breastplates and holding their long spears angled out in front of them. Their tunics were a deep purple, like Garet's vest, but their sleeves were a riot of colourful embroidery, running in spirals down their arms. At their waists, great, cross-hilted swords hung from gold baldrics. Black boots and silver helmets topped with long brushes of horse hair completed the heroic effect. Garet gazed at them in stark admiration. *These are what heroes should look like*, he thought, and he wondered if the Banes were really necessary with such men as these around. Then he remembered that the courage to face a demon was different from a soldier's courage; it was the courage not to attack but to withstand. Was a Bane's bravery a thing only capable of being learned in childhood?

The guard eyed him curiously as he approached his station. He was a young man, no older than Boronict. For an uncomfortable moment, their eyes met. Garet looked away and reddened. *How can I be braver than this hero?* He forced himself to look at the young man again. The guard had reddened also, and Garet realized suddenly that he was just a young man, with all the worries and joys of other young men. Had he ever faced fear before? Wrapped in metal and armed with a deadly sword, what terror could he ever have conquered? Thinking this, Garet knew why he was a Bane and this young man a mere soldier. This time it was the guard who dropped his eyes.

Marick pulled at him. "Don't bother with the guards. They're just decoration!" He tugged harder. "Let's go before the sun sets and we have to return to the Hall!"

Allowing himself to be pulled through the gate, he was whisked past the guards without a nod or a challenge.

The plaza they entered was immense, grander than Old Torrick's, and Garet remembered at once the trader's tales he had loved so long ago. Far across the open space stood a building that would have spanned the new, wooden walls of Bangt and filled Old Torrick's market. The slanted light of the sun picked out a thousand glittering points that dazzled Garet's eyes.

With a trembling hand he pointed at the magnificent, four-story building and asked, "Are those jewels?"

It took a moment for Salick and Marick to understand the question, but squinting at the building, Salick finally saw what he was looking at and shook her head. "No, Garet, that's only the sun reflecting off glass and crystal. Any jewel King Trax has ends up on his clothes."

"Or on his consorts," Marick added. "Wouldn't you like the King to give you some jewels, Salick?" he simpered, batting his eyes at her and then scampering away to avoid her hand. "Don't worry. The King doesn't flirt with Banehall girls, even if they are of noble blood..." This time he wasn't fast enough, and Salick's hand caught him across the back of the head with a satisfying slap. Several people nearby laughed. An old man passing by with a huge basket of charcoal strapped to his back gave Salick a toothless smile and held up one hand, palm down and slapped down on it with his open hand to applaud her victory. Salick blushed a bit but kept her glare on Marick.

"Oww, Salick!" he said, rubbing the back of his head. "Don't fool around. Remember, we're supposed to be showing Garet the sights."

Garet shook his head. He did not doubt that the little Bane's plans went far beyond a tour.

Salick's expression had not changed. She said in her sternest voice, "Once around the plaza. Quickly! And then back to the Banehall."

"Of course, Salick." Marick grabbed Garet's arm again and pulled him towards the centre of the plaza. "No more trouble."

Salick followed them grimly.

By the time they reached the middle of the plaza, marked by a wide fountain of many jets, Garet felt as dizzy as if he had been spun like a top. He had of course imagined that the world held many more people than he had ever seen, but now, to actually see them all at once, thousands of people walking and talking, and jostling and yelling, and all in colourful tunics that flashed before his eyes until the colours merged, darkened, and....

"Hold him up, Marick," Salick said, her voice coming from a mile away. He felt cold water on his brow and found himself sitting on the curb of the fountain with Salick's anxious face held close to his own. "Are you all right? Do you have a wound you haven't spoken of?"

Garet shook his head weakly. He tried to speak, but could only mumble, "So many people."

"What's wrong with him?" Marick asked impatiently. He scanned the crowd as if looking for someone.

"Too much change in too little time, I think," Salick replied and scooped up more water to poor down the back of Garet's neck.

Marick groaned. "Is that all? Come on, Garet. There's a place here that sells the best sugar drinks in all the Five Cities." The young Bane fairly danced in his impatience. "It's just over by the Astrologer's stalls. Let's go!"

Salick grabbed his hand and pulled him down to sit on the curb beside her. "Wait! How do you think you'd manage if I plucked you out of the Banehall and put you on a little sheep farm in the middle of nowhere with a father and brothers like that?"

Marick stopped fidgeting for a moment and looked at Garet thoughtfully. "I see what you mean." He broke into a grin. "But I'd probably steal the sheep and run off before the end of the first week." He reached across and grabbed Garet's hand. "Sorry! I know that everything must be so strange for you now." He said, with one eye on Salick, "But don't you think that you'd feel much better with a cool, sweet drink in your belly?"

Salick sighed. "Marick, you are incorrigible." She slapped the young Bane's hand from Garet's arm. "Never let me hear you tease Dorict about his appetite again!"

While the two argued, Garet tried to get his bearings. Directly in front of them, although at some distance now, was the gate through which they had entered. He could see the bridge beyond it, climbing to its apex before it curved down to the other side. To his left were the stalls Marick was interested in. The alleys between the canvas and pole shops were rivers of moving people as merchants called out their wares and buyers paused to argue over the price. Far to his right, three bright buildings, domed in blue and with white pillar walls, dominated the west side of the plaza. With his head clearing, Garet realized that they were temples, like the one they had stopped at yesterday. But here, they anchored a complex of buildings with surrounding fountains, gardens, and artificial ponds. Beside him, his friends' voices rose angrily.

Wishing to make peace, Garet said, "That's all right, Salick, Marick. I'm feeling better, and maybe I could use a drink." He felt in his tunic pocket for the small bag of copper coins that Mandarack had returned to him. "I have some money."

Salick stood up resignedly and helped him to his feet. Marick was already ten feet away, turning back anxiously towards them and waving them on. "No need for that, Garet," she said. "As long as our requests are reasonable, no merchant in the city would turn us away." She looked at the disappearing form of the young Bane, as he wove his way through the crowd towards the stalls filling the east end of the plaza. She sighed again. "The trick is to keep the requests reasonable."

By the time they caught up with Marick, he was pleading with a beefy man presiding over a table filled with large glass bottles, each protected by a basket covering. The man, his thick mustache bristling and his eyebrows raised in surprise so high that they almost touched his short grey hair, shook his head.

"No, little Blue," he said firmly. "That is too much to ask, even for a Bane. Do you know how much the syrup to make a full bottle costs?"

Marick, catching sight of Salick coming into the range of hearing, interrupted the man. "A bottle? I think you misunderstood me, friend," he said, shaking his head vigorously. "I only asked for a drink for myself and my friends, apprentices of Master Mandarack!" He turned to smile and wave over Salick and Garet.

"Apprentices, eh?" asked the merchant. He eyed Garet's and Marick's sashes.

Salick reluctantly stepped forward. "Master, I am an apprentice of Master Mandarack, and these two have, uh, recently journeyed with him to the Midlands and back." She gave a little bow of her head. "If you could give these two a small taste of your wares, I would offer the thanks of the Banehall in return."

The man laughed. "It's a good thing the little one has you here to keep him honest!" He poured a sweet smelling, orange liquid into three rough clay cups. "Bring back the cups before you leave the plaza, please."

Salick thanked him warmly. After a small sip of her drink, which she said she found too sweet, she gave the rest to Marick, who had already gulped down his own.

Garet took his time, savouring the heavy sweetness of the liquid. His mother had sometimes found bee hives on their trips into the hills, and they would raid them by lighting small fires of moss and birch bark to blow the smoke into the hives and quiet the bees. But even the stolen honey combs lacked the sharp sweetness of this drink. Feeling the last drop slide down his throat, he wondered that the traders who came to Three Roads had never sung its praises, instead of going on about mere jewels and gold.

Salick collected his cup and put it back on the merchant's table. She looked for Marick, but he had wandered over to another stall, this one decorated with colourful drawings of the sun and moon. The young Bane was chatting with the woman behind a paper-laden table. He waved over his friends as the woman paused in a long and impassioned flow of words.

"Salick, Garet," he called, "this is Alanick: the Sage of the Shirath Market!"

Garet looked above the old woman to the painted sign tied above the stall. Two symbols were roughly written in a fiery red paint: the full bowl symbol for 'all' and the doubled eye of 'seeing.' The 'all-seeing' woman looked him over, shifting her large bottom on a small stool. With great drama, she pointed a finger at him and intoned, "You're a stranger in this city, aren't you?"

"Come on, Alanick!" Marick teased. "The black hair alone would tell you that." He leaned on the high table. "Why don't you give us a good show?"

The woman shifted again and swept a pudgy hand through her loose, grey hair. "A show, hmm? And what do I get in return?" The all-seeing eyes narrowed.

"All I can offer is the thanks of the Banehall," Marick replied, sounding suspiciously like Salick.

Garet looked at his companion, expecting an explosion, but Salick hid a smile under her hand.

The old woman was smiling as well. "If you'll pass my name around to your acquaintances, I'll take that along with your thanks."

Marick grinned and dragged Garet closer to the table. It was covered with charts of the stars, each constellation joined by inked lines to make the pictures people saw in the sky.

"What was the day and year of your birth, dearie?" she asked, pen paused above a blank scrap of paper.

"I don't know," Garet was forced to reply. "I know I was born in the fire year, but we didn't keep track of birthdays in my family." He blushed as he felt Salick's eyes on him.

The old woman seemed nonplussed for a moment but soon rallied. "Well dearie, that's a shame, but there are other ways." She heaved herself off the stool and maneuvered around the table. Instead of the colourful tunics of most of Shirath's citizens, she wore a red robe of some soft, shiny material. Her feet were bare.

"Now give me your hands, dearie." She took Garet's hands and examined the length of his fingers, the state of his nails, and then looked long and hard at the lines on his palms. Finally, she took his face between her soft hands and looked methodically at each part, to Garet's extreme embarrassment. He couldn't help but notice that several passers by had stopped and were chatting to each other about this performance. Their comments indicated that they appreciated the thoroughness of Alanick's method. After many minutes punctuated by her nods, sighs, grumbles, and one startling 'aha' when she found a tiny mole on his neck, the sage walked back behind the table and planted herself again on the stool.

"You were born under the pole star, dearie, which is also called the Shepherd because it guides all the other stars." She broke off her lecture to glare at Marick.

The young Bane was sputtering and choking out sprays of the sweet drink he had been sipping. Hand and cup were both dripping with the overflow of his fit. Salick pounded his back until he stopped coughing.

"Do you question my abilities, Marick?" Alanick asked. She drew herself up to her full height, and looked the young Bane straight in the eye. "You, who know them so well?"

"No, Alanick!" Marick said, one hand patting the air in front of him to calm the outraged astrologer, the other swivelling the clay cup to slow the drops that threatened to fall untasted to the ground below. "It's just that you really hit the mark this time." He gave one last cough and wiped his mouth on his sleeve. "Garet knew nothing of demons and everything of sheep before we rescued him from the Midlands."

At the word "demon," Alanick had quickly touched one finger to her ear and then flicked her hand to the side as if to throw away the word.

"Hush, Marick! The name makes or breaks the luck." Her eyes suddenly narrowed again, and she stuck her fists deep into the flesh of her broad hips. "And what do you mean by 'this time'?"

Salick rolled her eyes at Garet.

Marick was caught still trying to lick the rim of the cup clean of the sweet drops before they fell to the ground. From this awkward position, he looked sideways at Alanick and grinned. "Well, 'all-seeing one,' didn't you tell me before I left for the Midlands that I would soon die a horrible death far from home?" The cup more or less clean, he transferred it to his other hand so that he could lick his fingers. "I remember that you were very enthusiastic about it."

Alanick sat back down on her stool, one hand tapping the pile of star charts in front of her. "As the stars are often hidden from us by clouds, so are the true meanings of a horoscope often hidden behind its words." She leafed quickly through the pile and pulled out a sheet from near the bottom. "See here?" One pudgy finger pointed to a group of five stars joined by spindly lines into a picture of a fox with a crooked tale. "Your stars were moving through a zone of disaster. That usually means death, but it could also signify taking part in a some great upheaval or chaotic event."

"With Marick, that's a safe prediction," Salick whispered to Garet, who immediately had a coughing fit of his own.

"Now don't worry, dearie," Alanick said, turning towards Garet. "The Shepherd is in a good position right now." She pointed to a large chart pinned on the canvas wall. "I'll have to make a full chart for you, dearie. You're passing through a time of change. There's danger, but opportunity too, if you're brave enough to grab it with both hands." She winked at him and grinned, revealing many gaps between her remaining teeth. "But all Banes are brave, eh young Master?"

Embarrassed by this bare-faced flattery, he fumbled for a reply, but Salick saved him before he could offer words or money in thanks.

"Thank you, Mistress Alanick," she said in her most formal tone, "but Garet's Master forbids her students to consult astrologers. She says she doesn't believe in them."

Alanick came huffing around the table again. "And just who is this woman?" she said in a voice that rose over the noise of the surrounding stalls. Her nearest neighbours paused in their commerce to enjoy the spectacle.

"Master Tanock," Salick replied. She grabbed Garet by the shoulder and dragged him back towards the gate, calling back over her shoulder, "I'm sorry, Mistress, but there's nothing to be done." The sage's aggrieved voice followed them for some time.

"Perhaps," Marick intoned, his voice deep in his chest, "Mistress Alanick's star is passing through a zone of irritation."

"No doubt," Salick laughed. "I'm sure that zone follows you around like a puppy!"

"Salick?" Garet asked worriedly, "Isn't Mandarack my Master?" The thought of losing Mandarack's steady leadership and guidance, just when he felt he would need them most, made him panic. "I've never heard of this Master Tanock!" he wailed.

"Neither have I," Marick observed.

Salick smiled. "Let's just say that she is a very convenient Master for young Banes to pull out in difficult situations."

"Salick," Marick asked, his eyes opening wide, "didn't you tell me that you had a cat named Tanock when you were little?"

Salick ignored the young Bane and said, "Garet, no Black or Blue looks to any one Master as his own. When you become a Green, a Master will choose you to be their apprentice. That Master will train you until you become a Red yourself."

"But who will help me until then?" Garet asked frantically. He grabbed Salick's hand and pleaded, "Who will tell me what I have to do?"

"Everyone!" Marick yelled, startling Garet out of his fears. "Don't worry, Garet. Blacks never lack for supervision." He put his arm on Garet's shoulder. "And I'll always be around to let you know how to act."

"That's comforting," Salick said. She put her own hand on Garet's other shoulder. "I'll be there too. And even if Mandarack isn't your Master, I know he feels responsible for you." She gave him a little shake. "I know how far you've come, and how strange this is for you. But you have to keep going."

Garet took several deep breaths and then nodded at his friends. He followed Salick towards the gate.

But he came up short against Salick's back and saw that she had been stopped by the ring of an inward-facing crowd. Salick pushed ahead until the crowd parted slightly to let them see inside. Two men, armed with light swords, faced each other in the middle of the circle. The nearest, a tall man in his twenties with short cropped hair, caught sight of Salick and waved at her.

"Salick!" he called, "come over and judge this match." He swung the thin blade vigorously in front of him, making impressive noises as he cut the air.

Before Salick could answer, and Garet could see from the dark look on her face that that answer would have been no, the other young man stepped forward to intervene.

"Not a Bane," he drawled. "They can't stand the sight of any blood besides their own." He stopped, the point of the sword on the ground, and twirled the hilt back and forth between his long fingers. "Fetch a guard, Draneck." He carefully brushed a strand of long hair behind his ear. "They don't begrudge a drop of glory to the rest of us poor, ordinary folk."

There was no need to go to the gate, for the guards, curious as to what had drawn a crowd, had left their posts to join the ring of spectators. One handed his spear to his companion and stepped in between the duelists.

"First blood?" he asked. The sun glinted off his armour and sword, but Garet thought that the two men he faced might be more dangerous. Draneck nodded at the guard. He sidestepped to a position directly across from his opponent, thin sword held out at chest level and rear hand curled up and hanging slackly above the shoulder of his green tunic. Weight on his leading foot, he ground his toes into the paving stones to ensure proper traction.

"Not if it's just a scratch," the long-haired swordsman said, and raised his sword lazily til its tip pointed directly at Draneck's eyes. His nonchalant tone was betrayed by the flaring of his nostrils and a quick shift of his hips to set himself for the match.

The guardsman raised his hand between them then jumped back as he slashed down. "Begin!"

Garet could barely see the swords move, they flashed back and forth so quickly. Steel rasped and rang as the two young men jumped about the ring, each trying to drive the other back against the spectators. The speed at which they attacked and avoided each other reminded Garet of Mandarack's quickness in battle. These two men had the speed of a Shrieker! The crowd cheered each attack and gasped at close escapes.

Draneck slipped, his foot catching on a crack between the stones, and the other man lunged at him. Draneck desperately twisted his body so that the tip of the sword lanced past his head. He slammed his own sword's bell-shaped guard into his opponent's blade, forcing him back. Even in the back of the crowd, Garet could hear their breath coming like bellows as they kept up a continual exchange of thrusts and blows. Draneck had recovered his balance and now the two men slowed their pace. They circled each other, sidling cross-legged, looking for an opportunity to dart in under the other's sword. The young man who had mocked Salick took one such opportunity, trying to reach around Draneck's blade and stab him in the side, but he paid for it when Draneck circled the blade tightly, flung it to the side and then, with a twitch of his wrist, sliced back across the man's forearm.

Draneck jumped back and lowered the tip of his sword. Between gasps of breath he asked, "Yield, Shoronict?"

The guardsman had stepped between them, one hand raised and the other on his own sword's hilt. Everyone looked at the blood dripping from the young man's arm to stain the stone beneath his feet. Without a word, Shoronict turned and pushed through the crowd, leaving the circle. Draneck raised his sword and jabbed it into the air above his head while the people surrounding him slapped their hands in congratulations. He gave a low, exaggerated bow to his admirers, a nod of thanks to the guardsman, and strutted over to the Banes.

"So, Salick, you're back," he said. His face was red with the effort of his win, but he held himself tall, chest thrust out. "Well, Cousin, did you see? Shoronict has been bragging of his skill with the sword since he joined the duelists last spring." The young man smirked. "Let him brag now!"

Draneck smile faded as he caught the look on Salick's face.

"Cousin," she scolded, "does my uncle know that you're fighting duels in the street? What do you think he will say about this match?"

Draneck tapped the flat of the blade into the gloved palm of his left hand. Little drops of blood fell off the tip of the sword to the pavement between them. "I'm a third son. Father has two other, duller sons to make into merchants." He wiped the sword blade on the leather of his boot and slid it back into its sheath. "He's already given in to the inevitable and allowed me to join the Duelists Guild." He touched the silver-chased hilts of his fencing sword. "How else do you think I could afford something like this?"

Salick shook her head. "Dueling just causes trouble. Doesn't the Guild get enough excitement protecting traders?"

Draneck sneered, "Not enough missions for us all, and the higher ranks keep them for themselves," he said. His tone turned savage as he looked down into his cousin's eyes. "You know how it is, Salick. If you're not a Bane, you have to live a very ordinary life in Shirath. The only chance for any fun, any excitement, any glory is to become a Duelist."

"There are the games in the Banehall plaza..." Salick began.

"The games!" Draneck said, one hand slapping his forehead. "You know as well as I do that nobody plays in the games after they grow up." He looked down, breaking contact with Salick's eyes. "I've grown now. I don't have to listen to my father or to you. You're not a lord's daughter anymore, and I will be much more than a poor cousin." He turned and left without another word. Salick raised her hand but did not call out.

"Come on, Salick," Marick said softly. "The sun's almost down."

Each keeping to their own thoughts, the Banes left the plaza and walked up the swell of the great bridge to cross the river.

A New Life

Nothing in the Shirath Banehall was what Garet had expected.

It was worse.

Atop the Banehall roof, he could see almost the entire city of Shirath, save for what lay hidden behind the great Palace across the river. Unlike the roofs of the ward buildings, which were divided by high walls into easily patrolled sections, the balustrade of the Banehall roof was barely waist high. Garet knelt against it, feeling the grit of mortar and stone against his chin, gazing longingly at the vista beyond the walls. The clouds above were flat and white, the first sign of fall in the foothills. He wondered what autumn would be like here, with no tree higher than his hip allowed to stand inside the walls, and every strip of green boxed in and pruned to within an inch of its life. Maybe if he could get out into the fields surrounding Shirath, help harvest the spring-planted wheat or the last of the apples from the orchards beyond, he might feel more a part of this place. *But no*, he thought bitterly, as he had been told, *there are few things that a Black Sash does, and many they do not.*

Without rising, he turned slowly. Looking west gave him a strange feeling. Three more cities stood beyond even his vantage point, somewhere along the Ar. When he had travelled the prairie, he had felt as if the whole of the South was waiting for him. Now he wondered if he would ever be allowed to leave this city again. Looking east did not help. That way lay only memories and regrets. To the north and

139

east were nothing but the distant hills lining the river valley, as dark and oppressive as the hills in which he had been born. With a sigh, he leaned back against the wall.

He fingered the material of his sash and remembered how proud he had been to put it on in Old Torrick. Now, he wanted nothing more than to tear it off and send it fluttering down onto the faces of the people below. The clothes he had thought were a key to a free and adventurous life had instead become a prison of ritual and regulations. Even now, in the few precious, unsupervised hours he had each week, he was avoiding his 'duties'. According to Farix, the Gold in charge of the dormitory room Garet now shared with five other Blacks, all years younger than himself, each hour not spent studying, exercising, or attending the needs of higher Banes should be spent in memorizing the numerous lists of Shirath Banehall Masters and their deeds. He should now be crouched at the desk beside his narrow bed, reciting these lists over and over again because, as Farix would daily remind him, he needed to pass tests that most boys his age had passed years ago, and if he ever wanted to catch up, he should "apply himself."

The thought of going over those lists again had driven Garet to the roof. The pages lay folded within his vest so that, if he was caught, he could claim that he had only been looking for a quiet place to study. *Marick would be proud of me,* he thought with a smile. He desperately wished the young Bane was here with him now. But both he and Dorict were busy training with the other Blues, and they barely had time to wave to him at meals.

With an even deeper sigh, he lay flat on the roof and looked up at the thin curtain of clouds. He missed his friends. The other boys in the dormitory were half in awe and half contemptuous of him. They envied him his role in the killing of three demons, although none quite believed the rumours that he had dispatched one on his own. His ignorance of their customs, expressions, and traditions, however, made him seem like a halfwit to them. They had also seen how Master Adrix had treated him when he had arrived that first evening.

He could feel the heat on his face just thinking about it. When Salick had led him into the dining hall, Adrix had waved them over and questioned him in minute detail about his trip. For over an hour, he had tried to silence the grumblings of his stomach while those about him, Adrix included, ate. The Banehall Master, a muscular, florid man who bellowed his questions, pointed his finger at Garet when he had finished the interrogation and had said, "Midlander, we have rules here, rules that were set down by the first Banes!" He leaned back and continued, loudly enough to be heard by every Bane in the room, "One of those rules is that no one is taken into the Banehall without the approval of the Hallmaster." His eyes were pitiless. "I have not yet given that approval. Remove that uniform."

A gasp had gone up from some of the Masters at the head table. Behind him, Garet heard all talk cease among the lower Banes. Mortified by this attention, and fearing that he was to be expelled from the Hall, he had raised trembling hands and pulled the sash off to lay it on the table in front of Adrix, but the Hallmaster was looking at Mandarack, who sat several seats to his right. Adrix had a tight smile on his lips, as if he had just scored a private victory over the older man. Garet was struggling to loose the top button of the black vest when a woman to Adrix's left broke in.

"Master Adrix!" she cried out. "Is this necessary? I trust Master Mandarack's judgement that this boy has shown the qualities of a Bane. To treat him this way in front of the whole Hall is shameful!" Two crutches leaned against the table beside her and she grabbed them as if intending to stand and face the Hallmaster.

"Yes, Master Tarix," Adrix replied, his eyes now back on the shaking Garet, "we know where your trust, and your loyalties lie." He had then lazily waved a finger at Garet. "Continue, boy."

With the vest finally unbuttoned, Garet had slipped it off his shoulders and laid it on top of the sash. Out of the corner of his eye, he saw Master Tarix pull herself up on her crutches and limp slowly out of the room. With Adrix still staring at him, he had no choice but to begin to unbutton his tunic, but was stopped by the light pressure of a hand on his shoulder. Mandarack stood beside him.

"Hallmaster Adrix," the old Bane said, his voice as dry and calm as ever, "if you wish to review Garet's circumstances, I invoke my right as a Master in this Hall to meet on the matter after supper."

Several Masters had rolled their eyes at this. Adrix scowled but said nothing.

"Salick," Mandarack said to his apprentice, loudly enough for everyone in the dining room to hear, "take Garet to a guest room for the night." He scooped up the vest and sash in his good hand. "And return these to him tomorrow."

Salick, seeing the chance, had taken the clothes quickly and pulled Garet out of the dining hall. She turned left outside the door and escorted him up a narrow staircase to the third floor of the Hall. There, she had deposited him in a bedroom facing the river wall. Before she left, she had turned as if to speak but said nothing. She clasped Garet's vest and sash to her chest and looked at him, eyes flashing and the corners of her mouth pulled down. She had left, but not before he saw tears rolling down her face. Was he indeed going to be thrown out in the morning? After a very short time, Dorict had brought him a heaping plate of food and a mug of cool milk, but Garet could not eat.

After a restless night, Salick had roused him early and given him back his clothes as if nothing had happened. She spoke little to him as she guided him to a dormitory for Blacks on the other side of the building. To Garet, the Banehall was a warren of training halls, dormitories, corridors, and staircases. Old Torrick's Hall would have been lost in it, Garet realized. And now, after a month of living here, he was still getting lost, to the exasperation of Farix and the amusement of his roommates.

Farix had been cool to Garet since Salick introduced them that first morning. Although some Banes, even some Masters, would give him a kind word or an encouraging pat on the shoulder in the corridors, Farix obviously looked to Adrix for the slant of his opinions. As a result, Garet received a bed with broken slats under a lumpy mattress. His belongings, not that they were very valuable—an old shirt, a pair of canvas pants, and tattered leather shoes—were lost for days before Farix dropped them at the foot of his bed, a look of disgust on his face.

"Burn these, boy, or keep them out of sight—and smell," he said, while the others giggled behind the Gold's back.

The remaining days had been no better. Farix had refused to believe that he could read and so had him copying his letters out like a rank beginner while the other Blacks laboured through the Demonary. The Gold was so obstinate that Garet hid his own copy of the book, with its corrections, under his mattress when Salick returned it to him on one of her rare visits.

The physical training was not difficult. They ran around the Banehall's exterior for an extended period each morning before breakfast. Every afternoon, they would lift heavy clubs of wood or stone, rolling them around their shoulders or waving them above their heads. Used to the work of the farm and kept fit by the trials of his journey from the Midlands, Garet found this practice easy. His dorm mates did not. They had been raised in the comfort of a city. Most had done little or no hard physical labour, for the work teams that went daily to the surrounding fields and pastures were made up of adults only. No child could run quickly enough—or at all—if a demon was spotted, Garet supposed, so why bother training? The five other boys in his room, all less than twelve years old, had done nothing more arduous than play kickball or wash dishes before becoming Banes. They coughed and wheezed after every run and moaned when hefting even the lightest club.

What a waste of his life! He was already fit; he had proved that on the journey and in his encounters with the demons. What he really wanted to do was practice with weapons, like Dorict and Marick. He had glimpsed them in the smallest of the Banehall's three gymnasiums, standing in a line of other Blues and swinging wooden poles back and forth in a choppy rhythm. But he dared not even wave to them, as Farix had repeatedly told him that he was still not a real Bane, and that he was not to "bother" any students or Masters until he was deemed worthy enough to speak to them.

He rolled over and picked up a sliver of stone fallen from the low roof-wall and spun it at the lid of the trap door, left open and leaning against the opposite wall.

"Ow!" Marick yelped, as the chip skipped off his head. "I thought you might want some company, but if that's how you feel..." He stood on the ladder, rubbing his forehead and grinning.

"Marick!" Garet cried, rolling to his feet and hurrying over to his friend. "Sorry! Are you hurt? Is there any blood?" He pulled away Marick's hand to reveal a small scratch on the young Bane's head. Biting his lip in contrition, he sat back on his heels and apologized again, "I'm so sorry, Marick. It was an accident. I really do want some company."

Marick wiped a drop of blood off his forehead and set his hand on the rim of the opening. "That's all right, Midlander. If I were stuck in a room with that lot of babies, and with Farix sticking his long nose into my business all day, I'd be driven to violence as well." He pulled up his other hand, showing that it held the end of a long pole. "Look at what I've brought you!" He passed the staff to Garet, who held it up in wonder. "Consider it a birthday present." Marick announced grandly. His hands free, he climbed up on the roof and leaned against the wall. "You told the great seer, Alanick, that you don't know when that day might be, so it might as well be today."

Garet ran his hand over the training weapon. Two fingers thick and as long as a pitch fork, the pole felt heavy in his hand. He tried to bend it, but it wouldn't flex.

"It's made of ironwood from the hills north of Solantor," Marick told him. "Even Dorict's head won't break it."

"How do you know?" Garet asked suspiciously. He ran his hand over the shaft, tapping the wide bronze rings at the ends.

"Oh," the young Bane replied airily, "a training accident." He pulled Garet over to the corner of the roof, where the servants who maintained the Hall had left a pile of canvas and pots of dried tar. "Leave it under the canvas when you go back down." He looked at the clouds, which streaked half the sky in wispy sheets but threatened no rain. "It'll be a month before we get any serious rain. So there'll be no leaks to repair until then, which means that no one beside us will ever come up here."

"Us?" Garet asked, pausing his examination of his present.

"You need a teacher, don't you?" Marick asked. "And you're unwilling to wait for the moldy rules of the Hall to let you start training with weapons, aren't you?" He waited for a reply, drumming his fingers on the top of the railing.

"I don't want to give Master Adrix another reason to kick me out," Garet protested, but he ran his eyes along the pole and then stepped forward into a guard position, trying to copy what he had seen the Blues do at the beginning of their practice.

"You were found by Mandarack," Marick said. "That's enough reason for Adrix to hate you." He grabbed the end of the pole and pulled it down into the proper angle. "No higher than the top of your head!" He stepped back and crossed his arms. "Now, you'll never please Adrix or his toadies, so you'd best please yourself—and your friends. Step forward!"

Garet took a step forward, pole held steady.

"No, no!" Marick groaned. "Cross-step, don't march. You're not a guardsman on parade; you're a Bane!" He demonstrated a quick step, his right leg going in front of the other and his left hip pointed forward. "Keep your head at the same level, now. Try again."

They practiced walking back and forth across the roof until they heard the bell signal all the Hall to supper.

"There," Marick said, clapping his hand on Garet's back. "Even Tarix couldn't train you any better."

Garet slid the pole under the canvas and straightened up. "Is she your teacher?" he asked.

"Of course!" Marick replied, smiling. "Only the best for the best!" He looked down the trap to make sure the coast was clear. "She may be the Training Master, but she doesn't think she's lowering herself to train mere Blues." He listened for a moment. "Come on."

They went down the ladder, closing the trap door behind them. The storeroom below was empty, except for a few pieces of broken furniture that had been dumped here rather than carried down three flights of stairs.

"Aren't you glad I showed you this place?" Marick teased.

"Very," Garet replied. He cracked open the door to check the hallway. Only a few rooms were occupied on this floor, and the corridor was empty. "You're a good friend, Marick." He started to leave the room but was stopped by Marick's hand on his arm.

"Thanks, Garet," he said quietly. His face was serious, and he looked down before he spoke again. "You're like Dorict, he's the only other friend I have here." He looked back up and his smile returned, although it seemed a bit wistful. "Except for Salick, maybe. I know I'm better at making enemies than friends, so I have to value the few friends that I have." He slipped out and disappeared down the hall, leaving Garet standing in the doorway.

After a moment, he followed. Marick had already vanished down the stairs into the noisy life of the Banehall. *A quick meal and then back to my lists*, Garet thought, but the knowledge that Marick was willing to help him escape such mindless tasks and train him to be a real Bane was heartening. It gave him the courage he needed to descend into a world run by people like Farix and the Hallmaster.

City Lessons

Garet's tasks soon became, if not lighter, at least more meaningful. Another month had passed since Marick had joined him on the roof to begin his weapons training. Farix eventually excused him from the stamina-building exercises because, Garet suspected, the other Blacks thought he set too hard a pace for the rest of them. He still exercised, but only on the rooftop, sweating through the complex training pole forms Marick had taught him. What time was left over he spent finishing the Demonary and studying for his Blue Sash tests.

He was at his small desk, copying the illustration of a Crawler Demon, taking care to ink in each of its armour plates, when Marick raced into his dormitory room.

"Marick!" he gasped, "You almost stopped my heart!" He pulled out the notes he had jammed under the desk. "I thought it was Farix."

"Not likely!" his friend said. "Farix never moved this fast in his whole life."

Garet grinned in agreement. The Gold preferred a stately progression down the rows of beds, stopping only to criticize a wrinkled blanket or a dropped sash. "But what are you doing here? Shouldn't you be at practice until lunch?"

"I am at practice," Marick said, grabbing his arm. "Come on, Tarix wants to meet you." He pulled Garet up from his desk, barely giving him enough time to hide his notes beneath the mattress. "Come on!"

He led Garet at a gallop down two flights of stairs to the main level of the Hall. The Greens and Golds on the stairs, most just coming back from weary harvest duties in the fields around the city, saw Marick coming and stood aside, a resigned expression on their faces. When they reached the bottom floor, Marick took him down a narrow hall to the Blue Sash gymnasium. Garet saw that Marick was avoiding the more direct route, one that would have taken them by the Masters' Rooms, where Adrix directed the operations of the Banehall.

Tucked in a corner of one of the wings, the gymnasium intruded into the floor above, giving it a spacious feel after the claustrophobia of the hallway. The Blues were clustered at one end of the gym, swinging their poles at bags of sand suspended from a frame. With each hit, the bags made a muffled thump of a sound. Garet could see Dorict at one end, sweating and puffing as he attacked his bag with a grim determination.

"Marick!" a voice called from the middle of the gym. "Bring him over here."

A woman sat in a strange chair, waiting for them. The chair had four small wheels instead of the usual legs. The Training Master reached down and pushed to one side with a short crutch, forcing the chair to turn in their direction. She surveyed them calmly. Her hair, gold with a few strands of grey, was tied in a tight braid at the back of her neck. Her face had a pleasant, open feel to it but was marked by a scar reaching from her lip to her left ear. Garet, remembering her angry outburst on the night he arrived at the Hall, was relieved to see her smiling as they approached.

"Master," Marick said, pushing Garet forward and grinning at his stiffness, "this is Garet."

"Yes, I remember," she answered. "I saw you on your first night in the Hall." And seeing Garet's blush, she added, "Garet, you have no cause to be ashamed because of that night." Her eyes held his, forbidding him to drop his head. "It is we who should be ashamed of how we treated a new Bane." She broke off her gaze to check on the Blues striking the practice bags. "Charet! Use your hips, not just your shoulders!"

The Blue she had corrected turned and gave a slight bow to acknowledge the order. When he resumed his attack, twisting his hips as directed, the noise each strike made was noticeably louder.

"Come with me, both of you," she said, picking up a second crutch from her lap and twisting the chair again to align it with a door on the far side of the gym. The sound of wood on sandbags faded as they entered a spacious office. A cluttered desk was placed beside the door, and Tarix carefully maneuvered her chair in front of it. There was little else in the room save training bags, empty of sand, and a rack holding a bewildering variety of long and short weapons. Garet ran his eyes along them greedily. The weapons of a true Bane! Now that he knew something of the origins of the early Banemasters, he was not surprised to see versions of rather homely tools leaning in the rack. Beside the fisher's trident were spears hooked like orchard pruning tools. Flails for threshing grain, their wooden heads now bound in ridged iron, stood with axes and hammers that would not be out of place on a village farm. The one or two weapons that broke with this unglamorous tradition were so bizarre as to not seem to be weapons at all. Slightly dented shields such as Mandarack wielded lay among spiked gloves, weighted nets and hooked ropes. But what he had expected to see, swords and bows, were missing. *If they had started a Banehall in Three Roads*, he wondered, *would copper pots be displayed in the armoury?*

The crutches that Garet had seen Tarix use on that first night, longer than the pair she used to move her wheeled chair, leaned against the weapons rack. Tarix followed his gaze. "On good days, I can get around on those," she said, indicating the crutches. "On bad days, I'm trapped in this." She patted the arms of the chair and then her legs. Even though they were hidden under the trousers and boots of a Bane, Garet could see that they were not quite straight. He swallowed and quickly looked up when she spoke again. "Five or so years ago, a Basher ran me over in the stockyards of Ward Six. One of the less pleasant consequences of being a Bane." Her voice held no bitterness or anger. Garet nodded, thinking of the scarred face of Senerix who kept the stores in Torrick Banehall.

"But from what I understand from Marick," she continued, a slight smile on her face, "all the consequences of you becoming a Bane have been unpleasant."

"No, not at all, Master," Garet answered. "I want to be here." He glanced over at Marick, knowing that the young Bane would be enjoying his discomfort. "My friends are here, and I want to be..." He struggled for the proper word.

"A hero?" Tarix asked. There was no smile on her face now.

"No," he replied honestly. "I guess that I want to be useful, to be a part of something greater than a farm and a few sheep."

She nodded at that and picked up a piece of paper from the untidy desk. "Marick tells me that you have been studying the Moret Demonary." She held a hand up at his look of sudden guilt. "Don't worry, I won't tell Farix." She picked up a brush and dipped it in an open pot of ink. "What is the main attack of a Horned Demon?" She tapped off the extra ink while she waited for an answer.

"A charge, Master," Garet answered. "They use their head horns like a bull."

The brush made a small mark on the paper. Garet could not see what she was writing.

With the brush held ready again, Tarix asked, "And what will a Shrieker do if cornered?"

Garet thought for a moment before answering. "Moret says that a Shrieker will try to climb a wall to escape, but," he hesitated before gathering his courage to continue, "I have never seen a Shrieker try to escape." He stood ready for a charge of disrespect towards the ancient scholars of the Hall.

"Neither have I," Tarix replied. She made another mark. "Shriekers are not only the least common demons, they are also the most aggressive."

"But Moret says they are the most common!" he protested and then stopped, aghast at having contradicted this imposing Master. *Another mistake to mark down*, he thought with a sigh.

"They are indeed the most common, Garet." The brush made another mark. "What are the tactics used to fight a Rat Demon?" she asked.

The interrogation went on for half an hour. He was now so familiar with the Demonary that there were only a few questions he could not answer. When she finished with her questions, Tarix thanked Garet for his patience and told Marick to take him to the kitchens, on her authority, to eat a late lunch. Surprised, Garet realized that he had not even heard the bells for the mid-day meal. Tarix handed Marick a scrap of paper with her permission brushed on it and waved them out.

Marick was grinning from ear to ear as they left the gym. They ran into Dorict, still red from his battle with the sand bag, as he returned from lunch.

"Dorict!" Marick called and waved him over. "Come to lunch with us. Tarix gave us a note to eat in the kitchen and it doesn't say how many."

Dorict's face brightened noticeably, and he fell in with them immediately. Dropping his voice, he whispered to Marick, "Did it work?"

Marick clapped his hand on Garet's shoulder and whispered back, "He was amazing! I swear that he's memorized that clawed book."

Dorict's expression was smug. "I told you it would work. Salick knows Tarix better than either of us." He smiled up at Garet. "Congratulations!"

"For what?" Garet asked.

Marick pulled him into a cubby hole below the staircase. Dorict followed them. The space under the stairs was just wide enough for all three to crouch together, barely.

"Don't want to stand in the halls where any lazy Gold can give us a job," Marick said, then turned to Garet. "Why do you think Tarix was asking you all those questions?"

Garet sneezed at the dust they had raised and rubbed his nose. "She was probably deciding whether or not to let me keep reading the Demonary." He rubbed his nose again. "I was afraid she would confiscate it, but I guess I must have made enough progress to satisfy her."

Dorict laughed quietly, and Marick shook his head.

"You just passed your Blue Sash test, you idiot!" Marick hissed, trying hard to keep from shouting out the news. He rolled his eyes at Garet's look of incomprehension. "Part of the test is a basic knowledge of the Demonary."

"Part of it?" Garet asked. "Then the test isn't over?" His thoughts were spinning: Farix had dropped so many dark hints about the Blue Sash tests that Garet had expected something, well, much more frightening.

Marick turned towards Dorict. "Have you talked to Salick about the physical test?"

Dorict shifted in the cramped space. "Yes. She thinks that Garet will be excused, thanks to Farix." He ground out the name of Garet's supervisor. "That fool made it simple by excusing him from exercising with the other Blacks."

Garet looked at him curiously. He had never heard Dorict insult anyone except Marick. The stout Bane's expression was grim, and from the noise, he seemed to be grinding his teeth.

Marick poked him in the ribs. "Don't worry, Farix's day is coming." He saw Garet's questioning look and said, "Dorict hates Farix because he's a bully and loves tormenting the new Blacks." Dorict nodded in agreement. Marick continued, "But Farix is also one of Adrix's followers. That's why he won't be on top forever."

Garet's face must have kept its look of confusion for Marick, after a moment of hesitation, offered one more, cryptic comment. "You were there at Old Torrick, remember?"

The young Bane would say no more but pushed Garet out of the dark space and led him to the kitchen. Dorict trailed happily along, all his past bitterness about Farix forgotten in the anticipation of an extra meal.

Later that day, after supper, Salick came to find him. He had been sitting outside on the benches in front of the Banehall, watching two teams play kickball in one of the many sports fields in the Banehall plaza. The Demonary lay forgotten in his lap. A leather ball, as big as his head, moved back and forth across the field according to mysterious rules. Just when he was sure nothing had happened, the spectators shouted in joy or anger and the field master would throw his feathered wand into the air, signalling a goal. Garet sighed, promising himself to pay more attention next time.

In contrast to the glory of the palace and temples, and the busy commerce of the market stalls across the river, the Banehall plaza had a relaxed, playful atmosphere. The Banehall itself was imposing enough, four stories at its centre and three at the sides forming a 'U' shaped courtyard facing the river. There was a gate of iron bars and spaced wooden timbers to defend that courtyard, but Garet had never seen it closed. The rest of the plaza was uncrowded. The people who played on the grass fields or walked among the low-pruned gardens had none of the frenzy they displayed in the other plaza. Like Garet, they had come here to relax and enjoy a crisp autumn evening. He often sat in the plaza after supper, finding it, like the rooftop, a place where he could escape the worries of his life and just think.

He had a lot to think about. According to Marick, he was now a Blue, although his friend hadn't told him how he was to get a new sash. Thinking of how he had acquired the black one he now wore, he smiled and thought he had better ask Dorict instead. And there was still the matter of his physical test. He had already guessed that he could pass such a test easily, especially considering the lack of strength and stamina in the other Blacks. Since they were unlikely to pass a test that would be too difficult for him, he would pass the physical, unless Farix hated him so much that he failed them all. That thought brought a new flutter of nerves, but Dorict had hinted that he wouldn't have to take the physical exam. Garet idly thumbed the pages of the rewritten book and thought of his frail dormitory mates. No dragon-fighting heroes there. Like himself, they were depressingly normal. Whatever whim of Heaven chose Banes, it left out magnificent specimens like the ones that guarded bridge gates or swaggered about with Duelist's swords on their hips.

Then another, more unpleasant thought rose in his mind: Adrix. The Banemaster obviously hated Mandarack, and might use Garet to undermine or embarrass him. Sitting here and thinking in the quiet of the low autumn sun, he now understood what Marick had been hinting at under the stairs. There was a split in the Shirath Banehall, similar to what had occurred in Old Torrick's Hall. Adrix was obviously the leader of one group, but who led the other? Master Tarix had some similarities to the winning Master in Torrick, Corix, but in Garet's mind she didn't fit the part. She was too gentle. Could it be Mandarack? He helped force the change of power in Old Torrick, and Adrix certainly saw him as an enemy. Garet sighed. He knew that he owed more loyalty to Mandarack than any other Master. Whether he wanted to or not, circumstances were making him choose sides in this struggle, and probably suffer for his choice.

"Garet!" a voice called, stirring him from his thoughts.

He looked up and saw Salick coming towards his bench with another Bane, a Gold. It was Farix! *Why would she be bringing him to see me*, Garet wondered as he jammed the Demonary into his tunic, got up and sketched a slight bow for Farix's benefit.

Salick barely waited until she stood by Garet's side before she launched a question at the Gold. "Now did you or did you not excuse Garet from physical training?" Her voice was sharp, and Farix straightened as if being addressed by a Master rather than a lowly Green.

"I did, but what business of that is yours, Salick?" He looked flustered, and Garet realized that Salick must have dragged him from the Hall for this meeting. In the background, a cheer went up as one team put the ball through the wicker circle at the end of the field.

Salick pressed on. "By doing so, were you saying, as his supervisor, that he already met the requirements?" She crossed her arms and waited for his answer.

"No! I..." Farix replied, and then stopped. He looked hard at Salick and then Garet while he considered his response. "Yes," he said finally, drawing out the word as if he hated its taste. "He met the requirements—barely." With that, he turned on his heel, but Salick's hand on his shoulder stopped him.

"Don't forget to record that in the register."

Farix didn't turn, but gave a short nod of his head before striding away.

Salick gave that stiff back a savage smile. "Got you!" she said in a lowered voice. She turned to Garet. "That's that.

You've passed all the requirements for the Blue!" She dropped down onto the bench, and he slowly sat down beside her.

"Why did Farix agree, Salick?" Garet ran his hand through his hair and tried to put this new development into place with everything else. It didn't fit. Farix would never let him off easily, nor would Adrix.

Salick waved her hand at a pair of Banes leaving the Hall for nightly patrol. Vinir, just returned from Bangt, waved back and called something inaudible. The Red she accompanied, a short, bearded man, waited impatiently. Salick motioned her on and turned back to Garet. "If he said you weren't fit enough after letting you off the exercises, he could be accused of not training you properly." She leaned back and turned her face to the gold-tinted clouds above the city, obviously pleased with herself. "I gave him no choice, if he wanted to remain a supervisor, and Farix couldn't live with himself if he didn't have some Blacks to boss around."

The spectators at the kickball game cheered again and Salick craned her neck to see who had scored. "Let's go for a walk, Garet. I'm too excited to sit down." She jumped up from the bench and strode off towards the fields, Garet following.

"Salick," Garet asked, catching up to her, "will Mandarack be the next Banehall Master?"

Salick stopped dead and fixed Garet with a calculating stare. "I see you've been thinking again." Her tone was neutral. "And if he was?"

Garet's response was immediate. "I think it would be a great improvement."

Salick smiled. "I agree, but I also think that newly tested Blues, or even Greens for that matter, shouldn't be saying such things in public." She turned slowly and continued her walk, now a relaxed stroll around the plaza.

The game had finished and the winners were consoling the losers while the spectators paused to discuss the finer points of the match. Garet wished he knew the rules better, so that he could play it himself, though thinking about it, he had yet to see any Bane, young or old, taking part in the various games of the plaza.

Salick led him into one of the gardens between the fields. Lacking the delicious scents of the summer, the gardens were now mainly a treat for the eye. Birch and maple trees, restricted to a cramped life in clay pots, showed off their new fall colours. Garet felt as if he were moving through a miniature forest. Salick ran her hand lightly along the tops of the trees as she walked.

"These trees are so small," Garet said.

"Hard to hide a Basher in them," Salick replied.

When they came to a secluded place, Salick said to him, in a lowered voice, "Garet, I know that you think about what you see, so you must know what is going on in the Hall."

Garet paused before answering. Adrix's treatment of him when he arrived and Tarix's obvious dislike of the Banemaster were only two clues as to what was happening. Lately, the head table had become a mirror of the conflict, with Adrix's supporters crowding around him at the centre and his opponents pushed out to the ends. Garet had also observed that some masters would not speak to each other in the halls, and he had heard Golds cursing each other for following a Master on the opposing side.

"I know that there's a split in the Hall, Salick," he finally answered, "but I don't know what's causing it." He ran his hand along the top of a nearby maple in unconscious imitation of Salick. "Is it because Adrix is such a cruel person?" The red leaves felt smooth against his palm.

Salick picked up a fallen leaf from the ground and absently rubbed it against her cheek. When she saw Garet staring at her, she stopped and said, "This is something people do in Shirath." She held up the dry leaf. "All the age of your skin goes into the leaf, and you'll never get wrinkles." She dropped the leaf, reddening.

Garet had the sense to stay silent.

One hand firmly clasping the other behind her back, Salick continued walking and explaining. "Adrix is cruel, but that's not why so many are against him. Usually the other Masters can control a Hallmaster if he or she gets too arrogant, but Adrix has proposed something that has won him the support of at least some Masters." She paused in her speech while a young couple, holding hands and whispering to each other, passed by. The yellow of the girl's tunic was ablaze in the slanted light as she laid her head on the young man's shoulder and laughed. Salick watched them walk away, her expression unreadable.

When they were out of hearing, she continued. "Adrix is using this sudden appearance of demons in the Midlands and their increase in Old Torrick to press for more power here in Shirath." Coming to another stone bench, she sat down. Garet remained standing, looking down at her.

"Well don't just stand there!" she said crossly. "Sit down! You look like a tree waiting to be pruned."

Garet sat, wondering what had made her so irritated. "I'm sorry, Salick. Please go on. How can Adrix increase his power?"

"Not just his," Salick corrected, "but ours as well." She looked at the open gates of the river wall. Over the hump of the centre bridge, they could see the top floors of the Palace. "Adrix wants the King to cede him power over trade and the Ward courts, the two most important things the King does. Without those powers, Trax might as well go back to being just another lord."

"Why would Adrix want these powers?" Garet asked, suddenly very aware of Salick's nearness, the red tinge the sunset gave to her yellow hair, the curve of her jaw above her tunic's collar. He swallowed and looked away.

"He wants to peel the years back," she said, her voice soft again. "For a hundred years after the demons came, the Banehalls had much more power and privilege than the lords or the King." There was a soft scuffing sound as she swung her foot back and forth on the paving stones. "But the Banehalls eventually found it easier to let the nobles run the commerce and courts so that we could concentrate on killing demons. That division of power has worked fairly well for five hundred years." The sound of her foot stopped, and her voice tightened. "Now Adrix is making all sorts of ridiculous demands on the King. And Trax is not the kind of man to stand by and see his power disappear!"

"What kind of demands?" Garet asked. He looked down at his own feet.

"Oh," she replied airily, "little things like a personal servant for each Gold and Red Bane, a Banehall more magnificent than the Palace, approval on all trade missions and treaties, and a final say over all court cases, even those not involving the Banehall."

Garet shook his head. "Why bother with servants," he tried to joke. "You already have all us Blues and Blacks to wait on you now!" He looked up at her and saw her smiling at him. The world suddenly felt unsteady.

"You're beginning to sound like Marick!" she chided. "But I'm glad of your support—for Master Mandarack, I mean." She blushed.

"And what about for you?" Garet said, hardly knowing why he asked but needing to ask all the same. His nerves jumped.

"Me?" Salick asked, as if she didn't understand. But Garet saw in her eyes that she understood the question, if not how to answer it. She took a breath to speak but was interrupted by a distant scream.

A Change in Circumstances

They both jumped up and looked around for the source of that panicked voice.

"The Ninth Ward!" Salick said.

Garet's gaze followed her pointing finger. One of the Ward gates in the barrier separating the plaza from the city proper was closing. It was the gate nearest the river wall and not far from where Garet and Salick sat in the gardens. Salick leaped over the low hedge in front of her and set off at a run for the gate. Garet hesitated for only a moment, then followed at the same speed.

The gate, its carved symbols proclaiming it to be the entrance to the Ninth Ward, was almost closed when he slipped through, just behind Salick. She turned when he bumped into her and frowned. They were standing in a tiny plaza just inside the gate. Beside them a small stone gatehouse, an overturned stool in the entrance, stood unoccupied. A wheel creaked above them, moving a toothed pole that pushed the gate closed. The weighted rope that turned the wheel by its falling was slack. By craning his neck, Garet could see the catch that had held the weight. In the shadows behind the wall, he traced a cable down to the lever beside the gate house. Once the lever was pulled, the gate would close automatically, and the demon would be trapped in this ward.

Salick stopped suddenly. "We shouldn't be doing this," she said quietly.

"Why not?" Garet asked. The gate guard was nowhere in sight. Garet checked for bloodstains around the stool but found none. He became aware that Salick was glaring at him.

"That wasn't Master Relict or Vinir who called out. It was probably the guard," she said.

"Does it matter who called?" Garet asked, perplexed by her hesitation. "And where is the guard?"

"Gone. He ran. The demon came close enough to terrify him but was too far away to freeze a man with fear."

Garet remembered clearly the slow increase of horror he and his family had felt as that first demon had approached their cabin.

Salick turned her head, scanning the streets leading into the ward from the gate plaza. "Once a Master is on the hunt, only he or she can call for help." She took a half-step forward and stopped again. "Most wouldn't—for the shame of it, but Vinir's Master, Master Relict, is more open-minded than some..." her voice trailed off as they heard two voices, a man and a woman's, calling faintly to each other in the depths of the ward.

Salick straightened, having made up her mind. "We'll go take a look," she told Garet. "I can always say we were in the ward before the gate closed." She glanced at the massive wood and iron barrier. "There's no help for it anyway. They won't open the gates until the demon is killed." She set off at a trot, calling over her shoulder, "Stay with me, but do as I say!"

Her tone rankled him a bit, but he realized that Salick knew much more than he did about what was waiting for them. He ran after her down a narrow avenue.

After the main plazas, which along with the Banehall were the only parts of Shirath he had seen in his two months in the city, the streets of the Ward seemed claustrophobic and dark. The blank walls of buildings, pierced only by high, infrequent windows, ran unbroken, save for the occasional closed door, along the cramped lanes. Salick had paused at the entrance to one such street and scanned the walls and their dark windows, waiting for the calls to start again. Her head snapped up as, far ahead, several voices rose in frantic horror.

"Come on!" Salick cried as she waved Garet past her, then turned to swing shut another gate that would block the way they had come.

Garet put his shoulder to the wooden planks and together they pushed the heavy barrier. It groaned as it swung on its iron hinges. When it bumped against the gatepost, Salick threw a simple bolt to lock it. A small opening cut out of the gate's planks allowed a person on the other side to reach in and release the bolt. *Why no lock*, Garet thought, but had no time to consider it as Salick ran off down the uneven, cobbled lane.

They now passed higher walls pierced by two levels of barred windows and well-spaced, locked gates. As they neared the source of the screams, they came upon an open gate, and Salick shouted at the occupants of a small courtyard beyond, "Close this! Now!" An old man crept out from where he cowered behind a sheet drying on a clothesline and pushed at the gate. Garet stopped to help, but Salick called back, "No, Garet! Stay with me." He had no choice but to follow as other residents of the courtyard rose trembling and moaning to help the old man seal themselves in.

They finally reached the end of the lane, only to find another locked gate blocking their way. Garet wondered how many gates Shirath had, then he remembered what Mandarack had said when they approached the walls, that Shirath was designed to keep demons in, to trap them for the Banes to kill. His stomach did slow flips. He knew the demon was near. The screams rang out again, this time above their heads. Other voices rang out too, harsh, angry calls from the roofs above.

"Up there, on the roof!" yelled Salick. "They have it cornered on the roof!" But at that moment something dark and supple flashed across the space above their heads. Garet had no more than a glimpse of it, but the pointed beak showed it to be a demon. Wider than any he had seen, it looked almost square against the fading light. It disappeared onto the opposite roof, and Salick cursed, "Claws! It's a Glider." She stamped her booted foot on the cobblestones and looked wildly about.

"Salick!" a female voice called from above. "Up here!"

Garet looked up and saw Vinir and another Bane, a bearded Red, looking down at them. Salick waved at them and yelled up. "We saw it. It's on the opposite roof." She pointed to where the demon had leapt.

"We know!" the Red beside Vinir called. "We'll follow it. You two try to find a net or some rope and bring it up to us." He turned to Vinir and they began to thrust a wide plank out over the gap between the roofs.

They're actually going to walk across on that, Garet thought in amazement, but was pulled away before he could witness the feat.

"Come on," Salick said and led him to a gate below where they had seen the demon vanish. She reached through a hole and slid the bolt back. They both pushed it open, and Garet closed and bolted it behind him.

"Good!" Salick said. She ran into the courtyard and quickly scanned the interior. Several men and women, some with small children, crouched in their doorways or on the second floor balconies that ran around the interior of the yard. A child screamed in one of the dark apartments on the second floor. "Look for some rope or a net of some kind," Salick ordered as she ran into the nearest set of rooms, brushing past an old woman who blubbered unseeing at the sky.

Garet took the opposite door, finding nothing but a table with the remains of dinner and a chest of carpentry tools. There was no sign of the apartment's occupants. He ran to the next door, finding an abandoned loom, and the next, but still did not find what the Red had demanded. He was entering the fourth set of rooms on that side when he heard Salick yell, "Got it!" He ran out and saw her dragging a tangled net out of a door opposite. "Grab the other end!" she ordered, and as Garet scooped it up from the stones, she ran to a corner staircase, half-dragging him behind. The net caught on the carved balustrade, and Garet was forced to tear at it to get it free. He bundled it tightly to his chest and climbed to the second floor. Salick didn't stop there. She stepped over a child, eyes tight shut, squeezing a rag doll in her hands and rocking back and forth, to ascend another set of steps, leading to the roof.

The net caught on the child's legs, then the corner post of the balustrade, and Garet finally yelled, "Stop!" His nerves were jumping; the demon was close now. He looked down at the little girl, but she showed no recognition of his presence. Salick tugged on the net again, but he held firm.

"Give it to me," he yelled, "or we'll never get to the roof."

Salick hesitated for a moment then thrust the net into his arms. As he gathered in the trailing edges, strung with ball-like wooden floats, Salick disappeared up the final flight to the roof. The net bundled tightly in his arms, Garet followed as fast as he could. The awkward weight slowed him, and Salick had vanished when he emerged onto the top of the building.

The roof was flat, with shoulder high walls. Awnings and mats, books and food, even musical instruments were scattered across it. The dread that had been growing in him must have already driven the people relaxing here down into the courtyards below.

There was a flash of purple in the twilight and Garet moved through the shelters toward it, lugging the net. He came up against a high wall that split the roof's surface in half, touching the edge barriers at each side to prevent passage from one section to the other. *More walls*, thought Garet, but he could see no gate piercing it as he scanned back and forth for his companion. At the corner where the wall met the edge barrier, a water tank stood and Salick was there, jumping up and down, trying to look inside it. Giving up on that, she flattened herself against the staves and pressed her ear to the wood. After a long moment, she turned to Garet as he hurried up with his burden.

"I can't hear anything sloshing in there, and there's no demon in this section," she said, "so it must be on the other side of this wall." She stomped her foot. "Claws! We came in the wrong courtyard!" Her eyes judged the height of the wall. "Garet, boost me up so I can take a look."

He dropped the net in an untidy pile at the base of the wall and cupped his hands, but before Salick could place her foot in them, Vinir's voice called from the other side.

"Salick! Are you there?"

"Yes!" Salick shouted back. "What should we do?"

"Did you find some rope or a net?" Vinir asked.

"Yes, a fish pond net."

There was a scrabbling on the other side of the wall and Vinir's head appeared as she pulled herself onto the top. "Garet! I thought it was you. I'm so glad!" she gasped as she shifted her grip on the edge. "Salick, get some poles and stretch the net out." She turned her head and listened to a voice below her. Garet couldn't make it out. Vinir turned back and continued her instructions. "Master Relict and I will drive the creature over this wall. Keep the net stretched between where you hear our voices." Just before slipping back down on her side of the wall, she called out, "Hold the net high when I tell you!"

Salick surveyed their surroundings. "Quick, tear down that awning!" They quickly disassembled the shelter, using a dropped fruit knife to cut the lashings. The net was in a tangle, and with their nerves jangled by the demon's proximity, it seemed to take forever to tease it out to its full length. There was a substantial tear on one side. *Somebody was repairing this*, Garet thought. He threaded a pole through one edge, sliding the point around the wooden floats. Salick did the same on her side. From the other side of the roof, two voices grew louder, one high and screaming "Yahh!" the other lower and yelling "Hoy!"

"Over there!" hissed Salick, indicating a spot halfway in-between the two voices. They lifted the posts into the dark sky, the net stretching up above the wall but nearly invisible in the darkening sky. They pulled on their ends, trying to stretch the net tight. Garet braced the butt of the pole on one hip and pulled back with both hands. He looked at Salick and saw her whole body leaning back as she strained at the weight.

At that moment, a great clatter and hissing rose from just beyond the wall, and Vinir's voice screamed, "Now!" They hoisted the posts up to shoulder height, and held on. The poles were torn from their hands by an invisible force, and Salick, pulled off balance, tumbled after them, slamming up against an awning pole still set in its socket. She lay there, the breath knocked out of her. Garet pushed himself up from where he had dropped to his knees and ran to her, but she waved him after the moving net.

The trailing poles were dragged back and forth, ringing hollow notes as they struck against other posts. He grabbed the nearest pole to keep it from disappearing into the forest of awnings. The net pulled against him, but weakly, as if the creature could not get any purchase in its escape.

He looked back. "Salick, I've got it. Hurry!" But instead of Salick, Vinir appeared beside him, a raw scrape on one cheek and her long braids unravelling. She grabbed the other pole. "Haul it in!"

Together, they pulled back on the poles, dragging the net towards them. It came slowly, decorated with bits of broken furniture, torn matting, and a chipped teapot caught by its spout and sloshing its contents onto the roof.

"Pin it!" Vinir gasped. She pushed the end of her pole down on the writhing mass of cords. Garet copied her, though he probably caught more net than demon with his pole.

"Careful!" called a deep voice behind them. Relict, the Red who had called from the roof, stepped up between them, an axe held two-handed over his head. Searching for a target, he chopped a half-dozen times into the net. At least some strokes must have found the mark, because the net stopped twisting, and Relict's weapon dripped a dark liquid from its edge. Salick limped up beside them, one hand pressed hard against her side. "Is it dead?" she gasped.

Vinir dropped the pole. She threw a supporting arm around Salick who cried out in pain. "Salick," she asked, "are you injured badly?" She turned to Relict. "Master, Salick is hurt!"

Relict stood up from checking the corpse of the demon. He hurried over to examine Salick. She bit her lip as he felt her side. "It's her ribs," he said. "Cracked, I think, not broken." He smiled at the injured Bane. "Heaven shone on you tonight, Salick." She gave him a weak nod, sweat standing out on her forehead.

Relict turned to Garet. He looked at him for a moment before speaking. "You're Garet, aren't you?" he said, and then, not waiting for an answer, continued, "Vinir has told me about you." He clapped a hand on Garet's shoulder. "No wonder you did so well!"

"Master!" Vinir reminded him. She was supporting Salick, trying not to cause her more pain.

"Oh, yes," he said. "Garet, take Salick back to the infirmary. Ask the guards for help if she can't walk." He looked back to Vinir. "We'll take care of this." He pointed at the motionless net with the blade of his bloody axe.

Vinir nodded quickly in agreement, her braids unravelling further. "Take good care of her, Garet," she said, transferring the shaken young woman to his shoulder.

As he half walked, half carried Salick down the courtyard steps, he heard Relict say softly to Vinir, "You were right about him."

The walk back to the Banehall was slow, but Salick refused to be carried. With a look of grim determination on her face, she limped along, one arm around Garet's shoulders. When they arrived at the Banehall, most of its occupants were already in their rooms for the night.

The infirmary was located on the main wing's lower floor, close to the training gymnasiums. It was a large room of many beds, most occupied by elderly Banes, but some by victims of training accidents or unlucky encounters with demons. The man in charge was a non-Bane in his middle years named Banerict, a soft-spoken man with a greying beard who quickly confirmed Relict's guess about cracked ribs, and motioned Garet to put his charge on the nearest empty bed.

"Don't worry, young man," he said. He took a tray of long bandages from a cupboard and set it beside Salick's bed. "Salick will be up and around in two days, although she might not be chasing demons for a while." She smiled at his small joke but then grimaced as he eased the sash off over her head. He directed Garet to pull off her boots while he carefully removed her vest.

Garet stood there, uncertain of how to help. Banerict looked around and suggested, "Maybe you could inform Master Mandarack that his apprentice is not too badly injured?"

Garet looked at the bandages and realized that Banerict wanted to wrap Salick's ribs, a procedure that would require him to remove her shirt. Hurriedly leaving the room, he made his way to the section of the main wing that housed the Masters' rooms. He knocked on Mandarack's door once and then paused, suddenly afraid of disturbing the old Bane. Banerict had been preparing for bed himself when Garet had half-carried Salick into the infirmary. But his concern was unnecessary as the door opened promptly to show Mandarack wide awake and still dressed.

"Come in, Garet," he said, as if it was the most natural thing in the world for Black Sashes to call on Masters so late in the evening. Garet entered and Mandarack waved him to one of a pair of chairs flanking a small side table. There was little other furniture in the room: a narrow bed, a small shelf of books, and a tiny writing desk. The room had no window. Garet wondered if the spareness of the room was another sign of Adrix's disfavour or merely a reflection of Mandarack's disciplined personal habits.

When they both were seated, Garet blurted out the reason for his visit. Mandarack listened and quietly asked, "Was Salick badly injured?"

"No Master," Garet replied, "but Banerict says that her ribs are cracked and she'll be off her feet for two days." He paused as Mandarack rose and took two cups down from the bookshelf. He filled them with steaming liquid from a teapot on his desk. Garet asked the Bane, "Master, Salick called Banerict 'physician.' What does that word mean?"

Mandarack handed Garet his tea and paused, probably, Garet thought, to judge how much other information he would need to make sense of any explanation. Another reminder of his ignorance.

"In the North and among the Midlanders, there are few large concentrations of people. That, of course, is changing in the Midlands." He sat down in the other chair and sipped his tea.

Garet took a sip as well. He was surprised to taste something familiar, mint and strawberry leaves, the same tea his mother had served the Bane months ago in their rough cabin.

Mandarack put down his cup, the thin china clinking on the stone top of the table. "If people in those places are injured or ill, a man or a woman skilled in healing is called, even if they must come from a distant place. These healers pass on their knowledge to their children, or perhaps to an apprentice, but they work in isolation with no healer sharing her knowledge with another." He waved a hand at the walls of the room, indicating perhaps the city beyond. "In the Five Cities, healers learn from each other. They study together in special schools, write books of their skills, and train any student who shows promise in the healing arts. The Palace of Shirath holds one such school. If you graduate from that school, you are called a physician, one who heals the body." He looked at Garet to judge his comprehension.

Garet nodded. "Such men and women would be very valuable in the Midlands and the North," he suggested.

"And indispensable in the Banehall," observed Mandarack, taking another sip. "Tell me of the Glider Demon."

Garet described the battle, stopping now and then to answer the Bane's request for more details. When he had finished there was a silence in the small room as Mandarack pondered this information.

"The idea of a net was intelligent. Gliders are rare, and I doubt anyone now living in Shirath has experience with them, but Master Relict is a resourceful Bane."

Garet recalled the brief comment on Gliders in the Demonary. This type of demon was said to be half the size of a large Shrieker with flaps of skin stretching from their forearms to their back claws. According to the book, this allowed them to slide like a falling leaf through the air. The size of its jewel was not mentioned, but Garet thought it would be rather small, as the fear he had felt had not even matched that produced by the Basher.

He looked over at Mandarack and found him still deep in his thoughts. Something he had said earlier still confused him and he decided to use this opportunity to continue his education about Shirath.

"Master," Garet asked, "are there other schools?" He waited until Mandarack turned to him before he continued. "I mean, physicians have a school, and I suppose the Banehall is a school as well, but are there other workers in the city who have this," he paused, looking for the word, "training?"

Mandarack smiled slightly. "Yes. My brother has a school of what he calls mechanicals, people who make and repair machines." He rose and poured himself another cup of tea from the pot on the desk. It was the same size and shape as the one Garet had seen caught in the net earlier that night. "There are also schools for scribes and stewards, those who assist the lords in running their wards and the King in running the city." He sat down again. "The Duelists also run a school of sorts to train bodyguards for trade missions."

These new facts ran together with all the other facts in Garet's head, forcing a familiar frustration to the surface. More questions. Why didn't the Banehall have scribes and stewards when they had a physician? Who helped 'run' the Hall? He slapped the arm of the chair, the noise loud in the small room. "I'll never understand this city!"

"No, I don't suppose you will," Mandarack replied. "At least, not like one who was born here. Everything will always be new to you." He observed Garet closely.

"Then why did you bring me here?" Garet asked. "You could have left me at Bangt, to be trained by the Masters there, maybe by Boronict. At least I knew something of the Midlands and might have been of more use there."

Perhaps some bitterness born of the humiliations he had suffered since arriving in Shirath coloured his tone, for Mandarack's lips twitched into his dry, small smile.

"We had a conversation like this once before," Mandarack said. "Then, I said I could try to change something for you, but here, any change is difficult." He leaned forward and put his good hand on Garet's arm. "For six hundred years, we have created rules and habits to keep a balance in this city. We each have our role in Shirath, forced into it by the continual threat of the demons. But on the whole, it's a balance that has served us well. We have survived to create a society undreamed of by our ancestors." He stood and pulled up his bad arm behind his back and began to pace slowly from the bed to the door and back again. "If Banfreat, our Hall's founder, could walk the streets of Shirath today, he would marvel at the theatres, the libraries, and the great mass of humanity housed within this city."

Theatres, libraries: more words Garet did not know. His sigh passed unnoticed by the pacing Master.

"And yet, Garet, this success may be our undoing." He paused in his slow strides to face the young Bane. "You know that the situation with the demons has changed, perhaps forever, although Master Adrix claims it is but a temporary problem."

Garet nodded. "Demons now appear together and some cannot be tracked by the fear they send out."

"Simple facts that turn our world upside down, I am afraid." He started to pace again. "Yes, I fear that we will not be able to survive this change in our circumstances."

"But that is your duty," Garet said and then hurried to explain his answer when the old man stiffened. "I mean, you and the other Masters will find a way to deal with it, like bringing all the Midlanders into towns like Bangt, and putting Corix in charge of Old Torrick's Banehall."

"Perhaps," Mandarack replied, "but the demon we met at the temple may be a change beyond our ability to adapt."

"Why, Master?" Garet asked.

"Because it may have the ability to control other demons, to work with them for our destruction," Mandarack answered softly. "In the marketplace of that ruined town, we were attacked so that Salick could be lured into a trap—a trap that you managed to break open. The Shrieker attacked us at the other demon's bidding." His pacing became more determined. "And do we even know how many demons the one you drove off can control—one, two, an army?"

Garet took a breath. He saw the reason for Mandarack's concern. The thought of facing many demons, all attacking at once, and perhaps coordinated by some evil intelligence was daunting. He shook his head.

"But that still doesn't explain why you brought me here instead of leaving me at the new Hall in Bangt," Garet said to the old Bane, hands gripping the arms of his chair. Would he get an answer? Did Mandarack think he deserved one?

Mandarack relaxed his stance and sat again. *He looks tired*, Garet thought.

"I brought you here because I thought we would need you here," Mandarack said. He waved away Garet's attempt at another question. "No, I don't expect you to fully understand yet. But you are a Bane that can see the Banehall from the outside, without the burden of those six hundred years of Shirath tradition." He closed his eyes for a moment. "That is a unique ability. When whatever disaster is coming arrives, your observations may be vital to our survival." He opened his eyes again and rose slowly from the chair. "The hour is late, but we have one more task to complete before we may sleep tonight."

He opened the door and left the room. Garet gulped down the rest of his tea and followed. Mandarack's conversation had sent a thrill of anticipation through him. The thought of some great change coming to the Banehall was welcome. But that joy was tempered by the fact that Mandarack seemed to dread this change.

It was a short trip that ended in the Records room, a dusty office that stood beside the Hallmaster's suite. The door was open and Garet followed the Master inside. Tarix, leaning on her crutches, was standing by an old woman and shouting in her ear.

"Garet!" she said, her voice rising. "That's right, Garet! I want to register his change of sash!"

The woman, a faded red sash around her vest, shook her head and pulled down a heavy book from the shelf behind her head. "What symbols does her name use?" she asked querulously. Tarix yelled, "His name!" but looked nonplussed. Mandarack stepped up to answer.

"When I registered him two months ago, Master Arict, you yourself chose the symbols "night bird" and "wave" to spell out his name."

The Records Master grumbled and thumbed through the thick pages of the book.

Garet knew that the writing symbols could be used to sound out names, which rarely had a symbol of their own. His mother had said that was because few names had a meaning in the shared language of the North and South, so one could only borrow symbols, each of which had its own meaning, for their sound. His mother had chosen "stream" and "fall leaf" for his name, two symbols with similar sounds to the ones Arict had picked. Garet didn't think it was worth the trouble to correct the three Masters, especially if he would have to yell.

Arict found the page and dragged her bent finger down the entries until she stopped on his name. Garet, who had quietly come up to the table, saw that it listed the date he had arrived, his age, and that he was a Black Sash. The other entries on the page had much more information. Garet could see Ward numbers, parents' names, even the comments of different Masters.

Mandarack examined the entry. "Farix, the Gold in charge of Garet's training, was supposed to list his completion of the physical requirements," he observed.

"He sent a note," Arict said, pushing aside several leaves of paper to pull out a scrap with Farix's precise writing covering one side. She picked up a brush, inked it, and made an entry in the space below Garet's name. 'Physically fit,' she wrote and looked up at Tarix, the inked bristles dripping slightly on the page.

The training Master leaned forward on her crutches and took the brush. She wrote 'Passed basic knowledge' in a bold hand beside Arict's spidery symbols. Tarix looked questioningly at Mandarack, but he shook his head slightly. The weapons Master shrugged and continued writing. "There!" she said, straightening up and twisting around to face Garet. "You are officially a Blue. Come to training tomorrow after breakfast and we'll deal with the rest of it then." With a word of thanks to Arict and a nod to Mandarack, she limped out of the room. Garet saw that only one of her legs touched the ground as she walked, the other was twisted at the knee and ankle so that it hung swinging in the air.

"Get some rest," Mandarack said, and putting his good hand between Garet's shoulders, pushed him gently towards the door.

As if I will sleep, thought Garet, as he went back to the Black Sash dormitory for the last night. The hunt for the Glider Demon, Mandarack's unsettling talk, and on top of it all his concern for Salick's injuries chased each other within his tired skull. *I wonder*, he thought, adding one more worry to the mix, *if I will ever have a night when I can lay down my head with nothing in it but sleep?*

While no true winged demon exists, it is likely those legends refer to the Glider Demon. As with other demons, it is the jewel which causes fear, not the beasts shadow, though to behold one of these fearful monsters is to understand how these stories began.

Glider Demon

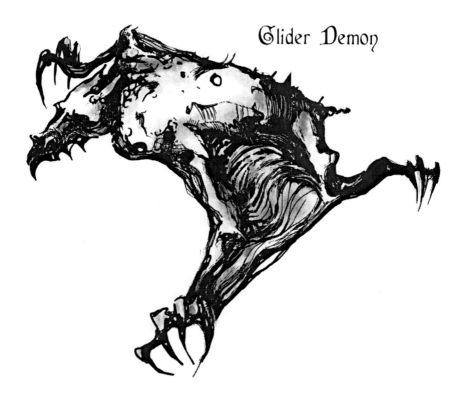

Like a falling leaf, the Glider Demon comes to rest far from where it starts. There are various methods of countering this fearsome skill.

While some will tell you that piercing the membrane which runs from the beasts forearms to the hind claws is critical to the success of fighting this foe

New Freedoms, New Problems

Life as a Blue was a vast improvement. Blues did not have a dormitory supervisor to approve, or more likely disapprove, their every action. They lived with two or three others of their rank on the upper floors, mainly under their own supervision. When Marick had told him this during one of their roof top training sessions, Garet had looked at the younger Bane suspiciously.

"Doesn't that give certain Banes," he paused significantly, "more opportunities for getting into trouble?"

Marick had shaken his head sadly. "Not at all. In fact, it's easier to fool a Gold than a fellow Blue," he replied. "And I'm afraid that the lack of supervision means that revenge is often swift and painful," Marick said, then added in a forlorn tone, "In the case of innocent Banes, that revenge can be totally unfair!"

Garet had laughed, knowing that however many beatings Marick had received, they were not equal to the trouble he had caused.

The young Bane had been waiting for him at the door of the Black's dormitory when he returned from the Records room. He chided him for his lateness while Garet hurriedly packed his few belongings. Marick bundled up his bedding and led him up to the third floor of the Hall's west wing.

There, in a room that reminded Garet strongly of the one they had appropriated in Old Torrick, Marick dropped his blankets on a freshly turned mattress and said, "Now we'll have some fun!"

Over the next few weeks, Garet spent a considerable amount of energy avoiding Marick's plans for fun, all of which involved schemes to irritate his superiors. The only ones, besides Mandarack of course, who seemed safe from his proposed pranks were Salick, whom he feared, Vinir, whom he seemed to like, and Tranix, whom he worshipped. The weapons trainer could do no wrong in Marick's eyes, and any Blue who complained about her after a hard training session was likely to wake up in the middle of the night drenched in cold water, or in the morning with their pants missing.

Garet also came to admire the no-nonsense Master. She drove him hard to improve his skill with the training staff, and soon moved him with a select few of the other Blues on to more complex weapons. Marick, who had also advanced, was given a shield-sword by Tranix, after a long lecture to the young Bane on how to use his speed and "trickiness" to his advantage in a battle. Marick listened, eyes wide and drinking in every word. Garet had never seen him so dedicated to anything other than mischief. Marick later took to practicing with the shield every moment he had to himself, causing Dorict, who had not advanced, to threaten to kick him out of the room just to save his neck from a misjudged swing.

The larger Banes received hooked spears or tridents, and Garet expected one of these weapons, since, being older, he matched the height of any of the others. Tranix saved his weapon for last. While the others watched, gingerly holding their own new weapons, the Master, in her chair today, pulled a square leather case off her desk and pushed herself over to Garet.

"It took me a long time to decide on what to assign to you, Garet," she said. "I spoke with Master Mandarack about your confrontation with the Shrieker at the Temple, and he praised your speed and agility."

There was a murmur from the assembled Blues. Rumours of the strange battle had been circulating among the lower ranks for months. Many refused to believe that two demons had been seen together, or that a mere Black had anything to do with defeating them. Garet felt their eyes on him, as they re-evaluated him in light of this confirmation. Tranix cleared her throat to get his attention again.

"Your abilities and your experience," she stressed the last word, "have convinced me to let you practice with a particularly difficult weapon, one that will take all your concentration and effort to master."

She had then pulled a coil of rope out of the bag and Garet groaned inwardly. It must be one of the hooked ropes that hung at the back of the training hall, behind the sand bags. Marick had told him that this was the very first weapon they had trained with, even before moving on to the simple training staff. Someone snickered behind him, and Garet realized that he wasn't the only one to recognize the weapon.

Tranix paused in her action, pinning with her hard, blue eyes the girl who had laughed. She then slowly drew the rest of the weapon out and several Blues, Garet included, gasped. There was no triple hook on the end of the rope. Instead, one end was connected to a heavy iron weight, studded with short spikes. The other end was tied to a short hafted weapon of some kind. Taking the wooden handle in his hand, Garet realized it looked familiar. Turning it over, he knew where he had seen it before. It was like a smaller version of the rock pick he had used to break stone on the farm. The metal head of the one he now held had two sides: one was a point a hand and a half long, shaped like a bird's beak, though more curved, and the other side was shorter, a squared snout of metal coming quickly to a heavy point. He hefted the thing. At least this was lighter than the tool he remembered, and its short handle would give him some control.

Tarix picked up the other end of the rope, letting the spiked weight dangle. "I hear that you are a master at throwing rocks." Marick grinned, leaving no doubt as to the source of her information. "This weapon requires both speed and accuracy." She smiled grimly at him. "Or the wielder is likely to be its first victim."

After that morning, Garet received special instruction in the rope-hammer, as Tarix called it, in the grey hours before breakfast. He would often come late to the table, sweating and bruised. Marick, who had managed only a few training cuts, was sympathetic, in his own way.

"Don't worry, Garet," he said one morning as Garet groaned into his seat, holding his elbow. "All you have to do is beat yourself with that Bane-killer in front of any demon we encounter and Dorict and I will attack the beast while it watches in amazement."

"If you don't cut my head off swinging your own weapon!" Dorict sourly observed. His lack of fitness and poor coordination had kept him at the training staff level with a crew of new Blue Sashes. Garet resolved to take him up to the roof to practice, as Marick had done for him. He didn't like the thought of the quiet boy, who was always ready to patiently answer his questions about the Banehall and the City, being left behind.

Marick didn't answer. He was staring open-mouthed at the front of the dining hall. Mandarack had just entered and was walking to his usual place at the end of the high table. Salick followed him, and, with a start, Garet realized what had caught Marick's attention.

Salick was wearing a gold sash!

She followed Mandarack to his place at the table, laying down some papers she had been carrying for him. Stiff as a spear and her eyes straight forward, she walked back past the whispering Masters, and under the unfriendly eyes of Master Adrix, to sit at the end of the Gold table. The nearest Golds shifted away, perhaps mindful of Adrix's displeasure. Salick silently began to tear off a piece of bread, ignoring the empty chairs around her. She loosened up, though, when Vinir and a few other Greens came over to slap her back and offer congratulations.

"That must be the fastest promotion to Gold in the history of the Hall!" Marick whispered. "Not that she doesn't deserve it. If a fool like Farix can wear the Gold, why shouldn't someone who has some sense?"

Neither Dorict nor Garet bothered answering the question. The glares coming from Adrix and his party were eloquent enough. Garet hoped he wouldn't single out Salick in the same way he had humiliated Garet on his first night in the Hall. The Hallmaster, however, did not attack Salick directly. His reply came, instead, in the form of a new rule.

Farix read out an announcement that night at supper.

"By order of the Hallmaster, all promotions will be first submitted for his approval from this day forth." Farix's voice had broken slightly on the last part, and Adrix motioned him to read it again. When he had finished, the flustered Gold sat down, the paper still clutched in his hand. There was silence in the hall, as much among the Masters as the lower ranks filling the long tables.

Garet saw Master Relict look over at Vinir, sitting forlornly with the other Greens, all hope of a quick promotion to Gold probably crushed in her. Relict sat back and stroked his beard with one hand while drumming on the table with the other. Seated beside him, Mandarack reached over to quiet the drumming fingers and spoke softly to him.

"Not all the Masters will approve of this. Even Adrix's toadies might think twice," Marick observed. The meal was completed in an unnatural silence.

As a Gold, Salick's training was solely at the discretion of her Master. She often had the time to stroll in the gardens of the plaza after supper and would sit and talk with Garet when she met him on these walks. Two weeks after her promotion, they were walking among the small trees, now mostly bare of leaf, talking of the changes in the Banehall.

"Adrix is a fool," Salick said bluntly. "He alienates the King with his demands, and he splits the Banehall with his petty rules!" She slowed to wait for Garet to catch up. He had grazed his shin with the spiked ball at practice and had a noticeable limp. Master Tarix had denied him the use of the padded armour used by some Blues lest he rely on it and become less careful. As a result, each new skill he developed with the rope-hammer was accompanied by a new set of bruises.

"Not only the Banehall," Garet said. Salick turned to listen. "Haven't you noticed that the people of the city are treating the Banes differently?" he asked.

Salick shook her head. "Aside from these walks, I rarely get out into the wards anymore. Mandarack has me searching through the records." She grinned at Garet. "So if I start shouting at you, I'm not angry, it's just a habit I've picked up from talking to Master Arict."

Garet smiled, remembering the old Master and her poor hearing. "Well, they are. Marick is trying to show me the Wards."

Salick stopped, her hands on her hips.

"Only on the Temple days," he hastily added.

Salick nodded and resumed her walking. "I suppose it's a good idea. Most children who come to the Banehall already know the general layout of the city, and their home Ward as well as they know their own fingers." They stopped and sat at their favourite bench, a wide stone seat surrounded by fragrant, trailing junipers.

"I'm just concerned by your choice of guides," she continued tartly. "I'm sure Marick knows every wine shop and alley in Shirath, but that's not all you need to know!" She leaned back, her hands behind her back for support and looked over at Garet.

"What else do I need to know?" Garet demanded. "And who else would be my guide?" He held his breath, waiting for her answer.

"I suppose I should," Salick replied casually. "I'm almost done with the Master's research, so we can start tomorrow, after lunch, if," she added slyly, "you can give up a session or two of inflicting pain on yourself with that menace you call a weapon."

"I think I could," Garet replied, smiling. "I don't have much in the way of studies right now." This was true. At Marick's and Dorict's insistence, he had already "corrected" the two Blue Sash texts, *The Rules of the House* and *The Tactics of Demons*. The process of rewriting them had made them familiar enough for Tarix to test him on that knowledge. She had so far withheld approval for him to start on the Green Sash books. He looked curiously at the young woman beside him and asked, "What were you looking for in the records? Maybe I can help you search."

Salick sat up straighter. "No, I don't think you can, at least not without Master Mandarack's permission." She brushed invisible dust off her new sash. "I'll have it done by tomorrow afternoon, anyway." The late autumn air was calling forth clouds of steam from their breath and they soon returned to the Banehall, arms wrapped around themselves for warmth.

By the next day, Garet's leg was much better. Dorict had helped him wrap it in cloth strips soaked in an herbal concoction provided by Master Tarix. She often tended to minor training accidents herself, rather than send an injured Blue to the infirmary. Marick claimed it was because she cared so much for her students. Dorict, however, was of the opinion that the Training Master was afraid the physician would order one of them to take a day or two off from training.

Garet waited for Salick in the entrance hall, near the passage leading to the Master's rooms. Looking down that corridor, he saw Salick speaking with Mandarack. He gave her a slip of paper that she tucked into the top of her boot.

"What did Master Mandarack want?" Garet asked as they passed through the gates. The plaza was quiet in the middle of the day; many of Shirath's citizens were out gleaning the last of the late crops or driving the herds to graze off the stubble of the already-harvested wheat fields before the snows came. Salick didn't answer for a moment. When they had walked some distance from the gates of the Hall, she rounded on him furiously.

"Don't you have any sense?" she hissed. "I thought you were more clever!"

"I can be clever," he said quietly, "if I know what's going on!"

Salick looked around. The only people close enough to hear were a trio of old men diligently arguing a point in their lawn-bowling game. She waved him further into the plaza before continuing.

"Mandarack asked me to take a message to his brother," she said, her voice still low, "and to keep my eyes open and report back to him on what's happening in the city."

"So this trip was only a blanket to cover your mission for Mandarack?" He couldn't keep the disappointment out of his voice.

"Yes. No!" Salick said, and then stopped to turn and face Garet directly, hands on her hips. "The Master asked me to do this after I told him of our plans." She tapped the leg that hid the letter. "This must be important. We both know the situation is getting worse in the Hall."

Garet nodded. Adrix's rules were concentrating all the power of the Banehall in his own hands. He had lately sent a formal message to the king, delivered by an embassy of his supporting Masters, demanding a reply to the list of changes he had sent at the beginning of the fall. The King had not yet replied to those demands. The skin on the back of Garet's neck prickled, and feeling eyes on his back, he turned quickly to see the old men looking at them, shaking their heads and muttering.

Salick followed his gaze. "What you said last night was true." The old men turned back to their game. "People are treating us differently. I always felt that the citizens of Shirath, well, 'owned' me." She looked to Garet to see if he understood. Seeing his questioning look, she continued. "I mean they were proud of us, like parents who depend on their children for support." She shook her head. "We were their children. Now they look at us as if they are the children, and we Banes are their parents," she said. "Angry parents."

Garet thought this over. Salick was right. Walking in the plazas, or watching people deliver food and stores to the Banehall, he sensed a resentment aimed at anyone wearing a Bane's sash.

Both were now silent, wrapped in their concerns as they walked together, shoulders nearly touching, up over the centre bridge and into the Palace plaza. Garet couldn't help but notice how crowded that plaza was, in contrast to the Banehall side. The stalls in the market were bustling with activity. Rows of worshippers lined up before the temples, and the Palace gardens were full of richly dressed people enjoying one of the last fine days of the year.

Salick led him through the gardens towards the Palace. They passed some workers raising an awning over one of the stages that were used by anyone from musicians to astrologers. She shook her head. "Why would anyone set up a theatre when it's so cold at night?" she asked the air around her.

A theatre. Dorict had explained to him that storytellers in Shirath acted out their tales on a platform, like children playing out their stories in the street. He had not yet seen such a thing, but he hoped they were better than the regular storytellers he had once set so much hope in. After much pressing, Marick had taken him to a small courtyard surrounded by wine shops and bakeries. There, a storyteller had been spinning his tales for a small, indifferent audience. He was an older man, his blue tunic stained with wine and Heaven knew what else. His words were so mumbled and slurred that Garet could not make any sense of his tale. The story had eventually dissolved into belches and then snores and the activity of the courtyard had continued without noticing.

Marick had wrinkled his nose at the smell of the old man. "There's only a few of these solitary tellers who are worth listening to. The best are in the theatre troupes." He had then pulled Garet out of the courtyard, anxious to be about his own business.

"If they're so bad, why do they keep at it?" Garet had asked. He pulled away from Marick's hand to turn back towards the courtyard. The old man was slumped against the wall, half slid off his stool.

"Avoiding real work, I guess," Marick had answered, with reluctant admiration.

"Do you think we could see this theatre?" he asked Salick as she skirted the east wing of the Palace to get to the Ward gates beyond.

"If we have time." She hesitated and then continued, "Garet, I have a personal errand to do as well." She looked at him to judge his reaction. "I hope you don't mind; you'll still get to see more of the city."

"Not at all," he replied. He was feeling more and more like an afterthought.

They approached the gate for the Palace Ward, directly behind the main wing of the Palace. From the maps Marick had shown him, he knew this Ward was much smaller than the others, and unlike them, did not stretch as far as the outer wall of the city. Marick informed him that it held the warehouses needed by the King's trading missions and housing for his retainers and servants. A full five Palace guards, breastplates and helmets brilliant in the sun, eyed them as they passed. Garet wondered if he imagined the disapproval in their gaze.

"So many now," Salick said, mostly to herself. She looked back at the guards and shook her head.

She turned to the right and skirted the edge of the small plaza common to all the Ward entrances. A lane led them between the wall and a row of narrow, brightly painted townhouses. After a short walk, they came to an angled compound and a small, open gate. Inside, in a triangular yard formed by the intersection of the ward and plaza walls, young men and women lounged on benches, talked, shouted, and practiced with their quick swords.

Duelists, Garet thought. Why would Salick come here? Was this Mandarack's task, or her own? The rasp of thin steel blades sliding over each other echoed off the high walls, but all quieted and died out as the duelists noticed Garet and Salick standing inside the gate. There was much muttering and dark looks among the knots of men and women. The pairs who had been kicking up the dust of the yard with their sparring now lowered their swords and joined their fellows against the walls. Salick stiffened her back.

There's something different about them, he thought, looking at their sullen, staring faces. Perhaps it was their attitude. He had seen a few duels in the months since his arrival, especially on his travels with Marick. But at the time, it did not seem to have anything to do with him or the Banehall.

"Why do they hate us?" Garet whispered to Salick.

She whispered back without turning her head from those staring eyes. "Part of it is the fight between Adrix and the King. The other part is older and harder to explain." She paused for a moment and deliberately turned away to face Garet, her back towards the Duelists.

"They play with swords and risk their lives in silly duels, but they all know that if a demon came into this place, all their skill, all their swords would be useless." Her lips twisted in a tight smile. "Every time they see a Bane's sash, they are reminded of how brittle their courage really is."

As Garet tried to puzzle this out, he saw Salick's cousin, Draneck, detach himself from a group of his companions and walk reluctantly up to them. Salick, seeing Garet's gaze, turned to face her cousin.

"What do you want, Banes?" Draneck asked in a loud voice. "I don't think you're welcome here."

Salick scowled at him, but Garet suddenly realized what had changed about the Duelists: the young man, and all the other men and women in the yard were wearing sashes! A narrow band of purple cloth, edged in red, cut across Draneck's chest and held the sheath of the sword bumping at his hip.

"Draneck," Salick snapped, "what under Heaven are you wearing?" She pointed at the sash.

Draneck smirked. "Do you like it? It's a favour from the King." He turned and waved a hand, indicating everyone else in the yard. "His majesty wished to recognize the loyalty," he stressed the word, "of the Duelist's Guild." He touched the sash. "King Trax even allowed us to wear the royal colour."

"And the red?" Salick asked tightly.

"For our willingness to shed our blood for the King," a new voice replied. Another Duelist, followed by several others at a short distance had joined Draneck. With a shock, Garet recognized the leader as the young, long-haired man that Draneck had fought in the Temple plaza, Shoronict. Now the taller man draped his arm around Draneck's shoulder and faced the Banes. "Surely the Banehall's demands don't include keeping all the colours for themselves?"

His friends laughed and Garet noticed that most of the duelists had gathered behind Draneck and Shoronict. He stepped closer to Salick and tried to look confident.

"Draneck," Salick said, ignoring Shoronict and the men and women grouped behind him. "Your father asked me to tell you that it's time you returned home, time that you left these games and took up your duties." She looked around the small yard with disdain and several Duelists lowered their own eyes in response. Shoronict merely glared and stepped forward.

Draneck grabbed his arm to stop him from advancing on the Banes. His tone was cold. "Tell my father that this is my home now. If he thought this was a passing fancy, he is mistaken." Several of his friends nodded their heads and murmured in agreement. Draneck's voice rose. "Tell him that, unlike the Banes, I know my 'duties'." He was yelling now, his face red and the muscles of his neck standing out. "And unlike you Banes, I serve the people of Shirath, and the King!"

The duelists exploded into cheers behind him, and Garet took advantage of the chaos to pull Salick out the gate and down the lane. The noise continued behind them, coalescing into a chant: "Our swords for the King! Our swords for the King!"

Salick allowed herself to be guided back to the Ward's main gate before she pulled away from Garet's grasp. Clearly shaken, she strode out of the Ward and kept walking until she found an isolated bench in the cold shadow of the Palace. She sat down, and Garet was surprised to see tears running down her face.

"Uncle will be so upset," she said, brusquely wiping her cheeks with the back of her sleeve. She looked up at Garet and sighed. "He raised me, after my...father...became a..." The word 'father' seemed to trip up her speech, and she spat it out after a moment's struggle. She shivered in the shade but made no move to leave the bench and return to the sunnier parts of the plaza. Garet sat quietly beside her.

"My father was like yours, only worse," Salick told him, her long braids hanging forward to hide her face from him. He leaned forward a bit to see her eyes. They were closed.

"He was a braggart and a bully, but he was also a man of power." She sighed, and then straightened up, still looking away from Garet. "He beat me, and my brothers and sisters. My mother died when I was born." Her voice broke. "It was my fault, I suppose."

Unsure of what to say, Garet put a gentle hand on her shoulder. She didn't pull away.

"My father was Lord of the Third Ward, the one with all the potters and coppersmiths."

Garet remembered the pure sound of ringing hammers and the deep hum of the spinning pottery wheels as Marick had dragged him past open courtyards on their way to wheedle sweets from one of that Ward's bakers. He nodded at Salick to continue.

"He was a drunkard and a womanizer, especially after my mother was gone. Finally, the King, Trax's father, wouldn't stand for it any more." She wiped her eyes again. "The people of the Ward were complaining, and he never held court or helped in the greater work of the city, so he was removed as Lord." She looked up at the windows of the palace; their glass eyes were black. "He killed himself, or maybe fell drunk off the city wall down into the herd yards. I was already a Green." Her smile was bitter. "I suppose he made me a Bane, with the beatings and threats and all. But for years before his death, I had lived with my uncle. He took all of us in, with the King's permission, and moved us to the Sixth Ward, behind the Temple."

A chill breeze ghosted along the walls of the Palace and lifted the hairs on the back of Garet's neck. Had his father also made a Bane of him?

Salick rubbed her face. "Come on. We both look a mess!" She led him to a small fountain by the Palace walls, perhaps put there for the servants to draw water. She washed her face. Garet followed suit, gasping at the bite of the cold, shadowed water. He blotted his face with his sleeve, as much for warmth as for dryness and looked up at Salick.

She was sitting on the curb of the fountain, looking back at him.

"I don't think I've cried like that for years, since my Uncle took me away." She pushed back a braid. "I don't think I could have cried with anyone else, Garet."

"Why not?" he asked, and belatedly realized his question should have been, 'why me?'

She looked down at the dark, reflecting water. "To Master Mandarack, I'm the apprentice he relies on, to Marick,

Dorict, and the others, I'm the one who's always sure of herself." She dipped a finger in the cold water and moved it in small circles. Larger circles expanded from her touch, and Garet watched the ripples continue to the far rim of the fountain.

"But you came from outside," she continued, still looking down. "I didn't have to be anything for you. And once I saw your father, I knew that you were like me, that you might understand what I'd gone through." She raised her eyes and smiled slightly. Her fingers rested on the curb and drops of water fell back into the pool. "That's why I was so hard on you at first, you know?" She raised her eyebrows in question, but Garet could only shake his head, not sure of her meaning. She sighed. "Well, I always felt that if I had been a boy, I could have stood up to my father. Or I would have pleased him more." She paused for the briefest moment. "I thought that not being a girl would have made him love me."

She stood up suddenly and looked off to the gate of the Third Ward. At this distance, only the shapes of people could be made out, none of the details. Salick turned to Garet and continued. "But your father treated a son with the same contempt mine treated a daughter, and at first I hated you for not being strong enough to make the difference, instead of realizing that nothing would have mattered." Tentatively, she moved beside him and laid her hand on his. "That's why you're the only person who could see me cry like that."

"Salick, I..." Garet began and then fell silent. Salick had said all that needed to be said. He nodded at her, patted her hand awkwardly and stood up. Silently, but with a deeper comfort in each other's company, they walked back into the sunlight edging around the Palace.

The Mechanicals

The pair remained silent as Salick led him across the Palace plaza towards the Temple. There were fewer people on this side of the plaza, and they moved slowly, their eyes on the ground before them. Many men and women walked in the gardens, travelling the twists and turns of the patterned walkways as if in a great, slow dance. Garet paused, captured by their peaceful movements.

Salick smiled and said, "Don't worry, we'll come back another day." Tugging lightly on his sleeve, she added, "We still have one task ahead of us. An official one, this time."

Garet reluctantly followed, skirting the smallest Temple on the north end of the complex. The white walls were blinding in the sun, making them waver before their eyes. The round blue-tiled roofs seemed to float above those blazing walls rather than rest on them. Salick had to keep her hand on his arm to guide him around Temple-goers as he refused to take his eyes off the buildings to look where he was going. The last of the Ward gates in the wall surrounding the plaza was only half open. A knot of men and women, most uncharacteristically, at least for Shirath, wearing drab grey tunics were working under the orders of men in the subdued leather and brass armour of Ward guards.

One stout guard was directing the group with a stream of splendidly abusive language. "Jaws bite you! Pull harder there!" He pushed a fellow guard into the effort. "All of you Beast-born weaklings, pull!"

189

The chains they had attached to the cross beams of the gate groaned as they tightened with the workers' efforts. After a squealing protest, and an ominous sound of snapping metal, the gate began to open wider. A cheer went up and the supervising guard removed his helmet, the brass scuffed and the plume bent, to wipe his brow.

"Gonect!" Salick called. "What have you done to the gates?" She smiled at the short man whose prominent belly strained at the straps of his armour.

He tossed his helmet through the open window of the gatehouse and grinned at the Banes. "Salick! I haven't seen you in weeks. And a Gold now!" He enfolded her in a bear-like hug. "Your uncle will be happy to see you again," he added, holding her at arms length. "And, for your information, these gates are trying to recover from another of our Ward Lord's brilliant ideas." He pointed to a set of bronze springs fixed to both the wall and the gates themselves. "Those are supposed to let one guard open and close the gates more quickly." He released Salick and waved angrily at the contraption. "But they don't allow us to open the clawed thing at all!"

Salick laughed and said, "Don't worry, Gonect. I have to see Lord Andarack today—as well as my uncle," she added, to forestall the guard's protest, "and I'll pass on your high opinion of his latest project." She turned to Garet. "Gonect, this is a friend of mine, Garet." She pulled him forward. "He's from the Midlands."

Gonect eyed him appraisingly. "So this is the boy Master Mandarack brought back." He held out a hand. "Welcome to Shirath, lad."

Garet grasped his hand and was rewarded with a friendly, if bone-crushing, clasp.

"I'm glad to meet you, Guardsman," Garet said, keeping the pain out of his voice.

Gonect released his hand and looked meaningfully at Salick. "A strong one, eh. And well-spoken too. You better keep him happy, or we'll steal him for the ward guards!" he laughed, slapping Garet on the back and propelling him several feet.

At least, thought Garet, as Salick steadied him, *the man shows none of the resentment and anger I've noticed in many other citizens of Shirath.*

A rattle of chains signified that the workers in grey were loading their equipment into a hand cart, ready to leave. Gonect waved the Banes on and turned to thank the workers.

Salick nodded to Garet. They crossed the small entrance plaza and took the left-hand lane. A high, blank wall loomed on their left. On their right, narrow townhouses, similar to what he had seen in the Palace Ward, sported many small windows, the bars across them mostly swung open, with boxes of herbs fixed beneath. Old men and women sat in the doorways, minding the children that climbed past them to run up and down the street. A boy no taller than Garet's waist almost ran him down with an iron hoop he rolled in great wobbles over the cobblestones.

Salick waved or stopped to say hello to many of the ancients on the steps. She smiled more often than Garet had ever seen. *The Banehall might be her home now*, he thought, *but this is the home of her childhood.* He looked around, wondering what a childhood spent surrounded by other children would have meant to him. On their left, a red gate broke the long sweep of walls. Stopping in front of it, Salick examined a rope hanging down from above. It had a wooden handle on its dangling end, but its upper end looped over a hook and disappeared over the top of the gate. A small wooden plaque hung from the handle. On the plaque was painted a single symbol: "pull." Salick shrugged and cautiously pulled the rope. A bell sounded dimly inside and a door cut into the larger gate was opened before the clanging stopped. The guard who opened it looked with some alarm at the two Banes.

"There's no reason to fear," Salick hastened to tell him. "We are merely on Banehall business and need to see your Lord."

The guard nodded, his plume flipping back and forth sharply as he beckoned them inside the door. He bade them wait by the gate while he ran to the house and summoned his master. Garet looked around. The courtyard fronted an impressive house, wide and two stories tall. The other three sides of the court ended in blank walls. Nearly as big as the Banehall's courtyard, the space was almost filled with a jumble of unharnessed carts, two draft horses munching on heaps of hay, piles of wood and bricks, and a curious wheel-shaped device, its central shaft reaching up into the air to connect by a gear with a similar shaft coming through a hole in the house wall. Spokes came out from the machine, but its purpose was not apparent. The draft horses were yoked to these spokes, but seemed unconcerned by the strangeness of their condition.

The guard came trotting back and asked them to go ahead into the house on their own as the Lord was presently engaged. If they would wait in the great hall, he would see them there. As they walked across the crowded yard, the gate opened behind them, and the grey-clad workers they had seen earlier came in, pulling their handcart full of chains and tools.

Once inside, the warmth of the house engulfed them. A servant was waiting, a silent, bent old man. He led them at an arthritic pace down the hall and through a stone arch into the great hall. Here, as Garet knew from Marick, a Lord would entertain, instruct his servants and retainers, organize trade missions with the merchants of his Ward, and hold court to punish or reward his subjects. But nothing in this explanation had prepared him for Lord Andarack's great hall.

It was as cluttered and bizarre as the courtyard. The timber shaft from outside pierced a roughly cut-out hole in the brick wall, connecting to what seemed to be a cider-press. The hearth was surrounded by sand-filled baskets, and several braziers sent smoke up to the high ceiling, explaining the warmth they felt on entering the house. Long tables, to be used for feasting, now stood haphazardly here and there, their scarred surfaces covered with tools, drawings, and half-eaten meals. What should have been the Lord's seat of judgement had been replaced on its dais by an anvil. More of the men and women in grey were already here, some hammering at metal, others shaping it with files and grindstones, and still more poring over plans and waving their hands at each other. Garet looked at Salick. Her mouth had dropped open as she looked around the room, eyes blinking rapidly as if she didn't trust them. *Well,* thought Garet, *at least this time I'm not the only one stunned.*

One of the men came over to them, wiping his hands on his grey tunic before holding one out in greeting. "Banes! You are unexpected but welcome." He stopped and looked carefully. "Salick? Is that you?" He beamed at her and pumped her hand enthusiastically. "This is a pleasant surprise. Have you been to see your uncle? Not yet? Well, I imagine he'll be just as pleased as I am." While he talked he led them to a side table that held several pots of tea and many cups, a few still unused.

"I have a message from Master Mandarack, my Lord," Salick said, her eyes still sliding from the man to the chaos of the room. "Lord Andarack, what have you done to your hall?" she blurted out, and immediately coloured as she realized how impolite she sounded.

The Ward Lord, however, took no offense. Looking him over, Garet saw that he was as tall as his brother, but thicker at the waist. Unlike his brother, his hair still had streaks of blond among the grey. He laughed and poured them both a cup of tea. "It is a mess, isn't it?" He handed Garet his cup and motioned them to three-legged stools by the table. "But the Mechanical's school was overcrowded, and there were several things we needed to build that wouldn't fit." He gave Salick her tea, then poured a cup for himself. "Dasanat! Watch the colour of the glass!" he yelled, jumping up and spilling the greater portion of his drink.

A young woman near the hearth looked up and nodded. Part of the hearth had been closed in with hasty brick work to form a glass-blower's furnace. Dasanat carefully examined the glob of molten glass on the end of her pipe. Shaking her head, she placed that end carefully back in the furnace before standing back and wiping the beads of sweat from her face.

Andarack sat back down and resumed his conversation with the Banes, but kept an eye on the furnace. "Forgive me, but if the temperature is wrong, the beakers made from that glass will shatter when heated." He reluctantly turned back to them. "I thank you for your troubles, Salick and..." he paused, his eyes on Garet.

"My name is Garet, Lord Andarack." He stood and sketched his best bow. "Your brother brought me here from the Midlands."

Andarack's eyes lit up. "Did he indeed?" He grabbed Garet's elbow and steered him to where several of the hall's chairs had been placed beneath the narrow windows. "Sit here," he directed and quickly sat beside him. He gently turned Garet's head this way and that, examining his black hair and brown eyes in the shafts of sunlight. "Is it true that the field snakes of the Midlands carry their young wrapped around them until they are grown?" he asked eagerly.

"I don't know, sir," Garet was forced to admit. "I lived in the foothills on the eastern borders of the Plains. We had no field snakes there." He paused, unsure what else to say.

"The foothills, hmmm?" Andarack said. He leaned back in the chair and tugged at a strand of his greying hair. "What do you know of the rocks in that area?"

Garet panicked for a moment, thinking for a wild moment that Andarack wanted him to show off his skill at throwing stones, but then realized that the Ward Lord was speaking of rocks in general.

Salick's patience announced its end with a cleared throat and a slight stamping of her foot to gain their attention. "Lord Andarack, I'm sure Garet can tell you much of the stones on his farm, which seemed to be all stones to me, but your brother said that this was an urgent message." She removed the slip of paper from her boot and presented it impatiently to Andarack.

"Of course, of course," he said, unfolding the letter and stepping with it into the light of the window. "But you and I, Garet, will have to speak of those foothills soon." He read the message quickly, then went over it again, pulling at the strand of his long hair. When he had finished the second reading, he frowned and folded the letter, putting it securely inside his tunic. He turned to the Banes again. "Your Master, my older brother, asks much, Salick." He held up a hand to stop her before she could rise to Mandarack's defense. "I know. What he asks is necessary," he added, voice lowered. "Though very dangerous, especially in these distrustful times." He looked at her carefully. "Tell my brother that I agree, but that I will need the help of a few Banes who can be trusted." He gave a slight nod of his head in dismissal. "Come again tomorrow, and we'll get started. Now, you'll excuse me for not showing you out, but she is always too impatient with the heating." He turned back to the bustle and noise of the hall, making his way to where Dasanat was again examining the ball of molten glass.

Salick shook her head and looked at Garet. He shrugged his shoulders in response, and they left the Ward Lord's house.

When they were standing in the lane again, Salick asked Garet if he would mind returning to the Banehall on his own so that she could have a private visit with her uncle. He readily agreed. Draneck's refusal to return home would be a hard piece of news for her uncle to hear. Salick would not want any outsiders there to witness his grief. He walked back to the Banehall, thinking of what he had seen at Lord Andarack's. The ability to surprise, he decided, must run in that family.

Later that evening, long after supper was ended and the evening patrols had left, Salick came to the room the three Blues shared. She tapped on the door, and when Dorict opened it, slipped quickly inside.

"I need to talk to all three of you," she said. Dorict shot her a worried look, but Marick rubbed his hands together joyfully.

"At last, Salick," he said. "You can tell us what's going on!" He pulled her over to sit on one of the room's rickety chairs. Dorict and Garet took the other two chairs while Marick perched nervously on the edge of his rumpled bed. "Go on!" he pleaded.

"You've all three proved yourselves to be..." she eyed Marick and searched for the a term that could include the young Bane, "...loyal."

Squatting on his bed, Marick executed a graceless bow.

With a sigh, Salick continued, "That loyalty will have to be as strong as a Basher's hide tonight. Master Mandarack wants us to assist him in preparations for defending this city, preparations that Adrix refuses to make!"

Garet held up a hand. "Wait a minute, Salick. Preparations for what? Does Master Mandarack intend to take over the Banehall?" Dorict's mouth fell open, and Marick leaned forward expectantly.

"No, he doesn't," Salick replied, regret evident in her tone. "But the Master feels that the way the demons attack this city is changing," she continued, her eyes challenging them. "And we must change with it!"

Marick sat back again. "What changes?" he asked suspiciously. "Demons appear and we kill them!"

"The two demons travelling together," Dorict supplied.

"We didn't need to change to kill one and chase off the other," Marick replied.

"The lack of fear near the Shrieker at the temple," Garet added.

"It still didn't save the beast!" Marick protested.

"And the demons appearing in the Midlands, in case you've forgotten," Salick concluded.

The small Bane held up his hands. "All right, all right! I know that things have been a bit different, but what can we do except deal with every demon that appears?"

"If we can't sense them, we can't find them," Garet said grimly.

"Except by following the bodies," Dorict added. He eyed his friend. "Marick, you're the last person I would have thought to be against change."

"Maybe it's because I've already had more changes in my life than even Garet here," Marick replied ruefully. He grinned. "Besides, chaos is no fun if it's not of your own making. It's harder to steal the furniture when someone is pulling the rug out from under your feet!"

Salick smiled at him. "Knowing you, you'll find a way to steal that rug before it's left the floor." Her voice became serious again. "The Master's brother is helping us. We are to go to his workshop tomorrow after breakfast."

"But we'll miss Master Tarix's practice," Marick protested.

"Master Tarix is aware of what's going on," Salick replied. "She will train with you when she coaches Garet, before breakfast."

Dorict looked unhappy at this news, but Marick nodded, relieved. Salick rose to go just as a bell sounded loudly from the floors below.

"A call for reinforcing the Ward patrols!" Marick cried. He darted for the door but was restrained by Salick. "No, listen to the pattern. It's only for Golds and any Masters left in the Hall." She opened the door, but turned to glare at them. "Stay here, all of you." She slammed the door in her haste to answer the alarm.

It was a long evening for the three Blues left behind. Dorict and Garet made an attempt to quiz each other on the House Rules text, but were too distracted to concentrate. Marick strapped on his shield and battled the air, well away from the nervous Dorict. By the time the candles had burned low, they heard the sound of returning Banes in the halls below. Marick had almost persuaded his friends to join him in spying out some information when a knock sounded on their door, and Garet opened it to reveal a tired and dispirited Salick.

"It's bad," she said, stumbling into the room. She collapsed on the chair Garet had been sitting in moments before.

He hurriedly poured a cup of water from the jug and handed it to her.

Salick gulped it down and held the empty cup out for more. When she had finished, she wiped her mouth slowly and looked at the three Blues. There were shadows under her eyes, and her nose was red.

"It's bad," she repeated. "A Basher got into those crowded three-story courtyards in the Fourth Ward." She rubbed her eyes and sniffed. "The patrol had no sense of it, until they heard the screams and the walls coming down. The people nearest it didn't run, or even try to hide. Sandact said they just stood there, as if they had no fear at all." She looked at Garet meaningfully, and he remembered the pull he had felt from the demon near the ruined Temple market.

"There are many dead, including two Banes, Shonirat and Dalict," she continued, her voice flat with fatigue. "Both Golds," she added for Garet's information.

She had not needed to, for Garet knew them both. They had often shown up to get in some extra practice before breakfast while Garet worked with Tarix on mastering the rope-hammer. They had both been friendly and curious about his unusual weapon. Dalict had even been willing to show him something of wielding a trident. Now they were dead. He put his head in his hands and rubbed his eyes.

"They died when the building collapsed," Salick said. "By the time they knew where the demon was, there was already so much damage that the walls were falling down. Over a hundred people are dead or missing. The Ward guards and Lord Andarack's mechanicals are shifting the rubble now."

She stood up and walked to the window. This high up, one could see over the plaza wall into the Wards. Lights appeared in window after window as the terrible news spread through the city. Salick let the curtain fall but did not turn.

Dorict asked, "Is the Basher . . ?" but his voice skipped and he couldn't finish the sentence.

"Yes," Salick replied, still facing the covered window. "Master Relict pushed a section of wall down on it. Vinir made the kill."

"Good!" Marick cried, jumping off the bed. "Adrix will have to make her a Gold now." He restrained himself when he saw Salick's face. "I just meant that, well, at least some good..." he trailed off, then sat back down, arms folded and glum.

"Was Farix there?" Garet asked suddenly. He jumped up from his seat on his bed, hands balled into fists at his sides.

"No!" Salick spat out, her tone savage. "Adrix kept his favourites out of trouble, said they needed to 'protect the Hall in these dangerous times'."

"So he finally admits to the danger?" Dorict asked, unbelieving. The young Bane had not moved from his seat since Salick had entered the room.

"Not from the demons, Dorict," Salick told him. "He fears he might be challenged for control of the Hall if he leaves it or loses any of his followers to demons."

"Does a Hallmaster usually fight demons, Salick?" Garet asked.

"All Banes fight," Salick replied. She walked slowly back to the door. "Remember to meet me after breakfast, by the west bridge gate." She yawned, covering her mouth with a hand and leaning against the door. "If anything, this proves the need for Master Mandarack's plan." As Salick opened the door slightly and turned to slide through it, the yellow light from the lantern fixed at the head of the stairs glistened on her wet cheek. She closed the door softly behind her, as if any noise would be an offense against the heavy silence the Hall kept this night.

Plots and Swords

After a restless night, the three friends made their way down to practice in the gymnasium. Tarix was glum, and merely set them on familiar routines before leaving the room. They moved dispiritedly through their swings and thrusts until the bell signalled breakfast.

None of the usual chattering of young Banes filled the dining hall this morning. The heavy silence was broken only by the scrape of chair legs on the floor or the clink of a spoon against a bowl. As they entered, Dorict led Garet towards the Golds' table where a line of Banes of all ranks walked slowly past two empty chairs. As each Bane passed, he or she touched the sash draped over the back of each chair. Garet did the same as he passed by, letting his fingers run over the soft gold threads. Master Branet, who had trained both Dalict and Shonirat, sat at the high table beside Tarix, his face grey and his shoulders slumped.

When everyone in the hall had paid tribute to the fallen Banes and seated themselves in their appropriate sections, Adrix rose.

"Banes of Shirath," he began, his small eyes moving back and forth across the faces turned towards him. "We have but one question to answer on the day after this disaster, on the day after the worst loss of life to demon attack in a hundred years." He paused to let a murmur of anticipation pass. He suddenly slammed a hand down on the table in front of him. "That question is, who is to blame?" he shouted. The hall erupted into surprise and accusation.

Master Branet, shocked out of his grief, made to rise, but Tarix laid a restraining hand on his arm.

Adrix continued, one hand out to the empty chairs. "This disaster is the result of poor training, of Banes advanced too quickly, and under poor supervision."

The colour came back into Branet's face and he shook off the Training Master's hand.

"That is why I now must act for the good of the Hall. Why I must demand that not only must all promotions be approved by myself, but that some Banes lose the rank they now so undeservedly have." He sat back down and waved one hand. "Master Farix, read the list."

"Master Farix?" Marick hissed. Surely enough, when the smug young man came forward, holding a long slip of paper, he was wearing a red sash.

"The following Blues are hereby demoted back to the rank of Black," he said, and began a list of six names. Dorict's, Marick's and Garet's were the first three.

Garet fell back in his chair. *So fast,* he thought, *and so easily accomplished.* All that had to be done to steal away his efforts, his studies, his struggles to fit in, was his name on a piece of paper. He heard crying and saw one of the other Blues mentioned had laid her head on the table and was sobbing into her folded arms. Marick looked stunned, but Dorict, usually so calm, was fierce in his outrage.

"Farix!" he yelled over the chaos of every Bane either speaking or shouting. "Claws shred you before you take my sash!" He threw his plate to the floor and started to climb over the table to get at the smirking Master.

Marick hauled him back. "Not here, Dorict!" he whispered frantically to his friend. "Not now! But don't worry, we'll pick our own time and place."

Farix had worked his way through the Greens. Marick fumed to hear Vinir's demotion. "Just after killing a Basher! Adrix is mad!"

The new Master continued his list. He read out the names of four Golds who were sent back to the Green level, but surprisingly, Salick was not mentioned. He shifted the list in his hand and called out, "The following Masters are hereby stripped of the Red Sash and demoted to the Gold level." The hall hushed and took a collective breath, waiting for the names.

"Relict is demoted for dereliction of his duties in patrolling the Wards. He failed to track and kill a Basher Demon in time to prevent much loss of life," Farix intoned.

Relict sat stone-faced beside Mandarack. Vinir, who had come up behind his chair to speak, perhaps plead with him when her own name had been called, stood unbelieving beside him. Not a sound came from the assembled Banes.

"Tarix is demoted for undue speed in granting promotions and her present inability to fulfil her duties as a Bane," Farix continued.

Now it was Branet who stopped the Training Master from rising up on her crutches to answer this insult. In the silence that followed, the grief-stricken Master spoke in a voice that reached the Blues' table. "Wait, my friend. I have a feeling Master Farix is not yet done."

Adrix leaned forward and gave Branet a small nod of his head, a smile twisting his lips. "Thank you, Branet. There are a few more names." He waved at Farix to continue.

"Branet is demoted for the poor training of his apprentices which led to their tragic deaths. Bandat is demoted for not providing the Hallmaster with the names of candidates before promotions were awarded. And Pratax is demoted for ignoring the rules of this Hall." With that, he folded the paper and formally handed it to Adrix before returning to his place at the Hallmaster's side.

Now the hall erupted in noise, the Banes yelling questions at each other. "Why weren't Salick and Mandarack demoted?" Dorict shouted at his friends.

Although it was almost impossible to be heard, Garet shouted back. "I think he will, but not yet. Look at who he chose, all Masters and their Golds who favour Mandarack over Adrix." They looked to the table. All the demoted Masters were grouped around Mandarack, who leaned forward to listen to their demands. "Without their support at the head table, what can he do?" Garet said, and banged his plate to the floor to rest beside Dorict's. The spaces between the tables were littered with broken crockery. "Adrix will demote him as soon as the Hall adjusts to what happened today!"

The noise was dying as Bane after Bane looked to the Masters' table, waiting for a reaction. Mandarack had risen and raised his good arm above his head, calling for attention. Ignoring him, Adrix and his party got up to leave.

"Not yet, if you please Hallmaster!" Mandarack shouted, his voice rasping across the fading din. Adrix turned to face him across the length of the table, his stance polite, but the mocking smile still on his face.

"The Rules of the Shirath Banehall allow for the demotion of a Master only if a council of Masters is called and a vote taken." Mandarack turned to the assembled Banes. "I think that those who lost their sashes today for dereliction and breaking rules would like to know that no rules were broken by their own Hallmaster." He turned back to Adrix, and Garet recognized in the old man's stance the same fierce energy he had seen him project in his battles with demons.

Adrix said nothing. He turned, still smiling, and swept out of the dining hall. Chaos ruled as the Banes left the hall, arguing and shouting. Garet heard a Gold say to her fellow, "But we have to do something. Over a hundred citizens died last night. We failed, the Banehall failed, and unless we fix it, unless we pay for it somehow, we will be shamed in front of the people." Her friend's reply was lost as they joined the river of Banes flowing out into the halls.

Salick had cornered them before they could join the others leaving. "Follow me," she said, and led them to the high table. The humiliated Reds were echoing the arguments of their students.

"Mandarack," Branet shouted, "how can you just sit there? You must do what you did in Old Torrick's Hall." He waved angrily at the doorway through which Adrix had left. "Get rid of that pompous fool and take your place as Hallmaster!" He thumped a fist on the table in front of the old Bane for emphasis, making the cups tumble.

Mandarack did not stir or start at this outburst. He held up his hand and replied as if they were speaking of common matters. "What happened in Torrick was already happening when I arrived there." He fixed Branet with his eyes. "Master

Corix was an overwhelmingly popular choice, mainly because Furlenix never bothered to gather supporters. What argument there was focused on the method of change, not that change should occur."

Branet collapsed back in a chair, still muttering.

Mandarack continued. "If we act now, it won't be a coup; it will be a bloody civil war." He looked from one Master to another. "And while we are killing each other in this Hall, who will be protecting our city? We are still Banes."

The Masters looked at each other and reluctantly nodded at that undeniable statement. Only Branet protested. "But Mandarack, you heard what he said about them." He pointed to the sashes still draped over two empty chairs. "Dalict and Shonirat were good Banes, bright, hard-working. Adrix's words as much as said that they got themselves killed. They don't deserve that."

"No, Branet," Mandarack replied softly. "They do not, and neither do you, or Relict, nor any of you." He rose and beckoned to the waiting Banes. "Salick, take Garet, Dorict, and Marick to Lord Andarack's house and do as he instructs. Whatever happens in the Hall, finding a way to counter this new demon power is our paramount task." He paused in turning and added, "And take your weapons whenever you go out into the city." He turned to the Masters. "The council will meet," he smiled slightly, "as per the rules, after supper. As your duties allow, spend the day talking with others, trying to gauge how they feel. I will do the same."

The outside air was biting and tasted heavy, a sure sign that the first snow was on the way. Garet hoped his father and brothers had got in enough wood for the family to endure the cold of winter, then realized that he had not thought of them for some days. How could he forget? Guilt rose in him. His mother's face, strangely unfocused, floated before him and he leaned against the gate post and swallowed hard.

"Are you all right, Garet?" Dorict asked. Salick and Marick were half-way across the plaza, heading for the west bridge. The Bane's round face was still flushed with anger.

Garet shook his head. "It's nothing." He pushed off the wall and followed the others.

"Master Mandarack will make sure we keep our sashes," Dorict assured him.

"It's not that," Garet replied. "I'm worried about my mother and sister, what with winter coming on so soon." *There*, he thought, *I've admitted it to someone else.* His head felt strangely light after uttering the words.

Dorict mused for a dozen steps. "Why don't you send a letter to Boronict, at the Bangt Banehall? He'll have lists of all the people in the area, and the Three Roads outpost will still be under Bangt's control." The young Bane looked up at him thoughtfully. "I know I couldn't think if I didn't know what was happening to my family." He grimaced. "Well, most of them. I'm sure Boronict can get a message through for you."

"Dorict, you're a genius!" Garet yelled, and grabbed the shorter Bane in a bear hug. He released him and ran after Salick and Marick, leaving his startled friend to try and catch up. *A letter, of course,* he thought. He was already composing it in his mind when he caught up with the others.

"What are you happy about?" Marick asked sourly. Since breakfast he had been as downcast and angry as the others. He muttered constantly, planning his revenge.

"Nothing...oh Dorict just suggested I send a letter to my mother," he burst out, unable to contain his enthusiasm.

Marick smiled in spite of himself. "I guess Boronict could help you deliver it," he said, then his expression turned dark again. "I might go join the Bangt Hall myself, if we can't stop these fools."

Salick nodded in glum agreement. "I never thought I'd want to leave Shirath, but how can we stay? Especially if Adrix attacks..." She didn't finish the sentence but they knew she was afraid for Mandarack's sake.

In their low spirits, they barely noticed the other people in the plaza. Garet bumped into one, a fat merchant in an expensive green tunic, and said, "Oh, pardon sir."

"Look where you're going, Bane," the man snarled, and Garet drew back from the hate in his voice. "But I suppose we all know how blind you Banes are now," he continued, words dripping with contempt. "My best apprentice lived in that building until last night—when your incompetence killed her!" The man pushed past them, his jowls quivering with rage.

Garet stood open-mouthed until Salick gave him a little shake and said, "Don't take it to heart, Garet. A lot of people are angry over their loss today." She pulled him towards the bridge. "Say nothing to them, or we'll just make the situation, and their pain, worse." The guards at the bridge watched them sullenly as they passed though the gate and climbed the span.

At the Eighth Ward gate, Gonect greeted them quietly. "It's a sad day, Banes," he told them as they huddled just inside the Ward walls. On this side of the river, the wind was keener. "The funeral processions are already lining up at the temples." He nodded at the three domed buildings. Deep bells and the crying of women were carried to them on the cold wind. "Is it true that two Banes died as well?" he asked.

Salick nodded.

"Claws!" he swore softly. "Though it's a better death to fall defending your people than to fall drunk off a bridge, I suppose," he shook his head sadly.

Garet thought about it and was forced to agree. As a Bane, he faced the possibility of death with each demon encounter. But at least he would die usefully. He looked at Gonect and suddenly saw him as one soldier—or citizen—might see his fellow. Impulsively, he grabbed the guard's shoulder in sympathy.

Gonect looked up and smiled at him. "Ah, young Bane, there's no joy for any of us today, just company in grief." And he waved them on, shaking his head and wiping his nose on a leather-bound sleeve.

Salick did not say another word until she spoke to Andarack's door guard, asking again to be let into his presence. The great hall was quiet, only a single woman worked at the great press, and it was several minutes before Andarack appeared. Salick and Garet gasped when they saw him. The Ward Lord had aged ten years in the short time since they last saw him. His eyes were bloodshot, his long hair wild and greasy, his face grey; he greeted them distractedly. "Come," he said and led them out of the hall.

They walked past the expensive hangings on the corridor walls to a narrow, back hall ending in a dark, downward stair. Giving each Bane a small lamp, and taking one for himself, Andarack led the way down the steps. The lights danced among the greater shadows as they descended. One flight, two, three, Garet counted. The walls became moist with condensation. Marick purposefully scraped the brass base of his lamp along the stone. He heard Salick whisper fierce reprimands at the boy. *We must be far below the level of the street by now*, Garet realized, jumping at the noise. Andarack paused for a moment and leaned against the wall. Dorict took his lamp while Salick and Marick supported him. Garet looked around. Although he was last in line, he was sure he felt another presence hovering behind him.

"It's all right," Andarack said, wiping the sweat from his brow. A drop of water fell from overhead, extinguishing Dorict's lamp. He yelped and hurriedly re-lit it from Salick's lamp. The Ward Lord looked at them curiously. "Don't you feel it?" he asked, his eyes shining in the flickering light.

Garet sucked in his breath—the demon-fear! He reached for his rope-hammer, dangling awkwardly from the hook Tarix had given him to fix to his sash. Marick pulled at the flat leather case on his back, and Dorict yanked at the straps that bound his pole to Salick's trident.

Andarack held up a weak hand. "No, no! There is no need to prepare for battle, my friends." He waved down the last flight of steps gaping darkly before them. "The demon jewel from the Glider that, I believe, you two helped kill"—he nodded at Salick and Garet—"is down these stairs, in the old ice-rooms of this manor." He took back the lamp from Salick and beckoned them to follow.

The Banes looked at each other. No one outside the hall was supposed to know about the jewels and their power. Salick cleared her throat. "My Lord? How did you, ah, acquire the jewel?" Her voice squeaked, and Garet felt his own anxiety rise as they neared the bottom of the stairs.

Andarack's answer was barely audible. "Master Relict...delivered it... on my brother's..." he stopped talking and slumped against the wall. "Listen carefully, I can go no farther with you. Even having that cursed thing in the house has driven off all my workers except Dasanat." He smiled weakly. "She's a true mechanical. Nothing except her current project ever catches her attention." He pointed to a door at the bottom of the stairs and handed Salick an ornate, brass key. "There are instructions to follow...on the table inside." He waved off their hands. "Leave me to rest here a while and I'll be able to go back upstairs. No doubt...Dasanat has ruined the mix by now."

Reluctantly, they left the Ward Lord sitting on the stairs and climbed down the last dozen stairs to stand before the door. It was made of a single plank of oak, but the door was as wide as all four Banes standing side by side. "What a tower that tree must have been!" Dorict exclaimed, running his fingers over the ancient, blackened wood. "There's none like it these days." Iron bolts the size of their wrists affixed its hinges to the stone wall. Salick held out her lamp to the lock, a massive affair of brass and iron, and tried the key. It turned smoothly and she pulled back on the heavy door. Garet got his fingers around the edge and did the same. With a horrible groan that tickled their stretched nerves, the door swung open and they lifted their lamps to see inside.

Bones! Stacks of them were piled here and there in the low-arched room. Some looked almost human, but were deformed in some, subtle way. Others were monstrous, gigantic arms and legs ending in hooked claws. Skulls were stacked on the room's single table, dark eye holes staring at the Banes, needle teeth bared in the yellow light.

"So this is what a demon looks like with the meat off!" Marick exclaimed, stepping cautiously into the room. "I can't say it's an improvement." For demons they were, the skeletons of Shriekers, Bashers, Crawlers, Slashers, and several others Garet could not immediately identify. A small hill of ice blocks, half-covered in sawdust, was stacked on either side of the door. A single piece of paper lay on the table, held down by a carved wooden box.

"There's the jewel," Salick said, her breath steaming in the cold room. Walking stiffly to the table, she brushed the box aside with her trident and picked up the paper. Holding her lamp low, she read the message aloud. The room brightened as Dorict found wall lamps to ignite, bringing the piles of whitened bones into sharp relief.

"Procedures for the Testing of Demon Protection," she read, then stopped to look quizzically at the others. "Demon protection?" she asked.

Garet shook his head. "I thought we were the demon protection," he said. "But if Andarack can do all this, why does he need us to protect him?" He waved at the piles of bones.

Marick picked up a skull of a larger demon, crowned with impressive, horn-like crests, and moved the jaw back and forth. He grinned back at it before answering Garet. "Oh, this isn't Andarack's work. Remember how he acted on the stairs? He's no Bane. More's the pity!" He replaced the skull on top of its pile. "These must have come from the Depository. I guess I haven't taken you there yet," he said, noting Garet's confusion.

"Unless there was a sweet shop nearby, or trouble to get into, I doubt you would ever have gotten around to it!" Garet replied. He folded his arms and glared at his friend.

Salick and Dorict chuckled, glad of some humour to break the effect of the jewel's proximity, but Marick was unfazed. "Trouble enough, it seems." he said, looking at the piles of bones. "The Depository is where we keep the jewels of all the demons killed in Shirath. It's in the hills to the north." He ran his fingers over the white bones of a Shrieker's snout, tracing the nostril holes. "There's a deep crevice in the earth. All the jewels are dropped down there, and the bodies are left on the hill top to be cleaned by birds before they get dropped in too."

Salick looked at him, open-mouthed. "Do I want to know how you came by this information, information that I only learned when I became a Green?" She crossed her arms and tapped one foot, causing Marick to step back, arms raised in protest.

"Salick, I can't help it if you're a bit slow!" He ducked behind the table. "Hadn't you better read the rest of that letter?"

Salick eyed the young Bane and picked up the paper again. "Against the walls are various objects and materials you are to use." They looked around the walls. There, behind the piles of bones, were stacked an amazing variety of objects. Planks of various woods, shields of brass, bronze, and iron, bolts of cloth, and doubled glass frames filled with powders and liquids were neatly lined up under the wall lamps. Salick continued reading.

"In an orderly manner, place each object or material in front of the jewel so that it blocks its sight from you. Stand then in front of the material. Determine if the effect of the fear the jewel projects is changed. If it is changed, place the material that affected it outside the door. Put objects that did not affect it back against the far wall. It is very important that you methodically test all the objects and materials provided for you."

"To block a demon's fear..." Dorict said wonderingly. He reached out for the paper and Salick handed it to him. She rubbed her recently injured side with the opposite hand and eyed the objects along the wall.

"But Salick, Garet!" Marick yelped. "If the fear can be stopped, even those popinjay Palace guards could slay a demon!" He looked terrified. "What is Master Mandarack trying to do to us?" He was shaken and reached blindly towards the table for support, only to yank his hand back when it brushed the wooden box.

"I don't think this is meant to destroy the Hall, Marick," Garet told the young Bane. "I think the Master wants his brother to find out why we can't always feel the demons now." He looked at Salick, and after a moment's consideration, she nodded.

"Garet's right," she told Marick. "And it doesn't really matter who kills them. But think of this: if we can't find them, each attack could do as much damage as that Basher did last night." Her expression was determined, and Marick wisely held his peace. "Come on. Dorict, Marick, you two bring that stuff over here while Garet and I get the jewel ready."

The rest of the morning they tested each material against the jewel. Between the closeness of the jewel and the cold of the room, it was an unpleasant job—and unsuccessful. Nothing produced more than a slight relaxation in the

feeling of terror projected by the jewel. Thicker objects seemed to have a slight, almost imperceptible effect, but as Salick said, after shifting a heavy brass shield in front of the jewel, "Maybe it's only what we want to feel. I couldn't really swear that there was any change at all!" She let the shield slide and held a hand against her ribs. Garet stepped over to help, but she stopped him with a glare and wrenched the shield back into place.

Garet was forced to agree about the experiment. In the end, they put three objects outside the door: the brass shield, a heavy tile of granite, and a glass frame full of what appeared to be grains of iron.

They trudged up the stairs, locking the door behind them. Marick kicked at the stone slab. "If we have to wear these to fight demons, we'll never catch one, unless they run into us." The young Bane grinned at the thought. The door disappeared into darkness as they carried the light of their lamps back upstairs with them.

When they came into the great hall, Andarack looked better. He was arguing with Dasanat over how much pressure to put on the ore sitting in the press. He turned as he heard them approach and smiled expectantly.

"I'm sorry, Lord Andarack," Salick told him. "We found only three things that might have had an effect." She ran a hand through her hair. Being around a demon jewel all morning was exhausting. "If you have more material ready, we can try again."

Marick suppressed a groan.

"No, my friends," Andarack replied. "Not until I get the shipment I am waiting for." He waved at Dasanat and she rolled her eyes. After another, more vigorous wave, the mechanical walked out of the room, hands on her hips and muttering curses. Andarack pushed a set of plans showing some type of tower off the table to join the wreckage on the floor and invited them to sit. "Dasanat will bring some lunch for us." He sat beside Garet. "Now we have some time to talk of your life in the foothills of the mountains!"

And that is what they did. While the other Banes and an impatient Dasanat ate food purchased from a nearby wine shop, Andarack questioned Garet about every aspect of life in

the foothills. He wanted the Bane to tell him the habits of every animal, the properties of every plant, and what the local farmers ate, dressed in, and used for building their houses. His curiosity was endless, and Garet began to fear that Andarack would never let him leave, at least until the first fifteen years of his life were fully described, when the guard from the compound gate interrupted them.

"The miners' guild has delivered those crates, my Lord," he said. "But they won't bring them any closer than the gate." The young man kept a hand on his sword hilt, feeling even at this distance the brush of the jewel's emanations.

Andarack rubbed his hands. "There! More materials for testing." He sent Dasanat off to bring in the boxes. The Banes helped, as it was obvious that one person could not shift the heavy loads.

"What are these full of?" Marick demanded, pushing a crate beside the unsociable mechanical. "Rocks?"

"Of course," she answered. They both pushed and hauled at it until the first box was inside the great hall.

Andarack was sketching something out on a piece of paper. "There!" He showed them a drawing of a small, flat cart, with a mast at one end fitted with a swinging arm and a pulley. "This will move those crates with a minimum of effort!"

Dasanat took the paper and looked at it sourly. "Shall I put it with all the others?" she asked, indicating a stack of papers as tall as the wine jug beside it. "Or should I use it to bring the other boxes in?"

Andarack snatched back the paper. "How amusing! Go get the guard to help."

With the guard's assistance, they soon had all three boxes in the great hall, and Andarack pried off the top planks. Inside were indeed rocks. Big and small rocks. Gravel. Slices. Bags of rock dust.

Garet shook his head. He agreed with Marick. If they were to stop demons with stones, he still preferred to throw them.

Dasanat took the first set out, a black, crumbly rock that stained her hands, and loaded it into the press' hopper. Andarack spoke to the Banes.

"There's enough for everyone to do. Each of these rocks must be crushed and put in labelled glass frames. The rocks that are too hard to crush must be labelled and, if necessary, wired together to make a big enough screen." He indicated Garet and Salick. "You two are bigger, so please help Dasanat with the press." He bent over the boxes and began to haul out rocks to place in separate piles on the table. After a moment's confusion, Dorict and Marick began to help him.

The afternoon passed in a cloud of choking rock dust, thrown up by the press as it crushed the samples, one after the other. As each pile was put between the iron plates of the press, Dasanat pulled a red cord that ran along the shaft piercing the wall. The shaft soon started rotating and the press lowered or raised depending on how she had set the gears. Curious, Garet went outside to see what the cord was doing. He found the end attached to a lever. The lever, when pulled by the cord, opened a small spout that dropped oats into the pans hanging just in front of the horses. As soon as the grain dropped, the horses walked forward, trying to reach the grain and turning the post, which transferred its power through a gear at the top to the shaft that ran through the wall and turned the press. When the press stopped, a spring pulled the grain to within reach of the animals' mouths until the red cord was pulled again. The horses looked well-fed and remarkably content with their circular wandering.

After the rocks were reduced to a fine powder, Marick and Dorict used funnels to pour the dust carefully between sheets of glass held apart by wooden frames. When they were full, they carefully slid in the top slat of the frame and put it aside to be taken down to the cellar. Andarack brushed the name of each rock on the top of the frames and supervised the much-irritated Dasanat. The shadows had lengthened in the room, and they had lit the lamps before all the rocks were prepared.

"Done!" Marick told Dasanat. "If I never see another crushed rock, I'll die happy." He washed his hands in the basin the mechanical had brought when the last sample had been finished. Surprisingly, she smiled in return and clapped the Bane on his back.

"You work better than I expected!" she said.

Marick rolled his eyes in astonishment. When she had taken the dirty water out to the courtyard he turned to Dorict. "I thought she was all gears and pulleys! Who would have thought that there was a person in there." He shook his head.

Andarack laughed behind them. "Even I could not design such a machine. No, Dasanat is an artist. Yes, my little friend, don't shake your head. She works in glass, wood, metal, and more importantly, ideas." He yawned and stretched out his arms. "Now I think we must stop until tomorrow. You go back to your Hall and rest, and I will persuade Dasanat to try to remember where her family lives so that she can do the same." He took them to the courtyard gate and bade them a warm good night.

The sky held only a touch of silver and the shadows between things were deepening as they approached the Ward Gate. Marick yawned, setting off all the others. "Come on, all of you, let's go back and sleep. I bet I'll dream of rocks tonight."

Salick paused after a guard waved them through the Ward Gate. Looking across to the west bridge, she said, "Marick, you and Dorict go back directly and report to Master Mandarack. Take my trident. I want to walk through the plaza and listen to what people are saying, and I don't want to stand out." She looked at Garet who quickly nodded in agreement.

"What!" Marick yelped. "Why shouldn't we go with you. Is this just an excuse to be alone together? Just because..." His protest was cut off by an annoyed Dorict who grabbed his friend's ear and pulled him towards the bridge. His yells receded in the distance. "Dorict, let go. I was just saying...Ow!"

Garet felt his cheeks flush and saw that Salick had reddened as well. She gave him an embarrassed grin.

"Oh well, it's not like we're avoiding work, just because we're together." She slipped her arm in his and they walked slowly towards the Palace. Garet felt as if he were walking on cracking ice, each step had to be perfect so as not to disturb Salick's hand curled around his forearm. Because he was taking such care, he soon tripped over his own feet and Salick had to pull to keep him upright.

"Garet," she laughed, "what are you so nervous about?" She turned him around and, placing both hands on his shoulders, looked into his eyes. "I'm not a demon, though you're acting like I had a jewel in my head the size of one of Andarack's rocks!" She gave him a little shake. "Haven't you ever walked with a girl before?"

How do I answer such a question? Never walked with a young woman before, never flirted with a girl before, never been in love before: all were true, but he chose the least difficult. "I've never walked arm in arm with a girl, that's all," he told her and managed to laugh with her.

"Well, neither have I, walked arm in arm with a boy, I mean," Salick said. "But it seems I've learned better from observing others." She slipped her hand in his. "Shall we try again?"

He took a deep breath and tried again.

The plaza was still busy with the people who had attended the many funerals that had occupied the Temple until late in the day, and the large awnings in front of the Palace were still up for the play they had seen being prepared the day before. As true night fell, the last peal of the funeral bells faded and bright music started up on the stage. They stood at the back of the crowd and listened to the sound of trumpets, drums, tambourines, and strummed and plucked string instruments that Garet had no name for. The beat was fast and the musicians raucous. Jesters, dressed in fantastic costumes and wearing masks of distorted human faces and wild beasts, whirled on the stage. Jugglers wove among them. Two of the clowns bumped into each other and staged a mock fight that soon involved all the dancers. The two Banes, hands still clasped and shoulders touching, laughed at their exaggerated actions.

"Should we take off our sashes?" Garet asked, remembering the hatred of the merchant who had cursed him in the street.

"We'd have to take off all our clothes," Salick replied, fingering the winter vest and tunic she wore. They were a bad compromise between mobility and warmth, but they also bore the traditional colours of the Banehall, purple and black. "I don't think we'd blend in that way, so let's just stand here at the back and try not to draw attention to ourselves."

The audience was also appreciative, and Salick whispered to him, "Maybe this is what the city needs after last night."

Garet agreed. He felt a twinge as he remembered the empty seats draped with gold sashes, but he was here, and alive, and Salick was holding his hand. He laughed with her as the clowns trouped off the stage in grand disarray.

More music followed, accompanied by a pretty harvest dance, and then the clowns returned. They appeared to be constructing something out of wood and rope. One clown, a tall man with the mask of an old man, a large wooden hammer in one hand and a sheathed sword in the other, gestured wildly at them in a futile attempt to get the structure erected.

"That's Lord Andarack!" gasped Salick, her hand covering her mouth. She saw Garet's confusion. "Not the real one, of course. Clowns often poke fun at the important people of the city." On stage, the Andarack clown tested the structure by whacking his hammer into a support. The tower, along with several grey-clad clowns clinging to it, collapsed in a heap. He threw down his hammer, stomped on it and drew his sword. He chased the false mechanicals around the stage several times, just missing them with his theatrical swipes and thrusts, before driving them off the stage. The crowd showed its appreciation by slapping the back of their hands.

Salick had briefly let go of his hand so that they could both add their appreciation. "Will Lord Andarack be upset at this?" Garet asked, although he couldn't imagine the scholarly, open-hearted man taking offense at anything, except perhaps Dasanat's obstinacy.

"No, not at all. It's considered a great honour to be picked by the clowns for one of their comedies." She pointed at the stage. "Look, the actors' ambassador is coming out to tell the audience about the main piece."

A flourish of trumpets announced a portly woman dressed in rich purples and a trailing fur cloak. She bowed low to the audience, who responded with the call, "Ambassador! Ambassador!" She held up her hands to quiet them.

"Friends, citizens of Shirath. We come to you in a time of sadness, when the foundations of our city are shaken." A sigh went through the crowd. "We come to take you from your sorrows, and lift your spirits," she continued, raising her arms to Heaven. A smattering of applause rippled around Garet and Salick. "But distraction is not the only duty of an actor," she continued. She lowered her arms to hold them, palms up, to the people surrounding the stage. "We must also be a mirror, held up to the citizens of Shirath so they might know themselves better, and know what actions to take!" The two Banes looked at each other. Salick gave a slight shake of her head to indicate this type of introduction was new to her as well. Many around them also shook their head in puzzlement. The ambassador did not pause to quiet the talking in the crowd. She pulled her fur cloak off and flung it behind one of the curtains bracketing the stage. She bowed low, and standing straight again, said, "For the education and entertainment of the people of Shirath, we present, 'The Necklacing of King Birat'."

As she swept off the stage, the murmurs of the audience became a roar of surprise. Several people nearby turned to Salick and Garet to see their reaction.

Salick's hand squeezed Garet's tightly. Her wide eyes stared at the spot on the stage where the woman had been standing. Seeing the people nearby regarding her, she regained her composure and pulled Garet a little ways back from the crowd.

"This is incredible, and perhaps very bad, Garet." She kept her voice low and her eyes on the stage. Several actors, dressed as Palace guards, had appeared, pushing various props into place. A golden throne dominated the set, occupying centre stage.

"Why, Salick? I mean, it's only a storyteller's tale, isn't it?" he asked, his voice as low as hers. The musicians were moving to take new places on the left of the stage.

She shook her head. "It's an old story about a fight between the Banehall and the Palace that took place hundreds of years ago." Her face was grim. "This is not the time for such stories."

"Not unless you want another fight. And some people do," Garet replied softly. "Salick, what does necklacing mean? I remember Marick said it on the barge, when he played that trick on those bullies; what does it have to do with demons and Banes?"

Salick began to answer, but saw that some of the people waiting for the play to start had drifted closer to try and catch what they said. She shook her head at his question and said, "We'll watch the play. You'll understand well enough by the end, and Master Mandarack will want to know all about this." She drew him back to the fringes of the crowd.

More torches were lit around the perimeter of the stage. When all was prepared, drums signalled the arrival of an imposing figure, who swaggered on stage and ascended the throne. His face bore no mask, but was covered with red paint save for a few strokes of black to emphasize his eyes and mouth. The crowd booed as soon as they saw him.

"That's King Birat," Salick said. "He was the third king after the demons appeared in the South." The figure on the stage gestured at the guards, his arm movements both wide and sinister. A man was brought in, chains on his wrists and rags covering his body. His face paint was white and blue. He pleaded soundlessly with the King, his arms stretched out from his prone position on the floor, but the red-faced actor laughed and waved him away. The guards dragged him out, to the boos and hisses of the audience. Not one of the actors had spoken, and Garet soon realized that the whole story would be told through actions alone.

It was a confusing story, but with Salick's whispered explanations, and the clear gestures of the actors, he pieced out what was going on. The King, Birat, was an evil man who wanted to kill his son, the man in chains. A woman with a blue face, who received thunderous applause whenever she came on stage, tried to restrain the King, but was generally helpless in the face of his perverse nature. Several other characters, their faces tinted in varying shades of red if they assisted the King, or blue if they stood against him, contributed to the progress of the story. Garet was not sure what they all were doing, but the main conflict was at least clear in his mind.

The drums and horns swelled, signalling an important event. The king thundered silently on his throne at the blue-faced lady, who wept behind graceful, trailing sleeves. He gave orders to the guards and they left, returning quickly with a short man dressed as a Master of the Banehall.

"No!" Salick cried in a tight voice. Garet could barely hear her in the tumult that this character's arrival had evoked from the crowd. He leaned in to catch her words. "Look! Look at his face!" she ordered, and he did so. The Bane slunk up to the King, who bent to whisper in his ear.

"I see his face. It's red like the King's," Garet replied. "What does it mean?"

"Red means evil," Salick said, her eyes never leaving the figure now bowing before the King. "The actors, or whoever put them up to this, are saying the Banes are evil!" The actor dressed as a Bane mimed agreement to the King's suggestion and strutted off stage to the sound of a single, sinister flute.

"Moret would never have acted in such a way!" Salick exclaimed. "He was the second of the Shirath Hallmasters. He was already an old man when Birat was on the throne." On stage, the man in chains was dragged in again by the guards. The King demanded and he refused. The woman threw herself between them, but at an order from Birat, she was dragged offstage. All the musicians joined together in producing a desperate crash of sound.

Salick cursed. "Claws! Moret stood against Birat. But the Banehall was betrayed by a Gold who was Birat's cousin." She shook her head as the drama continued between the man in chains and his murderous father. "Birat paid him to bring..." she stopped to look around her, but didn't have to worry about being heard, for her increasingly angry outbursts had cleared a little space around them, "... to bring him a necklace of demon jewels so that he could drive his son mad."

"But why would he want to do that?" Garet asked, before remembering that both he and Salick knew of parents who did not love their children.

"To keep his throne, I think." She paused for a moment, remembering. "The Ward Lords opposed him because of his cruelty, and they wanted his son to replace him." She looked back at the stage, where the woman in blue face paint, moving alone on stage, danced out her sadness and fear. The crowd was silent, following every graceful step. "If his son went mad, there were none of the King's other children old enough to take his place."

The King and his court returned, to the sound of royal flourishes, driving the woman, his wife perhaps, to hide by the right hand curtain, though in plain view of the audience and the other actors. The King did not appear to see her. The false Moret then came back on stage, carrying above his head a black, polished wooden box. The music swelled while he danced around the prone figure of the son. At a crash of the symbols, he placed the box in front of the prisoner and threw back the lid. The King and guards raised their hands ritually before their faces while the son writhed on the floor. With a leap, the Bane pinned him and drew from the box a cord of withered, pear-shaped objects. He pulled up the head of the prince and settled it around his neck. The crowd gasped as the prince leaped and rolled across the stage in a pantomime of mortal agony.

"How could they think this," Salick murmured, and Garet saw a tear of anger trace the line of her cheek and chin. She merely shook her head when Garet tried to offer his comfort.

On stage, the guards reversed their spears and prodded the twisting, shaking man off stage. The King and his court, laughing uproariously, followed, leaving the Bane on stage alone, rubbing his hands at the audience. The hatred directed back at him was like a wind, and when the woman left her hiding place and came up quietly behind him, someone in the crowd shouted, "Kill him!", and many took up the call.

But the woman did not attack the Bane, instead she pulled a pouch from her tunic and waved it in front of his face. He comically chased after it, to a frenzy of cymbals, while she held it just out of his reach. After a whispered exchange, she passed him the pouch and he left the stage. The King came back on stage, without his guards, and slumped into his chair, head on his hand and eyes closed. While the woman stood at the corner of the stage and watched, the Bane slipped back in carrying the necklace of wrinkled objects—they look like hearts, Garet thought—and placed it stealthily around the King's neck. Cheers and drums erupted as the King went through even more gyrations in his agony than the Prince had. He flung his crown across the stage and overturned the furniture. The guards ran in and, with difficulty, pinned him against his tipped throne with the butt ends of their spears. A minor, blue-faced character appeared, supporting the prince. The crowd roared its approval. The lady gave him the crown, which he set on his own head. With an imperious gesture, he ordered Birat removed, still wearing the necklace. The throne was righted and the prince, now king, sat down. The slinking Hallmaster came before him, bowing low, but the new king set his booted foot on his shoulder and set him rolling back among the courtiers, to the great amusement of the audience. The false Moret climbed to his feet and shook his fist at the King and the Lady, who were laughing at his predicament. He then turned and shook his fist at the crowd, before stomping off the stage to a chorus of boos.

A general celebration seemed to be taking place among the characters, but Salick pulled Garet away while the play continued. "Garet, let's leave now." Her expression was troubled, and he followed her without question. They were soon alone in the great plaza, the crowds still following the end of the play.

"It was an insult, I agree," Garet observed as they approached the centre bridge gates. "But I don't understand why you take it so seriously." A half moon gave them just enough light to see where they walked. He shivered a bit, now that the warmth of the crowd was gone. Dorict had already chosen winter cloaks for them all, but they were still hanging in their room, and so not much use to him. He rubbed his upper arms.

"You couldn't know, Garet," Salick began, her voice almost pleading. "No one in Shirath saw the Banes that way before these black days." She shivered as well and Garet put an arm around her shoulders. She didn't pull away. "And they twisted history! Moret was the one who freed the prince. He risked his life to hide him in the Banehall. When the King demanded him back, Moret and all the Banes of

Shirath threw their sashes down on the Palace steps." She leaned against him, sharing his warmth.

"Why did they throw their sashes down?" he asked. They had slowed their pace as they held closer together. They were still alone in the great empty space before the bridge.

"To warn the King that they wouldn't fight any demons as long as he sat on the throne," she replied. The cold wind pushed her braids across her face and she tucked the ends of them into the collar of her tunic before continuing. "The Ward Lords finally rebelled against Birat rather than live in a Baneless city. They forced the Gold that had betrayed the Hall to put the necklace on the king, against Moret's wishes. Then they turned Birat out of the city gates, to perish, mad in the wild countries beyond Shirath."

Garet shuddered at the image of the tormented king, necklaced with demon jewels, struggling across an empty land. Their cold increased as they passed through the gate and the river's wind cut across them. The Palace guards were statues in the darkness. Aware of eyes on them, the two Banes broke apart and walked up the incline of the arched bridge.

"Wait, Garet," Salick whispered as they reached the centre of the bridge. "What was that sound?"

He looked back towards the plaza they had left and saw the lights of the palace had disappeared. "They've closed the Palace plaza gates," he told her. "But why so soon? Some of the people at the play must live in the Banehall-side Wards."

Salick didn't answer right away. She was staring off at the Banehall plaza gates. No lights showed there, either. "Garet, something is wrong. The other gates are closed too. Come on. We'll cross and go along the river road until we get to the west gate." She grabbed his hand and ran straight ahead. They had not covered a quarter of the distance to the end of the bridge when a voice in front of them brought them to a sudden stop.

"Well, what's this?" a man whispered in a harsh mockery of polite interest. "Two Banes locked arm in arm! Ignoring your duties again, children." The voice came nearer and they saw two men, their heads wrapped in scarves to hide their appearance. Metal glinted in the moonlight and Garet saw that they both carried the thin swords of Duelists. He pulled Salick back, but the sound of steel on stone spun him around to see a third man waving his sword at the Banes.

Salick drew herself up and marched on the two men blocking their way. "Who are you, and by whose orders do you stop us?" She slowed as she neared them. Garet backed towards her, facing the third masked man who must have followed them from the Palace plaza gates. His hand fell against the coiled rope of the weapon he bore at his side. As stealthily as he could, he slipped it off the hook that held it to his sash and fingered the coils in his hand. The spiked ball clunked softly against the hammer.

The man who had spoken before laughed nastily. "Poor Bane. You still think you Banes are pulling our strings, don't you." He advanced in a crouch, sword pointed at Salick's face. "But the time has come to show you just how powerless the Banehall is!" He straightened and lunged at her, but she ducked under the blow, ramming her shoulder into the man's chest. He fell back with a grunt.

"Run, Garet!" she cried and leaped over her opponent only to be confronted by his partner.

"Claws take you, Salick!" he yelled and slashed at her face.

Salick screamed and fell back, hands pressed to her bleeding cheek. Garet's opponent paused, startled by the piercing noise in the quiet night. It gave the Bane enough time to begin whipping the spiked ball around his head in ever-widening circles. The man retreated, sensing more by hearing than sight that he was in danger. Timing his swing, Garet let enough rope slide through his hand to make up the distance as his attacker retreated. The spiked ball slammed against the swordsman's shoulder, knocking him flat to the cobblestones beneath his feet. The hammer end raised in his left hand, Garet turned just in time to fend off the rush of the man who had wounded Salick. The thin blade rasped along the curve of the pick as Garet pushed the sword to one side.

With a harsh grunt, the swordsman brought his elbow up into Garet's face, knocking him back against the stone railing at the edge of the bridge. By instinct, Garet dropped and rolled, hearing the sword slice through air where his head had been a split-second before. Coming up behind his attacker, he flung the hammer at his back, driving the assassin down to his knees. Desperately, Garet grabbed the rope and pulled in both ends, feeling for the ball and the hammer. Salick moaned on the ground nearby. He couldn't risk looking to see how she was, but her cries cut him to his heart.

An anger rose in him as the swordsman recovered and turned on him with a curse. Garet now knew this anger well; it was what had first marked him as a Bane. He knew what his anger was capable of. He began to swing the metal ball in slow, deliberate circles around his head.

"What's this," he taunted, "a Duelist afraid of a mere Bane?" He flicked the spiked ball at the man, barely missing the masked head as the swordsman threw himself to one side. "Come on then, Duelist," he called, drawing back the rope and resuming his slow circles. "Let's see which of us is truly powerless." He advanced on the man, flicking out the ball and drawing it back, the hammer held ready in his left hand.

Confronted by a weapon that greatly over-reached his own, the Duelist tried to cut the rope as it passed, but, as the line was braided of leather and flexible wire, his sword just bent around it, almost becoming entangled. Attack after attack drove him back across the bridge until he had no where else to go. Stone chips exploded from the railing as the metal weight just missed him. With a curse, the Duelist threw his sword at Garet, the spinning blade missing him by a wide margin, and ran back towards the Palace plaza gates. The man who had first attacked Garet stumbled after him, one arm hanging limp at his side. The last man still lay on the ground where Salick had knocked him, gasping for breath.

Garet ran over to her where she lay curled up on the ground. Blood covered her hands and the front of her vest, and his heart came into his throat in a panic sharper than any he had felt from a demon.

"Salick!" he cried out. "How bad is it?" But she wouldn't or couldn't answer. He dropped his weapon and picked her up in his arms, his concern giving him extra strength. On stumbling feet, he ran down to the Banehall plaza gate. It was closed and there was no sign of the guards. With Salick moaning in his arms, he kicked at the gates furiously, screaming to be let in.

A commotion sounded on the other side. Metal sounded on metal and then the gates began to open inwards. He stood ready to enter or run from new attackers when a familiar voice called, "Is that you, lad?" The tall shadow of a man transformed into Mandarack. He ran up to Garet, shield held ready on his arm. Marick, similarly armed, was beside him. Dorict, Vinir, and several other Banes crowded through the open gate. Master Relict and Vinir lifted Salick from his arms and laid her on the ground. Mandarack quickly knelt and examined her. He signalled the two to take her to the Banehall, and stepped in front of Garet when he made to follow. Relict and his apprentice linked their arms under the injured Bane and gingerly carried her across the plaza to the Hall.

"She is not badly injured, Garet," he said, looking into his eyes to force his attention away from Salick. "But you must tell me what happened. Who attacked you, and where are they?"

"I can tell you that, Master," a gruff voice called out of the darkness. Gonect, the guard from Andarack's Ward, came out of the darkness of the bridge, dragging a man by his long hair. Garet's rope-hammer was wrapped in tangles around the guard's other shoulder. His captive's scarf had been pulled from his face, showing new bruises. Dorict followed behind, holding his staff in one hand and two swords in the other.

"Duelists, by the swords, and by this one's face, for I've seen him fighting in the plaza." He pulled back on the man's hair, and Garet recognized him as Shoronict, the young man who had confronted them at the Duelist's yard.

Gonect grinned and shook the stunned attacker. "He was trying to get away when Dorict here caught up with him. Claws! I've never seen a staff applied with such spirit. It was a joy to see." He winked at the young Bane. "If I hadn't hauled him off this piece of offal, you wouldn't have the pleasure of questioning him before we turn him over to the King."

The bruised man smiled at that idea, and Mandarack eyed him coldly. "No, not the King." The smile disappeared from Shoronict's purpled face. "Gonect, can you find a place to hide him, out of sight of the Palace guards, for a few days at least?" he asked the burly guard.

"Not a problem, Master," he replied immediately. "If you'll lend me a hand cart, I'll bundle him up and take him into the Eighth Ward and sit on him until you want him back." He nodded at the still forms of two Palace guards crumpled on the cobbles of the plaza just inside the gate. "These two won't tell, even when they wake up!" He bowed to Mandarack, forcing Shoronict's head down as well. "We'll take our leave, Master," he said, and dragged his prisoner off towards the Banehall.

Mandarack signalled a Gold to follow the guard and help him with the unfortunate Duelist. After scanning the darkness of the bridge for a moment, the old Bane turned once more towards Garet.

"That was a near thing, lad," he said in his calm tone. "When you didn't return, I was about to send Marick to look for you, but I was interrupted by Gonect's arrival. He had overheard some disturbing rumours about a planned attack on Banes. Even after what he called 'considerable persuasion,' his source wouldn't give him the details, only that it would take place tonight." He turned briefly away and sent two Greens to fetch water to wake up the guards. They soon brought back pails from the gatehouse and doused the unconscious men. Mandarack addressed them as soon as they could stand. "Either through ignorance or malice you have conspired to harm a Bane. This shall be reported to the King and the Ward Lords." The guards, already unsteady on their feet, paled. Mandarack signalled the Banes to follow him back to the Hall. He walked beside Garet and continued his explanation.

"I gathered people I could trust and brought them with me. Most I sent to check on the regular Ward patrols, but a few came with me to find you." As they passed into the courtyard of the Banehall, Mandarack lowered his voice. "We were going to search for you in the Palace plaza, where Marick said you had intended to go, but when we arrived at the gate, the Palace Guards refused to open them for us. We heard a scream on the bridge beyond, but they still refused and menaced us with their spears when we tried to force the gates. Gonect, who had come with us, sneaked up behind them and banged their heads together." A slight satisfaction crept into the old Bane's voice, and Garet turned to see him smiling slightly. They came to the main door. Master Branet was waiting for them and hurriedly motioned them inside. "Gonect is quite capable," Mandarack said as they passed the threshold. "He is an excellent ally."

They padded softly down the halls to the infirmary. Banerict, barefoot and wrapped in a quilted nightgown, was applying bandages to Salick's face. He looked up as Mandarack, Branet, and Garet entered.

"She's got a nasty cut on her cheek," he said angrily. "I doubt I can keep it from leaving a scar." He handed the remaining bandages to Vinir, who hovered over her friend. "This was made by no claw. It's a sword cut! What under Heaven's shield is everyone up to, Mandarack?" the physician asked, holding his instruments and bristling with anger.

Branet answered for him. "She was attacked by masked swordsmen, physician. In case you haven't noticed, the city is up in arms against us!" He folded his arms and looked dourly at the healer.

"Not the whole city, Master Branet," Mandarack corrected, "but certainly the Duelists and perhaps the King." He slipped the shield off his arm and placed it on an unoccupied bed. Leaning over Salick, he studied her for several moments, then straightened. "I know you will do your best for her sake, Banerict, but please take care of her for mine as well." He picked up his shield, nodded to Branet and the two of them left the infirmary.

Garet, released from any immediate concerns, felt his legs go weak. Vinir grabbed him and called to the physician, "Banerict, I think you have another patient!" She hooked a stool with her foot and pulled it under Garet before he collapsed.

"No, I'm all right!" he protested as Banerict fussed over him.

"Nonsense! You may not be wounded, but you're exhausted and worried sick about your friend." He paused while prodding Garet's cheek, provoking a yelp from the Bane. "You've got a nasty bruise on your face." He nodded to Vinir and they helped him over to the bed beside Salick's. "You can stay here tonight," he said and smiled. "I suspect you would have anyway." With that, he picked up the basket of supplies he had used to bandage Salick and took them away.

Vinir pushed him back down on the bed when he tried to rise. "Oh no, Garet. You wait here and I'll get some hot tea and food for you." She left at a trot and soon returned with a towel-covered tray. The aroma of stew woke him a bit and he ate with enthusiasm. Vinir pulled up another chair and drank tea nervously.

"Dorict said that you fought three Duelists to protect Salick," she said. Her hands twisted around her cup, and her eyes shone in the lamp light of the quiet room. Salick murmured in her sleep. The strips of cloth wrapped from the crown of her head to below her jaw gave her a strange, matronly look. Her left cheek was swollen and the folded bandages under the wrappings showed streaks of red.

Garet sat beside her and took her hand until she quieted back into a deeper sleep. He lowered his voice to answer Vinir. "Only two, Salick knocked down the other one. That was the one Dorict and Gonect caught, that Shoronict." He ground his teeth down on an urge to shout. "They didn't have any reason to attack us! It's Adrix they're mad at."

Vinir patted his arm to calm him. "They just see the sashes, Garet," she explained. "They didn't know who it was." She looked at her friend's wounded face and started to cry, her tears rolling silently down her cheeks.

Garet shook his head. "But they did know, Vinir. We had talked to Shoronict just the day before," he paused for a moment then rushed on. "And I'm sure the one that cut her was her cousin, Draneck!" He tore furiously at a piece of still-warm bread.

"How do you know that?" Vinir asked, shocked out of her tears. "I thought they were masked."

"His voice, the way he moved," Garet replied, speaking around his mouthful of food, "and he called her by name."

"I know they weren't friendly as children. Salick and I were raised in the same Ward," she said. Tenderly, she pulled the covers up around the sleeping Bane's shoulders. "She's been my friend for as long as I can remember." She smiled. "We've looked out for each other."

Salick turned her head in sleep as if she knew they were speaking of her, and her friends fell silent. He could see Salick first coming in to the Hall, a small, skinny girl, her chin thrust out in a determination to conquer her own doubts, excel at being a Bane, protect her friends, and then growing into the young woman he felt such concern for. He sighed and returned to the other bed. Vinir helped him pull off his boots before she took the tray back to the kitchens. Garet had only enough time to think, *I've dreamed of so much but never of this. So much good and bad together.* But he knew that what he had now was worth more than all his old fantasies put together.

Meetings and Mysteries

The first thing Garet saw when he woke up late the next day was Salick's blue eyes open and looking over at him. She lay propped up in the bed, changed into a dressing gown with a bowl of porridge balanced on her lap. He rolled out of the covers to stand bare-foot and stupid on the floor between their beds. She smiled then grimaced at the effect of the movement on her cut cheek.

"Banerict used some threads to pull the skin together. And it tugs every time I talk! But I'll heal, so don't worry," she told him, putting the bowl on the covers. He sat down on the bed beside her and took her hand.

"I'm really all right," she insisted. Reaching out with her other hand, she touched a light finger to his bruised cheek. "Besides, you probably feel as sore as I do." She shifted the hand to his other cheek. "Vinir told me what happened after I was injured."

Garet smiled ruefully. "I could have killed them, I was so angry," he said and looked down. "I suppose those rages are in my blood."

Salick lifted her head. "There's more than your father in you, and he's not the biggest part. I have my father's anger too." She smiled carefully. "You should know that by now! It's how you use that anger that makes you a man or a demon. Remember, Garet, Draneck and I are of the same blood."

His eyes widened. "You know he was on the bridge?"

She dropped her hand and leaned forward. "I recognized his voice just before he slashed me. Garet, he used his anger to attack me, like we were children again. You used yours to defend me. That's something I will always remember." She leaned back and put one hand on her bandages, her face pale.

Talking was painful for both of them, so they spent a good hour in companionable silence, each remembering their close call of the night before. Banerict finally came by and shooed Garet out while he changed Salick's bandage.

With nothing else to do, he went up the two flights of steps to the Blue Sashes' rooms, but Marick and Dorict were absent. After a good night's sleep, his nerves were settled enough to want company, and answers. The foremost question in his mind was what would they do with Shoronict. Gonect was supposed to be holding the proud Duelist in the Eighth Ward, but he could not hold him there forever. Would the King punish Shoronict or reward him for attacking them? The only knowledge he had of a Shirath king was from the play he had seen the night before. Was that truly only last night? It seemed an age ago, and the memory was not comforting; the king of that performance was as mad as a crow in winter. Would Trax also prove to be insane?

Garet shook his head and looked out through the room's solitary window. Through the distortions of the wavy glass, the plaza seemed deserted. Even the old men had abandoned their bowling, despite the weak sunlight falling on their pitch. He put his hand on the cold glass. The snow he had felt in the air last night would not be long in coming. Craning his neck, he saw the gardens were likewise empty, and in the distance, the three bridge gates were closed. *Not good*, he thought. The plaza had the feeling of a crop of wheat under a hail-filled sky. As he turned from the window, he caught sight of something that sent him running from the room. The gates of the Banehall's courtyard were closed and chained. Men and women, all Banes, stood in the yard, their spears, tridents and other weapons shining in the winter sun.

Salick was not in her bed, and he stood frozen for a moment before rushing out of the infirmary to find Mandarack. The halls were empty except for Black Sashes trotting back and forth with folded papers and trays of hot tea. None of the non-Bane citizens who worked in the Banehall were visible. Mandarack's door was slightly open, and he breathed a sigh of relief to hear Salick's voice before he knocked.

"Come in," called the dry voice of the old Bane. He pushed open the door to find the small room crowded with those opposed to Adrix. Master Tarix's wheeled chair was set beside Mandarack's chair with Relict on her other side, one hand on her shoulder. Branet sat hunched beside Relict, his expression grim as he eyed the young Bane at the door. Ranged along the walls were the other Reds and Golds who had been demoted, although they still wore the sashes of their original ranks. Some few others of the higher ranks, whom Garet knew sympathized with Mandarack, had joined them. Dorict, looking uncomfortable in such company, stood by Mandarack's elbow. Salick sat in the only other chair.

"Good, we were looking for you, Garet," Relict said, smiling and waving him in, though there was barely any space left in the small room.

"There you are!" exclaimed Marick, who had come up behind Garet and now propelled him into the room, following him and closing the door to a tiny crack. The small Bane stood by that crack, one eye on the hall.

Mandarack continued. "Salick has told us much of your courage and skill on the bridge last night. I am pleased to say that those who know you were not surprised and those who didn't were greatly impressed." He waited to accommodate the murmurs of agreement that rippled around the room.

Tarix beamed at him. "All those hours and bruises paid off, eh Garet?" she laughed. Even Branet smiled with the other Masters but quickly regained his serious expression.

"The attack on you two changes everything. Have you seen the courtyard?" the burly Master asked the assembly. Several Banes nodded, and the rest were soon informed by their neighbours.

"We seem to be preparing for a war," Relict observed. He stroked his short beard and looked at Mandarack. "A war I'm afraid we will win."

Several in the room looked at him quizzically, but Mandarack nodded in agreement.

"You are right," the old Bane said. "Think, all of you; whichever side wins this war, our city will die."

Garet moved carefully in the silence this remark produced until he fit himself into the small space Vinir had saved for him beside Salick's chair. He remembered Mandarack's lecture on the balance of power in the city. The Banehall, the King with his Ward Lords, and the demons. It seemed all three groups were changing so fast that any balance was doomed.

Branet cleared his throat and looked up from his thick, interlocked fingers. "Would you rather the King and his assassins win?" he asked. Another uncomfortable silence filled the room.

Garet answered, surprising himself with his boldness, but he felt he could no longer remain silent. He had, after all, been on the front lines of this war. "Master Branet, I have been told that there are three forces in Shirath: the Banehall, those we protect, and the demons we fight. If we treat those we protect in the same manner as those we fight, where is the right of it? And if we can no longer win against the demons, where is our purpose?"

Branet looked up at him, surprised at the passion in his voice. Mandarack caught Garet's eyes and nodded for him to continue.

He swallowed, closing his eyes for a moment against the throbbing of his bruised cheek and said, "This fight with the King is like two men gambling in a burning house. No one wins! We must find a way to stop this war before it begins in earnest!" He pushed his black hair back from his eyes. "We are Demonbanes, the only defense against the most powerful threat to Shirath." He held his hands out, pleading for their understanding. "But if the demons can no longer be found, except by following the trail of their victims, this city will be destroyed."

The assembled Banes reacted to this speech with reluctant nods and murmurs of protest, perhaps shocked at being instructed by a mere Blue, but Mandarack immediately held up his hand for silence.

"Garet is correct. Adrix has created this distraction with the King for his own purposes, a distraction that must be resolved before our 'house' burns." He touched Dorict on the sleeve. The young Bane gave a start. "Dorict, please repeat the news you brought from my brother."

Dorict stepped a bit forward and began in a somewhat squeaky voice, "Marick and I visited Lord Andarack this morning and assisted him with his testing. We found a rock that stops the effect of a demon's jewel." The noise that accompanied this announcement was so great that Marick shut the door until it died down. "He is also making a..." words momentarily failed the young Bane, "...device that can be used against a demon." There was much scratching of heads, Garet's included, at this cryptic statement. Dorict looked at them helplessly, obviously unable to give more details.

"We will keep in contact with the Ward Lord," Mandarack said. "Marick and Dorict will continue to assist him." He looked at Marick who was still guarding the door. "But you both must take care. Do not go into the city in your uniforms. Wear the clothes of the mechanicals."

"That's how we came back, Master," Marick replied smugly. "It's easy to mix in with all of them. They finally came back to Lord Andarack's house after he sealed the jewel inside a box lined with that rock." He winked at Garet. "At least now there's no more crushing and sorting to do."

Garet smiled back, remembering the labour of the previous day. Master Branet stood up.

"I would like to see this stone," he said to Mandarack. "But I don't see how it could have led to the deaths of my students. The stones of that building were hundreds of years old, and I killed a Shrieker there myself not a dozen years ago, and with no trouble sensing it!"

Mandarack nodded. "I agree, Master Branet. While my brother's discovery may yet help solve this mystery, it is too soon to tell. We cannot as a group, however, leave the Hall at this point. Perhaps when Andarack has his device ready, we can travel secretly to view it." The old Bane rose. "Remember, for now the best thing we can do is keep up our patrols and try to build support within the Hall. We must bring more people over to our cause."

"Even if it splits the Hall?" asked Master Bandat.

"The Hall is split, Bandat," Relict told her. "We now have to work to see what can be saved."

Sobered by these words, the assorted Banes filed out of the room after Marick checked for any lurkers in the corridor.

Mandarack signalled the four friends to stay behind. "Dorict and Marick will be out of harm's way, I trust," he eyed Marick sternly, "but you and Salick must also be protected. I don't want you to patrol right now." He held up his hand to stop Salick's protest. "I know how seriously you both take your responsibilities as Banes, but I fear that the Duelists will try to harm you if you leave the Hall." He shook his head. "Your help is unnecessary for now. Adrix, and everyone else in the Hall, knows what happened on the bridge. He has doubled the number of Banes on each patrol to provide safety in numbers from any other attacks." The old man's smile was grim. "He has such a need of bodies now, that he hasn't found time to enforce his demotions." He helped Salick up from her seat. "Adrix hates both of you. He hates you because your behaviour is truly Bane-like, and that reminds him that his behaviour is not. He also hopes to strike at me through you." His eyes fixed them both. "Alone, or with a patrol made up of Farix and the like, you would be at Adrix's mercy," he rasped, "and, I don't want to risk you again."

For the first time in their acquaintance, Garet could detect a strong emotion in the old Bane's voice.

Mandarack put a hand on his shoulder briefly then shifted it to Salick's. "You are both dear to me," he said, then turned to the two younger Banes by the door, "as are both of you. Take care of yourselves so I do not have cause to fear as I did last night." Salick looked up at him, her eyes glistening. "No tears, Salick," he said. "You must stay in the Hall for now, in the infirmary. I have already told Banerict that you are not

235

ready to take up your duties." He dropped his hand and smiled again. "He has agreed with my diagnosis." He motioned the younger Banes out the door and closed it softly behind them.

So the next few days passed. Banerict fended off Master Farix whenever the haughty Red came to demand the two Banes return to duties.

"Not yet, my good Master," Banerict would say, shaking his head and going on in a doleful tone. "The infection, you know. Don't know what's to be done." He would put his arm around the confused young man and lead him to the door. "Well, we'll hope for the best, only time will tell." It was a testament to Farix's stupidity that the same ploy worked for three days in a row.

On the fourth day, Adrix arrived with his assistant. "Banerict!" he demanded, his florid cheeks shaking, "How can you justify keeping two healthy Banes in their beds when we need everyone to protect ourselves from the King's assassins?" He planted himself in front of the physician and glared down at him. Garet and Salick, who luckily happened to be in those beds, tried to look sickly.

Instead of placating the Hallmaster, however, Banerict surprised them all by blankly contradicting him. "No, Hallmaster. You know nothing of healing hurt Banes. I do." He waved at his patients.

Garet took the hint and coughed helpfully. Salick moaned.

"When it is my opinion that they are ready to return to their duties, then I will release them to you," the small physician said, his voice rising, "not a moment before!" And, although the Hallmaster towered over Banerict, it was Adrix who retreated, grumbling and scowling, with Farix stumbling in his wake. Banerict smiled. "I've wanted to do that ever since he became Hallmaster," he said to no one in particular. Humming a cheerful tune, he then returned to his rounds, chatting with the elderly Banes who either stayed in the infirmary, or came there during the day.

By the end of the fifth day, Salick and Garet were beginning to wish Adrix had dragged them back to work, no matter what dark schemes Mandarack saw waiting for them.

Freedom came on their fifth evening in the Hospital. Salick's great swaths of bandages had gradually been reduced to a small square of cloth held on with a sticky gum that she complained about more than the wound. The cut had closed, leaving a thin, curved scar that accentuated her high cheek-bones. Garet commented that it made her look rather adventurous, like a thief in the book they were taking turns reading to each other. The hero of the play was a young woman who became a thief to steal evidence of her father's innocence and so save him from exile. The scar on her face had been made by the villain of the piece, who had caught her in her first attempt at burglary. After Garet pointed out the physical similarities, he went on to list other points of comparison, such as the character's impulsiveness and hot temper. Salick had made her disagreement clear by throwing the book at his head. Garet caught it and calmly picked up reading where she had left off. Banerict shook his head and smiled. His two patients were amusing at least, though a bit too energetic for his infirmary.

Marick interrupted their arguments by bursting into the room.

"Salick, Garet, what are you waiting for, come on!" he cried, frantically waving for them to follow.

The two Banes slipped on their boots and collected their weapons. Banerict waved off their thanks and shooed them out the door. "Be careful, both of you. I mean this kindly, but with luck, it will be a long time before I see you again."

They left him standing in the doorway to the infirmary. Garet imagined he could hear the physician's sighs follow them down the hall like a soft breeze.

Mandarack was waiting for them in the Blues' training gymnasium. Tarix sat in her chair, fidgeting with some objects in her lap. Branet and Relict waited as well, grey winter cloaks thrown over their uniforms. Mandarack's cloak was held over his good arm, and a long dagger was thrust through his belt.

"Here you are," he observed. "My brother has finally sent word." He held out the cloak to Salick, who helped him settle it over his shoulders. Three more cloaks were produced from

Tarix's room. After the younger Banes had concealed their identity beneath the grey wool, Tarix called them over.

"Garet's rope-hammer can be easily concealed under his cloak, but you two must leave your more obvious weapons behind."

Marick looked at her and swallowed. Reluctantly, he placed his shield on the floor beside the wheels of her chair. Salick silently laid her trident beside it.

Tarix smiled. "Don't worry. I wouldn't leave you defenseless." She held out the objects she had been holding. Short wooden handles fixed to a metal shaft as long as their forearms ended in four curved tines, like a set of iron claws. Each had been sharpened to a needle point. The weapons master handed one to Marick, handle first. "These were once used for advanced training, long before my time. A Master would try to slash a Gold while the poor Bane tried to save her skin."

Salick blanched at the thought of facing such a test. Tarix handed her the other baton. "Ahh, for the good old days, eh Gold?" she teased.

"Hide them under your cloaks," Mandarack instructed. "And hope Heaven has not written that we will use them tonight."

The six Banes took their leave of the Training Master and left the Hall by way of a back door. Marick led them to a small gate that could be forced with a simple blow to the hinges. Branet struck the top of the gate with the heel of his hand. A few flakes of snow, which had been falling in patches all day, shifted down onto the Master's hand.

"Again," whispered Marick.

Branet hit it again, and the gate squeaked open before Marick could catch it. The party froze, waiting for a shout of alarm, but the only sound came from far away, behind the Ward gates, the faint murmur of the city's life.

Clouds had covered the city all day, threatening the first real snow storm of the winter. Now they blocked whatever light the crescent moon and stars might have given. Branet reluctantly lit a small, covered lamp and held it out before the party. The feeble light that shone through the round, glass eye helped them skirt the low hedges and the stands lining the playing fields to make their way to the west gate. Several figures waited motionless before the gates. The purple cloaks of the Palace guards whipped around their armour. Torches guttered in their iron brackets and threw an uncertain light over the approaching party, for which Garet was extremely grateful. At a sign from Mandarack, they pulled their hoods down low over their faces and approached the Guards.

"Hold there!" called one, squinting at Branet. "Who are you?" One hand kept the wind from his eyes and the other rested on the pommel of his sword.

Branet didn't answer, but pulled open his cloak. The Guard stepped back and waved them through. The big Bane turned to the others to motion them on ahead of him, and as he passed, Garet saw a strip of purple across Branet's chest and a duelist's sword hanging at his hip. Branet saluted the guards and followed the others across the high curve of the bridge.

When they were out of earshot of the gate, Branet leaned over to Garet and said, "Ask your little friend here how he got this sash. I'm sure it will be an interesting story." He slapped Marick on the back, nearly knocking the young Bane over. With a laugh, the first real sound of pleasure Garet had heard the man express since the loss of his two students, Branet pushed up to the front of the party to light its way.

As Garet steadied him, Marick shook himself and grinned at Garet. "It would make a good story though. If we survive this, I might try to sell it to that drunken storyteller we saw by the wine shop!" Garet smiled back and shook his head, though not in doubt, for he knew Marick would try anything.

Branet's bluff got them through the Palace-side gate just as easily. The cold had emptied much of that plaza as well. At the far end, lights winked out one after another as merchants closed up their stalls. The stage was also dark. The only sign of activity was at the Palace. Lights blazed from every window in the magnificent building. Guards packed the entrances, and, even at this distance, Garet could make out the knots of Duelists scattered among them.

Mandarack paused to examine the distant scene. Beside them, the Temple complex showed only a few lamps lit around the pillars of the main shrine.

"Something's going on there," Relict said, looking at the Palace and pulling the edge of his hood out to block the wind. "Should we return to the Hall?" The others crowded in to hear the answer.

"No," Mandarack said. "We could only tell Adrix that we saw many Guards and Duelists at the Palace. He could do nothing more than he has already done to protect the Banehall." He looked at the others. "Remember that this is a distraction. We have to remember who our enemy really is."

The party resumed its path towards the Eighth Ward. That gate, unlike those of the other Wards, was opened a crack, as though it awaited their arrival.

"Here you are!" a rough voice called out over the wind. Gonect appeared, a lantern held high to illuminate the approaching party. "I've been waiting for half the watch for you," he complained as they filed through the gate into the shelter of the smaller plaza. "My Lord is waiting for you. Hurry! My bones tell me that there's a blizzard coming tonight."

The Banes quickly walked the distance to the Ward Lord's house and were shown into the great hall. They drew back their hoods and opened their cloaks, glad of the fires roaring in the twin hearths of the room. At the furnace opposite the entrance, Dasanat fiddled with a glass-blower's pipe, pointedly ignoring their presence. No one else was in the room.

Salick pulled out a chair for Mandarack and helped him off with his cloak. The others took theirs off as well, placing them on top of the tools and plans covering the table. They looked about the room, Branet and Relict taking in the chaos for the first time, the others used to it by now. A small figure came running through the entrance and skidded to a stop before them.

"Dorict?" said Marick. "I haven't seen you run that fast since we were Blacks!" He shook his head in wonderment at his friend's energy.

Dorict ignored him and spoke directly to Mandarack, his words coming out between gasps and wheezes. "Master...Lord Andarack is coming up from the ice cellar...he wants to show you..." here he stopped for a great clanking sound had grown behind him and all the Banes turned expectantly towards the entrance. At the other end of the room, Dasanat sighed and doggedly went on cleaning out the pipe.

Whatever the Banes had expected, they were not prepared for the vision that marched slowly through the entrance arch. Andarack it may have been, or anyone for that matter, for the figure's head and torso was covered in a bizarre mesh of brass and stone. Frames of the metal held thin slabs of rock over some sort of linked mail, giving the wearer the paradoxical look of being both angled and curved. The figure raised a bare hand, for the arms as well as the legs wore only the grey cloth of the mechanicals, and lifted the visor of the helmet.

"There!" Lord Andarack said, breathing hard but smiling. "This armour weighs what you would expect, considering its materials." He lifted the helmet and its neck-skirt of rasping stone off his head. His greying hair was plastered to his head. "Now then, who is going to try this next?"

Branet and Relict looked at each other, but remained silent. Mandarack's face bore the shadow of a smile.

The Ward Lord took the silence as a rebuke. "It's perfectly safe, if a bit uncomfortable," he said, laying the helmet down on top of their cloaks. "And it will block the effects of a demon's jewel, at least most of it." Dorict began to help him untie the lacings under his arms that held the breast and back-plates together.

"Most of the effects, Lord Andarack?" Relict ventured. He stroked his beard and regarded the massive helmet. "Could you please be more...detailed?" He used a cautious finger to trace the rim of shiny brass holding a stone slab on the forehead of the helmet.

"Ahh, thank you, Dorict," the Ward Lord said, slipping out of the armour.

Dorict, almost crushed by the weight of the armour, frantically motioned for Marick to help. His friend stifled his laughter and rushed over to prevent a disaster.

"The effect of the jewel is felt most in the head and torso," Andarack told Relict. "By covering these parts with the silkstone, the fear the jewel creates is reduced to a mere unease." He waved at Dasanat. "I myself have stood in front of the jewel, wearing this protection and have been able to think and move." The frowning mechanical waited by the furnace, still holding the pipe. "Dasanat," Andarack called, "bring refreshments for our guests."

The woman's curses could be heard all the way down the length of the room.

"Master Mechanical," Branet asked, "it may seem a small point after such a great achievement, but how do you see out of this contraption?" He was holding the helmet in his large hands, looking perplexedly at the complex face plates.

"Silkstone has a high concentration of crystals in its composition," Andarack answered. "The small plates in front of the wearer's eyes are a mosaic of chips bearing the largest crystals we have. The view is distorted, though perhaps fragmented is a better description." He helped Branet slip the helmet over his head. "If you move carefully and think about what you are seeing, there should be no trouble."

Branet's voice rumbled from inside the helmet. "The trouble, Lord Andarack, is that I now see several of you, which means that my confusion shall surely increase many times over!" He pulled off the helmet and handed it to Relict, who slipped it on with difficulty.

That Master now tried to walk around the room, bumping into tables at first, but then slowing down and showing every indication of knowing where he was going. After a minute, he too removed the helmet. "Lord Andarack is right, Branet. It just takes some time to get used to it."

Branet grunted noncommittally. "This still does not solve the mystery of why we could not sense two demons: the one you encountered on the road from Torrick, Mandarack, and the Basher that killed so many in the Fourth Ward ."

Mandarack nodded. "That is true, Master Branet." He turned to his brother. "Andarack, is this silkstone a common mineral?" he asked, indicating the helmet, now returned to its place on the table.

"No, brother," Andarack replied, "it is not, at least not in the South." He smiled at Garet. "In fact, it comes from the same place your parents did, the North." He took an egg-shaped piece from his tunic pocket and passed it to him.

The black stone felt a bit oily in his hand, as if it had been polished, though the surface was still rough. As he turned it back and forth in the glow of the lamps, a thousand points of light shone back at him from the embedded crystals Andarack had mentioned. It felt heavy in his hand. He made to hand it back to Andarack, but the Ward Lord smiled and shook his head.

"Keep it, Garet, as a reminder of your Northern heritage and in payment for all my questions the other day." Then he turned to the others and said, "That is the last of it, anyway. If we want to make more armour, we must find other sources for the stone, for there is not another chip of it in Shirath."

Dasanat returned, glowering over a pot of tea and small bowls of nuts and fruit. She placed the tray on the nearest open space on the table and scurried off before she could be importuned again.

"What do they use this rock for in Shirath that we had any at all?" Salick asked. Garet passed the stone over to her and she rubbed it against her palm, feeling the oily sheen before handing it back to him.

"Those who work in glass use it to polish and grind their creations," Mandarack told her, "or did, until I collected it all." He lowered his voice and added, "That's why Dasanat is in such a foul mood. She's had to put off several important projects until we can import more of it."

A sharp clang of metal on stone seemed to confirm Andarack's assessment as Dasanat threw the pipe against the furnace and plopped down to sulk on her stool.

"She'll recover," Andarack sighed. "In time." He turned back to the Banes. "The mystery you spoke of, Master Branet, may yet be solved," he said, a gleam in his eye.

Even Mandarack leaned forward to catch his next words.

"This suit allowed me to examine the jewel in detail," he said, his voice rising in excitement. "And to discover something of its properties!" He pulled a sheaf of papers from another pocket. "My first teacher, Barat of Solantor, made special jars that he filled with weak acids and certain metals. In these jars, he could capture a force that was similar to the spark that goes from your finger to the handle of a door." He saw their incomprehension. "Surely you have all felt a stab of pain when you almost have your hand on a metal door catch, especially in dry weather, and most especially if you have walked across thick rugs to get to that door?"

There were slow nods of agreement, and Marick said, "My mother said that those were spirits sent by heaven to remind us to be good!"

Very ineffective spirits, Garet thought, but held his tongue when Mandarack nodded. "So our own mother told us, Andarack, when we were small. Now you say such pain can be captured in a jar. What has that to do with a demon's jewel?"

The other two Masters nodded and looked to the Ward Lord for an answer.

"Ah, brother, so she did. But what our mother, nor young Marick's mother, nor anyone else knew before Barat discovered it, was that the tiny spark that causes it, a flash of light that looks like the sparks one can strike off a flint with a piece of iron, is really a river of force. It can be stored in such vast quantities that touching it will knock a man flat on his back." He held his hand up at their disbelief. "Before Barat died, he visited me here in Shirath and we constructed such jars together. Believe me, Banes, I was careless once and paid for it with a jolt that threw me against the wall and left me unconscious for several minutes." He gave them a twisted smile. "Barat was furious with me because I had broken the jar in my fall." He turned to Dorict. "Please fetch the jewel, lad."

Dorict turned and ran out of the hall. Marick shook his head again in wonder.

"Such force can be moved or drained off with wires made of copper," the Ward Lord continued. "And I have improved much on Barat's original designs." He waved them over to a small model of a water wheel, connected at the hub to a strange wire-wrapped device and trailing more wires from a series of glass jars. Using a wooden rod, Andarack pushed a loose copper wire onto a circle of the same metal set on the rim of the last jar. To their amazement, the water wheel began to turn, a strange, high-pitched whirring noise coming from it.

Marick clapped his hands and the rest craned their necks this way and that to see what was making it turn. Relict got down on his knees to look under the table, but found nothing to explain the movement. He got back up, staring in wonder at the wheel.

"Lord Andarack, surely this is a great thing under Heaven!"

The others agreed, all except Branet, who stood back, arms folded and glowering. "Yes, my Lord, it is a pretty toy, but what does this have to do with demons?" he asked.

Mandarack held up his hand to calm the impatient Master. "I'm sure my ingenious brother is about to get to that very point," he said. "Is that not so?" He gave Andarack a meaningful look.

"Of course!" Andarack said, flipping the wire off the rim and bringing the wheel to a halt, much to the disappointment of the younger Banes and, it might be noted, Relict. "If I try your patience, I must ask forgiveness, but let us then get to the point, as my elder and wiser brother demands." He smiled and bowed to Mandarack. "I know my curiosity and distraction have always tried your patience!"

Mandarack smiled and said, "Then it was my patience that was at fault, not you."

Garet looked closely at the two brothers, trying to imagine them as young children, arguing as brothers might do, but Andarack's continued explanation brought him back to the present.

"To put it bluntly," the Ward Lord was saying, "the jewel in a demon's skull works like one of these jars, storing the spark force and using it to create fear, among other things."

Branet's arms dropped slowly to his sides, and Relict looked blankly at the Ward Lord. Salick turned to Garet, but he shook his head, not yet sure what to think.

Dorict returned at that moment with the jewel, encased in a box made of silkstone. Two wires stuck up through tiny holes drilled in the top. Andarack took the opportunity afforded by Dorict's entrance to pour tea for his guests. Garet sipped his tea thoughtfully while examining the spark-powered wheel. Salick came up beside him and whispered, "Do you think all this is true?"

He shrugged. "In the Northern sea," he replied softly, "there is a fish that can knock a man out of his boat in a way that sounds like the sparks Lord Andarack describes, or so my parents told me." He looked at her. Salick's expression was doubtful.

"Andarack," his brother asked while they sipped their tea, "what did you mean when you said, 'among other things'?" The old Bane's eyes were bright, and Garet saw the energy building in him. *Sparks*, he thought.

Andarack laughed. "If you will all gather around the box, you will see what I mean." He hooked the wires that bristled from the box to another set of jars, this one complicated by a series of levers, each connected to many wires. With great precision, Andarack pulled three of the levers and said, "I will open the box now, brace yourselves."

"But what about you..." Garet cried, but it was too late and he wondered why he had worried at all. It was going to be all right. In fact, everything was perfect. And then it wasn't because Andarack had closed the box.

Relict was leaning on the table. "What just happened?" he demanded. Branet stood, open-mouthed behind him.

"Just a moment," Andarack requested, and changed the levers before opening the box once more.

This time, sadness welled up in Garet, a grief so profound that he took Salick's hands and they both wept, their faces and collars wet with their tears. Then, as suddenly as it started, the feeling disappeared. Embarrassed, they let go of each other and turned to see the others wiping their faces and sighing.

"Sorry," Andarack sniffed, "but those are the only two variations I can produce with any consistency. However, Dasanat and I have stumbled on joy, anger, fear, and even, er...attraction," he added, face reddening.

"Have you evoked a feeling of deadness," Mandarack asked quickly, "a lack of feeling?"

"No," Andarack admitted. "But that may only mean that we haven't found the right amount of spark to project such an effect." He untwisted the wire connections and turned back to his brother. "Based on this and your own experience, Mandarack, I think we can safely say that at least some demons can alter their jewel to change the emotions they project."

"But why?" Branet exploded. He waved his arms furiously, almost smashing Andarack's wheel. "Why would a demon need to project anything but fear? What good would it do them?"

Andarack, a Ward Lord in his own house, was not cowed by the larger man's passion. "What good would it do them?" he asked. "It could be used to call a mate, to control others, or as we have heard, to hide from Banes!" He pointed to the box and the surrounding equipment. "I don't know why they have this power or how well they can use it, Branet, but I know that it can exist in them."

Relict sat down heavily on one of the scattered chairs. "To control, eh? That maybe explains something. Something I haven't told any of you yet." He looked up at Mandarack. "I didn't want to say anything because I thought she might be wrong," he said. Then he added bitterly, "And I didn't want to give Adrix an excuse for demoting her even further!"

Branet stepped beside his chair and put a hand on his shoulder. "Go on then, tell us now, Relict."

The usually cheerful Master nodded his head somberly. "All right. On the night the Basher killed Dalict and Shonirat, Vinir told me she saw something in the dark, beyond the Basher and just after she killed it. I was on the ruins of the floor above and saw nothing, but she claimed there was something staring out at her, something that gave off the dead feeling that had delayed us so long in finding the beast." He looked up at Mandarack. "But it was like no demon she had ever seen, she said, for all she could see of it was a single, yellow eye, blazing in the dark." He shuddered a bit, in spite of himself and added, "There was nothing there when I climbed down and joined her. We looked, but whatever it was, if it had really existed, was gone." He leaned back in the chair. "And that's when we started to feel the Basher's jewel." He looked at the others. "What if it was another demon? Two together, like you found near Torrick, Mandarack? And one controlling the other and hiding it from us until it was too late?"

Garet's tea went down the wrong way and he began to cough. This was the fear Mandarack had confessed to him the day he became a Blue Sash.

There was silence in the room as the assembled Banes considered Relict's words. Branet protested, "But how can we think there is a demon out there with the power to block its fear, to control other demons, and to do Heaven alone knows what else." He rubbed his bushy blond hair. "I can tell you that no such demon exists in our Hall's records."

"But it does!" Garet cried. He stood up, bumping the table and knocking over several cups.

Salick hurriedly set them aright as Branet glared at the young Bane. "I'm not used to a Blue telling me what I do and don't know about demons!" he growled, but Garet had no time for Branet's anger.

"In the Moret Demonary, Master!" he said to Mandarack. "You remember how I cleaned it up and rearranged it?"

Mandarack nodded slowly, waiting for him to continue. Branet threw up his hands and sat down beside Relict.

"There were some leftover references to demons that didn't fit in anywhere," Garet continued. "Like a picture of a claw with no name under it, or a name of a demon with no description." He saw Salick's worried look and smiled at her reassuringly. "Well, there was a line that fit no demon in the book. It was so strange and I took so much time trying to find a match for it, that I still remember it." He paused to get the words right. "It said, 'This demon calls and sweetly sings, but only bloody death it brings'."

Mandarack nodded, and Relict said, "Yes, I remember the line, now that you quote it." Branet started to speak but then stopped.

"At first I thought it was a joke left by some Black or Blue, to confuse later readers." Garet saw Relict hide a smile behind his hand. Branet smiled a bit too, and nudged Relict with his elbow.

"If so," Mandarack observed, "this joke precedes even my generation, for I too read that line as a Black." He held his tea cup and stared into its steaming contents. "There is no older Demonary than the Moret, even in Solantor. Perhaps the Wheel of Heaven has finally turned far enough to let some old terror Moret knew loose upon us again."

"Then I may have a way to help you counter that terror," Andarack said quietly. He stepped into the middle of the group. "My brother says that this demon can call you to come to its claws." He hefted the helmet. "Wear it, and this demon can sing as sweetly as a desert bird and all it will get is a shield-point in its throat."

There was nothing more to say on the matter. Andarack requested that the armour stay with him for now so that he could continue examining the jewel. But before the Banes left, he took three more of the silkstone boxes from the table and asked Relict, "If you wouldn't mind, Master—and it would be better if they all came from different demons, so that I can test them against each other."

Relict smiled. "Of course, Master Mechanical! In times like these, I'm sure we will find many demons willing to surrender their jewels just to slake your curiosity," he said, bowing as he took the small containers.

As they left the hall and entered the courtyard, its collection of gears and harness now muffled by a coat of fresh snow, Branet turned to block the party's path. The tall Bane put his hands on his hips and growled, "Perhaps now that we have seen these marvels and mysteries, Mandarack, we may at last turn our attention to the very minor matter of our imminent destruction by the King?"

"Perhaps," replied the old Bane, walking around Branet and breaking the soft snow as he went to wake the door guard in his little shack.

Claws in the Night

The snow continued to fall heavily as the Banes left the Eighth Ward. Gonect was not there to see them off.

"Probably sitting on Shoronict," spat Dorict, who had taken a strong dislike to the arrogant young Duelist.

"Don't worry. With the beating you gave him, he'd have to crawl back to the King even if he did escape," Marick told his friend. Dorict smiled smugly and wrapped his cloak about him to keep out the falling snow.

The wind had died by the time they entered the Palace plaza. The gently falling flakes picked up the light of the lamps beside the Ward gates and the Temple's pillars and spread it softly over the whitened ground. There were no tracks in the snow between their own footprints and the west bridge gate, and Garet realized that the storm would help them return unnoticed to the Hall. The guards, seeing they were the same party who had passed earlier in the evening, merely waved them onto the bridge.

The guards on the other side were equally lax, and Marick shook his head. "Snow is the friend of both thieves and Banes, or so it seems," he said, grinning at his friends.

"How is it our friend?" Salick asked, brushing flakes from her eyes. Garet grimaced as a drop of melted snow trickled down inside his tunic.

"Salick," Marick cried, "it just got us past those guards. Maybe I should have said that it's our friend when Banes act like thieves."

Garet stopped dead as they merged with another set of tracks. He knelt and touched the snow, his fingers coming away sticky. Salick knelt beside him, her breath sending puffs of steam over the footprints.

"What is it, Garet?" she asked.

Mandarack and the other Masters paused when they realized the younger Banes had stopped. They returned to stand over Garet and Salick as they looked at Garet's fingers. Bloody snow melted against his warm skin and dripped back down to the white ground. Garet stood and followed the tracks back from where they had come, casting for more clues.

"Masters," he reported when he was done, "at least four people came here, very recently." He paused briefly. "One of them was wounded badly."

"How do you know it was a bad wound?" Branet demanded.

Salick bristled at the implication, but Garet calmly replied, "There is a lot of blood, and it has spurted out, not dripped, whenever they stopped." He pointed at the Banehall. "They were travelling towards the Banehall from the Tenth Ward."

The party looked back towards the Tenth Ward Gates. The gate's lamps were visible as a pale glow through the mass of falling snow. Mandarack signalled for attention.

"Master Branet and I, along with Marick and Dorict, will follow the tracks to the Banehall and give what assistance we may." He turned to Relict. "Take Salick and Garet with you and follow the tracks back." He looked at them, his expression grim. "All three of you have encountered this new demon, so I don't have to tell you what you might be facing. Remember your training and don't be fooled by whatever tricks you encounter."

Relict took the lamp Branet held out to him. Overburdened, he handed to his friend two of the boxes Andarack had given him. "I'll keep the one," he said, "in case I can fill it."

Branet smiled. "My friend, let's hope the beast has been prepared for you!"

Marick began to protest about being left out, but was cut off by Branet grabbing the hood of his cloak and dragging him after Mandarack and Dorict. Their outlines quickly blurred and then vanished in the dark areas between the plaza's scattered pools of light.

"Come on," Relict said. He held the lamp low over the ground so as to light the scuffed tracks even now filling with snow.

Garet trotted beside the Red on the other side of the tracks. More and more sprays of blood appeared and Garet began to fear the worst. It was difficult to believe that a person could lose so much blood and survive. They arrived at the Tenth Ward gate to find it had been pushed open, creating a small drift of snow which prevented its closing again.

The gate guard did not greet them, and it was soon apparent why. Salick pointed to the small gatehouse. A middle-aged woman, her leather and bronze armour torn half-off her body, lay face down in the doorway. Salick put a finger to her neck and felt for a pulse. After a long moment, she turned to the others and shook her head. Turning her over, they discovered a tight grouping of four punctures had pierced her throat.

"A Crawler," Relict said. He looked up, holding the lamp high and scanning the tall gates and the surrounding walls. "Keep your eyes up," he instructed, "and listen for its movements. They hiss before they strike." The Banemaster turned in a slow circle, trying to feel the demon's presence. "Nothing," he growled. "Do you two feel anything?"

Salick shook her head and Garet did the same. The same dead feeling had fallen over the Ward, hiding the demon's projected fear the way the soft snow covered the sound of their steps as they crossed the Ward's small plaza.

The tracks continued, now mere depressions in the snow, into the main avenue of the Ward. They passed the Lord's walled manor and then the brightly painted houses of rich merchants and retainers. Soon, they were walking past the plainer entrances to the two- and three- level courtyards where the majority of the Ward's residents lived. None of the street gates meant to trap demons had been closed. Relict ignored them as he jogged, keeping his eyes swivelling between the ground and the walls above their heads. The tracks continued past these poorer compounds as well and finally ended in a heavy gate that opened on the storage buildings and stockyards, placed by each Ward against the outside city wall. It was also open. Relict touched the handle of the wide gate.

"More blood," he whispered. "Ready your weapons." He shifted the lamp to his right hand and drew a Duelist's sword that hung from a sash similar to the one Branet had worn. He hefted the sword, his expression showing distaste. Salick drew out the clawed baton Tarix had given her, and Garet loosed his coiled rope.

The Master advanced as quietly as possible, and motioned Garet to close the gate. He and Salick pushed the gate closed against the weight of the drifting snow. Inside the wall, the warm smell of cows and sheep met them. They lifted the lamp as high as possible, Relict looping its top ring over the tip of his sword's sheath and raising it to check the roofs of the nearby warehouses. Finding nothing lurking there, they continued to follow the tracks. The dead feeling continued, and Garet felt his frustration grow at being unable to locate the demon.

"There," Salick said, pointing at a large structure bordering the fenced livestock yards. "The tracks go in there." She gripped her baton tightly, trying to see into the darkness beyond the building's open door.

"With only the one lamp, we can't separate," Relict said. He paused for a moment, looking over the building. "Follow me through the door, then split to the right and left," he ordered. "And keep your eyes up!"

Once inside the door, Garet slipped along the wall to the right. Salick disappeared over to the other side. The building was an immense barn. Stalls holding cattle ran along each of the long walls. Overhead, beams crossed and lost themselves in the darkness. Relict lit the lamps fixed to the door posts and walked forward, neck craned and eyes searching above. The cattle stood apathetically in their stalls, not bothering to moo at these late-night trespassers. The narrow route between the stalls forced the three Banes back together, and

Relict waved Salick to stay near the door while he and Garet continued.

The centre post that supported the intricate web of beams above them had another lamp fixed to it. Relict lit it and motioned Garet to stay there while he patrolled to the end of the barn. Dragging his eyes from Relict's back, Garet strained to see the roof above him. A slight sound drifted down, like a rat scrabbling along the beams. He shifted the spiked ball to his right hand and played out enough rope to swing it at an attacker. Dust drifted down on him and the noise vanished. Was that the gleam of eyes at the top of the centre post, or only his imagination? He looked quickly to the ends of the barn. In their little pools of light, Salick and Relict were unmoving, scanning the darkness above them.

He was just turning his face back to that darkness when the fear slammed into him. The dead feeling had been switched off like one of Andarack's spark jars, and the barn exploded with the bawling and crashing of the cows in their stalls. He collapsed against a nearby railing, but was knocked back by the impact of a cow smashing against it from the inside. Garet fetched up against the centre post, stunned and fighting to resist the screaming of his nerves.

Over the bellowing of the animals, he barely heard Salick scream, "Garet! Above you!"

Without looking up, he dropped to the straw-covered floor and rolled down the central aisle towards Relict. Something hit the pillar where his head had been, and he came to his feet, hammer end of the rope ready in his hand.

"Are you..." Salick gasped, sliding to a stop on the other side of the pillar, the hooked baton held ready for a strike. She swung her head nervously back and forth, struggling to control her breathing. Relict was beside her, sword pointed up at the shadows. The Red's brows were squeezed down, and his eyes darted rapidly in search of the demon.

"I'm fine," Garet said, his voice shaking a bit. "But something almost nailed my head to that pillar." Four close holes had been spiked into the wood where he had been leaning a moment before.

The cows crowded into the corners of their stalls now, too frightened to do anything but roll their eyes. In the silence, the scrabbling noise came again, barely louder than the Banes' rapid breaths. Garet pushed the fear down and tried to calm the beating of his heart. His head cleared. Beside him, Salick and Relict were going through their own rituals of denying fear. The Red muttered something over and over again under his breath. Salick twisted the baton, her breaths slowing to match the movements of her hands. The animals' rolling eyes shone back at them in the glow of the lamps.

"It might not attack three of us together," Relict whispered. "You two go back to where we came in, and I'll stay here." He took the sword hilt in both hands and slowly lowered the point.

Garet and Salick backed away from him, eyes still looking above them for the Crawler. As they neared the door, Garet saw Relict stiffen. Salick pulled at his sleeve. "There," she whispered in his ear.

Garet looked up to where she pointed with the baton. Just below the roof beams, a demon's head, beak slightly open to reveal needle teeth, peered around the central pillar at Master Relict. A thin, clawed hand reached around the post and four dagger-like claws curved inwards to dig into the wood. It pulled itself downwards, slowly advancing on the Bane below it. Relict stood unmoving, perhaps trying to fool the demon into seeing him as a victim of its projected fear. Salick and Garet stood perfectly still, tiny puffs of steam escaping from their mouths as they waited for the demon to strike.

When it was still twenty feet above Relict, it hissed and dropped like a stone. The Bane thrust his sword upward, but the blade bent against the demon's leathery skin, and he was borne down by its weight. He dropped the sword and grabbed the creature's thin wrists, trying to keep the stabbing claws from his face.

Salick reached the struggling Bane slightly before Garet. The hooks on the end of her baton caught the creature around its neck, and she hauled the beast back. With a cry and a twist of her hips and shoulders, she flung it against the pillar. Garet was ready. He whipped a great loop of rope around the pillar, pinning the demon. Salick quickly drove the baton into its head, slamming the bulging skull against the wood and stunning it. Before the beast could recover, Garet shifted the hammer to his right hand and drove the pick deep into the creature's throat. The heavy, curved point did what Relict's flexible sword could not, and dark blood spurted over the weapon as he pulled it out. The two young Banes stood with weapons ready for another attack, but the demon's eyes glazed over as it twitched into death.

"Well killed, Banes," Relict said, getting up unsteadily from the floor. Blood dripped from shallow scratches on his face and hands. His back and hair were covered with straw and muck. He raised his arms and held out his cloak, wrinkling his nose. "Echh! Tarix will kill me. She always says I come back looking worse than the demons." He took off the cloak and shook what he could from it. "You two make a good team," he said, as he reluctantly re-settled the soiled cloth around his shoulders.

Garet and Salick grinned at each other, nerves still twitching from the battle and the renewed effects of the demon's jewel. Relict brought out the box and borrowed a stunning hammer from the tools hanging on the back wall of the barn. The cattle pushed against the rails of their stalls, the wood groaning in protest. The Red quickly broke open the demon's skull and scooped out the jewel. The closing of the box brought blessed relief to them all. Garet smiled when a nervous cow stuck its head between the rails to nuzzle against him for comfort. He scratched the sensitive spots behind her ears and thought of Saliat, the cow on his father's farm.

Salick and Relict wrapped the demon's corpse in a piece of canvas and pulled it outside. The snow had finally stopped and the clouds had drifted off, leaving the edges of roofs and fence posts more visible in the weak moonlight. Relict hefted the demon on his shoulder.

"You two go to the Lord's house and wake his guards. Tell them to see to the guard at the gate and to search the Ward for more victims." He shifted the canvas covered burden on his shoulders. "I'll take this through the outer gate to the fields. Vinir can take it to the Depository tomorrow." He looked back at the barn. "From what Andarack told us, we can guess that if there was another demon, it was gone when we were able to sense this one again." He looked at Garet and Salick, who nodded in agreement.

"That's what happened at the old Temple," Salick said. Relict nodded and walked through the yards, leaving them to carry out his orders.

Salick raised the guards by banging on the gates of the Ward Lord's compound. They had come as quickly as possible back down the main street, their progress slowed by the many frightened people woken from their sleep by the sudden broadcast of fear. Salick reassured them as best she could.

"No, the demon is dead," she told them over and over again. "Go back to your beds."

The citizens of the Ward did so reluctantly, perhaps no longer believing that Banes would tell the truth.

The Ward guard captain accompanied them to the plaza gate, running ahead of them on the slippery cobblestones. He turned pale when he saw the dead woman. Collapsing on the ground beside her and taking the body in his arms, he yelled at the Banes, furious in his grief, "Claws take you! How can we live if we can't trust you anymore?" He put his head down and wept over the slain guard.

Salick knelt beside him. "Captain, no one is more worried than we are over these attacks." She put a hand on his shoulder, and he raised a tear-stained face to look at her. He was an older man, and the sadness was busy carving new lines into his weathered face.

"Why, Bane?" he sobbed. "Why?" He held the body closer. "This is my cousin. She honoured the Banehall, as I did. Why did you let her die?"

Salick's eyes were shadowed under her hood, but her voice was clear in the cold air. "I don't know the answer, friend. But I share your grief." She let go of his shoulder and stood up. "If it helps you to know, a Bane was badly injured fighting the demon that did this. That Bane may now be dead."

The captain did not answer, but rocked back and forth with the body held tightly in his arms. The thin moon shone through the open gate, covering the grieving man in a ghostly light. Knowing they could do no more, Salick and Garet walked quietly through the gate.

The Banehall Besieged

The corridors of the Banehall were deathly quiet when Salick and Garet crept in through the back gate. It had been opened for them and Salick left it that way for Master Relict's return. They made their way to Garet's room to see what news could be had from Marick and Dorict.

The two Blues were waiting for them, Marick still incensed at being left behind. It was some time before he would forgive them, but the description of the Crawler's attack on Relict shocked him out of his sulking.

"He tried to take on a demon with one of those toy swords?" he asked. The young Bane grinned at Dorict. "Maybe it's a good thing we didn't go along; my heart would have stopped to see it." He slapped Garet on the arm and immediately withdrew his hand. "Ewww! What have you been rolling in?"

Garet smiled and took off his cloak. "The same things Master Relict was forced to roll in. We did fight the thing in a barn, after all." He bundled the offending garment into a ball and dropped it by the door.

Dorict shook his head. "If Master Relict is in the same state, Master Tarix will have his head this time," he said.

Marick nodded vigorously in agreement.

"But why would Tarix object?" Garet asked them. "After all, she only trains Blues, not other Reds."

Salick had to answer because Marick and even Dorict had broken out in great gusts of laughter at this question. The Gold twitched a smile herself as she replied, "Don't you realize that Masters Relict and Tarix are married?" She lost control at Garet's look of astonishment and choked out between hiccupped laughter, "Really, Garet! Didn't you think that Banes ever got married?"

He reddened and stood embarrassed until their laughter died down. Marick poked him in the ribs with his finger.

"The way you and Salick carry on, I thought you had already consulted Alanick for the best date to go to the Temple!" he whooped.

Garet started after the little Bane, but Marick dropped to the floor and rolled under his bed, out of Garet's reach. Salick put a hand on his shoulder, her laughter gone.

"Don't bother with him," she said quietly. "Marick!" There was no answer from under the bed. "Come out now. I'll protect you."

There was a shifting and scrabbling as the young Bane edged out cautiously. Salick assisted him by grabbing an ear and pulling him the rest of the way.

"Oww! Salick! You said you'd protect me!"

"I am," she replied, lifting the boy to his feet. "I'm protecting you from Garet, who probably wants to throw you through that window rather than twist your ear." She let go and Marick backed quickly into a corner.

"I'm sorry, Garet. I'm sorry, Salick," he said contritely, then added with a grin, "but you two have been pretty obvious about it."

He covered his ears with his hands, but Salick did not move. Garet watched them both.

"Don't worry about that fool," Dorict said anxiously. "He says too much at the best of times." He pulled Marick out of the corner and dragged him over to sit on his own bed.

Salick eyed him dangerously. "And do you have anything to say about it, Dorict?"

The usually quiet boy surprised them by answering, "Yes, I do." He swallowed and then ploughed ahead, looking down at the knots in the floorboards. "I'm glad you two are in... close." After saying such dangerous words, he floundered for a moment before continuing. "Ahh, what I mean is...well, it's good, that's all, that you're happy, I mean." He trailed off and stood there in front of them, rubbing the sides of his feet together.

Marick was desperately silent behind him. Dorict waited for the claws to fall.

Salick paused for a moment, took a deep breath, and then folded the stout boy awkwardly into her arms. "I'm sorry, Dorict," she said, then looked at the shocked face of Marick. "I'm sorry to you as well." She held out an arm and Marick leaned into her embrace in a daze. "You two have given me more grief and irritation than any ten other Banes," she continued. "Except, maybe for Garet here." She smiled at him over the heads of the two Blues. "But I am happy, at least as happy as any Bane can be in these times. Oh, and I'm even happier that I can share it with both of you." Tears ran down her face and she held out her arms to Garet who took the place of the Blues, who wisely retreated to allow this new embrace. Dorict and Marick stood by and watched, managing to look embarrassed and pleased at the same time.

She looked over Garet's shoulder at the two Blues. "But don't think I won't be as hard on you as before..."

"Good!" Marick laughed. "I can deal with changed demons, murderous swordsmen, and even mad Hallmasters, but a gentle Salick would be too much to take!"

Garet's heart beat so loudly that he was sure it would wake the Hall. He held Salick for what seemed a very short time before Dorict timidly interrupted.

"We should tell you what happened to the other Banes from the Tenth Ward," he sniffed, wiping his nose on his sleeve. Marick nodded in agreement, one hand still absently holding his ear.

Salick and Garet sat down on two of the room's three chairs while the two younger Blues sat on Dorict's bed and filled them in.

"There was a badly injured Bane," Marick began, "just as you said, Garet. It was a Green, Rablick."

Salick gave a small cry. "She's almost a Gold! How did..."

"It's Farix's fault," Dorict cut in, his round face clouding over. "He made her wait by herself while they, Adrix's bunch, patrolled in pairs." He bit his lip. "Rablick said that Farix even knew it was a Crawler when he left her to guard a courtyard gate. I heard her tell Banerict. It just dropped on her. There was no fear to warn her; so she was clawed pretty badly around the face and shoulders before help could come."

Salick snarled, one hand unconsciously reaching up to touch the thin red line of her scar.

"We checked with Banerict," Marick added. "He kicked us out pretty fast, but he was ready to carve Farix up over it." The young Bane lowered his voice. "He said she might lose the sight in one eye."

There was a silence as they digested this news.

"Was Farix hurt?" Garet asked. The thought of that bullying, false Master leaving a Green alone to face a demon that could almost kill a Red sickened him. He remembered the arrogant smile on Farix's face as he read out the names, Garet's included, of those to be demoted at Adrix's command. A rage similar to that he had felt on the bridge rose in him. He was imagining the pleasure he would get by wiping the smile off Farix's face, when Salick interrupted his thoughts.

"At least now everyone will see that Adrix isn't taking the new demon threat seriously," she said quietly, "although I doubt that will cheer Rablick up." She got up and paced the room. "This can't go on! If we keep losing Banes like this, we won't have enough of the higher ranks to patrol the Wards!" She stopped and leaned her shoulder against the door.

"Don't worry," Garet told her, concerned with the desperate look in her eyes. "Banerict fixed you up, twice now! He'll keep patching us up, at least enough to fight a few more demons." He smiled at her and was rewarded with a rolling of her eyes.

"I suppose," she replied. She opened the door and said, "I'm going to see how Rablick is..." she stopped in mid-sentence and listened, her head cocked towards the corridor. Garet made to speak but she shushed him and continued listening. Without a word, she disappeared into the narrow passage. The three Blues exchanged confused glances, then rose as one to follow her.

They found Salick at the top of the stairs leading down to the second floor. She was listening to voices that floated up from the floors below. She heard the others coming up behind her and waved them over to the railing.

"No, only loyal Greens and Golds," a voice said. "The rest will fall in line after we've defeated the King's Guards and those murdering Duelists!" The voice drifted off as the speaker moved out of range.

"That was Farix!" Marick whispered. "I'd know that smug tone anywhere."

Dorict squeezed the railings in his hands, a snarl on his face. "I hate that beast-born fool!"

Salick looked at the young Bane, not used to such emotion from him, but Garet remembered the look on Dorict's face after he returned from capturing Shoronict; quiet or not, the Blue could be as wild as a demon when finally provoked.

"Come on," Salick whispered. "We have to warn Master Mandarack that Adrix is going to attack the King."

"Is that such a bad thing, Salick?" Marick asked, holding her sleeve. "We should let them kill each other. Maybe some sensible people will be left."

Salick shook her head. "If we win, Adrix is King as well as Banehall Master. Do you want to live in Shirath if that happens?" she asked.

Marick let go, grimacing at the thought. "Let's go find the Master."

They avoided Adrix's supporters by taking a back staircase and coming to the main floor of the Hall near the infirmary. Salick hesitated by the infirmary door, but Garet pulled her away.

"Later. We have to talk to Master Mandarack first," he told her.

She nodded reluctantly and took the lead again.

Marick stopped her. "I know a better way. If we take the main corridors, we'll run into Adrix's lot for sure. Follow me."

The route he took them on was a maze of back halls, rooms with two doors, and even a brief stint outside, slipping from a first floor window to a storeroom entrance. Finally, and unexpectedly for Garet, they found themselves in the back of the Red's section.

After checking for any witnesses, Salick took the lead again. With a quick, light step, she ran to Mandarack's door and tapped.

There was no answer. After a moment's hesitation, she opened it and called softly within, "Master?" But there was no answer, and she entered, the others following.

The room was in a state of chaos. The mattress had been dragged off the bed frame, and the bedding was torn and draped over it. Books had been thrown from the shelf, and the two chairs were smashed to pieces on the floor. Garet bent down and picked up a fragment of a tea cup. He felt the sharp edge of the broken china. He had used this cup all those weeks ago when he had questioned Mandarack's decision in bringing him to Shirath. Marick interrupted his thoughts.

"Salick, they've taken the Master!" he whispered fiercely. Salick started to nod, then stopped. She lifted the mattress up to look underneath. Sweeping the bedding back on top of the bed, she turned to survey the damage. A slow smile lit her face and lifted the small scar that rode her cheek.

"I don't think so, Marick," she said, kneeling on one knee, and signalled the others to listen. They squatted beside her. "His shield isn't here," she told them.

Garet scanned the wreckage. She was right.

"Adrix might have taken it," Dorict said doubtfully.

Salick shook her head. "Then why leave everything else?" she waved a hand at the mess surrounding them. "Marick, can you make it to Relict and Tarix's room, and check on Master Branet as well?" she asked, but the only answer she got was the young Bane's swift disappearance into the corridors. She turned to Dorict. "Go back to your room and get the weapons ready. Garet, wait here for Marick, then follow Dorict back upstairs," she instructed. She made to get up, but Garet stopped her.

"Where are you going?" he demanded.

She smiled at him. "Don't worry, I'll go out by the infirmary garden and sneak back in through the kitchen yard. With any luck, I'll get some help and join you in your room in no time!"

Before he could protest further, she slipped out through the door and was gone. Dorict looked at Garet and he nodded. The young Bane followed Salick, leaving Garet alone in the ransacked room. He picked up some of the scattered books and placed them on the desk. Marick found him straightening the bed when he returned.

"Where is everyone?" he demanded, and Garet relayed Salick's orders. Marick nodded, face grim. "All the Masters on our side are gone. Branet's room looks worse than this; he must have put up a fight." He lifted an iron bound club, nearly as tall as himself, the head bristling with lethal spikes. "This was on the floor. I guess Master Branet didn't get away." He handed the heavy weapon to Garet. "Relict's axe was gone, but there were several other weapons there. I think Master Tarix was fixing them..." he said, then stopped short, choking back tears.

Garet put a hand on Marick's shoulder. He knew how much the little Bane idolized the weapons Master. "Don't worry. If Relict got away, I'm sure he wouldn't leave his wife behind."

Even as he said it, he felt strange. His wife. He had never noticed the two of them together, working together as a husband and wife did on a farm. Was married life in the Banehall essentially a separate life, couples coming together only in the rare moments of quiet in the evening? He shook his head. This was no time to think about such things, though he would have given much to be able to stop for an hour now and remember the feeling of Salick's arms around him.

Marick tugged at his sleeve. "Wake up!" he hissed, and the two Banes slipped out to retrace their steps before climbing the stairs back to the third floor.

Dorict was waiting for them. He pulled them in and thrust weapons into their hands. His own pole, still sporting a deep nick from disarming Shoronict, leaned in the corner nearest the door. They waited for Salick, each conjuring possible disasters in their thoughts. With great relief, they heard a tapping and opened it to let in the Gold, followed by Vinir, wearing only tunic and pants and with her long blond hair unbound. Both carried tridents, which they propped beside Dorict's pole.

"All right, Salick," Vinir demanded, stifling a yawn. "Tell me what's so important you had to ruin the best night's sleep I've had since that idiot Adrix demoted me!" She glared at her friend, the intimidating effect weakened by another yawn. "Oh, it's cold in here!" she said, standing on one bare foot.

Salick dragged her inside the room, and the confused Green sat on the nearest bed, folding her long legs under her for warmth. After a moment, Garet went to his trunk and pulled out his old shoes. He had clung to them, along with his other farm clothes, as a reminder of his origins and perhaps his future. They had been carefully repaired with a piece of leather from the storeroom and wrapped in his old tunic. He reluctantly presented them to Vinir, face red.

"Thank you, Garet," she said, and slipped the battered shoes on her feet. She smiled at him.

"Are you finally ready to listen?" Salick demanded crossly.

Vinir grinned at her friend and waved her hand imperiously, holding out her legs so she could better admire her new footwear.

Her smile vanished as she listened to their report of what had been found in Mandarack's and the others' rooms.

"Master Relict's axe was gone?" she asked Marick, who had sat beside her on his bed.

The small Bane nodded glumly. "Master Tarix's chair was gone as well, but both pairs of crutches were still there."

Vinir thought for a moment and said, "Master Relict could well be on patrol, but as for Master Tarix..." She left the sentence unfinished and put a hand on Marick's shoulder. "Don't worry. There's not a Bane in the Hall of Blue level or above that doesn't respect her—and the sacrifices she's made for the Hall."

"Except Adrix," Marick replied, head down.

Vinir ruffled his hair and asked Salick, "How can we get word to Master Relict or Mandarack if they are out of the Hall? They could be walking into an ambush if they come back tonight."

Salick paced for a minute while the others waited. "The roof," she said finally. "We'll go up on the roof and call down to them when they return." She looked at them, her shoulders set and her chin thrust forward. "Get as many blankets and cloaks as you can find. It will be a cold wait."

Vinir groaned and looked at the thin shoes she now wore. Marick shyly offered her the blanket folded at the head of his bed. She smiled at him. "Well, let's all go freeze together."

Bearing their blankets and weapons, they climbed the ladder to the west wing's roof. This was a different section than the one where Garet and Marick had practiced. It was a floor shorter than that centre wing, but from it one could see the Banehall's courtyard and all the plaza, save that which lay directly behind them. The curved moon hung a hand's breadth above the retreating bank of storm clouds, turning their tops silver. Their feet brushed aside the powdery drifts and Garet looked down at the empty, snow-brushed plaza, knowing that the peacefulness of the scene was an illusion. Angry voices drifted up from the courtyard below.

Salick had crawled to the parapet. She waved the others over, palm down to signify that they should keep low.

Garet crawled beside her and lifted his head cautiously to peer over the edge. A mass of Banes crowded around the low stairs leading to the Banehall doors. Adrix stood at the top of the steps, listening to an anxious looking Gold on the step below. The young man was speaking rapidly and pointing to the centre bridge gate. Twisting his head, Garet looked and saw a line of torches approaching the Banehall. He pointed them out to the others.

Salick drew back her head and the others huddled with her below the lip of the parapet.

"I see about seven Masters who answer to Adrix, their Golds and Greens, and a few frightened Blues and Blacks," she whispered. "Those torches might mean a patrol is returning."

Vinir nodded. "Not even half the Banehall's down there. The rest must be on patrol." She pulled the blanket tighter around her.

"Very convenient," Garet observed. "All Master Mandarack's people are on patrol or taken prisoner so that

Adrix and his followers can do something stupid." He pulled the hammer-rope from under his cloak, but he knew the weapon would never reach the Hallmaster.

Salick put a restraining hand on his arm. "Don't do anything that will let them know we're here," she warned. "Our job is to find out what we can and then warn whoever was sent out on patrol before Adrix made his move!"

Garet reluctantly nodded. He eased his head above the wall again as Adrix began to speak to the assembled Banes.

"Some of you have questioned my attempts to gain more power from the King, and to use those powers to protect us from those who wish Banes harm!" he said, his voice ringing off the courtyard walls. "Let those Banes who questioned now look at the King's guards approaching our Hall to try and destroy us." He pointed at the approaching torches. "Trax has shown himself to be a traitor to this city. He attempts to destroy the only people who can keep Shirath safe from the demons." The Hallmaster raised his hands above his head. "The people fear demons. Now, let them learn to fear Banes as well!"

Several voices were raised in support of his speech, but many Banes looked at each other in wonder and doubt.

"Spears and tridents to the gates!" Adrix called. "Keep those horses back!"

His supporters ran to the high iron gates that closed off the courtyard from the plaza. They stuck their weapons through the rails to present a deadly defense to the approaching guards. Banes with shorter weapons or no weapons at all milled behind them, standing on tiptoe to see their enemy.

"Don't worry," Adrix said, coming down the steps and pushing to the front of the line, "we only need to hold them for a little while. We will soon have the weapons we need to drive these fools back into the river." He laughed and slapped the back of the Master nearest him. "Let them float all the way to Solantor, and good riddance!"

Laughter sounded below as the party on the roof drew back again. Salick bit her lip, then told Dorict to watch in the opposite direction to see if any of their Masters were returning. The Blue took up his position but soon turned to the others, shaking his head.

"We can't do anything except see what happens so that we can tell Master Mandarack," Salick complained.

Garet agreed, just as tense and nervous as Salick. If only they could do something. He leaned back against the parapet, thinking. Vinir shivered beside him, and he took off his cloak and gave it to her absent-mindedly. Salick was looking at the column of guards, some mounted and some on foot. A man on a tall, black horse led them, his steel and bronze armour shining in the moonlight. He was accompanied by footmen carrying lamps and standards.

"It can't be," Salick said, her voice rising unwisely. She raised her head for a better look and Vinir reached over to pull her back down.

"Are you mad?" she hissed. "What is so interesting that you want to get us caught?"

"I think," Salick began, "no, I know that the man leading the Guards is Trax. The King!" Her eyes shone. "He's a proud man, as proud as Adrix, but with as little reason," she whispered. "Let's see Adrix try to bully him!"

Vinir shook her head. "You know the King better than I do, or most people, I'm sure," she agreed. "But Adrix knows he can't back down without losing the confidence of those Masters down there. Most of them support him just because he's the Hallmaster, not because they agree with him." She stuck a lightly-clad arm out of her wrappings and pulled her trident closer. "If he backs down in front of the King, they'll demand another vote."

Garet straightened up. "Maybe he doesn't intend to back down," he said. "Salick, what did Adrix mean about getting weapons to drive Trax back into the river?"

Salick shrugged. "I don't know," she replied. "He has all the weapons of the Hall there already." She thought for a moment. "He could be talking about others supporting the Hall," she said, but then shook her head. "But that's not very likely the way most citizens feel about us now." She looked questioningly at Garet. "What do you think he means?"

"There is one weapon that he can use," he said, after desperately trying to find other possibilities. "How deep is the crevice at the Depository?"

"No!" Vinir cried, shocked enough to raise her own voice now, but Garet doubted anyone below heard her over the shouts and curses.

"How deep?" Salick asked, her eyes widening as she realized the reason for his question. "You can't mean that Adrix would use demon jewels against our own people!" she whispered.

Dorict came back to see what the commotion was and Marick told him, "Garet thinks Adrix has sent for jewels to use against the King and his Guards."

The young Bane shook his head. "Salick was right, Adrix must want to become King. He'd use the jewels to control the city through fear, just like the demons."

A clear voice rose above the hubbub of the enclosure below.

"The King comes to seek parley with the Master of Shirath Banehall," a young man's voice rang out. "Let him come forth to speak!"

Garet looked down. A youth in a tunic of royal purple stood in front of the massed spears and tridents, their points barely an inch from his chest. If he was nervous, he didn't show it. One hand was held up in sign of truce and the other held a tall banner, its brocade a raging bear under a crown and starry heaven. The young man spoke again.

"Let Hallmaster Adrix come forth and speak with his King!"

Adrix pushed his way to the front and yelled through the bars. "My King? Why does 'my King' come to the Banehall with armed soldiers and bearing fire?" The voices of the Banes beside him rose in support.

"Because your King is troubled by the actions of the Banes of his city," spoke a voice from behind the herald. The King urged his mount forward, the big black edging nervously close to the massed points of the weapons. Trax was a man of thirty or so, broad shouldered and smooth faced. Not tall, he stayed on his horse, perhaps to maintain the advantage of height.

"Your King comes before you to ask you to take up your duties, as you have for the six-hundred years since the founding of Shirath." The voice rose to reach all the Banes in the courtyard and those looking down from the windows facing the plaza. In the torchlight, the King's armour shone and sparkled with the richness of its gilt and jewels. Trax calmed his prancing horse and continued.

"The left hand does not fight the right," he shouted. "Nor does it act on its own." His voice grew angry. "The people of Shirath die in their homes because you Banes forget what you owe to this city: six-hundred years of generous support! Stop trying to take powers and privileges that were never yours. Do your duty before the demons slaughter us all!"

The Herald and several soldiers near the King touched their ears and flicked away their hands as Garet had seen the Astrologer, Alanick, do in the Plaza so long ago. Born to a fear that they feared even to name, Garet realized, the people of Shirath now had to confront the possibility of facing it without the Banes. No wonder they would take up arms to try and force the Banehall to protect them again. How would they feel if they knew how helpless the Banes really were in the face of this "Caller Demon" and its ability to attack without warning?

Adrix answered the King, his voice dripping sarcasm. "Well, Trax, you speak of duty and support. Yet for six hundred years, we have died protecting the people while Kings have polished the throne with their backsides. You sleep in your beds because we leave ours to patrol the Wards. You live whole because our blood is spilled." His voice rose to a howl. "Powers and privileges that aren't ours? Can you fight the demons, Trax? What powers and privileges do you claim that you truly deserve more than we do? From this night on, there is no useless King in Shirath! We Banes are the rulers of Shirath!"

The roar of approval from the massed Banes drove the Herald back until he stood beside the King's black horse. Trax put out a hand and grabbed the banner from him, hoisting it high above his head.

"My house is as old as this Hall!" he growled. The horse reared and the herald scrambled for safety. Dragging the bit back cruelly, Trax got the animal under control. "We cannot fight the demons, but we can fight you." His voice rose. "We can force you to remember what you owe this city." He wheeled his horse and called, "Force the Gate!"

The palace guards, their ranks bolstered by Duelists and now looking less decorative than fierce, lined up facing the ranks of spears and tridents. Garet saw that all they would need to do was chop down the Bane's weapons with their great swords until they could approach the gate and force it open by mass of numbers.

"Fools!" yelled Adrix at the Guards advancing in step towards the courtyard. "Any guard who attacks this Hall will face King Birat's fate!"

The rank of guards faltered and then rallied as Trax rode up behind them, shouting, "Steady! You fight for your own lives and the lives of your families, the lives these pampered, beast-born fools would throw away." He drew his sword and swung it about his head. "Forward!"

Garet held his breath, and Adrix drew back from the gate, yelling, "Where is Farix? We need those jewels now."

"Adrix!" a woman's voice called. The Banes looked across the courtyard to the side door leading into the gymnasiums of the east wing. Tarix was crawling out the door, pulling herself along on her elbows. "Adrix!" she called again, and the Hallmaster turned to sneer at her.

"Do you come crawling for forgiveness, Tarix? I'm afraid it's too late. I'm rather busy, and I've never had time for traitors." He signalled two Golds to grab the Red.

The two men pulled her up and were dragging her back into the Hall when she wrapped her arms around the railing at the edge of the steps and held tight.

"Listen to me," she screamed at the Banes massed behind the defenders. Many turned to look at her. "Shame!" Tarix yelled at them, her voice shaking with effort. "Shame on us all! Adrix has twisted six-hundred years of honourable service into a crown for his own swollen head, and you help him set it there!"

Several Reds and Golds lowered their heads at this criticism, but the Hallmaster merely laughed.

"A swollen head, eh? Let's see how yours feels when I drop a necklace of demon jewels around it. Even a Bane can't stand that forever!" he observed, and signalled the Golds to pry her off the railing.

Marick tried to run back to the ladder, but Garet grabbed him. "Wait 'til we know where they're taking her," he told him. The young Bane resisted for a moment, then nodded. He jabbed the point of his shield into the snow and looked back down at the courtyard.

A Red grabbed Adrix's arm. "You threaten to necklace a fellow Master?" he cried.

Adrix shook him off, shrieking in his fury, "Yes! And anyone else who defies me."

The Red stumbled back in shock, his spiked club dropping from his hand.

From above, the watchers could see a space begin to clear between two sets of Banes, those who followed Adrix and those who now feared what he might become. The Red who had questioned Adrix pulled several other Masters aside and spoke urgently to them. Steel rang on steel as the Guards attacked the forest of points arrayed against them.

"Heaven's shield," Vinir whispered. "Do you feel it?"

None of the others needed to ask what it was they were supposed to feel, for a great tide of demon-fear began to wash over them. Garet crawled shakily to the other side of the roof and peered over the side. A large party of Banes approached the side of the Banehall, making for the kitchen yard entrance below their perch. As they got nearer, Garet could see their stiff movements and jerky steps. *How many jewels do they have*, he wondered, fighting against more fear than he had ever felt in his life.

He groped his way back to the others. Vinir was breathing hard, mumbling over and over, "Fear is outside. I build a wall." Dorict and Marick clung to each other, their breath ragged. Salick's eyes were dark with her inner battle. The fear filled Garet's stomach. He tried to push it out with his breath, but there was always more pushing in. His eyes watered and the very moon seemed to tremble in the sky. And then it was gone.

Salick collapsed beside him, gasping. Garet pulled her up into his arms, afraid the mental attack would start again. Vinir coughed and retched beside them.

"Wh-what happened," Salick stuttered. "Is it the demon, the one we saw near the old Temple?"

"No!" cried Marick. The young Bane stood beside the parapet, looking down into the courtyard. "It's something much, much better."

They pulled themselves up beside him and looked down. Mandarack stood on the Banehall's steps, holding Farix by the collar. The young Red had his hands tied behind his back and looked terrified. Relict stood nearby, one of Andarack's silkstone boxes in his hand. Behind and beside them, arrayed on the steps leading from the door to the courtyard, stood many of the Banes who had suffered during Adrix's reign as Hallmaster. Garet saw Pratax and Bandat on the lower steps, tridents pointed at the man who had tried to demote them. Even the Records Keeper, Arict, roused from her sleep by the jewels' horror, stood in the group, her nightcap still on her head and a rusty spear in her hand.

"The King!" Salick whispered. She pointed beyond the gate.

No guard stood in the light of the dropped torches. The royal banner lay on the ground among the litter of abandoned swords and spears. *Adrix was right*, Garet thought. The jewels did drive them away. But how had Mandarack escaped to capture them? Below them, the old Bane spoke to the crowd.

"This Master," he said, pushing Farix down the stairs, "and others, have betrayed the honour and history of this Banehall to aid his own mad ambition."

As Farix stumbled down the last steps, Pratax reached out and tore off his red sash. The young man tripped and rolled to the ground at Adrix's feet.

"There will be no necklacing of Kings or Banes tonight, Adrix," Mandarack said, his eyes steady on the glaring Hallmaster. "Let those who wish to return to their duties stand with us."

Many of the Banes in the middle of the courtyard and some from the line at the gate moved slowly over to stand beside the steps.

Adrix grabbed a Gold from the remaining defenders and twisted him to face Mandarack. He waved the others to follow. "We will cleanse our own Hall before we deal with the King." He pushed the Gold forward and turned to pull others up. "Kill them! Kill them all!" he screamed.

Mandarack came down the steps, signalling his followers to stay back. He faced the young man, who pointed a spear at the old man's throat, and spoke a single word, "Choose." Mandarack bore no weapon nor made any move to defend himself.

The Gold looked at him.

"Do it!" screamed Adrix. He pushed the rest of his ragged line forward.

"Forlinect!" Tarix cried.

The Gold looked at her. The Training Master still clung to the railing, though now only to remain upright. The two Golds who had tried to remove her had moved to Adrix's defense. Her face was smeared with blood, and one eye was swollen shut. She looked at Forlinect out of the other eye and waited.

He looked at her and then back to Mandarack. Ignoring the screaming Hallmaster behind him, he dropped his spear into the slush of the well-trodden snow. Without a word, he walked over to Tarix and pulled her upright, an arm around her waist for support.

More spears and tridents followed as Bane after Bane dropped their weapons and ranged themselves on the steps behind Mandarack. The few remaining loyal to Adrix backed away as they saw the numbers now against them. The Hallmaster glared at Mandarack and cursed him, spittle falling from his mouth.

"You clawed cripple!" he snarled. "I should have dealt with you at the beginning of this." He twisted his neck and saw how few and how frightened were his followers.

Mandarack stepped forward, leaving his supporters farther behind, to face the Hallmaster in the middle of the courtyard. On the roof, Salick gripped the parapet and whispered, "Careful, oh Heaven, please be careful!"

Garet looked around for a weapon that would reach Adrix if he decided to attack Mandarack. The tridents were useless for throwing with any accuracy, his rope would not reach that far, and neither Marick nor Dorict carried anything that would serve. He cast desperately about the roof for something useful. Below them, the mass of Banes stood unmoving, paralyzed by the confrontation between the two Masters.

Adrix's breath came in huge gulps, his florid cheeks were a deep red, and Garet wondered if the man would survive his own rage. With an incoherent roar, the Hallmaster scooped up the club the protesting Red had dropped and charged Mandarack.

Salick screamed and below, Pratax and Bandat, shocked out of their paralysis, started to run forward to protect Mandarack, but the distance was too great. Relict was flying down the steps and Tarix was pushing at the Gold when they all stopped. Adrix fell to the ground, clutching his knee and howling in pain.

The Banes on the roof spun to look at Garet. He was still twisted from the throw, his fingers stretched as if reaching out to the man on the distant ground. Beside Adrix lay the fragments of the silkstone Lord Andarack had given Garet a thousand years ago that same night.

Dorict fell to the roof in astonishment and relief. Vinir stood staring down, trident dangling from her hand and the blanket and cloak in a forgotten pile at her feet. Salick knelt, her head on the parapet, face covered with her hands. Only Marick seemed to retain the power of speech.

"Garet! How did you..." he squeaked. The young Bane stumbled over to where Garet was slowly straightening, eyes still on the moaning figure on the ground. Marick touched his outstretched hand in wonder. "That was amazing," he said simply, and then with a whoop of delight, ran for the ladder.

Garet saw Mandarack raise his arm in salute to him, but he made no motion in return. The screaming Hallmaster had been lifted from the ground and was being carried noisily into the Hall. Tarix had also disappeared and in a moment, only a few stunned Banes were left in the courtyard, to be herded inside by Arict's rusty spear and antique curses.

His mind still some distance from his body, Garet slowly turned his face up to the moon, and saw its thick crescent bright against the black sky. He felt arms come around him and heard Salick's voice.

"You did it! You saved him," she whispered fiercely in his ear.

He could feel her body shaking and drew his arms in around her, suddenly aware again of the cold, the noises around him, even the silkstone's oily feeling left on the palm of his hand. A shiver overcame him. His muscles slowly relaxed.

Marick clambered back up the ladder and gasped out his news. Mandarack had summoned them to the dining hall. The Masters were to choose a new Hallmaster, and decisions were going to be made about the King. They followed him shakily down the ladder, their legs unsteady on the narrow, wooden rungs. Vinir grabbed Salick's hand and promised to meet them in the dining hall as soon as she was properly dressed. She dashed off towards the back stairs and the Golds' rooms on the main floor, the shoes Garet had lent her leaving wet marks on the corridor floor.

The dining hall was full of Banes talking, banging tables, or just sitting in their chairs, trying to take in the night's events. Mandarack sat in his usual place at the high table, but the centre section was empty. Relict sat beside his wife, using a cloth to gently wipe the blood off her face while she smiled at him through her bruises. Branet slowly limped into the hall behind Dorict, rubbing his wrists and glowering happily. The big man caught up with Garet as he pushed into the hall and grabbed his shoulder.

"Well thrown!" he bellowed, causing a sudden silence in the buzz of the hall. Mandarack looked up momentarily before turning back to argue with Bandat and Arict. Several Golds and Greens took up the call, however, and the dust was shaken off the ceiling beams with the stomping and banging that accompanied the shouts.

Garet stood there, embarrassed beyond movement, but Salick took his elbow and led him past the chanting Banes to the end of the high table. The calls died down as Mandarack stood and motioned for silence.

"This has been a night that will be remembered for the next six-hundred years!" he began, to nods of agreement and nervous laughter. "Never before has a King of the Five Cities attacked a Banehall. That will be remembered. Never before has a Hallmaster led his Hall so near to disaster."

At this, several Banes lowered their heads. Branet scowled at them, his injured leg propped up on a stool in front of him, Banerict fussing over it.

"That will be remembered as well," Mandarack warned. The dining hall was silent as each pondered how future Banes would judge them. "But be cheered," Mandarack continued, "for it will also be remembered that some who had been wrong saw their mistake in time, though it was only at the very last moment that it was given to them to choose."

Beside Master Tarix, the Gold who had refused to attack Mandarack with his spear shivered and a little hot water spilled from the bowl he held for Master Relict. Tarix reached out from her wheeled chair and put a hand on his arm to steady him.

"But, when all else is forgotten or changed, it will be remembered that Garet, a Blue of this Hall, by a single courageous act, changed everything," Mandarack said, looking down at the discomfited young Bane. "And saved everything."

A cheer went up in the Hall. Even Adrix's erstwhile supporters found themselves caught up in the celebration, raising their voices, building fellowship again and beginning to heal the breach between themselves and the victors.

Garet, still not sure of how he felt about crippling a fellow Bane, hunched his shoulders and took the nearest route out of the dining hall, into the kitchen. The air was warm and moist as a few sleepy cooks, summoned at Mandarack's orders, set about making a very early breakfast for the Hall. Garet stood there, smelling the baking bread, and the aroma of the onions and spices to be mixed into the huge pots of porridge simmering in the hearths. The cooks ignored him, too concentrated on their own tasks to worry about a Blue wandering into their kingdom. Salick caught up with him. She was alone.

"Garet?" she began, tentatively. She stood beside him, not touching him, her eyes concerned.

"I'm not that!" he said. The smells and noise of the kitchen seemed the only protection he had against what he feared in the dining hall.

"What?" she asked. She moved to stand in front of him and bent a bit to look into his downcast eyes. "What aren't you?" She still did not touch him.

Garet took a deep breath full of the scent of bread. "I'm not someone worth cheering for," he told her, looking up to see her blue eyes. "What I did was..." he hesitated, "...wasn't done for cheering, or congratulations." He stomped a foot in frustration. "If I were my father, I'd be in there accepting their praise and their drinks, bathing in that glory like a pig in a mud hole. But I'd rather be necklaced then be like... Oh, I wish no one had ever seen me throw that clawed stone!"

A slow smile spread over Salick's face. "No, I don't suppose you acted for the fame of it," she said. Then she did take his hands in hers. "You did it to save Master Mandarack."

"Yes..." he said, thinking for a moment. "I did. But that wasn't a demon I hit. It was a man," he explained. He turned back to her, eyes pleading for understanding. "When I did it, I didn't care what happened to Adrix, and when I saw him on the ground, I felt nothing, not at first." He wiped the moisture off his face. The great bread ovens set in the hearths had been opened to reveal dozens of brown loaves. The cooks slid in long, wooden paddles to lift them from the hot bricks and set them on wooden racks to cool. Looking at them, Garet suddenly remembered that Banfreat, the first Banemaster of Shirath, had been a baker. He wondered if the first weapon used against a demon had been a baker's paddle.

"Why should you feel anything for him?" Salick asked, puzzled at his words. She brushed back a limp strand of hair.

They stood to one side as wooden trays, stacked high with loaves, were carried past them into the dining hall.

"Because he's a human being, not a demon!" Garet said. "He lay on the ground screaming, maybe crippled for life, and all anyone can say is 'good throw'!"

When the remaining cook looked up from stirring one of the porridge pots and frowned at this outburst, Garet strode out into the kitchen yard. The moon had set, but the sun was now just below the horizon, giving the baskets and carts a pearly grey sheen. It was so cold that the snow had crusted into ice, and the Banes' feet crunched through this thin layer as they walked out into the yard.

"But he is an evil man!" argued Salick, her hands stuck under her armpits, and her breath steaming.

"And so is my father. And your father. And Marick's mother who left him alone on the streets of Torrick. And how many men and women in this city?" he asked. The sky was moving from grey to the fragile blue of a cloudless dawn. "Should they all be crippled? What right do I have to judge them, to hurt them?" he spat out the words. "And what right does anyone else have to tell me what I did was right?"

"None, I suppose," spoke a quiet voice behind them.

Garet turned and saw Mandarack standing in the doorway.

"You had two choices, Garet: to act or not to act," the old Bane said. He drew his twisted arm behind him with his good hand and took a step out into the yard. "Adrix's crimes would have become even more terrible. You chose not to let that happen," he said.

Garet hesitated for a moment then nodded for the Master to continue. Salick stood to one side, watching them and shivering a bit.

"We applaud your skill, because it is a true skill, whatever use it is put to. And we applaud your decision to act, because it shows that you are a true Bane—you protect your people," Mandarack explained. He turned to Salick. "I do not rejoice at Master Adrix's pain, even though I know he meant to kill me," he told her. "He has acted in an evil way, but he has also killed many demons in his day—and bears the scars to prove it."

Salick's hand went to her cheek, one finger touching the small, curved scar. "I'm sorry, Master," she said, hand still on her cheek. "It is wrong to enjoy another's pain, but when I saw him attack..." she trailed off. Her hand dropped and she looked at the ground.

"I honour your concern for me, Salick. And," he added, turning to face Garet again, "your protection. But this war with the King, and within this Hall will not be won through hate, but through forgiveness and agreement." He nodded at them and turned to go back into the Hall.

"Master!" Garet called. "Would you have killed Adrix if I hadn't stopped him?"

Mandarack paused for a long moment in the doorway and finally turned his head to answer. "Yes, if there was no other way, I would have tried. But like you, I would have found no joy in it."

When they were alone again, Salick shook her head and said in a low voice, "I'm sorry, Garet. Maybe I don't understand you, either of you." She stepped close to him and put her arm around him. "I can't help but take satisfaction in Adrix's pain. He got what he deserved." She sniffed in the cold air. "I suppose I'm just more cruel than you," she joked, but her eyes brimmed with tears.

He shook his head and touched his cheek to hers. "No! Remember that night on the bridge? You can't imagine how I felt when you were injured!" He took a deep breath. "If Adrix had been attacking you in the courtyard instead of the Master, I would have smashed his skull with that stone and danced on his corpse," he said savagely.

Looking a little shocked, Salick held him out at arm's length and looked into his eyes. "I suppose I'm glad then that it wasn't me he was after," she said. She linked arms with him and they went quietly back through the warm kitchen into the dining hall.

Rare, Heaven be thanked. Ware its tail, which it swings like a soldier's mace.
The legs are as a child's, though the arms are powerful and heavily clawed, moving
solely to the front and down to dig.

Digger Demon

Fear fouls the air
Yet nothing is there
Listen for the sound
Of the Beast below the ground

A New Hallmaster

After a quick breakfast, Garet slept throughout the day and woke again just before supper. Dorict and Marick still snored gently under their blankets, so tired from the night before that they had only pulled off their boots before dropping into sleep. He sat up and scratched his head, feeling nothing more than a great need to be clean. A fresh tunic and pants under his arm, he threw on a robe and slipped out the door. The floor was icy on his bare feet and he half skipped down the hall to the stairs. Two flights down, the common washrooms were thankfully empty. He dreaded more congratulations for his actions of the night before. Filtering through the frost on the small windows, the late afternoon light spun with dust motes when he dropped his clothes on the counter. He bent over a basin of water, picked up a sponge, and began to scrub and shiver himself awake.

Clean, invigorated and freshly dressed, he ran back up the stairs as fast as he could, keeping his head down when he met other Banes. *Not that that's much use*, he thought; his black hair marked him more clearly than any sash or uniform. He ignored any calls in his direction, rubbing at his ears with a towel to pretend temporary deafness. Marick was pushing at Dorict, trying to rouse him when Garet re-entered their room.

"Get up, you slug!" Marick demanded, pulling at his friend's shoulder. Dorict only grumbled in response and burrowed deeper into his blankets. With Garet's help, Marick got him upright and then pulled the blankets out of the sleepy Blue's reach.

Dorict shivered and opened his eyes a crack. "Why are we getting up so early?" he grumbled. One toe touched the floor and he jerked his foot back.

"Look at the light!" cried Marick, waving one hand towards the window. "It's practically night again. Anything could have happened by now!" He threw Dorict's clothes at him and scrambled into his own uniform. "Hurry up!" he said, pulling the tunic over his head. "I refuse to be left out just because I'm a Blue!"

Towing the protesting Dorict, his two friends dashed back down the stairs to the front of the hall. There was much coming and going through the front doors. Garet could see four armed Golds standing in the slanting light of the courtyard. Someone called down from the roof, and they opened the Gate to let in a patrol of fifteen Banes, led by Relict. The Red waved to them as he entered the hall but, much to Marick's disgust, did not pause to give them any news. Instead, the Master passed them by and practically trotted to the Records room. Marick managed to get a peek inside before the door was closed on him.

"Master Mandarack is there," he reported. "So is Master Tarix and Master Bandat." He pulled them into the dining hall. "Lots of Golds too. I saw Salick there." He smiled smugly. "At least we'll know sooner or later."

Garet wasn't so sure. Salick's sense of duty towards the Hall was absolute. He doubted that even her new feelings for him would cause her to break trust with the Masters. As they entered the dining hall, he pushed Marick and Dorict to the back of the cavernous room, away from the other diners.

Marick looked at him quizzically. "Does the praise you've gotten really bother you that much?" he asked. "Don't worry, people will forget it soon enough." Looking darkly at the few Masters seated at the head table, he added, "It's the bad deeds that are never forgotten."

"In that case, you'll always be a legend in this Hall!" Vinir's voice sounded behind them. When she raised her hand to ruffle Marick's hair, Garet saw by the flash of gold that she had been promoted to the rank she deserved.

Tongue-tied, Marick could only grumble happily.

"Can you tell us what's been happening?" Garet asked Salick, who had appeared on his other side.

"Eat first," she said, and sat down heavily beside him.

Vinir nodded. "Certain Blues might sleep away the day in their beds, dreaming of glory, while we Golds labour for the preservation of the Hall," she said. "Well, at least since noon," she added with a smile that dimpled her cheeks.

Dorict pulled Marick away to get their food. As Garet followed them with his eyes, he saw that a certain quiet chaos raged in the dining hall. Although the Reds maintained their pride of place at the head table, the lower ranks had abandoned their sections of descending importance to sit in large, mixed groups, eating and talking, mostly at the same time. As he watched, Garet saw a Red, Pratax, come in and signal to one such group. Stuffing the last of the food in their mouths, they picked up their weapons and followed him out of the hall.

"A patrol," Salick explained, seeing his confusion. "Master Mandarack says that no small patrols can go out anymore." She leaned against him slightly, and Vinir grinned at her friend and rolled her eyes. Salick glared back but moved slightly away from Garet before continuing. "Large patrols are going out to the Wards, checking each one before moving on." She slid a hand under the table to touch his. "Another patrol comes along soon after, so that a demon can't do much harm before it's caught." She paused as the two Blues arrived with trays of food. "The only problem is that it takes so many Banes. That's why Blues and even some Blacks are going out on patrol—even if they can't fight, they can watch so the older Banes aren't ambushed." She turned to Marick. "And I suppose you want to know what's going on too."

"No need," the boy replied airily, waving away her comment. "The cooks told us all that and more." Dorict nodded, busy at his first meal of the day. Marick pushed over a plate of bread and a bowl of stew across the table to Salick and added, "Old Tarlax and his helpers haven't left the kitchen since last night, but I think they've been trading sweets for information all that time." He popped a sugar-dusted cookie into his mouth.

Dorict finished his first bowl of stew and took up the conversation for his friend. "Tarlax says that the King has ordered that no Palace guard or Duelist cross the bridges without his permission." He wiped his mouth and asked Salick, "Did Master Mandarack really use the jewels to drive off the king, or was it Farix doing it before the Master caught him?"

Salick glanced around the nearest tables to make sure their occupants were involved in their own conversations. "Yes, the Master did it," she answered reluctantly. "He knew that whoever won inside the Hall, the King's men couldn't be allowed to defeat us, nor could the jewels be left anywhere Adrix and Farix could get at them." She put a piece of bread in her mouth and spoke around it. "He told the other Masters that it was the hardest decision he had ever had to make." She raked them all with her eyes. "That does not need to be repeated."

"I don't think anyone at this table would think of doing so, Salick," Garet said quietly. He touched her hand. Marick and Dorict nodded, and Vinir leaned over and punched her in the ribs.

"Oww, Vinir!" Salick cried out. "That's my injured side!" She rubbed her ribs and glared at her friend.

"Well then, it'll likely be some time before you insult your friends again by showing so much distrust," Vinir replied calmly.

Marick snickered a bit and even Dorict smiled around a mouthful of cookie. Garet put his hand on Salick's shoulder and gave her a little shake.

"All right! All right!" she said. "I'm sorry, but with all these plots and counterplots, I'm seeing shadows in sunlight." She lowered her head, picked up her spoon, and ate her stew.

Relict came into the dining room, looking around the tables. Vinir waved at him and the short Master came over.

"Ah, Vinir," he said, pulling at his beard, "I was looking for you." His sharp eyes scanned the table. "I was looking for all of you as a matter of fact." He broke into a wide smile. "And here you are conveniently gathered just for my sake."

Reaching over, he pulled up a chair from another table and sat down near the two youngest Blues.

"First of all, I need Marick and Dorict here to go out on a patrol with my group," he said, then held up his hand at the Blues' excited reaction. "It may not be anything more than watching our backs while we search the Wards. But we will be crossing the bridge." His tone turned serious. "We have been searching the Palace-side Wards for the whole day, and no one has tried to stop us," he explained. "But night is falling, and that will doubtless make things more dangerous." He turned to his apprentice. "Take them to get their weapons and cloaks please, Vinir."

The blond girl smiled and winked at Salick and Garet. She led the two Blues out of the hall, Dorict trying to finish his bread on the run.

Relict turned towards the two remaining Banes. "I'm afraid that you two will have something more interesting to do than go on patrol," he told them. Standing up, he motioned them to do the same. "You won't be able to finish your meal. Master Branet wants to see you immediately."

Salick had already risen and was tugging on Garet's sleeve to get him to follow. Relict nodded at them and said, "Good luck to both of you. I approve of the Masters' choice for this mission, having had the pleasure of seeing you two work together." He smiled, the scratches left by the Crawler Demon still visible on the left side of his face. Signalling to more Banes on his way out, he left to organize his patrol.

"And to think that I once thought being a Bane was boring," Garet said, shaking his head.

Salick laughed. "All of us think that when we're Blacks. With any luck, we'll live long enough to be bored again." But there was a light in her eyes, and Garet had to agree that he felt more excitement than fear. Very shortly, they stood in front of the Records room door, brushing the crumbs off their vests and sashes before knocking.

A Gold opened the door and led them to the great table where Garet's status as a Blue had been registered before turning and leaving the room. Branet sat behind the desk, a map of the city laid out before him. Pieces of paper lay on top of the map, some with lists of Banes and schedules of patrols, others with notations on supplies, and a few that Garet couldn't decipher from his position across the table. Branet swept a portion of the map clear, revealing the Palace plaza. The semi-circular space had the outline of the Palace in purple ink and three blue dots to signify the Temple complex. A section on the east end was labelled "market" and each Ward gate had its number drawn beside it.

"I hope you are both well-rested after last night's excitement," Branet said to them. He did not wait for an answer. "The skirmish with the King was not conclusive," Branet said. He waved them to sit across from him and continued, "He was forced to retreat, but he will not surrender." He looked at Salick for a moment, and she nodded.

"The Ward Lords are not decided in their support," he said. "Hallmaster Mandarack's heightened patrols have reassured many that we have no intention of abandoning our duties, but they fear that we cannot deal with this change in the demons, even though they are not sure of what that change is."

He picked up a list of Banes and studied it. "We don't have enough Banes in the Hall to continuously patrol every Ward," he told them. "With the King's help, we could have eyes in every part of the city, night and day. But first we must make peace with the Palace." He looked at them, his mouth set. "That is why you must undertake a dangerous assignment. You two will go and see the King."

The words dropped into a profound silence; the stacks of papers and bound ledgers seemed to lean towards them, waiting for a reply. At first Garet did not believe his ears. See the King? Any sight of a Bane's sash near the Palace would bring out a mob of Guards and Duelists, competing for the glory of killing them! He looked over at Salick. She was shaking her head, her eyes wide in disbelief.

"Master!" she said. "How can you send us there? You know what will happen!"

Branet held up his hand to stop her protest. "I know that it sounds dangerous, even foolhardy, but we believe that you can do it and return safely." The calmness of his voice contrasted bizarrely with the outrageousness of his suggestion. With a thick finger, the Hallmaster traced the curved wall separating the Wards from the plaza. "All our patrols are shadowed by one or two guards when we patrol the Palace-side Wards. The only way we could get past them to the Palace without bloodshed would be to use the jewels again." His mouth twisted at the thought. "But that would only increase Trax's suspicions. We must make him understand that the real threat to this city does not come from the Banehall or even," he added grimly, "from the King."

Garet nodded. "All the resources of Shirath are needed to counter this new demon, Master," he said. "I can see that." He turned to Salick. "Any Bane with sense can see that," he added.

Salick gave him a wry smile for his compliment. "But is it this new demon, this Caller that Garet spoke of?" she asked, looking at the Red.

"The Hallmaster believes that it is," Branet replied. "And it explains why my two Golds died so strangely."

Branet stopped for a minute and his hand clenched into a fist, crumpling the pages he held. He glanced down, opened his fingers and looked up at the two Banes.

"It is a demon the South has not seen in centuries. Heaven knows how they survived it six-hundred years ago!" He dropped the list of Banes on the table. "Without Trax's help, Shirath will become a city of the dead. We must make the King see this."

"But will the King understand?" Garet asked Branet. "The Banehall hides its knowledge, keeps it like a rich man keeps a treasure," he explained. The big Bane listened carefully.

"What if the King simply doesn't have enough knowledge to make the right decision?" Garet asked, then stopped. He was sure that he was right, but was a little nervous at criticizing one man of authority to another.

"Trax is no fool, Garet," Salick said. "He'll guess more than he's told." She turned to Branet. "What does Hallmaster Mandarack think of this?" she asked.

Master Branet tapped the table between them with one beefy finger.

"The Hallmaster does not agree with this, but he has been overruled by the other Masters." He broke into a sudden, savage smile. "It has been a long time since we had a Hallmaster who would listen to the other Masters, even if he didn't want to. We agreed on the need to send a message to the King, and, since Mandarack's idea of going by himself is lunacy, you two are going to find a way to deliver it."

Garet stared at the Master, his thoughts spinning. Branet had still not said how they would even reach the King before being murdered by the Duelists or the King's guards. How could they accomplish what he said Mandarack could not?

Did he expect them to just walk up to the palace door and ask if Trax was receiving guests?

Salick stood up and crossed her arms.

"I know why you chose me, Master, but why Garet?"

There was steel in Salick's tone. She stood across the table from Master Branet, eyes narrowed. Garet wondered what would make her act so defiantly.

Branet tapped the table again, harder. He growled out his answer, "He's a curiosity, an outsider who can present Trax with an unbiased view." He stood and hit the table again, this time with his fist. "Are you Banes? Do you question a Master's commands? Keep still, learn from your betters and obey, Gold!"

Garet stood up and moved beside Salick. "Like you obeyed Adrix a few days ago?" he asked. Part of him quailed at defying Branet, a man who in size and temperament resembled his father, but, after many so months in this Hall, he was tired of bullies.

"All right, I agree that Trax might want to hear my 'outsider' viewpoint, even if he doesn't believe it, but that doesn't have anything to do with Salick, does it? Why does she have to risk her life?"

Branet looked angry enough to break the table in half then throttle them both, but a voice from the door stopped him.

"Master Branet, the vote went against me on this, but these Banes answer to me, not to you. Please restrain yourself," Mandarack said. He stepped into the Records room, a puzzled Master Arict shuffling in behind him, her arms full of scrolls and ledgers.

Branet grumbled back into his chair. "The vote went as it did because there is nothing else to do! We dance on the tip of a claw here, Mandarack. If we are to have a chance against this Caller Demon, we need to make peace with the King first, and remember, you are no stranger to desperate strategies." He turned to the two young Banes standing between the two Masters.

"There is only one question to answer; will you stand by and let the Banehall fall?"

Garet held up his hand, trying to think it through. Branet was right about one thing, the situation with the King had to be settled first. They couldn't face the demon if the King's sword was at their back. And Trax might listen to him, at least in gratitude for ridding him of Adrix. He could understand that, but, despite what Branet said, there was still one more question to be answered.

"Why Salick? Why would the King listen to her?"

Branet shrugged and looked down at the table. "There's her former status, of course, as the daughter of a ward lord, and there is her...personal history with Trax."

"My personal history?" Salick asked. The steel in her voice was now ice, and Branet didn't reply.

Mandarack stepped to her side and put his good hand on Salick's shoulder. "I have told the other Masters of the dangers of this idea, and of the disrespect they show a fellow Bane by forcing you to face Trax again." There was a real anger in his voice.

Branet kept his gaze on the table top.

Salick looked from Mandarack to Branet and then to Garet. Doubt showed in her eyes, but she pressed her lips together and nodded.

"Very well, Master Branet, I will obey—not because of your rank, but because I do want to save this Hall." She smiled, though her eyes remained narrowed. "Besides, seeing me will give Trax such a shock that Garet will at least get in a few words before the guards are summoned."

Branet let out a whoosh of air and stood again.

"And besides," Salick added, "I'm not letting him walk in there alone."

Garet shook his head. They had faced danger together before this, but what Branet was proposing seemed like suicide.

The Red gathered some more papers and made to leave the room.

"A moment, Master Branet," Mandarack said. "You should witness this."

He held his hand out to the Records Master, and, after much fumbling, she placed a ledger in his hand.

"Garet may be seen as an 'outsider' by some, but he proved himself to be a true Bane before he ever set foot in Shirath." He opened the book to the first blank page and dipped a pen in an ink bottle.

"I am promoting you to the rank of Green, although I'm afraid that you won't be able to wear your new sash—or any sash—on tonight's mission." He entered the change into the book and left the page open on the table for the ink to dry.

If Master Branet had any doubts about Garet's promotion, he kept them to himself.

"I suggest that you not wear the mechanicals' clothes Marick and Dorict used earlier," Mandarack said. "Lord Andarack has been arrested, and doubtless any mechanical will be stopped if he or she approaches the Palace."

Garet froze in the action of bending over to look at his name written in the book of promotions. Salick gasped, her hand going to her mouth.

"Master," she said. "Your brother! How did they...Trax wouldn't dare arrest a Ward Lord without the Ward Council's approval."

"I doubt they gave it," Branet said. "The Duelists arrested him. They captured Gonect as well and freed Shoronict."

Mandarack gestured for Branet to open the door. He shook his head and said, "If any good may come of this, my brother's capture should make the other lords see their only hope lies in restoring the balance between the Hall and the King, if only to protect themselves from the Duelists." He motioned Arict to place the remaining records on the table and said to the two Banes, "Tell the King everything," he said. "Garet is right. If Trax has all the information, he might make the right decision."

In the corridor outside the Records room, Salick looked at Garet, her eyes troubled. "I don't like you going with me," she told him.

"And I don't like you going with me!" he replied fiercely. "Why do you think that you'd be safer than I would?"

"Trax won't harm me!" she answered. "It's more likely to be the other way around." Her cheeks flushed and the scar was a thin line against the blush.

"And what about Shoronict?" he shot back. "Or Draneck?" He reached up to touch her scar, but she pulled her head back out of reach, glaring at him.

"All right!" she said. "Get killed, just to prove you're a 'true' Bane." She stepped back, hands on her hips.

A passing Gold turned to look at them, and Garet took a breath to calm his own anger. "Salick, it's not about proving anything. Branet is right; I might be the only Bane he would listen to," he said. "You know him, that's obvious, but will he trust you?"

She didn't reply at first, but her shoulders sagged a bit. "Probably not. Our last meeting wasn't pleasant."

"But if I'm there, backing up your arguments with my Midland point of view, then we might succeed," he continued, hands held out to her. "This is the most important thing we might ever do for the Banehall. If you think about it, it's no more dangerous than the patrols are now, hunting for that strange demon and avoiding the guards and Duelists."

She took his hands and answered him, her eyes shining. "I know. I know all that, Garet. It's just that I don't want to risk losing you." Her voice trembled, and she looked around, embarrassed, but the Gold had wisely continued on her errand.

"And I don't want to lose you," he said, his voice low but fierce. "But I must be true to myself, as well as true to you, now that I'm beginning to know who I am."

She sniffed a little and asked, "Who are you then?"

He smiled. "The crow who escaped the cage. A fatherless son. A Bane, which is a greater and stranger thing then I ever could have imagined." He took her hand. "And your friend, which is also a greater and stranger thing then I ever could have imagined." He watched her smile. "And the man who will one day marry you." He waited for her reaction.

"Marry?" she said, her voice soft. "Oh Garet, that's so far away. Banes don't marry until they become Masters." She saw his disappointment and rushed to continue. "But that doesn't mean that...claws! I'm not doing this well, am I?" She pulled him into an embrace. "Of course we'll marry! There's no one else I could stand...I mean that I love...Oh, you know what I mean," she said, hugging him tightly.

She then held him off to examine his face. "What's wrong?" she asked, seeing his somber expression.

"I wish we could get married sooner, tonight," he said.

"Garet," she said, confused, "there will be time. It's best to wait until we can share quarters as Masters and have more control over our lives. Why rush into it?"

"Because Master Mandarack made me a Green tonight," he replied.

"But that's a great honour! You've only been a Blue for such a short time. No one advances that quickly," she replied. "And besides, what does that have to do with when we should marry?"

"It may have much to do with how much time we have left," he replied. "Why would he give it to me so quickly, unless he feared that it might be his only chance to do so?"

Salick had no answer. Silently, she led him to the front doors to see if they could catch Marick and ask him if he knew of anyone or anything that could help them in this mad plan.

The King's Chambers

"No dearies, it won't do," Mistress Alanick told them. "You'll be stopped and gutted before you get through the front doors of the Palace."

They were sitting in the old astrologer's rooms in the Fifth Ward, directly behind the palace. She poured more tea for the two Banes and smiled at them.

Garet looked around the sitting room, and tried to come up with a better plan than sneaking up to the Palace doors and demanding an audience. The walls were covered with tapestries of night skies, done in deep purples and black, the stars embroidered in gold and silver threads. The shadows of the room were punctuated here and there with silver vessels on inlaid stands. The light of the many wall lamps reflected back from these, as it did from the silver tea service on the tray in front of them. Two desert birds chirped brightly in a wire cage in the corner. It was a room of some wealth, Garet decided.

He waved a hand at the walls. "Did you get all this from telling fortunes, Mistress Alanick?"

Salick scowled at this distraction, but Alanick beamed a beautiful, toothless smile.

"No, my lad. Astrology is my life, not my living," she replied. "I have over two hundred sheep in the city flocks, and enough pasturage to feed them all." She leaned forward, straightening the red velvet of her robes.

My family could work for five years and not make enough selling our skinny lambs to buy that cloth, Garet thought.

She crumbled a biscuit into her cup. "I hire youngsters like yourselves to watch the sheep, while I attend to more important things," she said.

"Mistress," Salick pleaded, "you have to help us find a way into the Palace. Marick says you know everything about this city and its rulers. You do their star charts, visit the wealthy in their homes, but have you ever been in the Palace? Do you know a safe way for us to get inside?" She twisted the linen napkin in her hands, mauling the embroidered flowers along the edges.

"Eh, careful with that, dearie," Alanick said, taking the napkin from her. "Those are worth a pretty penny in the market, I can tell you." She re-folded it and placed it near her on the low table. "Have I been in the Palace? Of course I have. I used to live there, you know," she said, enjoying their stunned reaction.

"Lived there..." Garet began, but she held up her hand to stop him.

"Yes, dearie, when Trax's grandfather, Sortick, was on the throne, I was his favourite concubine," she said, smiling until her eyes almost disappeared into folds of wrinkled flesh.

"You, er, were a concubine?" Salick asked. The cup the Bane held was suspended half-way to her lips and seemed likely to remain there.

"That's right, dearie, and the prettiest one of the lot, or so old Sortick used to say," Alanick replied. "He was always giving me gifts, sheep mostly, because he had much too many of them at the time, but as I say, eat what's on your plate, so I became a shepherdess when Sortick passed on, and I made a good living thanks to him." She slapped her round stomach and leaned back, sighing, temporarily lost in her memories.

This gave time for Salick and Garet to look sternly at each other until they could speak again. In the silence, he heard a potter's wheel rumbling in the shop below and wondered how many people in the city would be unable to sleep in these dangerous times.

Garet asked, "In your time in the Palace, Mistress, did you see anything that would help us now? You know what's at stake."

The old woman's smile disappeared. "Yes I do, lad, perhaps even more than you do." She heaved herself off the cushions of her chair and walked over to a set of drawers. Rummaging through them, she pulled out a small square of silk, framed in ivory and brought it over to show the two Banes.

"Careful with this! It's the oldest star chart in the city, maybe in the Five Cities combined," she told them, laying the yellowed silk chart on the table before them.

It showed familiar constellations, all in their right places, as far as Garet could discern. Writing symbols, though oddly shaped, ran in ornate notations beside each major constellation.

"These are our stars, now, this very night," he said. "But don't they change over time, pass through the different, ah 'zones,' as you said in the market."

"So, you remember that, dearie," Alanick said, smiling a bit. "I knew when I saw your stars that you would be involved in great things." She slapped a hand to her chest. "Let your Master Tanock dispute with me now!"

Salick bit her lower lip and, after a few deep breaths, said, "That Master has...retired, Mistress." She leaned forward and pointed at the chart. "But isn't Garet right, I mean, why should an old chart show the exact pattern of tonight's stars?"

"Because the greatest of all cycles in Heaven has just completed itself," the astrologer replied, her voice deepening to its professional level. "The stars are as they were six-hundred years ago, when Shirath was founded. It was under these stars that the first Banehall Master and the first King together laid the stones of the city wall," she explained. "Here," she said, pointing at the symbols on the side of the chart. "Here is where the zones are listed. The stars that govern all our fates now pass through the Zone of Change, just as they did six centuries ago. Things are occurring now that have not happened for six hundred years." She folded her arms and looked down at them.

"Does that mean that the Caller De..." he started, then stopped as he saw her eyes widen at his intended word, "I mean the new beast that's loose in the city now, is that what's returned?"

"Perhaps," was all she would say.

"But what about the Midlands?" Salick asked. "There were no problems there six hundred years ago!"

"How do we know that?" Garet said, before Alanick could bristle a response. "And besides, change doesn't mean the same change, over and over again."

Alanick nodded at that, and after a moment's hesitation, put away the chart and poured more tea to replenish their cold cups. Planting herself on the cushions again, she leaned forward, all business, and began to speak.

"If you want to get into the Palace, you'll have to get past the guards and the Duelists who surround it day and night now," she began. "That prancing fool, Shoronict, is back and in charge of them. He's always putting his nose into everything. Some say he means to be a Lord himself, perhaps he'll take Andarack's place if the King has him banished." She shook her head and took a sip of her tea and biscuit mix.

"How do we get past them?" Salick demanded. Her hands curled around the cup, the contents trembling a bit inside.

"I'm getting to that, dearie," Alanick said. "There's a baker in this street who delivers to the Palace. Trax likes his sweet buns for breakfast, Tomick says. He delivers them at the beginning of the fourth watch, only an hour or so before dawn. He owes me money, so I can convince him to let you two take the delivery there for him." She sat back, satisfied with her plan. "He owes me too much to ask questions, though it'll worry him half to death!" She seemed pleased with the prospect.

"But Mistress," Garet complained, "that will only get us to the kitchens."

Alanick held up her hand, the fingers bent and swollen with age. "Easy there, dearie. I won't leave you halfway." She leaned forward again and grinned. "You two will take the Beauty's Way into the King's chambers." She fell back on her cushions and cackled. It was some time before she could speak again.

"There's a hidden corridor from the servant's section of the Palace to the King's rooms. Not many know about it. The Kings used it to bring their concubines to their chamber. That's why it's called the Beauty's Way. Very handy if the king was married," she said, wiping her eyes and wheezing slightly.

"But couldn't their wives stop them?" Garet asked

"If there were no children yet," Salick told him, "the King might try to produce an heir using a concubine." Her tone was flat. "The Ward Lords do that sometimes as well."

"Yes, that's true, dearie," Alanick agreed, reaching across for Salick's hand and patting it. "There's many as is hurt in that business, but I'm glad to say that Sortick's wife had already passed, so I never had to sneak around her. We just used the Beauty's Way to stop the gossip; the Palace is a terrible place for it, you know." She shook her head.

Salick slipped her hand away and held it folded in the other on her lap. Alanick clucked her tongue and smiled at her.

"How will we find this secret corridor, Mistress?" Garet asked.

"Once you two are in the kitchen, drop your wares off with the cook and make for the washing rooms. Tell them you have to wash up before you go back. When you get there, look in the last bathing stall. The closet behind the tub has a false backing. You can lift it out. The Way starts there," she explained.

In the street below a voice called out, "All clear here, Master," and was answered with a faint, "Come back then." Footsteps echoed on the cobbles below as the patrol passed.

"Thank Heaven you Banes are back on patrol!" Alanick said. "Else we'd all wake up dead in our beds." She pushed herself up and signalled them to follow her. "Come on, dearies, let's go give Tomick the bad news."

The baker grumbled, but Alanick backed him into a corner, physically with her considerable weight, and financially, with a threat of immediately recalling his many loans. In the end, he sourly directed the two Banes to cover the colourful tunics they had secured from Marick with the white canvas aprons of baker's apprentices. Their weapons,

Tarix's steel clawed baton and Garet's rope-hammer, were too obvious to try to smuggle into the Palace and were left in Alanick's care. The two Banes were forced to settle for long, serrated bread knives thrust through their belts.

"If we meet a demon," Garet complained as they pushed a handcart of steaming bread and buns through the freezing, pre-dawn streets of the Ward, "maybe it'll be kind enough to stand still while we saw it to death!"

The iron-rimmed wheels rang on the stones beneath as Salick pushed beside him. "Don't worry about demons," she said, cursing as they maneuvered the ungainly cart around a tight corner. "Leave them to the Banes, we're just a pair of poor bakers."

The Fifth Ward guards let them out without comment, used to seeing the delivery rattle through the gates on their watch. The flatter paving stones of the plaza quieted their wheels as they pushed the cart through the rear gardens of the palace towards the servants' entrance.

Before they could reach the door, a man's voice called out, "Halt, who comes to the Palace?" and two guards stepped out of the shadows to confront them. They held their spears ready but lowered them at the sight of the cart.

The other guard, a woman with a sharp, hawk-like face, held out a hand to stop them. "Where's Tomick tonight?" she demanded. Her spear's point hesitated at a spot between the ground and their hearts.

"Ate too many of his own wares last night, and now he's in bed with a sore gut and leavin' us to do his job as well!" Salick said, all in one breath. She pushed her baker's cap back on her head and asked, "Where are we supposed to take these, Mistress?"

Her companion was pawing through the cloth-wrapped bread. Garet saw him pocket a few of the buns. "This stuff's all right, Silat," he said.

The woman eyed them for a moment and then barked, "Show me your hands!"

The two Banes held them out for her inspection. She grabbed Salick's hand and felt the calluses on her palm. White flour came off on the guard's own fingers when she released her.

"All right, take the cart to the right, into that archway," she told them, wiping her hand on the wrappings covering the cart's contents. They faded back into the shadows, probably, thought Garet, to eat their stolen buns.

As they approached the archway to the kitchen yards, Salick whispered, "Alanick was right about rubbing our hands with flour. She's sharper than I thought."

Garet nodded. "Now we know what Marick will be like if he grows up!" But it was true, the old woman had planned their invasion of the Palace as cleverly as a King or a Hallmaster. The cart made it easily through the wide kitchen-yard gate, and Salick propped it against the curb of the yard's well. They stacked the trays, one on top of the other as Tomick had shown them, and shouldered them before entering the kitchens.

Despite the early hour, a dozen cooks bustled about their tables and hearths, preparing a breakfast that could feed an army. And there was likely an army of the King's fighters to eat it, Garet thought, as he lowered the trays on to an empty table.

"Not there!" a middle-aged woman yelled at him. She wiped her hands on a stained apron and bustled over to them. "Where's Tomick? Have you got all the order?" She pulled cloths off trays and counted items. "There's some buns missing," she cried, then waved off their excuses. "Never mind, it's those guards outside, I know." She threw up her hands. "Claws! They think they should eat like the King just because they serve him. Heaven save us from mad times!" She called over apprentices to take the trays.

Salick gathered up the cloths and tied them in a knot over her shoulder. "Mistress," she asked timidly, "could we wash up before we go back?"

"What?" the cook demanded, already turning to deal with a new disappointment. "Oh, of course, child. Over there, down that hall to the left." She stomped away to direct a biting flow of language at a pot of burnt porridge, and the apprentice who had ruined it.

"Come on," whispered Salick and they slipped out of the kitchen and down the hall the cook had indicated.

A gust of warm, moist air showed them the door to the washing room. Inside, rows of wash stands and tubs of water gave their heat and moisture to the air and made them feel they had stepped out of winter and into a humid summer day. The back wall had stalls, each with a huge tub, and each tub large enough to hold four people. Three of the stalls had the curtains drawn across their entrance. That, along with the sound of splashing water, indicated their present use. As they tip-toed down the row, Garet saw with a sinking heart that the last stall had its curtain drawn as well. He looked at Salick and she held a finger to her lips.

Edging closer, she listened, then shook her head. Garet listened as well, but no noise came to his ears at first. Then, starting softly, but growing in volume, he heard the unmistakable sound of a person snoring. He looked at Salick. Her relieved expression showed that she had heard it as well. In fact, the snoring grew so loud, that it cut across the splashing from the other tubs.

A woman's voice called out from behind one of the other curtains. "Tirint! Listen to that; old Barick's fallen asleep again," she said. Laughter answered her from another stall and water splashed out from beneath the curtain.

"Do you think he might drown this time?" a man's voice answered.

"The stars would never be so lucky for us. Claws, he's louder than a sick cow!" the woman laughed back.

The snores continued, unabated by the criticism. Salick edged the curtain open and dropped to her hands and knees, motioning Garet to follow her. The floor was swimming in water that washed over the side of the massive tub. Looking up, he could see a massive, grey-haired head propped against the wooden rim. Garet's hands and pants legs were soaked, and he slipped slightly on the flagstones, bumping the tub.

The snores changed timbre and the two Banes froze. The head moved slightly and a tide of water sloshed over the side, drenching Garet's head and back. Salick fingered her knife doubtfully for a moment, then carefully reached for a wooden bucket resting on its side behind the tub. She hefted it. Garet held his breath. The snores resumed, perhaps a bit deeper than before, and Garet sighed with relief.

They crawled to the cupboard behind the tub and silently removed the bright green tunic and other clothes hanging there. The tension of the moment and irritation at his soaking caused a sudden urge for mischief, and Garet placed the clothes on the floor where the water was deepest. Salick tried to stop him with soundless words and exaggerated expressions, but in the end she just shook her head and smiled. The back panel of the closet was only loosely hanging on hooks at its top and bottom. They lifted it off carefully and slid into a dark passageway, replacing the panel behind them.

The corridor was narrow and dusty. High above, the walls were pierced in tiny, decorative patterns of outside light. They could hear faint voices through these small holes, but no words could be made out.

As his eyes adjusted to the gloom, Garet saw the corridor turned some fifty yards ahead of them. He took the lead, leaving Salick to follow. Just around the corner, a stairway led up past the rills of light into the darkness beyond.

"Alanick said this staircase leads to the King's chambers on the third level," Salick whispered. She held the knife in front of her so tightly that Garet put a hand on her shoulder for reassurance. She smiled at him, relaxing her grip. "Don't worry about me! It's just that I hate this place," she whispered, and squeezed past him to climb the stairs.

Their boots made no noise, softened by the inch of dust on the steps, and Salick held her nose to keep from sneezing at the small clouds they created with their passage. When they reached the level of the wall holes, the voices became more distinct. Salick paused. She held up her hand for Garet to listen. One of the voices was Shoronict's, the other was Draneck's. The taller Duelist was speaking in a condescending tone.

"Don't worry, Draneck," he said. "The King may have been routed, but that doesn't mean he, or should I say we, are finished. If we can't kill them with swords, we can kill them with hunger."

"That's not how I want to end this!" Draneck said. "What about that armour you took from Andarack's house?"

"It may have its uses, but for now, Lord Andarack is unwilling to tell the King, or anyone, just what they are." He gave a short laugh. "His Majesty does not want to persuade him to be more forthcoming, lest he lose the support of the other Ward Lords. Perhaps..."

"If that armour is what we think it is, we won't need the Lords," Draneck cut in, "or the..."

"Quiet, fool!" Shoronict hissed. There was the sound of something heavy being pushed against the wall, just below the holes. "If you talk like that, we'll both end up banished, and the Duelists will cease to exist in this city!"

There was no audible reply and the two Banes made to continue when the sound of running boots sounded from the other side of the wall. Shoronict's voice came to them again, fading as he moved away. "What's that? No, don't bother the King, I'll..."

Now it was Garet's turn to grasp the handle of his knife and squeeze. He hated Draneck for wounding Salick, and Shoronict for assisting him in the attack on the bridge. Salick tapped his shoulder and pulled him after her as she slipped up the stairs, one hand out in front to feel for obstacles.

After many more stairs, her fingers brushed against a panel similar to the one that had hidden the entrance to the Beauty's Way. Listening for a long moment, she looked at Garet. He drew his knife and nodded, muscles tense. She removed the panel, only to be confronted by a dimly lit closet full of silk and fine linen.

Garet moved up beside her, and they carefully pushed them aside. Garet paused to use a thick tunic to press the water out of his hair and mop his neck. The doors to the closet were not quite closed and gave them a narrow view of the room. A faint light came from somewhere out of sight, reflecting off dozens of surfaces in the small room beyond the closet. Garet looked out wonderingly as they slowly pushed open the door. Each wall, even the outside of the closet, was covered in mirrors. *Incredibly expensive*, Garet thought, *but why go to the trouble?*

"Dressing room," Salick whispered, and slipped out, her many reflections mimicking her movement on every surface. A connecting room was occupied by a single man, sitting at a desk beside a large, curtained bed. His back was to them, and as he held up a large square of silk to the light, Garet saw it was a map of the Banehall plaza, a twin to the map Mandarack had shown them of the Palace plaza earlier that night. What was he planning?

The King, for so he must be, ran a hand through his thick, blond hair. He wore only a shirt, its collar open half-way down his chest, and black silk trousers. His feet were bare, a pair of shoes tucked under a second chair where rested a purple tunic and jewelled sword sheath. The bare blade rested on the table in front of him. Dropping the map on top of the sword, he stood and left the room, walking into some other room beyond their sight.

"Get the sword," Salick whispered. "We can't talk to him if he's trying to kill us."

Garet slid the knife back into his belt and crept into the room. Lifting the corner of the map, he grasped the hilt of the heavy broadsword. Trax's voice froze him in place.

"Those are horribly hard to use," the King said, standing in the doorway and holding a Duelist's rapier in his hands. "Takes years of practice just to keep from cutting off your own limbs. You'd do better with one of these."

He walked across the room towards Garet, whose hand was still on the hilt of the sword beneath the map. Trax moved confidently, making little swishes with the rapier's tip.

"You couldn't have brought Birat's necklace with you tonight, my young friend. So I suppose this comes down to steel." He kept advancing, and Garet retreated, the broadsword held up awkwardly in his hand.

"Lower it," the King commanded. His voice was sure.

Garet obeyed. He had no illusions that he could use the heavy weapon he held, or his knife for that matter, to disarm the King and overwhelm him before he could call for help. *Where is Salick*, he desperately wondered. His back hit one of the carved posts of the bed. The King's blade hovered a few inches from his face.

"Now, let's see who you are under that cap," Trax said. He pushed it off Garet's head with the point of the blade, revealing the black hair the cap had hidden so far that night.

"Ah! You must be the 'skinny Midland crow' Shoronict is always harping about," Trax said. "It was wise of you to use a disguise to try to see me. But for what purpose, hmm?" The blade floated down to settle at the base of Garet's throat. "Why did you want to see me?" Trax asked, his eyes suddenly hard and bright. "To kill me?" he demanded. He drew his arm back slightly, but stopped in mid-motion. Salick's knife was across his throat.

She stood behind the King, one slim hand tangled in his blond hair, the other holding the knife, its serrations pressed into the skin of his neck.

"While murder sounds so satisfying, your Majesty, we really just wanted to have a word with you," she told him, pulling back on his collar to move him away from Garet. "Get his sword," she commanded.

Garet did so, dropping the larger sword on the bed and making a wide circle so as to stay away from the hovering point of the dueling sword. This blade felt like a toy in his hand after the broadsword, but he already knew how dangerous it could be in the hands of a trained fighter.

Salick pulled Trax backwards into the chair he had recently vacated. She moved around to the front, the knife ready in her hand. Garet stood beside her, the point of the rapier an inch from the King's chest.

"Salick!" he said. "Is that you?" He made to get up, but stopped when the sword point touched his shirt. "What do you mean by this?" he demanded. "What are you doing here?" His eyes flashed dangerously, undaunted by his disadvantage.

"I told you, your Majesty," Salick replied, dumping the clothes and sheath off the other chair and pulling it up to face the King. "We came to talk to you."

"As I recall, Salick," Trax said, leaning back into his chair and ignoring Garet and his sword, "you told me you never wanted to speak to me again." He smiled. "And I believe it was in this very room."

"I remember it perfectly," Salick said, her tone icy.

Garet glanced at her, but she kept her eyes on the King.

"That match was my father's idea," she continued. "Not mine. The fact that you went along with it against my will and against the laws of this city should be to your shame, Trax!" After several deep breaths, she continued. "And I was already a Bane."

"Yes," Trax replied. "Though it was an impolitic move on your part to join the Banehall. Your father was drinking himself to death quite quickly, and you could have traded that piece of green cloth for a whole Ward, or a city." He ran his hand through his hair, careless of the sword at his chest. "My father beat me for my part in it, you know," he said, and seeing her surprise, added, "He was furious. He told me if I couldn't convince a girl to love me without force, I was not fit to be a King of Shirath." He grinned ruefully. "He said that love might come in spite of the parents, but never in spite of the girl."

"Trax, you must know that you can't win against the Banehall," Salick said.

"Oh, I don't really know that," he replied airily. "Shoronict has all sorts of clever plans to make life difficult for you." He looked up at Garet for the first time. "How much food do your Masters have squirrelled away, lad?" he asked. When no answer was forthcoming, he continued. "What would happen if your well was poisoned in the night? Eh? Or your patrols ambushed from afar by archers. We still have a few archers in the guards you know, though they practice mainly for competition and tradition's sake." He waited politely for an answer.

"Very good plans, your Majesty," Garet replied calmly, "but if you succeed, what then?" He lifted the sword to rest the blade against his own shoulder. Salick held her breath, but Trax did not bother to move. "Will you use the clever Shoronict against the demons?"

Unlike his guards, Trax did not blanche at the word. He merely continued looking at Garet.

"Perhaps," he said, "we will no longer need the Banes, if Lord Andarack's new devices work." He crossed his ankles and waited for a response.

"All the silkstone in Shirath barely made one suit of armour, your Majesty," Garet reminded him. "And you have twelve Wards to guard, not to mention two rather large plazas and miles of fields and woods. Whoever wears that armour will be very busy."

Trax grinned at him and stood up. He waved a hand at Salick to calm her nervous reaction. "No, cousin, don't worry, I like this conversation," he told her. "Even if so far, we have only proven that we all know what we already know." He took a bottle of wine from a sideboard and gathered long-stemmed glasses between his fingers. "But let us continue this talk in a more civilized manner," he suggested.

He led them into the next room, a large sitting room, well-lit and appointed. Garet kept the sword, pointed diplomatically downwards, and Salick placed her knife back in her belt. Trax put the wine and glasses on a round marble table and waved them to the chairs around it.

"My advisers pester me here daily," he explained. "So there's no reason why you shouldn't do the same." He poured the wine and took the first sip. "There, you see, not poisoned. Rather good, in fact. From Solantor."

Garet had no taste for expensive vintages; it was just wine to him, but Salick raised her eyebrows at her first sip and said, "I see that you still know how to impress—especially if it helps your plans, your Majesty."

"Call me Trax, Salick. You too, Midlander," Trax said, smiling. "A king should always have one or two people in the city who can freely express their disgust with him." He took another sip and looked over the silvered rim of the glass at Salick.

"Now tell me what Mandarack thinks I should do," he said.

"How did you know that Adrix was..." Salick began, but Garet cut her off.

"The cooks," he said, and Trax nodded.

"So you see, I know things that you didn't think I knew." He smiled at Garet. "I wonder if there's anything you know that I don't expect."

"You're afraid of the Duelists," Garet told him, and smiled when the King's face went stiff with surprise. "You need them to fight the Hall, because your guards aren't enough, but you fear that one of them, Shoronict probably, plans to take over, to make himself King when you finish with the Hall. And from what we heard on the way here, you're right." He raised his glass to the King. "Did I hit the mark?"

"Yes," Trax replied, regaining his composure quickly. "But I hear you're very good at hitting a target."

"Enough games, Trax," Salick broke in. She leaned forward, pushing the wine glass to the side. "Master Mandarack said that if you had all the information we had, you would make an intelligent decision, and I, Heaven shield me, agreed with him." She folded her hands on the marble table top. "So I am now going to tell you everything."

For over half an hour, she spoke, with little interruption from the King, just a question now and then about Banehall procedures, or the nature of demons. Garet watched and sipped lightly at his wine, not used to the taste, but wanting to be occupied while Salick told Trax of the Caller Demon's threat.

"And these jewels, which I assume replace the traditional demon hearts on that necklace Adrix threatened me with, can truly be blocked or shielded by Andarack's armour?" the King asked.

Salick nodded.

"Is it possible this new demon is using something like it?" he asked.

"No, the demons we kill who are blocked are not armoured, or changed in any way we know. Master Andarack believes it is a property of this new demon's jewel to be able to hide the fear, to cover it with a dead feeling, or some other strong emotion," she explained.

Trax ran his hand through his hair again. "I can see how dangerous this is, Salick. I'm no fool," he said. "But things have gone very far already. Adrix's greed and the Hall's failure to protect..." He held up his hand to stop her protest. "I know. You tell me that failure was unavoidable, but in the eyes of the people, those deaths were the fault of the Banehall. Now the Duelists are treating those deaths like the first casualties in some war out of the dynastic records!" He stood up to pour more wine. "They are hard to control. They want this war to prove themselves, and they will take violent offense to any attempt to make peace."

"Yes, I believe we would, your Majesty," a sardonic voice said behind the King. Shoronict stood in the door to the bed chamber, sword in hand. Behind him was Draneck, grinning at the shocked look on their faces.

"So the Beauty's Way is not just a servant's joke," Shoronict observed, stepping languidly into the room. "When the guards told me that old Barick was screaming about someone attacking him in his bath, I went to see," he said, waving his rapier languidly. "For the diversion. Your Majesty's butler is always amusing when he's in a fit, but I did wonder why anyone would simply dump his clothes on the floor rather than, say drain out the tub, or pour in ice cold water, if they wanted to play a joke on the poor wretch."

Draneck stepped in lightly behind him. "A wet boot print on the closet floor led us to this traitorous meeting!"

The two men stopped a few feet within the room. Salick had moved behind the king and stood beside Garet. Knife in hand, she now reached over to take the knife from Garet's belt as well. He held the King's rapier in his hand, the point fixed on Shoronict's movements.

"Oh, please, Trax," the Duelist continued. "Don't think I'm angry with you. In fact, you've made us very happy. All of you have! Isn't that so, Draneck?"

The young man beside him whipped out his own blade and smiled. "Very happy. I'm sorry to say, Salick, that you and this crow are about to be killed for assassinating the King."

"That is a lie, Draneck," Trax said, his voice tight. "They are here to talk. I gave them my bond." His fingers were tight around the neck of the wine bottle.

"The bond of a dead man is worthless, Trax," Shoronict replied. "For, you see, they succeeded in killing you, perhaps with one of those pathetic knives Salick is holding. We followed them, but only came in time to avenge your death." The point of his blade was suddenly alive, trained on the King. "No one, not even those craven Lords of your Council will need any more proof of the Banehall's treachery." The point of the sword seemed tied by an invisible thread to Trax's throat. "I will defeat the Banes, despite their cowardly use of those clawed jewels, and then there will be no

310

difficulty in being chosen as the next King of Shirath." He smiled and dropped into a fencer's crouch. "Let us do this quickly, your Majesty."

"Lad," Trax said to Garet, "give me that sword, unless you fence as well as you throw."

Garet tossed him the sword and kicked his chair at Shoronict, who leaped to the side to avoid it. With a howl of rage, Trax flung the wine bottle at the Duelist, barely missing Shoronict's skull, and rolled over the table to confront him, blade to blade.

Garet looked wildly across the room at Salick and Draneck. The young man, his face frozen in a mask of hate, was jabbing over and over again at Salick's face and chest, trying to break through the guard of her two knives. She was slowly being backed into the wall next to a hearth. Garet ran to join her. Behind Garet, the rapid clash of swords told him that Trax was holding his own against the man who wanted to replace him.

Scooping up Trax's chair from where it had tumbled to the floor, he flung it at Draneck, but the Duelist ducked and jabbed at Salick's legs. She barely leaped back in time, but too far, coming up against the wall hard enough to knock the breath out of her.

Draneck swept his sword around to slash at Garet's face as he grabbed for the Duelist, causing the Bane to twist to one side and fall into the iron grate of the hearth. The tools stacked beside the fireplace fell over him. Brushing aside the bellows and tongs, he grabbed a poker, shorter than the one that, on a summer night so long ago, had set him on the road to this even deadlier night. Short it may have been, but the iron rod was heavy and comforting in his hand. With a howl of fury, he rushed the Duelist again before he could close in on Salick for the kill.

The first blow of Garet's weapon knocked aside Draneck's blade as it flashed towards his cousin's heart. The next drove Draneck back as he jumped to avoid a crushed skull from Garet's desperate back-handed swing.

Recovering his stance, Draneck screamed at him, "You clawed crow! Ever since that night on the bridge, I knew that I would kill you with my sword!"

"You lost your sword!" Garet yelled back. "You threw it away and ran like a whipped dog!" He drew the poker back for another attack.

But Draneck lunged forward, his arm a perfect line from the shoulder to the tip of his blade, and drove the point into Garet's thigh.

The pain burned through him like a lightning strike. He dropped the poker as Draneck moved forward, pushing the blade deeper into the muscles of his leg.

"Can you stand that, Bane?" the Duelist hissed. "Or is the courage of your lot overrated?" The hilt was almost touching Garet's leg before he stopped. "And now for my dear cousin."

He started to withdraw the blade, but Garet grabbed the rapier's bell-shaped guard with both hands. Draneck cursed and twisted the blade. Garet screamed, but held on.

The Duelist drew back his left hand to strike him, but screamed himself when Salick raked the saw-like edge of her baker's knife over the hand that still held the sword. Draneck fell back, both hands pressed to his body, trying to staunch the blood. Before he could look up, Salick smashed the hilt of her knife down on the back of his neck, dropping him like a polled ox.

"Good night, dear cousin," she hissed, and then knelt by Garet.

The sword was still in his leg, and he could not stand. Propped up on one hand, he reassured Salick.

"I'm all right," he gasped, then grimaced as the lightning ran up his leg again. "Or at least I'm not dying. Help the King."

The King did need help. Trax had fought well early in his battle against Shoronict, but his lack of training was beginning to tell. Unlike the Duelist, he had neither had the time nor inclination to devote his entire life to fencing. A trickle of blood from his left shoulder and a clean cut on the shirt above his stomach showed that the match would soon end.

Salick looked desperately at the sword still stuck through Garet's leg. He gritted his teeth and tried to pull it out, but she grabbed the poker instead and leaped over him.

"No!" he cried after her. "Take the sword!" But she was already racing towards the King.

It was too late for her help. Shoronict disarmed Trax with a flick of his wrist, sending the King's sword cart wheeling across the room. He smiled slightly and drew back his arm for the killing blow.

Trax stood, desperate but unmoving in the face of his death. But the blow never fell. Shoronict gave a small start, and the smile faded from his face to be replaced by a look of wonder. The Duelist fell forward, revealing the King's broadsword sticking out of his back and a fat, terrified man in wet clothes shaking behind him.

"You...your Majesty," the man stuttered, his grey hair raining drops of water on the floor as he trembled, "I, I came up those stairs to see if you needed me. I found your sword— you left it on the bed again." He pointed a shaking finger at the body of the Duelist lying on the floor. "Then I saw this man attacking you, and..." He stopped speaking and started to weep, great tears curving down his round face.

"Excellent timing," Trax told him, holding his wounded shoulder and gasping for air. He leaned back against the table and turned his head to the two Banes, Salick caught half-way to the King, poker still raised above her head. "May I introduce my butler, Master Barick."

From his position on the floor, blood flowing around his fingers where the sword stuck out of his thigh, Garet looked at the wet clothes on the poor man and said to the King, "Your Majesty, I think we have already met." The last thing he heard before fainting was Salick's near-hysterical laughter.

Swords in the Banehall

Garet half-woke several times before coming to full consciousness in the Banehall's infirmary. His earlier rousings were a jumble of voices and images. In one, the hawk-faced Guard who had stopped him outside the Palace held him, pinning his arms against his chest. She looked down at him angrily and said, "I knew something was wrong about you," before the lightning went off again in his leg, and he dropped back into unconsciousness. Another fragment was the voice of the King saying, "I don't care how many of you it takes, Captain. Disarm all of them and send them back to their homes." And then an image of a red dawn swinging overhead and the sound of wheels on stone.

Banerict was bending over his throbbing leg when he came fully awake. The physician was dabbing a stinging liquid on the wound and cleaning away the blood. Garet's pants had disappeared.

"So, you've finally decided to join me!" the physician said, smiling at him. "You'll be glad to know that a sword is no longer sticking through your leg, and the blood has stopped leaking out of you and staining the blankets." He bent to examine the wound. "Yes," he muttered, "if I were foolish enough to want such a wound, this would be the kind to wish for, clean, straight, and thankfully missing the bone and major arteries." He straightened and smiled again.

"Where is Salick?" Garet rasped, his throat dry as dust.

Banerict helped him to a sitting position and gave him a cup of water from the small table beside the bed. "She is with Mandarack and some other Masters at the Palace, making peace with the King and his Council of Lords," he told him. "But other friends of yours are waiting. Shall I summon them?"

Garet nodded weakly. He closed his eyes for only a moment, it seemed, when he heard Marick's outraged whisper to the physician.

"I thought you said he was awake, Banerict."

"He is, more or less, Marick," Banerict replied calmly. "He's lost enough blood to make him sleepy for a few days, and that leg will take a fortnight to heal, but he will recover fully."

It didn't seem worth the trouble to speak, and soon it was quiet again. He must have slept, for when he opened his eyes, he was thirsty again, and Master Tarix, not Marick, was there beside him in her wheeled chair, offering him a cup of water.

"So, the rumours are true, Garet; you're not dead after all," she laughed. "I'm glad, especially with all the time I've invested in your training." The bruises on her face were fiercely purpled, making her look more damaged than the young man in the bed.

Garet eased himself up carefully and drank from the cup again. Feeling at last able to speak, he asked, "How are you, Master?"

"Bruised and sore, but otherwise happy," she answered, and bent in her chair to look at his leg. Banerict had tied the edges of the wound together with silk threads dipped in some liquid to discourage infection. The threads pulled and stung whenever he moved.

Satisfied, she sat back and asked, "How are you?"

"Light headed, Master," he replied truthfully. "The King gave us wine."

"And trouble, too, I see," she said, clicking her tongue.

"That was Shoronict and Draneck," he said. "Who did this, I mean." He pointed to his leg. Still thirsty, he reached to the table for more water, but found none. Turning back, he found Tarix studying him carefully.

"I wonder if you know what a name you have made in this Hall, Garet."

He did not answer.

"You have forced many of us to look at things as you must—from the outside," she laughed. "It's an uncomfortable view for many of us. Even Master Mandarack couldn't split open six-hundred years of tradition on his own."

"I know I am an outsider, Master," he said quietly. After all he had seen and done, he knew it was still the most important fact of his life.

"No one is born to the Hall," she replied, laying a hand on his.

"But won't you and Master Relict have children in this Hall?" he asked, then apologized when he saw Tarix flush. "I'm sorry, Master, that was rude. I should never..."

She shook her head, taking away her hand and stifling a laugh. "No, Garet. I'd forgotten how all-encompassing your curiosity can be." She looked down. "If Heaven blesses us, we might try reducing our patrols and other duties in the Hall for a few years to raise a child. Some Banes even leave the Hall and return to their old homes to do so." She gave a small, self-conscious sigh. "But it is difficult to live more than one life. That is why most Bane couples give up their children to be raised by relatives. And there is, of course, no guarantee that the child will be a Bane."

To live two lives, Garet thought. He remembered Salick saying, long ago, that a Bane had no time to be anything else.

"Then why get married?" he asked, more to himself than to his visitor.

Her startled whoop shocked him out of his reverie. "Garet," she said, fighting back tears of laughter, "there are some questions that you just can't expect people to answer!"

He ruefully shared her amusement, the tension easing from his tired body. She picked up the long crutches from her lap and slid them onto the bed beside him.

"Take these. You'll need a pair for a while."

"But Master, these are yours," he said. "You'll need them!"

"Don't worry," she reassured him. "That crazy woman Dasanat and our own Banerict are conspiring to try and fix this leg," she said, slapping her bent limb. "He wants to re-break it to let it heal straight; he still curses the last physician we had when I broke it, and Dasanat swears she can cobble me some sort of brace to hold it steady when I walk." She thrust out the smaller set of crutches and rolled her chair towards the door. "Whatever happens, I'm sure I'll need this chair for a while longer, even if they're not mad."

"Why is Dasanat here?" he asked. The last time he had seen the Mechanical, she had been so involved with her work that she barely left Andarack's house to eat or sleep.

She paused at the door and wheeled her chair around to face him again. "She's the one who brought word of Andarack's capture," she told him. "That's been fixed, by the way. Once the Duelists were broken up and sent packing, he was found at their training yard, along with Gonect, both chained to the wall and spitting mad." She laughed. "The other Ward Lords were so incensed that the King had their full support, and all their Ward guards to help get rid of those pompous bullies!"

After a moment of silence, she spoke again. "You're a Green now and should apprentice to a Master. I know that you owe Mandarack much, but if you decide to look to another Master, I would be pleased to accept you as my apprentice, if Banerict can make me fit for patrolling again, that is."

Without waiting for a reply from the stunned Bane, she twisted her chair to line up with the door and propelled herself quickly back towards the gymnasiums.

Choosing a Master, Garet thought. He had forgotten all about his promotion. Looking at his uniform, folded at the foot of his bed, he saw a green sash peeking out from below the tunic. Leaning back on his pillow, he shook his head. No wonder, with all this excitement he would probably forget his own name if people didn't keep calling him by it.

"Garet!" a voice called from the doorway, and he spent a pleasant hour with Marick and Dorict learning of the latest events. The Council of Lords was holding Draneck for trial.

The Duelists were suppressed, and the King was singing the Banehall's praises, at least publicly.

Later in the day, Salick came rushing in. After many welcome, though awkward embraces, she explained why she had been absent.

"Honestly, if the Council could decide anything faster than mud crawling uphill, we would have been done in an hour," she complained, sitting on the bed beside him and transferring the tray of food she had brought from the chair to his lap.

He asked her a question that had been on his mind, now that he had time to think again. "Where is Master Adrix?"

"In his quarters, with Farix and a few others," she said. "There's only a few that didn't accept Master Mandarack as the new Hallmaster. They've all given their promise to the other Masters that they won't try anything."

"Adrix is screaming bloody murder," added Marick, who had followed her in, clucking his tongue at their displays of affection, "but only Farix is there to hear it."

"How do you know?" Salick asked suspiciously.

"Oh, I had business outside his door today."

Salick rolled her eyes. "Well, he can scream all he wants, his name wasn't even mentioned at the Council meeting today. I think that they've all decided to pretend he doesn't exist," she said. "It's more convenient that way for the King and the Hall."

"Did the King support us in Council?" Garet asked around a mouthful of roast chicken.

"Don't talk with your mouth full, Green!" she teased. "Of course he did, but every Ward Lord except Andarack had to be listened to while they droned on about tradition and duty and how none of this was their fault." She grimaced. "Finally Master Mandarack shut them all up by explaining why this new demon is so dangerous, and telling them what they needed to do to help us." She stole a chicken leg from his plate. "After that, they practically got down on their pudgy knees and begged him and the King to make peace," she said, waving the drumstick in the air. "They signed the agreement an hour ago."

"If you're done taking the food from a wounded Bane's mouth," Garet laughed, "maybe you can tell me if the Caller has reappeared."

Salick shook her head. "Not yet. In the last two days, patrols have encountered two normal demons, if the word can be used to describe such things. One was another Crawler and the other a Rat Demon," she said. "Both were broadcasting fear. They were easily tracked and killed before they did anyone harm."

"Do you think it's gone?" Garet asked.

"Perhaps the stars have shifted into a less dangerous zone," Salick replied and deepened her voice to add, "dearie."

Marick grabbed his neck, as if choking.

Garet had already become heartily sick of staying in bed during his last visit to the infirmary and was even more vocal about it this time, so Banerict soon gave him permission to travel anywhere on the main floor as long as he used the crutches and rested his leg wherever he ended up. He got in many people's way until he found a bench in the Green gym. There, he watched Master Branet limp bear-like around the room, yelling at the sweating Greens and assuring each one that, "any demon that catches you out in the fields is welcome to you, as none of you is any use to the Banehall until you can thrust that trident like a real Green!"

Garet watched and trembled, hoping he would do well enough to please this demanding Master. He came back often to try to learn what he could before he had to perform with the others. Branet, busy with his cajoling and disappointments, mostly ignored him.

As his wound began to heal, he leaned on a single crutch and practiced with his rope-hammer in the infirmary garden, aiming at rocks Marick or Dorict placed on top of the low wall for him to hit. This activity was eventually stopped by Banerict, who complained that the noise was driving his patients back to their duties before they were fully healed.

Garet sighed and wished for active employment. Salick answered this wish by sending him to help Master Arict search for information about the Caller Demon in the oldest records of the Hall. This was the research she herself had attempted earlier at Mandarack's orders, without much success. After a week of dust and shouting, and cryptic references that after much reflection actually meant nothing at all, he stopped making wishes.

Several Banes came by to speak to him: Blues he had trained with, several Greens and Golds who worked under Masters sympathetic to Mandarack, and some he did not even recognize. Vinir stopped by between patrols, smiling and bringing him treats from the kitchen. They spoke of the progress the Ward Lords had made in finding ways to alert the Hall if the Caller Demon returned.

"They have citizen patrols to bolster the Ward Guards," she told him. "My old Granny is out every evening with her friends, peering into every alley and scaring the life out of couples looking for a quiet place to kiss." She laughed at his sudden blush. "I suppose you and Salick will have to be careful!"

Garet's embarrassment deepened. He and Salick had not yet kissed, but it was very much on his mind.

"I never guessed she would lose her heart so soon," Vinir continued. "And to someone from the Midlands, when all she could ever talk about was the Shirath Hall and the duty of the Shirath Banes." She shook her head in wonder.

"I don't know why she, we..." Garet faltered.

Banerict came by with a tray of cordials for the aged Banes clustered around the hearth at the far end of the infirmary. He smiled at them but did not stop to chat.

"Don't you?" Vinir asked, grinning. "Well, at least you're not puffed up! She chose you because you came from outside, idiot!" she said. "You don't fit into her expectations of other Banes, which are rarely met, I might add. When Master Mandarack chose her, many said it was because both were from noble families, and she really didn't deserve such a great Bane as a Master. Salick met that resentment and returned it, doubled. It isolated her. Plus, she's always been careful about whom she would allow to get close." She held up a hand and ticked off fingers. "Myself, mainly because we came from the same Ward, and she saw me as a Ward sister to be protected." She pulled one finger down. "When I first came here, I was a little mouse..." She giggled at his raised eyebrows. "Yes, yes, I don't seem very shy now, do I? Salick protected me from the cruel ones like Farix. You should have seen her, a Black telling off a Green and getting away with it!"

She was silent for a moment with the memory until she noticed Garet's impatience. "Don't worry, I'll get to the point in a week or two! Now, let's see...oh yes! Marick and Dorict soon followed as part of her new family, but never a boyfriend or even a crush." Two more fingers were pulled down. She looked at him thoughtfully, her smile disappearing. "I thought for a long time that she would measure every man against her Master and they'd come up short, because the only other measure she had was her drunkard of a father." She poked the last finger held up into his chest for emphasis.

"I'm neither as good as the Master or as bad as her father," Garet protested.

"No, but you argue with her. I mean, you stand up to her, but you don't bully her," Vinir said. "You accept her for who she is. What else could she want, difficult as my friend can be?"

Garet nodded slowly. He remembered how she had slowly come to accept him and listen to him. With difficulty, he conjured an image of Salick as he had first seen her, an arrogant, sneering girl who had almost made him run away from his new life as a Bane. He shook his head. There was no sense looking back; he had been a different person too.

Vinir stood and put a hand on his shoulder. It was long-fingered and delicate, but traced with the thin, white lines of training scars. *A true Bane's hand*, he thought.

"Salick's happy," she said. "Or at least as happy as she allows herself to be. So I'm happy too." She kissed his forehead and left the infirmary.

Between visits and research, he took one more duty upon himself. With Dorict's help, he gathered paper, ink, and pen and finally wrote to his mother. The letter was long. He wrote of what he had done, of what he had learned, and of his hopes to see her and his sister Allia again one day. Dorict promised to send it with the next messenger to Bangt and so on to Three Roads. A burden whose true weight he had not known was lifted from his heart.

So occupied, he healed as quickly as he could, and after another week and a half of complaints, Banerict took away his crutches and begged him never to be injured again. Garet grinned and sincerely thanked the physician before limping happily out of the infirmary.

The two flights of stairs to his room made him less happy, and he stayed on the third floor for the rest of the day, reading a Gold text and enjoying the victory of at least sitting on his own bed. That evening, he told Salick that he intended to apprentice under Master Tarix, as soon as she recovered from the breaking and re-setting of her leg.

"Oh, I see," Salick said, her voice becoming somewhat distant. "May I ask why you didn't choose Master Mandarack?"

Garet took a deep breath. He had known this conversation might be a difficult one. "Because Mandarack is your Master, Salick," he told her.

She thought about it for a minute and nodded for him to continue.

"Well," he said, "I think it's partly a matter of ah, rank. I don't mean to reject him! You know how much I respect him, and I know that you think of the Master as your father." He rushed on before she could speak. "That's why you care for him so much, and I wouldn't want to intrude on that," he said.

She shook her head, either in doubt or confusion, but did not say anything.

"And," he said quietly, "if I apprentice to Master Mandarack, you'll always be my superior. We won't be equals."

"I'll still outrank you either way," she said. "And besides, I've been your superior since you got here." Her voice was not as cold, but her eyes were still guarded.

"It's not the same if we look to different Masters, and you know it," he argued. "Would you want to be ordering me around all the time?"

"Maybe I would," she replied, smiling at him. "But I think I see what you mean. There could be times when I'd have to order you to do something dangerous, and I don't know if I could, after what happened to you at the Palace." She leaned her head against his. "I was so afraid," she said.

Garet relaxed. He had been worried that Salick would not understand his decision. There was another reason he had not given her. He knew himself now, enough to realize that it was his nature to question everything, including his Masters. Tarix knew that and still asked. But what if Mandarack was his Master? Salick was fiercely, perhaps even blindly, loyal to Mandarack. Any dispute between Garet and the Hallmaster would force her to choose between them. It was a risk he did not want to take. It was hard truth to face, but he was afraid that in such a competition, he would lose.

There was a tap on the door.

Garet sat up and put some distance between him and Salick. They had kissed earlier, a nervous, awkward event, and he had been thinking of improving on that first attempt. The tap sounded again. *Later*, Garet thought, happiness warming his chest now that 'later' was once again assured. "Come in!" he called.

Dorict opened the door and entered, followed by a grumbling Marick.

"I don't see why we have to knock on our own door," he complained.

Dorict ignored him and settled on his bed. Marick paced.

"What's wrong?" Salick demanded.

The little Bane stopped pacing to answer. "There are calls out from six Wards that demons have been seen moving through the streets without spreading fear," he told her. "Dorict here," he added, pointing a disdainful finger at his friend, "thinks that it's just more false alarms."

"Six different Wards?" Salick asked, getting to her feet.

"Six people seeing the tail of a stray dog or some such thing in six different Wards," Dorict said. He shook his head. "I don't know if the watch system the King set up is doing more harm or good."

Marick nodded. "Every time some tipsy citizen sees shadows through the bottom of a wine bottle, half the Hall is turned out."

"Practically the whole Hall tonight!" Dorict said.

"Except us!" Marick replied, scowling.

"We're on special duty," Dorict argued with his friend. "We can't go running out to chase every shadow!"

"Special duty!" Marick sniffed. "That's just the Master's way of keeping us out of the action. Salick," he said, turning towards her, "you've got to ask Master Mandarack to let us go out on patrol again! I'm going to die of boredom if I have to stay here every night waiting for messages to deliver." He flopped face-down on his bed, grinding his face into the blankets.

Used to his dramatics, his friends ignored him. Garet looked up at Salick, who had replaced Marick in pacing across the room.

"Six different sightings? They must be like Dorict says, false alarms," he told her.

Salick shook her head. "I suppose." She turned to Dorict. "How long ago did the reports come in?"

"Over the last hour," Dorict replied. He cocked his head. "You don't think that many demons could be in the city at one time, do you?" he asked.

"We don't know what's possible or impossible these days," she answered shortly.

Garet had been watching her pace, an absent expression on his face. He stood up. "Quickly, Dorict! Did the reports say what kind of demon was seen?"

"They were all sightings of Glider Demons," he answered, looking wide-eyed at the two older Banes. "That's why I thought they must be mistakes. Gliders are so rare!"

"Gliders," Salick muttered. "Well, they can be easy to lose, especially if there's no fear to track."

"Could one Glider cover that much space in an hour?" Marick asked. He looked at Garet. "You've seen one fly."

"I don't think so," he replied. Absently fingering the edge of his new green sash, Garet looked over at Salick again as the Gold resumed her pacing. "They only sail like falling leaves or a sheet blown off the wash line."

Salick shook her head and continued walking. For a long moment, no one spoke.

Dorict broke the silence. "In any case, the Wards that reported are on both sides of the river. How could even a Glider pass over the bridges without being tracked and killed?" he demanded, his usual calm replaced by a nervous energy that pulled him off his bed to put his hand on the training staff leaning against the wall.

Salick stopped dead and whirled to face the others. "There's something wrong with this!" she said. "It may be some new trick of this Caller Demon, or the King may be planning something and is trying to distract us for some reason." She strode to the door, pulling it open. "I knew we couldn't trust him! Quickly, arm yourselves and follow me. Master Mandarack must be told." She waited impatiently while Marick and Garet grabbed their weapons.

The upper Hall was quiet. Those Blues and Blacks who were not out serving as extra eyes for the patrols were asleep in their beds, exhausted by the stress of the increased efforts of the Hall. Salick hesitated, looking at the closed doors of potential allies.

Marick grabbed her sleeve and pulled her down the stairs. "No time, Salick," he told her. "Besides, if something really is wrong, we can sound the alarm after we see the Master."

Salick allowed herself to be pulled quickly down the stairs, and they soon reached the main floor. Garet was last, still limping slightly. Salick led them through the maze of small hallways until she reached her own room. In a moment, she emerged with the baton she had used against the Crawler Demon in the stockyards. "Vinir's gone," she told them.

Garet stared at the three claw blades curving out from the weapon in Salick's hand and asked, "Your trident?"

Salick moved across the hall and knocked on the nearest door. "Too long to use in these passageways if the King's Guard attacks." she explained as she moved to the next door and banged again.

Dorict, Marick, and Garet did likewise, trying each door along the hallway. No one answered their calls. The floor boards squeaked harshly in the unnatural silence of the normally busy corridors. The four moved with increasing speed and anxiety down the hallway. At the far end, Salick gathered them together.

"There's not a Gold or a Green left in their rooms." she said, one hand pushing back a strand of bright hair that had slipped in front of her eyes. "They must have all been called out for these supposed sightings. We'll go to the Masters' rooms now."

They walked past the entrance of the dining hall. That cavernous room was dark, a single lamp burning within the kitchen and casting a narrow slip of light over the empty tables and chairs. Salick paused to peer within.

"We should check to see if the evening cooks are still there," she said. "Garet, go with Marick to take a look in the kitchens. If the cooks are there, find out what they've heard and tell them to go home, even if they haven't finished cleaning up." She waved at Dorict to follow her down the front gallery to the rooms reserved for the Reds.

Garet walked into the dining hall, Marick following close behind. They followed the sliver of light on the polished floor to the kitchen entrance at the back of the hall, near where the Blacks traditionally sat. The gloom and silence daunted the two Banes and they slowed a bit to avoid any clatter of knocked-over chairs or squeak of scraped table legs.

The kitchen entrance had no door, and Marick peeked around the corner.

"No one here," he told Garet.

Looking inside the room, Garet couldn't see anyone working at the small mountains of dishes piled in their wooden tubs. Cleavers and ladles lay scattered about the slate table tops. The lamp that had attracted their attention was fixed to the far wall beside the entrance to the kitchen yard. That door was slightly open, a chill breeze seeping in to raise goose bumps on the backs of their arms.

Garet tugged down his tunic sleeves and turned to go, but a flash of brightness on the floor stopped him. Something lay between the hearth and the unwashed tubs of dishes. He signalled Marick to stay where he was and crept in to investigate. A copper pot, used for heating water in the hearth, was overturned, the water flooding the fireplace and making a slurry of ash and charcoal that dripped down over the lip of bricks to the floor below. Raising his head from this small disaster, he saw two still forms lying, out of sight of the doors, underneath one of the large preparation tables. He started to move and then froze. Looking around, he saw no demon or waiting human attacker. He crawled quietly until he was beside them. The two men, kitchen apprentices of the Hall, had been tied hand and foot to the thick legs of the table. They were breathing but unconscious, the hair on the back of their heads matted with blood.

No demon, not even one as odd as the Caller, would tie up its prey. Garet took a sharp knife from the wash tubs and cut the bonds holding the two. He rolled them to a more comfortable position, but they did not stir. Banerict would have to be called. Garet edged out from under the table and slipped the knife into his belt.

Like Salick, he wanted a weapon he could use in tight quarters.

"Marick!" he hissed. He skirted the puddle of wet ashes and called softly again, "Marick!" but there was no answer. The doorway to the dining hall was empty. *Where is he?* Marick's frivolous behaviour was well-known to him, but the small Bane was usually dependable in a dangerous situation. Shifting the haft of the hammer end of his weapon to his right hand, he let out two coils of rope and walked slowly to the door where he had left his friend.

With the light from the lantern behind him, he could see that Marick was nowhere near the door. He cast around, trying to hear movement. He stood for a long moment, but instead of a sound, a dreadful impression grew in his mind. The room felt dead. Not the feeling of an empty room but the awful sense of life extinguished. He had felt this strange emptiness twice now: the first time at the ruined Temple, and then in the stable yards of the Ninth Ward. *The Caller Demon is in the Hall, and maybe others too*, he thought. Marick's absence now took on a sinister aspect that sent him running through the hall to the far entrance, knocking over chairs and careening off the edges of tables in his haste.

He had floundered half-way across the dark room when a hand stopped him short by grabbing his collar and yanking him backwards. He struggled, but stilled himself when cold steel pricked the side of his neck, just below the jaw line. The hand that held his collar dragged him towards the front of the hall, and he stumbled with his captor, the blade forcing his cooperation. As they neared the Masters' raised table, the lights of the main gallery cast a dim illumination and let him see a pair of people waiting near the door. One of them was very short.

A black-wrapped figure held Marick tight. As they came close, Garet saw that it was a woman who held his friend captive, a Duelist's sword held in her raised arm so that the needle point, like the one at his own throat, held the small Bane motionless.

"Now we will settle all accounts, Midlander," a harsh voice whispered in his ear.

A chill of recognition ran through him. The voice belonged to Draneck.

The Caller's Claws

The point of Draneck's sword dug into the skin of Garet's neck and the voice snarled. "Did you think that you and my precious cousin had defeated us? Even the King will pay for his crimes!"

Garet's eyes ran up the length of the sword pressed to his throat. The hand that held it was wrapped in a blood-encrusted bandage. Bits of straw stuck to the bandage, giving him a hint as to how Draneck had avoided the King's patrols after his obvious escape. That hand trembled a bit and the movement travelled along the blade to force Garet's head back against his captor's shoulder.

"Drop that clawed rope," the voice ordered. Garet let it slip from his hands to pile in a jumble at his feet.

"Kill him!" whispered the woman who held Marick. No older than Garet, she was clad in a grimy cloak. Bits of dirty, blond hair stuck out from the edges of her hood. A long scratch ran from her forehead to her cheek, adding to her wild look. She glared at him, eyes filled with a desperate hate.

"Draneck," Garet said, swallowing against the pressure on his throat, "there's a demon in the Hall. If you kill us, it will take the both of you." The hand on his collar shook him, but he continued, "Your swords won't help you. You know that!"

"If there's a demon," Draneck asked, hauling Garet up on his toes, "why don't we feel it? Or is it one of your imaginary demons that can't be sensed?" He shook Garet again, the point of the sword waving dangerously in front of his face before settling again below his jaw. "Such tales might frighten the King, but I know better."

The woman spoke again, more urgently. "Kill the Midlander and make this one tell us where the Hallmaster is." She twitched her sword and a thin trickle of blood dripped down Marick's neck to stain the purple of his tunic. "He'll tell us where the Hallmaster is hiding!"

But she found out that Marick was never easy to control. The young Bane's lips tightened in determination and, with a lightning quick twist and stomp, he wriggled out of the woman's grasp and darted away to crawl under the high table. He pulled himself up on the other side, one hand pressed to the price of his freedom: a long, freely bleeding gash in the skin of his neck and shoulder.

"Claw you!" she screamed, forgetting caution and half-falling over her bruised foot. She raised her sword to slash across the table at the boy as Marick ducked behind a Master's chair to escape out of the hall.

Garet pulled against the hand on his collar to try and stop that blade from reaching his friend, but his leg, still weak from his injury, gave way and he almost fell. He was yanked down to his knees, and Draneck shifted the rapier from his neck to a point on his back just below the left shoulder blade.

"Don't worry about your friend, Midlander," he said. "He's in good hands."

The tip of the sword parted the fabric of his tunic as the pressure on his back increased. He arched his spine away from it but, on his knees and with no way to twist away like Marick, he could only wait for the point to penetrate his skin and work its way to his heart.

"Don't bother crying for help," Draneck told him. "It was pathetically easy to send your patrols chasing shadows. We still have friends and allies in Shirath!" The voice drew near and Garet could feel the Duelist's hot breath on his cheek. "This is where your meddling ends. Farewell, crow!"

Garet threw a desperate hand backwards to try and grasp the blade, but just as he attempted this impossible strategy, the floor bucked and split beneath them. Draneck tumbled backwards as slate tiles and the wooden beams beneath cracked and fell back into a dark pit that opened under the

Duelist's feet. With a sharp cry of surprise, he dropped his sword and disappeared from Garet's sight.

Garet rolled back from the crumbling edge of the hole. Sharp fragments of tile dug into his hands and knees as he pushed himself up and backed away.

Moans rose from the pit. Garet looked at the young woman, her sword forgotten in her hand. Marick had already disappeared into the main gallery of the Hall. The woman's eyes were fixed on Draneck's sword, rocking slightly back and forth on its bell-shaped guard on the ground between her and the pit.

They both flinched at a snapping sound from the dark hole. Draneck's moans transformed into high-pitched screams, screams that were abruptly cut off and replaced by a low, inhuman whistling of breath.

Garet's back hit the Masters' table before he knew he was backing away from that hollow, hooting voice. The Duelist stood rooted in her tracks, only a few feet from the cracked lip of the pit. Only the tip of her sword moved, jerking back and forth.

A long, heavily muscled arm, its colour indistinct in the gloom, rose out of the hole and felt along the floor. It swept aside the sword, and the woman, as if released from a spell, stumbled back onto the Masters' dais, to stand side-by-side with Garet. A second arm joined the first, the claws on the end of the stubby hands each as thick as a wine bottle's neck. The weight of the arms collapsed more of the floor into the pit and the demon had to scramble to pull itself up onto the floor.

Even more heavily muscled than a Basher, the demon's thick arms were fixed to a barrel of a torso that tapered to a flat tail still dangling down into the pit. Back legs no bigger than a child's were pressed tight to its flanks. Its head was as round as a water cask; its crests mere nubs against the thick plates of skin over its skull. Weak eyes peered about the room, and seeing them, it opened its short, blunt beak to reveal rows of bloodstained, needle teeth.

The woman beside Garet swore and raised her sword. Without the demon's usual, paralyzing fear, now deadened to her, she seemed ready to attack the beast as it slithered towards them. With a cry, she launched herself at the demon, her sword lancing towards its eyes.

"No!" cried Garet, for he had studied these demons and knew what they could do. But she ignored him.

With a lightning twist of its body, the demon turned, switching ends and lashing out with its flat tail. The woman's sword merely skidded over the plates on the thing's back, and she was thrown to the floor by the slap of its tail against her ribs. She slid for several yards and lay gasping for breath, barely conscious as the demon pulled itself quickly after her.

Garet reached to his waist for the rope hammer but felt nothing but the hook hanging from his sash. Where was it? Scanning the dark floor in front of him, he could not see it and realized with a sharp drop in the pit of his stomach that it must have fallen into the hole with Draneck.

The thing was almost on top of the woman now. She had revived just enough to realize her danger. One hand on her ribs, she was trying to crawl away, pulling herself along with her other arm and kicking with her feet. But it was no contest. The demon moved over the floor with the fluid grace of a snake, using its tail as well as its arms to propel it towards its victim. She kicked at the beast's massive head, but it barely paused. One stubby hand came down on the Duelist's leg, pinning her, and the mouth opened.

Garet leaped onto the demon's back, praying to Heaven that he was right about what he was fighting. At first, the beast seemed to ignore him, but then it reared and hooted in pain as Garet plunged the small knife he had taken from the kitchen into the thing's eye, stabbing down over and over until his sleeve was splattered in its blood.

The arms tried to reach back for him, but seemed unable to bend that far. Garet felt triumphant; he had been right about this thing. It was a Digger, a demon built for attacking its prey from beneath the soil. Its arms, like its whole body, were formed to move forward in the dirt, sweeping tunnelled material back and down, but not up over its back. It swam through the earth, sensing its prey walking above before it attacked. Moret had been right for once, Garet realized gratefully, hanging on to the demon's shoulders with one hand and transferring his knife to the other eye for a renewed attack.

But the demon had a trick Moret had not mentioned. It twisted itself over on its back, pinning Garet beneath it and crushing him as beneath a large stone. The breath wheezed out of him. The small knife dropped to the floor. With a hissing cry, the demon flipped back upright beside him, leaving him winded on the ground. It lifted itself off the floor with one arm and raised the other above Garet's head, ready to slam his skull to jelly against the stone tiles of the dining hall floor.

The blow never fell. Above Garet, a thin line of steel flashed across his blurred sight and buried itself in the remaining yellow eye of the demon, finding the only path that could breach the thickness of that burrowing skull to slice into its brain. The demon writhed like a fish on a hook, snapping the Duelist's blade. She pulled Garet out of the range of that thrashing tail, and the two huddled together like brother and sister until the demon stilled, its upper body now dangling back into the pit from which it had crawled.

His head clearing now that he could breathe again, Garet turned towards the woman beside him. She stared with horror at the demon, her face pale in the dim light from the passage outside the entrance. With a groan, she released Garet's arm and fell back, both hands now pressed to her ribs, her broken sword forgotten beside her.

"Are you badly injured?" Garet asked. "Can you walk?"

She bit her lip and shook her head, making no attempt to rise. Touching her ribs, Garet could feel them moving freely under the skin. *Badly broken*, he thought. He remembered Salick's pain when her ribs were bruised during the killing of the Glider Demon; it would probably be better to bring Banerict to this woman than to try to drag her to the infirmary.

"Stay here," he told her, perhaps unnecessarily, for she seemed on the verge of fainting. "I'll get the physician."

She nodded weakly and mouthed some words that Garet could not make out, but her eyes were worried.

"Don't worry," Garet said after a moment's thought. "I—we won't turn you over to the King." He grinned at her. "You helped kill a demon after all!"

She smiled weakly.

"Perhaps," he continued, "we should make you an honorary Bane."

Her eyes widened in alarm, and she struggled to speak.

"Don't worry," he said. "I'm sure your fellow Duelists would understand."

He left her lying on the floor and stumbled out of the hall to find the others. The strain of the encounter was telling on his injured leg and he had to keep one hand on the wall to stay upright. No one was in the main entrance way. The doors to the courtyard were closed and only the night lamps lit to help returning patrols find their way to their rooms. *But those patrols are still out in the Wards*, Garet thought, *chasing shadows as Draneck had boasted*. He heard movement nearby and limped forwards, stopping at the first corridor on his right, one of two leading into the Masters' rooms.

Looking down that dark corridor, he thought he caught a glimpse of light and shadow flickering at the end of the hall. He moved as quickly as he could towards it, one hand tracing the doors of the Masters' rooms to steady himself. At the end of the corridor, he looked left for the light he had seen. It seemed to come from around a corner, from within another corridor in this warren leading back towards the main gallery of the Hall. *It must be a dead end*, he thought, for there was no third entrance that broke the wall of rooms at that point. He wished Marick were with him. His friend knew every corner of the Banehall. The thought of the missing boy increased his determination, and he moved forward towards the light, his hands still empty of weapons.

A grunting and the scrape of metal on stone stopped him and he peered cautiously around the corner. A man was on the floor, leaning against a door, groaning, not far from Garet. One hand pulled a small oil lamp along as he tried to inch his way down the dark passageway.

It was Adrix, Garet realized with a start. The former Hallmaster's leg was splinted and wrapped in bandages. His face, as he persisted in his struggles, was tight with concentration. With another groan, he pushed the lamp ahead of him and inched his back across the wooden door supporting him. It was a moment before he realized Garet was standing over him.

"Who is it?" he rasped, holding up the lamp. His face darkened. "You! What do you want?"

Garet was silent. He stood looking down at the man, hatred and guilt struggling inside him.

"It was you who did this to me," Adrix said. He dropped a hand to his immobilized leg. "Banerict tells me I'll be as crippled as that clawed traitor Tarix because of you." Spittle formed at the corners of his mouth as he raged at Garet. "You never belonged here! Crow! Mandarack should have left you to rot in the Midland pig sty where he found you!"

One beefy hand reached out to grab him, but Garet backed just out of reach.

"What are you doing here?" he asked, his voice as neutral as he could keep it.

Adrix placed the lamp on the floor. The flame sputtered for a moment before settling back into a steady glow. "There's something in the Hall, Midlander. Some demon, or maybe assassins from the King." He passed a hand over his sweating brow. "Farix is dead. I called for him to bring me the medicine Banerict had given me so that I could sleep, but he didn't answer. I finally crawled to his room and found the door smashed open." His eyes bored into Garet's. "They locked him in, you see, so he couldn't run away. But thanks to your stone, they didn't see any need to lock my door."

Garet reddened a bit, but nodded for him to continue.

"Something had got in and cut him to shreds. He had no weapon to defend himself, just like me. That's why you find me here. I'm looking for allies, some of my old friends who might protect me since your precious Mandarack won't."

Garet looked back down the corridor. It was silent, like the Gold and Green dorms they had checked earlier.

"Two Duelists tried to attack the Hall," Garet told the ex-Hallmaster. "They are the ones who drew off the other Banes with false reports of demons in the Wards."

"Where are they?" Adrix demanded, the natural redness of his face paling at the news.

"One is dead and the other badly injured," Garet told him. "A Digger Demon got them."

"A Digger," Adrix muttered. "No, that's not what killed Farix, though it might have been what broke down the door. His wounds were more like a Shrieker's." He picked up the lamp and held it out to Garet. "I assume the demon is dead, or you wouldn't be here. Take this lamp. Since I felt no demon-fear, Mandarack's crackpot idea of a Caller Demon could be true. It might attack at any time. Try to force some doors and find weapons for us."

Garet took the lamp cautiously. "I need to find Master Mandarack first, and my friends."

Adrix's eyes blazed. "Claws take you, boy! Are you a Bane or not?" he demanded. "Find us weapons and we'll be able to kill this demon. Hesitate and it will escape to kill others."

"I thought you didn't believe Master Mandarack when he said that two demons could be in the same place," Garet said. He looked at the injured man and waited for an answer.

When it became clear that Garet would not move without a response, Adrix reluctantly said, "It seems he was correct." Adrix ground the words out, looking down at the floor. He raised smoldering eyes and asked between clenched teeth, "Does that satisfy you?"

"Yes," Garet said. "It does." He stepped over Adrix to try the nearest door. It was locked and so was the next. The first unlocked door led to nothing more than a bare room, devoid of furniture or other items. The next, however, showed signs of being used. The bedclothes were in a jumble at the foot of the bed and a cup of water sat half-full on the small table nearby. *This must belong to a Master who was called out tonight in the middle of his sleep*, Garet thought. Too befuddled to lock his door against mischievous Blacks and Blues.

No weapons caught his eye at first, and he threw open chests and cupboards in his search. Under the bed, he found a leather case which he dragged out. Opening it, he found a short, heavy club. It was thick and iron-bound, its point decorated with blunt spikes. The leather strapping on the handle was loose, and the wood showed small cracks, but it was a weapon.

He ran back to Adrix and handed him the club. "Here, defend yourself, if you can." He helped the injured man down the hall, pulling him into the empty room. "Stay here," he told Adrix. "Bolt the door. I'm going to find help." Leaving the injured man lying on the floor of the room, he limped back down the corridor. He heard the bolt on the door of Adrix's refuge slide shut before he was three steps away.

Now, to find the others and see if whatever shielded the fear of the Digger was within the walls of the Banehall. He guessed that power was not in the Digger, for when it was dead, the Caller's jewel, according to Lord Andarack's theories, should have returned to its normal, fear producing state. Something was still blanketing that fear.

He retraced his steps until he reached the back corridor. From there, he came to Arict's room and turned back towards the front of the Hall, coming to a stop before Mandarack's door. The door was locked and knocking brought no response.

Stymied, he paused in front of the door and tried to think. Where would they be? He needed help. Adrix was almost defenseless and the woman in the dining hall was badly injured. *The infirmary*, he thought, and managed a hopping trot to the main gallery, turning right and coming to the long corridor of the east wing. His footsteps rang in hollow tones off the stone walls. Never had the Hall seemed so empty— and so threatening to him.

A light glowed to his left, coming from the door to the Green gymnasium. But to his right, the door to the infirmary was open and also showing the glare of a lamp. He heard Marick's voice from that direction and quickly made his way to the infirmary's door.

"No, that's not the way," the young Bane said, his voice irritated. "Here, bend your head. Now, Banerict, together. Lift!"

Garet stood in the doorway, squinting into the room. At least a dozen lamps were lit inside the infirmary. Some were wall lamps, others were set on bedside tables or the floor. They illuminated a bizarre scene. Marick was standing on a bed, the mechanical Dasanat standing on the floor beside him. Banerict was on her other side, assisting Marick in trying to lower the helmet of the demon-proof armour onto the protesting mechanical.

Dasanat was already struggling to stay upright under the weight of the breastplate and back plate that hung on her like a man's tunic on a child. She was trying to fend off the heavy helmet with her hands while Marick lectured her.

"Stop that, Dasanat!" he scolded. "How are you going to help us if you're paralyzed?" He forced the helmet down and quickly secured the buckles before she could get it off again.

Her protests came muffled from the breathing tubes sticking out the back of the helmet.

"Marick, take this off. I don't know anything about fighting a demon, I'm a mechanical!"

"Garet!" Marick cried, and jumped off the bed to wrap his arms around the startled Bane. Dasanat, deprived of support on the one side, fell over onto Banerict, who struggled to sit her on the bed.

"Are you all right?" Marick demanded, examining him hurriedly for wounds.

"Yes, I'm fine, Marick," he replied. "What are you doing? Where are the others?" he demanded.

"It was my idea," Banerict gasped. He held one hand on the side of Dasanat's helmet, striving to keep her upright. "Salick and Dorict came here when they couldn't find Mandarack. I think he went out with the patrols." He sat beside the overburdened mechanical to support her better. "They went to check the rest of the Hall, and then Marick came, telling me about the attack in the dining hall." His keen eyes scanned Garet, and apparently satisfied, he returned to his explanation.

Dasanat's protests started up again, but they were stifled enough to ignore.

"Between Duelists and a Demon, we thought we were overmatched, so I persuaded Dasanat here to put on the armour."

At this point much waving of arms from the mechanical threatened to slide her to the floor. Marick grinned and hopped back onto the bed on her other side to stop her fall.

"She demonstrated the power of Lord Andarack's spark-powered jewel when she first arrived," the physician said, "but I'm afraid Dasanat is still the only one who can operate the device. We hoped she could get near enough to your attackers to use our jewel to counteract the others. But," Banerict tapped the helmet, "I knew from your reports that the demon's fear could start again at any time, paralyzing both of us, so we were taking precautions," he said, a satisfied smile on his face.

Shaking his head at the ingenuity of the plan, Garet told them of the deaths of the Digger Demon and Draneck, and of the injuries to the other Duelist. He thanked them for preparing to rescue him, although he knew by the time they would have finally arrived at the Hall, he likely would have been dead from one or another of the killers there. Mistress Alanick would have called it fate.

"Banerict, can you go to see to that Duelist? There should be no danger, unless the fear is let loose again."

The physician was already gathering his materials. "Of course. And don't worry about me. I have one of Andarack's boxes here," he said, opening his belt pouch to show Garet one of the small, silkstone boxes Andarack had given Relict. "I can remove the jewel immediately and place it inside so that I won't be struck if the other demon withdraws its power." He hefted a hammer and a thick chisel, dropping them into his basket of supplies. Garet nodded and swallowed, thinking of the recent re-breaking of Master Tarix's leg. He could see the Training Master in a far bed, drugged to unconsciousness by the physician. Banerict swept past him, snatching a lamp from the table before he ran out the door.

Marick shot off the bed, leaving Garet to grab Dasanat before she tumbled over.

"I have to get my shield back from the dining hall!" he said, and ran after the physician.

Ignoring the mechanical's pleas for release, Garet leaned her against the pillows and ran through the room, searching. Aside from Tarix, the other beds were all empty. Some of the oldest Banes had, at Mandarack's request, moved back in with relatives in the Wards, to provide more eyes and ears outside the Hall and to help re-build the bonds of trust between the Hall and the city. Everyone else, that is everyone who could still walk on their own, was probably out with the patrols. Finally, standing in a back corner, he found what he was looking for. He grabbed them and ran back to Dasanat.

"Here," he said, pulling her to her feet and fitting the crutches under her armpits. "Use these to keep upright. Now where's the device?"

She lifted one crutch carefully off the floor and pointed towards Banerict's room. Garet retrieved the tray of batteries and the silkstone box with its wires and imprisoned jewel. He urged Dasanat to follow him as quickly as possible, and the poor mechanical hobbled behind him as Garet moved out of the room, even with his limp still faster than the woman.

Once in the corridor, he looked up the hall towards the gymnasiums, where he had seen a light before. It was still there, casting faint shadows on the opposite wall as someone moved within the Green gym. He led Dasanat in that direction. She stumbled a bit in the gloom, but neither of them had a hand free to hold a lamp.

The light within the Green gym grew and steadied. A figure stood in the doorway, using a taper to light the lamps beside the door. Salick! Garet put the tray down on the floor and hopped towards her, leaving Dasanat farther behind. He reached her in a moment and grabbed her hand, startling her into dropping the burning candle.

"Garet!" she said, putting a hand over her heart. "You frightened me." She pulled him inside the gymnasium where Dorict was coming out of the storeroom, struggling with an armload of training weapons.

"What have you found?" Garet asked. "Is Mandarack in the Hall?"

Salick started to answer and then stopped. The look of concern left her face and she smiled serenely. "It's all right, Garet," she said softly. "Everything's all right now."

And Garet realized it didn't matter who or what was in the Hall. Demon or not, everything was perfect. He smiled back at her. "Yes, I can hear it calling."

Across the gym came the clatter of wood and metal on the floor as Dorict dropped his load of weapons to stand slack-armed and grinning.

Garet took Salick's hand. They left the Green gym and turned right, towards the peace and happiness calling to them. Someone said something, but the muffled voice was easy to ignore. At the end of the corridor, the door of the Gold gymnasium stood wide, the light from the hall lamps illuminating the way to joy.

They entered the gym and saw the demon. It was on the far side of the room, standing over the body of a Black, a small body that lay twisted and torn in a pool of blood. Training dummies and mats had been pulled to the wall to make a kind of nest. The creature's snout was painted with blood, and its claws dripped with it. A single yellow eye burned in its face. It raised a hand, the sickles at the end of its fingers spreading in anticipation. The Banes smiled.

Hand in hand, they walked forward, seeing nothing but happiness. A small part of Garet's brain said to him, you fool, it's like in the clearing by the old Temple, only it's stronger now, much stronger. It's a false peace, fool. Stop!

But he could easily deny the voice; there was no joy in it.

They had crossed half the length of the gym when a pair of arms wrapped around his waist and pulled him to the ground. He tried to get up but whatever held him was heavier than he was. Still bruised from the Digger, he couldn't shift the weight. With a desperate wrench, he managed to twist around to see his captor.

It was Dasanat. The mechanical had grabbed him from behind and the weight of the armour aided her in keeping him from what he must reach. Salick seemed to notice the struggle and his missing hand for only a moment before turning to walk on.

Dasanat screamed within the helmet, the voice echoing oddly before reaching Garet's ears.

"You have to fight it, Garet," the woman yelled. "Oh Heaven's shield, please, please fight it!"

He struggled again, but the mechanical's arms were strong from their long acquaintance with hammers and the forge. He could not break free. With a groan of effort,

Dasanat flipped him over to her other side, shielding his body with her own from the gaze of the waiting demon.

A cloud passed over Garet's mind. Where was he? He looked at the mask of the helmet in front of him. He could dimly see Dasanat's eyes within, split into multiple images by the crystals, each one pleading with him to listen. The feeling of joy was still there, but as Dasanat clenched him to the protective armour, the little voice he had earlier dismissed gained strength.

"Dasanat!" he said. "What's happening?"

The mechanical yelled back, "It's the demon, Garet! It's controlling you!" Her voice was frantic.

Looking up from his position on the floor, he could see that Salick was almost within the creature's grasp. Groaning with the effort, he lifted the mechanical to her feet, keeping her between him and the demon.

"Go!" he yelled, pushing her ahead of him as fast as he could. "Grab her!" he instructed Dasanat as they reached Salick.

The mechanical wrapped her arms around Salick's waist, as she had done with Garet, and they both struggled to drag the protesting Bane back from the death she was so willing to embrace.

The demon hissed and screeched in frustration. It climbed off the body of its first kill and onto the piled mats of its nest, preparing to leap on the three struggling figures. With a gut-tearing wrench, Garet pulled them all down onto the floor as the demon sailed over them to land in a heap beyond.

The feeling of joy ceased, as abruptly as the closing of a door cuts off noise. Salick cried out, and Garet shook his head at the suddenness of it. He rolled out from under Dasanat and pulled Salick to her feet.

"Help me get her up," he told Salick, and they both lifted the limp mechanical. The helmet lolled to one side, and Garet feared that he had knocked her out by pulling her down to avoid the demon. He positioned the armour-clad figure in front of him and Salick, taking what protection he could against its recovery.

The Caller, for that was what it must be, shook itself off the floor and glared at them from one, yellow eye. This close, Garet could see the other eye socket was gouged and empty, the effect of his stone thrown so long ago near the abandoned Temple market. The demon seemed to recognize him as well, for its single eye never left his face as it advanced on the trio.

Salick pulled her clawed baton from her belt and thrust it forward but the short weapon was unable to reach much beyond the armour that protected them. Garet could not take it to wield against the demon and support the unconscious Dasanat at the same time. There was little they could do except back away as the demon advanced on them, claws raised.

No joy came from it now, nor any other emotion, as if in its anger, it would do nothing else but rend and tear the Bane that had once maimed it. Ignoring Dorict, who was closer to the beast than the others, the demon quickly outpaced their awkward backwards shuffle and struck at the mechanical facing it. The blow passed in front of the helmet, a few inches from the silkstone surface.

The demon hissed in frustration and struck again, with the same result. It launched itself at the armoured figure, but came up short against it in mid air, obviously before it expected to make contact. Dazed, it stumbled backwards a few paces.

What's wrong with it? It's as if it can't tell where things really are. A memory of his life in the Midlands came to him. His brother Gitel sitting at the table after losing a brawl with a neighbouring farm boy, his left eye purpled and closed. He remembered his father's mocking voice telling his brother, "Don't bother trying to even up the score just yet. You're useless for now! No one can land a blow with only one eye!"

That was it, the one thing that might save them. But he had forgotten the beast's other powers. The frustrated Caller paused in its slow approach and opened its pointed mouth in a prolonged hiss. Fear flooded the room, curling around the edges of their protective shield and gripping their minds. Salick bowed her head against Garet's back, moaning a little. Garet made himself as small as he could behind the armoured woman he held to them, but even then, he could barely breathe. Dasanat was safe in the armour, but unable to fully protect them.

Just as the sense of joy had been stronger than they had experienced before, the fear hammering at them was far worse than any they had encountered. It was as if the creature's rage increased the power of its jewel. The fear ran along their windpipes and closed them off. It twitched their muscles and plucked at their racing hearts. Garet felt it as a physical pain in his skull, much worse than Draneck's sword through his leg, or the beating he had taken from the Digger.

Unable to command his body any longer, he let Dasanat slide to the floor at his feet. He collapsed to his knees beside her, dimly aware that Salick had done the same. His universe had collapsed to a single yellow eye that set fires in all the far and near reaches of his being but would not let him die, not yet.

The demon crawled towards them, carefully on all fours, like a dog. It seemed to savour their pain and paused to run its forked tongue between the rows of needle teeth. A clatter behind it made the beast shift to look with its good eye over one shoulder.

Mandarack and Marick had entered the far door. Leaning against the Red, the small Bane held the tray of spark jars and the silkstone box. With clumsy hands, he tried to connect the wires to the jars, but the jerking of his own muscles defeated him. With a cry, he dropped the tray to the floor and fell backwards, clutching at his temples. Mandarack advanced, leaving Marick pinned to the ground by his terror. The old Bane moved slowly, leaning forward into the waves of fear like a traveller into a heavy wind. His withered arm hung limply at his side while the other, clad in its shield, was held out, as if feeling for the proper path. The Hallmaster shuffled painfully towards the demon, passing Dorict without a word or a look.

With an effort almost beyond him, Garet held his head up to look at the advancing Bane. As he came closer, Garet wept to see a trickle of blood flowing down Mandarack's chin from where he had bit his lip in the struggle to keep moving. More blood dripped to the floor from the straps of the trembling shield, as the Hallmaster used all his resources to fight the crushing fear.

The demon turned to face the old man, reared back on its hind legs and spread its thin arms as if in welcome. The waves of fear intensified, rolled them over and over, drowning them and exploding like soundless thunder in their heads. Mandarack cried out, a drawn-out groan that came from the depths of the stoic Bane. Salick's own tears fell on Garet's neck and she clutched at his tunic in her distress.

The two were almost within reach of one another. The creature drew back one arm and held the other out in an attempt to judge the distance. Mandarack stumbled a bit and came to a stop, the outstretched tip of his shield touching the claws of the Caller's reaching hand.

Both Bane and demon struck, struck at the same instant, the claws slashing at the Bane's neck and chest as the tip of the shield tore through the tough hide of the Caller's throat in Mandarack's last, desperate lunge. The creature threw back its crested head and tried to screech, but a horrible, bubbling hiss came out of its blood-frothed mouth. It collapsed across the legs of the Hallmaster, both bodies motionless on the gymnasium floor.

The reduction of the fear was disorienting, and at first, Garet could not move. He could only retch weakly as Salick crawled over him to Mandarack's still form. She kicked the corpse of the demon off Mandarack's legs and pulled her Master's grey head up into her lap.

Garet finally managed to crawl after her. She was using her gold sash to dab away the blood from Mandarack's face. There was no sense trying to stop the blood from the ruin of his chest. The demon's claws had lain open the Bane's heart and cut the life from it. Garet removed his vest and laid it over the wounds. Salick wept over the body, rocking slightly back and forth.

Garet looked up at the drawn faces of Dorict and Marick and said, "Help me with Dasanat." He looked at Salick. "Then we'll take care of the Master."

"I'll stay with him," she said, one hand caressing the pale cheeks of the man she held.

The Temple

The third Temple dome, closest to the river, was traditionally reserved for the King and Lords of the city. There they looked up at the night sky dome, their expensive leather boots held by servants outside the ring of pillars, and pleaded for whatever the powerful might still desire. Their daughters and their sons joined hands in marriage on those cool tiles, and when they died, the priests laid them there to rest, to look up with sightless, open eyes, to study the way they must go.

Banes, even the most revered, were laid like any citizen in the northernmost dome before being carried with songs and tears to the burning grounds outside the walls. But today the traditions were remade. The funeral procession of Hallmaster Mandarack came sighing and rustling over the centre bridge and weaved its way through the wintered gardens towards the Temple dome of the Lords of the City.

No sound came from the ranks of Banes who had cast off their cloaks to show the sashes and uniforms of their Hall to a city that once again accepted them. Equally silent were the Ward Lords who stood side by side with the Masters, carrying the bier. Lord Andarack led them on the left, the pole held tightly to his shoulder and tears flowing down his cheeks. Branet, the new Hallmaster, led them on the right, with no tears but a stricken look on his face. Tarix limped beside her husband's place, her newly-braced leg supported by a single crutch. Behind them all came the men and women of the city, their bright tunics like fire trailing from the darker mass that preceded them.

A small group stood on the terrace in front of the Temple, broken up into pairs and trios, waiting for the procession to cross the plaza. Some were priests, awaiting the body, others were Mandarack's remaining relatives. And there were four others. Garet stood with Salick at the edge of the terrace. Dorict and Marick stood a little ways off, rubbing their red noses and taking what comfort they could in each other's company.

"They'll be here in a moment," Salick said. She held a long, white cloth folded over her arm. Behind her, the Temple bell sounded the first of the many booming notes that it would give voice to that day.

Garet waited for the vibrations to end before he spoke. "Why don't they speak, or sing, or shout?" he asked, nodding towards the crowds still coming through the centre bridge gate.

"The bell speaks for all of us," Salick replied. She hugged the cloth to her and leaned against his shoulder. Tears flowed down her cheeks, tears that had never really stopped over the last two days.

Garet had found her crying over the body of her Master when he returned with Banerict to the gymnasium. The physician, who had been paralyzed by the powerful fear the Caller Demon finally broadcast, had roused himself at the creature's death and was helping the injured Duelist to the infirmary when Garet found him. Garet had borrowed the physician's tools to remove the Caller's jewel, for as Andarack had predicted it had still been broadcasting fear. With the jewel secured in the silkstone box, Banerict was able to enter the gymnasium to assist the Banes. Together, they had laid Mandarack's body in the cold air of the infirmary's garden. They had covered him with a blanket and left him to be watched over by Salick and by more and more returning Banes. Even when Relict had finally forced her to rest in the infirmary, she had cried silently in her fitful sleep. In the confusion and meetings that followed, he had seen little of her until this morning.

Now she wiped the tears away and stood straighter as the procession advanced. It was a heartbreakingly clear winter day, the sky a cutting blue and the wind gusting cold across the open plaza. Salick's hair, released from its braids for the funeral, whipped out and across his face, covering him for moment in warmth. He did not move.

She did. Turning to face him, Salick asked, "Where did you go? After, I mean."

"I had to report to the new Hallmaster," he replied. "Master Branet was chosen as soon as they all assembled in the Records room. Relict nominated him. Then Andarack and the King were sent for, and I had to tell it all again." He yawned, hiding his open mouth behind his hand. "Andarack wanted to examine the Caller's jewel. It was incredibly large, twice the size of a Shrieker's jewel, but it was," he paused to search for the word, "normal again. No worse than any other dead demon's." He shook his head, and then yawned again.

Salick bit down to stop an echoing yawn. "I want to rest so much when this is done," she said wistfully. "I feel such a need to do nothing but think and remember for a long, long time." She pulled back the whipping strands of hair from her eyes to watch the procession. "There's Trax," she said, pointing.

Garet looked. The King was indeed there, far across the plaza. He walked just in front of the bier carrying Mandarack's body. In golden robes and a bejewelled baldric, the short, muscular figure drew all eyes as he set the pace for the Banes and Lords behind him. But no crown sat on his head, and no sword rested in the jewelled sheath at his hip. Out of respect for the man he escorted to the Temple, Trax carried only one symbol of authority this day. Across his outstretched arms lay Mandarack's red and black sash.

"He honours us," Garet said.

Salick nodded reluctantly. "I suppose he does, but it still rankles, him being part of this. I will never trust him!"

In the two days since the Caller's destruction, only one other demon had been caught within the city walls, a small Rat Demon that was easily dispatched by the now-frequent patrols. Hopeful that things were finally returning to normal, the people of Shirath had emerged like bright-winged butterflies from their homes, ready to build and repair, to buy and sell, to celebrate and mourn. Every citizen who could walk or be carried had travelled across the three bridges early this morning to take part in the funeral march.

The procession had stopped half-way across the plaza. The guild leaders and minor aristocrats met them in a folding line of purple and silver. They pushed gently between the Banes and Lords holding the bier to touch the black cloth draped over Mandarack's body. The King's face was somber as he led the pallbearers at a slower pace to accommodate the greater crowd. That crowd now flowed up behind them, engulfing the bier and filling every space between the gates and the Temple's terraced walls.

Garet and Salick stepped aside as priests moved around the raised area at the head of the ramp, brass censors swinging back and forth in their grips, the smoke giving a brief scent of burning herbs before the breeze blew it away. The purification of the terrace complete, the priests replaced the censors in ornate cages on the posts supporting the cylindrical bell. As it sounded again, a priest, his robe just a shade of blue darker than the winter sky above, opened his arms and chanted.

The wind slapped at the two Banes again. The last group of notables had touched the pall draping the bier, and the procession resumed its slow progress. Trax glittered at its head. Salick and Garet paused in their conversation, taken by the way the swaying, bright mass of citizens parted to let the King and pallbearers through.

The bier paused at the entrance to the only straight path through the Temple gardens. A pair of priests joined Trax, ceremoniously taking his elbows to escort him to the ramp leading up to the Temples. Salick and Garet waited on the terrace. Their part in the ceremony would not come until later.

The procession slowed again, allowing the pallbearers more time to carry the bier up the incline. The two Banes moved back, merging with the small knot of relatives holding strips of blue or white cloth.

Salick turned towards him. "I can't imagine my life without him, Garet. I know he freed me from a life of anger and resentment. He gave me a greater purpose."

Garet reached across and drew the yellow strands away from her eyes. "I know, Salick. He did the same for me. He saved me from..."

He didn't want to finish his thought, but Salick's eyes, pleading for any distraction from the grief approaching them, forced him to continue.

"He saved me from the life of a dreamer who never left his dreams to live a real life. And that would have been the best I could have hoped for."

"What would have been the worst?" she asked.

"To become a man like my father," he answered. There, he had said it.

"Never," Salick said, taking his arm in hers. "If there was even the smallest chance of that, the Master would have left you in that pesthole. No, Garet, he knew your quality, and he knew that men like you would be needed—especially now."

He knew she had given him a great gift with these words, greater than he deserved, perhaps, but for a gift, one must give a gift—truth for truth.

"I thank you, Salick. But I could never match him. The best I can hope for is to be someone the Master would have respected. Someone like you."

He felt her shiver against his shoulder. He slipped his arm out of hers and put it around her waist, holding her until she was still.

"But whatever I become, I'll never be my father's son—you saved me from that," he said. "You, the Master, Marick and Dorict. You gave me this new life." He took his other hand and traced the small, crescent-shaped scar on her cheek. He had several scars to match it on his own body. "A dangerous life, perhaps, but I wouldn't trade it, even if I could make those old dreams come true."

Salick leaned against him, the tears coming again.

An old woman turned and shushed them fiercely. The bier had reached the top of the ramp and the King was passing in glory before them.

Salick, ashamed, stiffened and took a deep breath to control herself. A priest came up behind them and laid a kindly hand on Salick's shoulder.

"Don't worry, Bane," he said. "The dead are listening to other things now, other voices. Let your tears flow as they will. You are not the only one crying in the city today." He led her and Garet, along with the small knot of relatives, around the temple to wait on the other side of the pillars while the Hallmaster's body was lifted from the bier and carried under the dome to lie on the cold, marble tiles. He then left them to listen to the chants of the inner priests. Lord Andarack came forward and knelt by the head of the corpse and opened the unseeing eyes. The words of the priests seemed to echo back from the dome until the terrace rang with a harmony of prayers. For many minutes the chanting continued, and then, at some signal Garet missed, it ended on a single, soaring note.

Salick clutched the cloth in her hands and backed into Garet.

"I can't do it," she said, her voice rising.

The woman who had shushed them earlier was twisting a strip of blue cloth nervously around her fingers.

He took hold of Salick's shoulders. "You can," he told her. "I'll be there with you."

She took a tentative step forward and looked back to see if he had indeed followed. The relatives came after, murmuring prayers and holding their strips of cloth. With uncertain steps and great love, Mandarack's people came forward to dress his body for its last journey.

Later, there would be the fire, and the smoke rising, and many sleepless nights. But as Garet looked up to the bright patterns laid out on the ceiling above them, he knew there would also be life and love, danger and friendship. His bare feet touched the ground of his city, Shirath on the Two Banks, and the stars of Heaven shone down on his bare head.

Author Biography

Photo by Karen Holland

Kevin Harkness is a Vancouver writer who has just finished a third career as a high-school teacher. His first two careers: industrial 911 operator and late-blooming university student, were nowhere near as dangerous and exciting as teaching Grade 10s the mysteries of grammar and the joys of To Kill a Mockingbird. He also taught Mandarin Chinese—but that's another story. Outside of family and friends, he has three passions: a guitar he can't really play, martial arts of any kind from karate to fencing, and reading really good stories.